"How can you tell without glasses?"

"I don't need them to see up close," he said softly, moving nearer until there were but inches between them. She looked into his eyes, deep, gray, intense, and felt she was gazing into his soul.

"I love your mouth," he murmured. He removed his glove and his skin was firm and a little rough as he traced the bow of her upper lip with his forefinger. "So perfectly shaped here. And smooth and rounded like a ripe fruit here." The edge of his thumb stroked the length of her lower lip.

The wind and chill receded and it might have been summer. His breath felt warm on her cheek. Her lips parted in anticipation.

He was going to kiss her again.

Romances by **Miranda Neville**

THE DANGEROUS VISCOUNT
THE WILD MARQUIS
NEVER RESIST TEMPTATION

MIRANDA NEVILLE

The Dangerous Viscount

AVON

An Imprint of HarperCollinsPublishers

This is a work of fiction. Names, characters, places, and incidents are products of the author's imagination or are used fictitiously and are not to be construed as real. Any resemblance to actual events, locales, organizations, or persons, living or dead, is entirely coincidental.

AVON BOOKS
An Imprint of HarperCollins*Publishers*
10 East 53rd Street
New York, New York 10022-5299

Copyright © 2010 by Miranda Neville
ISBN 978-0-06-180872-2
www.avonromance.com

First Avon Books paperback printing: October 2010

Avon Trademark Reg. U.S. Pat. Off. and in Other Countries, Marca Registrada, Hecho en U.S.A.
HarperCollins® is a registered trademark of HarperCollins Publishers.

Printed in the U.S.A.

10 9 8 7 6 5 4 3 2 1

To Jill
I shall always be grateful I went to Albany.

The Dangerous Viscount

Chapter 1

Mandeville House, Shropshire, England
July 1819

It all began with a glimpse of stocking.

Women's stockings were not something he'd ever thought about. He didn't know they were made of silk. Or that they could be pink.

He walked through the arch into the stable yard and saw her. Already mounted, she leaned over to adjust her stirrup, revealing the arc of a calf, the rounded angle of a knee.

His breath hitched. Instead of turning on his heels like the sensible man he was and always had been, he found himself propelled forward, captivated by the expanse of shapely leg bracketed by an ankle-high boot and a green cloth habit. A leg encased in pink silk that—although this fact was unknown to him—had been christened Maiden's Blush by the exclusive Bond Street haberdasher who sold the stockings.

A name, as it happened, quite appropriate for Sebastian Iverley, a man whose carefully arranged existence included the avoidance of all things female.

But the first time he saw Diana Fanshawe, Sebastian

had no idea his life was about to be ruined. When he walked into the library at Mandeville, he anticipated an undisturbed afternoon browsing the Duke of Hampton's collection of ancient maps.

Instead he found representatives of three classes of people whose company he scorned. Four men of fashion whose collective heads contained scarcely a full-sized brain between them. Three ladies, youngish, one of them giggling. And his cousin, the Marquis of Blakeney.

Blakeney could have been included in the first group, but to Sebastian he was *sui generis:* the single person in the whole world Sebastian disliked the most. Though not without competition for the title, Blakeney was an easy winner.

"Blake," Sebastian said.

"Owl—er—Sebastian," his cousin said. "I didn't expect you."

"And I didn't know you were here," Sebastian replied. "I met the duke at White's on his way to Brighton. He told me I'd have the place to myself."

He looked about him, willing the unwelcome company to magically dissolve into a vapor. Or failing that leave the room on foot. Alas, Blakeney remained both concrete and present. Sebastian, an unfailingly reasonable man, conceded that his cousin, as only son and heir to the duke, had the right to be there. What he disputed was the attitude of superiority with which Blake had regarded him since they first met at the age of ten.

"We were bored to tears at Blenheim so we left early." Blake's careless tones always set Sebastian's teeth on edge.

The giggling girl reacted to this evidence of brilliant wit on the part of her host by modulating her tone. She tittered.

"Decided to come to Shropshire early and a few of the fellows joined me. And ladies too." Blakeney turned to his companions. "Are you acquainted with my cousin, Mr. Iverley? Lady Georgina Harville."

One of the ladies curtsied, a plumed mess on her head bobbing with her. She reminded Sebastian of his female cousins, Blakeney's sisters.

"And her sister, Lady Felicia Howard." The giggling girl. *She* reminded him of his female cousins before they grew up. Their giggling had always been directed at him. Lady Felicia he absolved of that offense. Her mirth appeared completely lacking in discrimination.

The elder of the two eyed him curiously. "Mr. Iverley," she said, "I don't believe we've ever met." What to Sebastian was a cause for celebration, Lady Georgina seemed to take as a personal affront. "How very odd. I'm Blakeney's second cousin by marriage on his mother's side and my husband has known the family forever."

Sebastian ignored this riveting piece of information and waited impatiently for Blakeney to finish his introductions and leave him alone.

"Lady Fanshawe." His cousin indicated the third lady. In the two seconds of attention he afforded her, Sebastian noted that no birds had been harmed in the arrangement of her hair, and that she did not giggle. Remaining blessedly silent, she evinced no interest in him whatsoever. With Lady Fanshawe he found himself in mutual agreement.

Blakeney moved on to the men in his party. With the exception of James Lambton, Sebastian knew none of them, nor did he wish to. He promptly forgot their names, though he did register that one of them belonged to the woman with the dead avian on her head. With Lambton he exchanged greetings of barely concealed disgust. Then he adjusted his spectacles and looked longingly at a corner of the library where the largest folios were shelved.

"We came in here because this window gives the best view of the coverts. We're planning some rough shooting for tomorrow. I don't suppose you'll join us. You never did enjoy sports." It was clear Blakeney actually thought his comment an insult. Sebastian refused to waste another minute on these ridiculous people.

"If you don't mind," he said, "I'll find the atlases I came to see. No doubt I'll see everyone at dinner."

Unfortunately.

Diana Fanshawe assured the groom she would prefer to ride alone and dismissed him, prematurely it turned out. Her stirrup leather was an inch or so too long. She gave a quick glance around the empty stable quadrangle, pulled up the skirt of her riding habit, and removed her left foot from the stirrup.

Botheration! How had she forgotten to change her stockings? The pale pink ones were a favorite pair, and too fragile for riding. She cursed silently as she struggled with the stiff buckle, not realizing her solitude had been interrupted until a deep voice, a few feet away, asked if she needed help. Not a servant's voice.

She looked up to discover Mr. Iverley staring at her exposed limb. At least it wasn't Lord Blakeney. Normally she would have been pleased by the chance to "accidentally" display her hidden assets to the marquis and allow him to admire her seat on a horse. But today she had a particular reason to avoid him, so she'd timed her ride to coincide with the shooting expedition. Had she given him any thought, she'd have supposed Blakeney's peculiar cousin immured in the library. He'd barely spoken at the dinner table, addressed not a single word to Lady Georgina sitting next to him, and shown no interest in the house party's plans.

He was, however, showing considerable interest in her leg.

"May I help you adjust that?" he asked.

Really! She twitched the skirt so it covered her knee. Then realized he meant her stirrup. Why not? The alternative was to dismount. She was impatient to be on her way before the two weird sisters decided to join her. Or the gentlemen appeared. There was always the chance they'd take it into their heads to seek alternatives to avian carnage as a way to pass the morning. Iverley didn't seem the sort to take liberties. If he did, she had her riding crop in hand.

"Thank you, sir. One notch shorter, if you please." Her well-trained horse from the Mandeville stable was fifteen hands or more, yet Mr. Iverley's head reached the level of her waist. He had to stoop to undo the buckle. All she could see was the crown of his hat, but she sensed his fingers at work and felt his arm brush her silk-clad calf.

"Is that high enough?" He mumbled the words

and when he looked up he avoided meeting her eye, as far as she could tell through steel-rimmed spectacles. Color tinged his cheekbones.

Diana aimed at the stirrup and missed. Grasping her ankle, Iverley deftly guided it into the metal hoop. While his hand on her booted foot was unexceptional, she felt a little frisson at the contact.

"Very good, thank you," she said, letting her skirt down and adjusting her reins.

He gave a little grunt of acknowledgement. She expected him to step back and let her ride off. Instead he hesitated a moment. "May I accompany you on your ride?"

"I am going to call on my mother and father at Mandeville Wallop," she said.

"That's at the north end of the park, if I recall correctly. Three or four miles perhaps?"

"Just over three. If you wish to ride with me to the Wallop gate I'd be glad of your company," she lied. Double botheration. She'd gone to considerable trouble to make sure her duty visit to the family was made on her own.

At that moment the groom appeared leading a handsome bay stallion, saddled and ready. "Here's my horse," Iverley said. He mounted with easy grace. Bookish or not, Iverley was more than capable of handling a challenging animal.

"Do you know the way?" she asked as they rode abreast through the stable arch, "or will you follow me?"

"I know it."

"Do you stay here often?"

"I came as a boy," Iverley replied. "I haven't in several years."

"Don't you enjoy Mandeville? I think it must be the most beautiful house and park in the world."

The only response was another grunt. The joys of Mandeville didn't inspire Iverley to an eloquence to match her own. Growing up just beyond the vast encircling wall, the park had always seemed like paradise and the great Palladian mansion a palace, shared with the duke's less fortunate neighbors in carefully dished out tastes on public days and the occasional dinner or ball.

"It feels a little odd to be staying here, with my family only a step away. Lovely, of course. I am enjoying getting to know the house better." She intended to know it very well indeed, but that thought she did not share.

Her uninvited companion wasn't much of a conversationalist. Without appearing inattentive, he failed to reply to any of her openings, merely staring down at her. Diana didn't believe his face expressed admiration. More like bafflement.

Tired of trying to draw him out, she urged her mare to a canter and gave herself up to the beauty of her surroundings on a clear summer morning. With the superior strength of his mount, Iverley passed her and she was able to confirm her impression of a skilled rider with an excellent seat. On horseback his ill-fitting and old-fashioned garments were hardly noticeable. Instead she discerned that he had the muscular thighs necessary to control a spirited horse. In the final half mile stretch to the gate he accelerated to a gallop. Her mare followed and both of them, rider and mount, were panting by the time she drew to a halt.

"Good girl!" she said, leaning forward to praise and pat her horse. "What a splendid ride."

The north access to the Mandeville park was a more modest affair than the triple-arched main entrance. A pair of rusticated stone pillars bracketed the iron gate, used mostly by tradesmen and farmers. Diana exchanged greetings with the gatekeeper, an old acquaintance, as he emerged from his cottage, then turned to Iverley.

"Thank you for your company," she said. "But don't let me keep you."

"The village of Mandeville Wallop lies beyond this gate, I believe," he said. "I don't ever remember seeing it."

"There's not much to see. When the first duke came to Mandeville in the last century he built Duke's Mandeville as a kind of model village. That's where all the elegant houses and most of the shops are to be found. Everything in Mandeville Wallop is old."

"Your family lives here?"

"Yes, at Wallop Hall."

"An old house?"

"Very old."

"I'm interested in antiquities."

Without being shockingly rude, there wasn't much else Diana could do. "In that case, you'd better come with me. If you have a taste for the Gothic, or perhaps the poetry of Sir Walter Scott, you'll probably like Wallop Hall. My father, Mr. Montrose, will be glad to point out the parts that go back to the Middle Ages."

It wasn't the end of the world. Since Iverley was obviously an eccentric, he should fit in perfectly with the Montrose family.

Chapter 2

Sebastian followed Lady Fanshawe up a drive lined with ancient oaks and wondered if he'd lost his mind. Two constant principles guided his life: avoid all women, at all costs; and eschew meaningless social discourse with chance acquaintances. So why was he going to call on a family he didn't know and had no reason to believe he'd find congenial? Worse still in the company of a person who was, definitely and without question, female.

From his vantage a couple of yards behind, he had a splendid view of Lady Fanshawe's figure. She sat on her horse with perfect posture, showing off a fine high bosom and slender waist. But not her legs. He'd never been interested in a woman's legs before, or in any part of her except in a general, theoretical way that he had no difficulty dismissing. Now he couldn't stop thinking about them. That little tease of calf and knee had him thinking about ankles and thighs too. The complete legs, both of them, not in rationed sections but in their glorious entirety. Clad in pink silk.

Not that there was the least chance of his seeing them, so what on earth was he doing here? Conversely, if there was any chance—or danger—of seeing Lady Fanshawe's legs, common sense demanded he turn around and gallop off in the opposite direction, never stopping until he reached the haven of his bachelor household in London.

"Lady Fanshawe," he heard himself say. "Is your husband planning to join you at Mandeville?"

Where the hell did that come from? He didn't give a damn about her husband's whereabouts. Or hers for that matter. He'd be much happier if she wasn't here, happier still if he wasn't. But ever since he'd caught sight of her in the stable court he seemed to have lost control over his movements and his powers of speech.

She turned her head at his question and his heart performed a jig in his chest. He'd already observed, in a dispassionate, almost scientific way, that she had blue eyes fringed in thick lashes that matched shining, dark brown hair. Nothing to get excited about. They were just features on a face. Agreeable ones—well, beautiful if you were being honest and Sebastian prided himself on his honesty—but nonetheless just eyes. Everyone had them, along with forehead and chin, nose, lips, and so forth. It was quite illogical that the sight of her cheek, plump and curved and the color of rich cream, should do strange things to his sense of balance.

"Sir Tobias Fanshawe died nearly two years ago," she said.

He made some kind of noise in lieu of a more appropriate response. He feared she'd start weeping. Weeping, he had some idea, was what widows did when their late spouses were mentioned.

Lady Fanshawe, however, remained dry-eyed and showed no appreciable grief, or even agitation. She continued their progress at a slow trot that displayed her seat to advantage, until coming to an abrupt halt. "Min!" she cried.

"Di!" The response came from a girl perched on a stile, reading a book. She closed the volume and waved. Lady Fanshawe descended nimbly from her horse and met the girl by the side of the road. They embraced.

"What are you doing here?" asked the girl. *Min?* Was that a name? "We didn't expect you before to-morrow at the earliest. Why are you riding? Where is your luggage?"

"I am staying at Mandeville for a few days. I rode over."

"Really?" In the mysterious manner of females, "Min" managed to invest the simple word with a wealth of meaning.

Lady Fanshawe nudged her head in Sebastian's direction with a little frown. "Mr. Iverley has been good enough to ride over with me."

"Not Lord Blakeney?" Min didn't giggle but she did smirk.

"Lord Blakeney is out shooting with the other gentlemen of the party. I had intended to come alone."

Min nodded. "Of course."

"But I met Mr. Iverley at the stables."

"I see."

Obviously important information had been exchanged and he had missed it. It took Sebastian back to his childhood and the company of his girl cousins, whose conversation always appeared fraught with hidden meaning. He waited, teeth on edge, for the inevitable peal of giggles.

"Mr. Iverley, allow me to present you to my sister, Miss Minerva Montrose. Min, this is Mr. Iverley."

He dismounted and sketched a bow. Min, despite her age, which Sebastian estimated to be in the teens, curtsied with admirable gravity, then somewhat marred the effect by complaining to her sister. "You know, Di, since you are married I should properly be introduced as Miss Montrose."

"I do beg your pardon! Mr. Iverley, this is my younger sister, *Miss Montrose*." This last came with a smile that scrambled his insides. In addition to her other manifest attractions, Lady Fanshawe possessed lips like ripe plums and straight white teeth. "Really, Min. When did you become such a stickler?"

"Since I determined on a diplomatic career."

For a moment Sebastian had made the mistake of judging Miss Minerva rational. She held up her book and Sebastian seized with relief on the reassurance offered by an ordinary object, despite the lunacy revealed by the girl's statement.

"What are you reading, Miss Montrose?" he asked.

"Monsieur de Pradt's history of the Congress of Vienna."

"Is it good?"

"I haven't finished it yet. But evidently the diplomats could have done better."

"You speak of becoming a diplomat. An unusual ambition for a lady."

"I know it is impossible. I shall have to marry one and become a power behind the throne. Or perhaps I shall wed a statesman and become a famous political hostess. Either way, it is important for me to know the forms of polite society. That's why I have become a stickler." She cast a triumphant look at her sister, making her appear very much her age despite the precociousness of her conversation. Sebastian half expected her to stick her tongue out.

"It's very hard living in Shropshire," she added. "I hardly meet anyone worth practicing on. I have to learn everything from books."

"Don't underestimate the virtues of the printed word," Sebastian said. "Books are usually coherent and never answer back."

He found himself in the position, once his impression of her common sense was restored, of tolerating female company. He was almost disappointed when she declined to accompany them to the house. Miss Montrose, unlike her sister, did nothing to upset his internal equilibrium.

"No thanks," she said. "I haven't been through the front door in three months."

"Is Papa is his study, then?" Lady Fanshawe asked.

"Yes."

"We shall have to sneak around to the garden door."

Obviously he'd overestimated the intelligibility of the sisters' conversation.

He and Lady Fanshawe continued up the drive on foot, leading their horses. "You must forgive my little sister, Mr. Iverley," she said. "She does tend to run on about subjects that have taken her fancy."

"It's good to be interested in something."

"Then you have come to the right place. Wallop Hall is full of enthusiasm."

The drive veered off to a modest stable block where they consigned their mounts to the care of a groom. As they rounded some thick shrubbery a low, sprawling stone house came into view. As promised, the building appeared to be of considerable antiquity, covered with thick ivy right up to an arched front door of scarred oak planks. Although the glossy vine almost obscured a small window to the right of the entrance, Sebastian detected movement behind the diamond-paned glass.

Lady Fanshawe stopped and placed a restraining hand on his arm. "Don't look," she said softly. "Keep to the left and don't let your feet crunch on the gravel."

He did his best to comply, intrigued by the air of mystery and a little dizzy from her proximity. She exuded a subtly perfumed warmth as she leaned on his arm and whispered directions. They'd almost made it to the corner, another few paces would bring them out of sight of the front, when his booted foot slid on a large pebble and sent up a shower of stone, shattering the summer silence. He was not generally so clumsy, but how could he concentrate when she touched him? It was her fault.

For a few seconds they froze. Without any idea what they were trying to avoid, he prepared to run, pulling her with him.

Too late. The front door opened and she muttered a mild oath.

"Diana! My dearest child!"

"Now we are in for it," she muttered, releasing

his arm. She turned to greet a man with a bald pate, gray whiskers and a paunch, a very caricature of the jolly country squire.

"Papa!" she cried, further confusing Sebastian by sounding happy to see him. "How are you?" He swept her into a great hug.

"Who's this?" he asked, after his daughter had briefly explained her presence.

"Mr. Iverley. Allow me to present my father, Mr. Montrose."

"I am acquainted with Lord Iverley."

"I'm surprised, sir," Sebastian said. "My great-uncle never leaves Northumberland."

"We may have met in years past," Mr. Montrose amended. "I don't perfectly recall. But we exchange correspondence from time to time."

"You must be interested in machines, then. Uncle Iverley rarely writes a letter on any other subject."

"I do like to tinker with all sorts of mechanisms."

For some reason this seemingly innocuous remark made Lady Fanshawe tense. "Is Mama in the garden?" she said. "I think I'll just run around and find her."

Her father seized her arm to prevent her escape. "Nonsense. You haven't been here in six months. And Mr. Iverley has never been. You must both come into the hall."

She let her father guide her through the oak door. Though not given to fancy, Sebastian detected the desperate air of a prisoner approaching the gallows. What could this affable man threaten that so oppressed his daughter?

Coming in from bright sunlight was like entering

a cave and it took a few moments for his eyes to adjust to the gloomy hall and notice something out of the ordinary: a wooden seat suspended by a chain from a metal contraption. Whatever it was, it looked relatively benign, certainly not the instrument of torture suggested by Lady Fanshawe's agonized expression.

"Up you get, my dear," Mr. Montrose ordered. She looked around as though contemplating flight, then climbed into the swinging chair.

Watching her father conduct some business with blocks of metal hanging from a horizontal bar, Sebastian realized the device was a weighing machine.

"Eight stone, two pounds," Mr. Montrose announced. "Let me see." He picked up a vellum bound volume from a small table and flipped through the pages. "Five pounds more than last time."

"I'm wearing a riding habit. This cloth is very heavy," she said.

Her father wagged his finger at her then pointed at the entry in the ledger. "None of that. Last time you wore a winter gown and full-length fur-trimmed pelisse. See? You made me record it in the book." He dipped a pen in an inkwell kept handy for the task and entered his daughter's new weight.

Although not in the habit of judging people's emotional reactions—men, thank God, didn't have them—Sebastian noticed Lady Fanshawe looked as though she were about to cry. Was she, for some reason, upset about the increase in her weight? He couldn't imagine why. He found her figure absolutely perfect. Its diminution by even an ounce would be a sad loss.

If he cared for such things. Which of course he didn't.

"I've never been weighed," he said.

Mr. Montrose beamed. "Of course you must take your turn. All the visitors to the house do. Get down, Diana."

The ordeal with the weighing machine over, Diana obeyed. Honestly she'd like to murder her father. He had no idea how acutely he'd embarrassed her, in front of a stranger too. She could only be thankful that Iverley, not Blakeney, had witnessed her humiliation. How sound was her instinctive determination not to allow the latter anywhere near her childhood home. His cousin, on the other hand, seemed to fit right in with her eccentric family.

Iverley took her place in the hanging chair. It was on the small side for his frame and sank several inches from his added weight. He had to tuck his legs under the seat to keep them off the floor. His long arms hung limply at his sides, putting her in mind of a Guy Fawkes effigy on a bonfire.

Her father looked him up and down. "With new people I like to try and guess their weight. Eleven stone, I think, perhaps eleven and a half." He adjusted the balancing weights. "God bless my soul! Twelve stone, five pounds. You carry more muscle than appears."

It was apparently a good thing, Diana thought bitterly, that Iverley weighed more than he looked. A fleeting recollection of his thighs crossed her mind. There might be a fine figure beneath his long coat and waistcoat, a good decade out of style, and breeches that she assumed were made for comfort since they lacked any discernable shape.

"Tell me, sir," Iverley asked. "What is the object of collecting this information? Have you been able to draw any conclusions from your observations?"

"That's a good question. I purchased the scale after I saw the jockeys weighed at a horse race. It's only a simple steelyard and I had some notion of improving the mechanism for reading the weight. But nothing came of it and I moved on to other things. I like to record the changing weights of my family and acquaintance over time. The children love it, don't you, my pet?"

He looked at Diana who managed to bite her tongue. How could Papa be so oblivious to her feelings? The boys didn't mind, of course. And their mother hadn't been weighed in years; since her weight never varied by so much as an ounce she refused to waste her time. But Papa couldn't get it into his head that his daughters didn't enjoy being the subjects of this particular scientific experiment.

"I haven't used my records to pursue any particular line of enquiry," he said in answer to Mr. Iverley's question.

"Might I suggest you record the heights of your subjects as well as their weights? Then there would be more of a basis for comparison."

"God bless my soul. That's a fine idea. I might have expected a relation of Iverley to have such a fine grasp of the sciences. What are you? Six feet, at least, I think. I shall set up a device immediately. Next to the bootjack would be best. For of course people must remove their shoes before their height is measured."

And off he went, into his own world. Since the measurement of height presented little challenge, he would no doubt come up with a needlessly complicated and ultimately impractical invention, perhaps a water-powered bootjack. Diana loved her father dearly but he made her want to scream. Often.

"Run along, Diana," he said. "I daresay you'll find your mother in the drawing room."

As she led Iverley from the hall she heard her father thinking aloud. "Boot removal, hmm. I wonder if people should disrobe before they are weighed."

Before he could act on that particular notion, she closed the drawing room door behind them and found herself in a small outer circle of hell. With every window open the room was yet stifling. On an unusually warm July day a fire burned in the stone hearth, a massive affair doubtless designed for the roasting of whole oxen in days of yore. Diana's mother knelt on the floor talking to the reason for this madness: her favorite foxhound bitch stretched out on a blanket with a litter of tiny blobs, attached and noisily suckling.

Mrs. Montrose looked up. "There you are, darling. Locket pupped yesterday. We had the devil of a time getting her pregnant. I'm breeding for longer noses so I sent her to Squire Mostyn's Bobbity over at Charlton. Bobbity did his business but it didn't take until the third time. Locket just didn't fancy him. But the clever girl had ten in the litter and not a runt among them."

This was a good deal more information than Diana wished to hear.

"Congratulations, Mama. I've brought Mr. Iverley for a visit. He's interested in antiquities."

Her mother rose from the floor, looked dubiously at her doggy hands, shrugged, and wiped them on the skirt of her shabby riding habit. "How do you do, Mr. Iverley," she said.

Iverley accepted the proffered hand without apparent reluctance. "How do you do, ma'am."

"Do you hunt?"

"Not with any regularity, though I have done so occasionally," he replied.

That was enough for her mother. In short order Mr. Iverley was cornered on a sofa and Mrs. Montrose proceeded to interrogate her guest on his acquaintance with different packs of hounds. In the old-fashioned drawing room Mr. Iverley no longer looked so odd. His appearance fit in with the solid oak furniture, dark paintings in crooked frames, piles of books and journals, and dog hair everywhere. He didn't even seem to mind the heat. He and her mother made quite a pair. Like Iverley she was tall and thin and dressed only to please herself. Her idea of suitable attire for a London ballroom still gave Diana nightmares.

To be fair to Mama, her aged riding habit fit her well, for she never stinted on those garments. Her fair hair contained hardly a hint of gray. Were it not for the ravages to her complexion wrought by days in the hunting field, she might have passed for a woman much younger than her forty-eight years.

Margo Montrose was a very handsome woman and her younger daughter resembled her. Diana took after her father, dark with a tendency to plumpness.

Avoiding dog hair on her forest green habit and thus the displeasure of her French maid, Diana took a plain wooden chair with the advantage of proximity to a window. With a jerk of her head she summoned Minerva, who had managed to creep into the house without attracting her father's notice, and was sitting in a corner with her book. Waving her hand in a vain attempt to encourage cooler air, she whispered the dreadful news. "I put on five pounds."

Minerva examined her critically. "You don't look it."

"Too much good food during the season, too many dinners with a dozen dishes for each course. You wouldn't believe how delicious the meals are at Mandeville. I have to stop trying everything." She looked enviously at her sister's slender figure. Of course poor Minerva didn't have much of a bosom, but there was still time for it to develop. And if it didn't, the right modiste would take care of the problem. Min would not suffer the humiliation of making her bow to society inadequately dressed. She had a sister with the knowledge and the purse to ensure she found the husband she wanted, first time out.

Meanwhile, Diana had her own problems. Some of her gowns had grown a little tight and her maid was complaining. "I thought," she said softly, "I might stop eating the dishes I particularly like, then I won't be tempted to eat so much."

"That's a stupid idea," Min said. "Why don't you

only eat the dishes you particularly like and leave the others. Then you'd eat less and enjoy it."

"I like your plan better. I could try that."

"Now, while you have the chance, tell me how you come to be staying at Mandeville."

"It was a miracle!" Diana said. "My leader cast a shoe near Wolverhampton. While I was waiting for the coachman to return from the smith's, Blakeney and his party drove up and offered assistance. He insisted on taking me up so that I could wait at an inn in comfort."

"Did he recognize you?"

"Of course he did. He's known me forever."

Min looked skeptical. "But did he *recognize* you?"

"I can safely say I have gained his attention this time." Excitement made it hard to keep her voice low, but a quick glance told her Mrs. Montrose was happily occupied. "He invited me to join his guests for a few days before I return home to Wallop." Reliving the moment made her almost giddy.

"I don't understand why you care for the opinion of a man who has ignored you for most of your life. What is he like? He has certainly never paid any attention to me."

"You've seen him, Min. He's as handsome as ever."

"And?"

"His clothes are superb. In all of London only Tarquin Compton is better dressed. And I believe Blakeney has the better figure, though he isn't as tall."

"Is he intelligent?"

"He excels at every kind of sport."

"You hate sports."

"It doesn't matter. When I look at those blue eyes and golden hair I forget what he's saying. Besides, everything sounds good in his voice."

"That's idiotic, Di."

"You'll understand one day."

"I hope not. And don't smirk at me in that odious way as though you know something I don't."

Poor Min, only sixteen and buried in dull, rustic Mandeville Wallop, had no notion of what delicious things could happen between a man and a woman. Diana's smile broadened. She spent a good deal of time thinking about what she'd like to do with Lord Blakeney in a large bed.

"Who is Mr. Iverley?" Minerva asked.

"Blakeney introduced him as his cousin. I'm not sure of the connection. He doesn't speak much, though he grunts quite a lot."

"He's talking now," Min observed.

On the other side of the room Mrs. Montrose, having exhausted the enumeration of Iverley's hunting experiences, had moved on to her other favorite topic, the breeding of hounds. Her guest displayed a level of interest that could only lead to trouble.

"Do explain, ma'am," he was saying, "exactly how you go about enhancing the various desirable characteristics in your animals."

Diana hastened to the rescue before her mother could get into embarrassing detail about the mating habits of dogs. "Mama! Pray recall that Mr. Iverley is interested in antiquity."

Mrs. Montrose gave her a suspicious look, then turned back to their visitor. "If you want the history of the house you'd better see Mr. Montrose. I know it dates back to Henry IV or Henry VI or some other Henry, but I have no time for such stuff."

"Papa's had *an idea*," Diana said.

"Oh dear. Minerva, be a good girl and run to the kitchen. Tell Cook dinner will be an hour late. No! Better make it two. There's no saying when your father will be ready if he's inventing something."

Minerva winked at Diana and tossed Mr. Iverley a grin on her way out. Mrs. Montrose put her head out of the window and yelled. "Stephen! Come in please." A few minutes later the youngest Montrose joined them.

"Hello, Step," Diana said.

"Hello, Di." Being fourteen, he didn't kiss her.

"Stephen," said their mother. "Would you take Mr. Iverley into the garden and show him something ancient? I need to speak to Diana."

That sounded ominous. Though she was twenty-three years old, three years married and almost two widowed, Diana, like everyone else, found it hard to resist her mother's will when she chose to exert it. Luckily that wasn't often.

"Minerva tells me," Mama began once they were alone, "that you are staying at the House. Is the duchess in residence?"

"No. I came with Lord Blakeney's party. It's perfectly correct, Mama. Lady Georgina Harville is there with her sister. And may I remind you that I am a married woman and do not need a chaperone."

Really it was the outside of enough for her mother to be bothered about propriety at this stage. She'd been completely inadequate as the mother of a debutante, making no secret of the fact she found the whole business a dead bore. Diana's clothes had been all wrong and she hadn't met the right people. Small thanks to her mother that Diana had made a good match.

"You are there as Lord Blakeney's guest?"

"Yes. With several others. I daresay we'll all stay a week or two and then I shall come home."

"Blakeney has a ramshackle reputation. I worry for you, Diana."

"Oh really, Mama," Diana scoffed. "He's no different from any other gentleman of the *ton*. He won't offer insult to a lady."

"Don't be naïve. You are a widow now and gentlemen do not see widows in the same light as they do unmarried ladies."

Diana rolled her eyes. Did her mother think she was stupid? "I have no intention of succumbing to Blakeney's seduction. Quite the contrary."

"I doubt he'll be allowed to marry you. The duke wouldn't have it."

Diana said nothing. What was the point arguing?

"Take that mulish look off your face." Mrs. Montrose's voice softened. "I don't want you to be hurt. Fanshawe wasn't a man to make a young girl's heart race, but he was a decent man. Your father and I wouldn't have let him have you otherwise. I understand you want to find a younger husband, but don't lose sight of what is important. Mr. Iverley seems a nice young man."

Iverley? Her mother had finally lost her mind if she thought Diana would prefer that scarecrow to his cousin anytime in the next millennium.

* * *

"I'm afraid I don't know much about history," Stephen Montrose said apologetically. "You need my father or Diana for that. Or Rufus, but he's abroad."

"It doesn't matter," Sebastian replied. "I'll just look around your garden." At first glance there wasn't much to see: an unkempt lawn and some shrubs. Not that he was any expert.

"Are you an antiquarian?"

"I collect old books, otherwise I wouldn't say so. I'm no scholar."

"Just like my mother to get it wrong."

"It's not her fault," Sebastian said. "Your sister invited me to accompany her because I expressed an interest in old things."

"Are you a friend of Diana's?"

"We only met yesterday. I am staying at Mandeville."

"I didn't think you looked the sort. You seem to be quite a sensible fellow. Girls!" Stephen invested the last word with a wealth of meaning that Sebastian completely understood. They walked for a minute or two in companionable silence, broken by the younger man. "Do you have an estate?"

"Not at the moment," Sebastian replied. "I live in London."

"Poor you. London is awful. I much prefer to be at home, but they make me go to school. Papa already listens to me about the management of the farm. That's what *I* am interested in."

"Perhaps you could find a situation as a land steward," Sebastian suggested.

"Perhaps. Eventually I shall have Wallop."

"Forgive me, I was under the impression you had an older brother. Rufus, did you call him?"

"Actually I have three. Rufus is the second. But Papa doesn't believe in primogeniture. He thinks everyone should do what interests them."

"My guardian had something of the same notion. He encouraged my interest in books from an early age. Being a viscount, of course, he cannot get around the laws of inheritance. Your father's attitude is unusual, and quite enlightened."

"He'd probably even leave Wallop to one of the girls."

"As if Diana or I would want it!" Minerva joined them. "Diana has simply pots of money and I have no intention of moldering in the country for the rest of my life. It's so dull here. I'm going to ask Di if I can stay with her in London this autumn."

"Good," Stephen said. "Maybe the parents will be lonely by themselves and let me leave Harrow."

"They won't even notice. Until one day it will occur to Papa he hasn't weighed anyone in months and he'll wonder where we all are."

"And Mama will say," Stephen added, "that explains why the butcher's bill is down. She thought it was because the dogs were off their feed."

"How tragic it is to have a mother who prefers a pack of hounds to her own children! Diana *must* let me come and live with her."

"I also prefer London, Miss Montrose," Sebastian said.

"Good. I look forward to seeing you there. You will call on me, won't you?"

Sebastian promised he would. It was odd to find a young lady neither foolish nor alarming. In fact Minerva amused him. There was something very appealing about the entire family. So different from his cousins. He imagined for a moment what it would have been like if when he first came to Mandeville, he'd found Minerva and Stephen instead of Blakeney and his sisters. He suspected the Montrose children wouldn't have mocked a shy, gauche boy. They wouldn't have called him Owl. They might have laughed at him but he probably wouldn't have minded.

"What are you two doing here? Or did you just come out to escape the heat?" Minerva asked.

"Mama told me to show Mr. Iverley the garden."

"What is there to see?"

"Not much." Stephen turned to Sebastian. "I'm afraid I've brought you out here under false pretenses. But we can't go in yet. Mama's giving Diana a lecture."

"I'm sorry to intrude. I must be in your way." Sebastian felt awkward. It occurred to him that Lady Fanshawe had shown no great enthusiasm for his company. Suddenly he felt a fool, something that happened often when he ventured into polite society and another reason for avoiding it. He never seemed to register the unspoken nuances behind other people's words and conduct. Women particularly were incapable of communicating their wishes in a straightforward manner.

Minerva Montrose, for all her diplomatic aspirations, responded with glorious and unfeminine frankness. "Don't worry, we always welcome a new face at

Wallop Hall. Anything for a distraction. And don't worry about Diana. Even if she's a little grumpy I can promise she'd prefer you to a sermon from Mama."

"Should we rescue her?" he asked.

"It can't be done," she replied. "Mama would just tell us to go away again. You might as well look at the garden."

"I know," Stephen said. "We'll show you Will's clock."

He took off over the lawn, and Sebastian followed, careful not to trip on any of the more robust tussocks of grass, until they reached a circular flowerbed with plants set at intervals in seedy clumps around the periphery. The three of them stood in a row and regarded the unpromising sight.

"How is this a clock?" Sebastian asked. He would have expected a sundial in the center.

"It's a botanical clock," Stephen explained. "Linnaeus said you ought to be able to construct one since different plants bloom at different times of the day. Our oldest brother decided to test the theory."

"That's clever," Sebastian said.

"It would be if it worked," Minerva said, "but the plants never to seem to behave the same way from one day to the next. At one time Will used it instead of a watch. He was either early or late for everything."

"Do you remember, Min?" Stephen said. "He swore the problem was that Shropshire is on the wrong latitude. I wonder if he's managed to build one in South America."

The activities of the Montrose family made Sebastian feel a little dizzy. "South America?" he asked.

"Yes," Minerva said. "He's hunting specimens in the Amazon jungle. Rufus, the next oldest, is searching for Roman ruins in Anatolia. And Henry's at Edinburgh University reading medicine."

What a marvelous family, Sebastian thought. The table talk must never be trivial. He wished he were staying at Wallop Hall instead of Mandeville. Dinner the previous night had been sheer misery with Lady Whatshername babbling in his ear, trying to draw him out. Her sister had giggled while Blakeney and his acolytes droned on about their ludicrous pursuits and brayed with laughter for no discernable reason.

Unfortunately it was time to leave this haven of rationality and return to the tedium of the ducal household. Lady Fanshawe appeared on the terrace next to the house and beckoned. On the bright side, Lady Fanshawe beckoning was a sight to behold. From the lawn he took in the full splendor of her figure.

"Are you ready to ride back?" she asked. She smiled at him.

At least he'd have something attractive to look at during dinner.

Chapter 3

Lady Georgina Harville, née Howard, had come out the same year as Diana. The daughter of an earl with a healthy portion, Lady Gee had been invited everywhere while Diana languished on the obscure fringes on the Beau Monde. Nevertheless they'd been distantly acquainted, then and since.

Lady Gee made little secret of her displeasure at Diana's addition to their group. She and her sister, Felicia, spoke to her as little as possible and with the barest excuse for civility. But this evening, during a convivial dinner, the entire party agreed to address each other informally. Given that level of supposed intimacy, Lady Georgina could hardly maintain her standoffish attitude when the three ladies of the party retired to the drawing room. She was not, however, lacking resources when it came to putting a perceived upstart in her place.

"Remind me, Diana dearest, in which county is Sir Tobias Fanshawe's country place?"

"Coghill Hall is in Essex."

"I thought perhaps he was one of the Yorkshire Fanshawes."

"Goodness, no. No connection at all. He was a

'Madras Fanshawe.'" Diana had learned that the best way to deal with malicious attacks on her husband's antecedents was to acknowledge them with an ironic smile. As Lady Gee knew well, Diana's late husband had been the son of an India merchant named Shawbottom whose name change preceded the purchase of his baronetcy by a matter of weeks.

"I believe you have no children. Did the estate pass to another branch of the family?"

"The 'Madras Fanshawes' have no other branch. Coghill belongs to me now," Diana replied, taking the opportunity to remind Georgina that her fortune was far greater than either of the others. "So convenient to have a comfortable house near London."

"My husband's family place is in Cheshire, not very far from Mandeville. Sir Charles and Blakeney are childhood friends."

"My family lives three miles away at Mandeville Wallop."

"Really? It seems very strange that Charles never encountered your family during his visits over the years."

Diana skirted the gibe about the Montroses' low social standing. "I'm not surprised I never met Sir Charles before, being much younger than Blake. And I wasn't out."

Georgina frowned in deep thought. "I vaguely recall that we came out in the same year. We must have encountered each other at some affair or other."

Pretending not to know someone you'd met on numerous occasions was an affectation Diana found especially tiresome. Nevertheless the set-down was a

compliment of sorts, a backhanded recognition that
Diana was no longer naturally beneath her notice and
needed to be actively snubbed.

She smiled sweetly. "I do believe you are right,
Gee. We must have married at about the same time.
Such a coincidence that we both wed baronets."

Whether that was a winning thrust could be open
to interpretation. Sir Tobias Fanshawe was by far
the richer. Sir Charles Harville was younger, with an
older title. Lady Gee's luck at attracting the attention
of Lord Blakeney, the biggest prize of all, had been no
greater than Diana's, but with her birth and fortune
she should have landed a peer. While Diana's marriage was something of a coup for her, Lady Georgina
might have expected to marry better.

Lady Felicia Howard nodded her head from side
to side as she followed the exchange, exuding the
occasional pointless titter. Now she fixed her eyes
on the door.

"Look," she giggled. "Mr. Iverley has come back
with the other gentlemen. What a quiz."

Felicia was an exceptionally silly young woman,
but Diana couldn't argue with that opinion. The
other gentlemen might not be as pleasing to the eye
as their host, but they were people of the highest
fashion, as were the Howard sisters. And Diana's
own lemon yellow silk was brand-new, perfect in its
extortionately expensive simplicity for a lady visiting
a ducal seat.

Iverley offered a comical contrast, both to the
grandeur of the room and its modish inhabitants.
To put it bluntly, he looked like a country bump-
kin. Not slovenly precisely: his garments were clean

and well brushed, his linens white. But Diana could scarcely credit that this scarecrow in sagging evening breeches, a shabby coat with shiny elbows, and well-worn though polished buckled shoes, was cousin to the elegant Blakeney. The piece of muslin wound about his collar hardly deserved the title of neck cloth.

"How exactly is he related to the family?" she asked. Lady Georgina hadn't previously been acquainted with Iverley, which in itself was odd, but she knew who was connected to whom, and how.

"I was puzzled at first, then I realized he's the son of the duke's sister, Lady Corinna. She's lived abroad for years. I don't know the details, but she married an Italian."

"He doesn't look foreign," Diana remarked, "and nothing like any of the Vanderlins, either."

The Vanderlins, family of the dukes of Hampton, tended to be very fair. Mr. Iverley was darker, his longish hair brown. Diana hadn't noticed the color of his eyes, obscured as they were by his spectacles.

"The Italian was her second marriage," Lady Gee explained. "She's a contessa or something now. She was married before, to an Englishman. A nephew of the Viscount Iverley."

"Mr. Iverley is obviously not addicted to fashion," Diana remarked. "His interests tend toward the intellectual, it appears. I gather he is here to inspect some of the famous rarities in the Mandeville library."

"I didn't know you were bookish, Diana." Georgina Harville had her eye on Blakeney for her sister and was trying to brand the competition a bluestocking.

Diana had waited years for this chance. Nothing

was going to stop her from becoming Marchioness of Blakeney and eventually a duchess.

"By no means," she said, and asserted her superior knowledge of all things Mandeville. "But growing up in the neighborhood I know a great deal about the duke's collections."

Mr. Iverley stood in the middle of the room, looking uncertain. Diana sensed his eyes on her and thought he was headed in her direction when Blakeney, moving faster, reached her side.

"Would you care for a walk on the terrace, Diana?" he asked.

Yes!

Lady Georgina looked sick, Lady Felicia puzzled. Diana tried to keep her face from registering triumph, muted only when Blakeney invited one of the other gentlemen to come with them.

It was one of those midsummer evenings when twilight lingered after sunset, the mysteries of night promised but postponed. Dusk clothed the horizon in stages. First the distant elm groves, then the lake, dissolved from sight. The scent of roses drifted from the walled garden below, flooding the broad raised terrace on the west side of the great house. Inside the crimson and gold drawing room the candles had been lit, but their glow through the open French window wasn't needed for Diana to see the face of the man standing next to her.

"What a glorious night!" A sweeping gesture encompassed the rose garden and achieved its real purpose, which was to brush against Blakeney's arm. Blake, she amended. Blake's arm.

"Look at that climbing rose," she said. "The profusion of white flowers appears magical in this light." Her statement happened to be true, but she'd selected that particular bloom for notice because of its location. In pointing at it she had to lean across him. She could feel the fine cloth of his evening coat through the thin silk of her sleeve. She trusted Blake was appreciating the sight of her bosom. The low-cut bodice displayed her assets to great advantage, she knew. Mr. Iverley, seated opposite, had barely taken his eyes off them throughout the evening meal.

The marquis, however, was proving elusive. She was ready to resist the kind of improper advances hinted at by her mother, but none had been forthcoming. So far, Blake hadn't said a word to her that couldn't have been overheard by anyone. She'd hoped for more when he'd asked her to take a stroll outside. She told herself that Blake was paying homage to the proprieties by inviting James Lambton to accompany them. Though Diana had nothing against Lamb, an amusing charmer and one of Blake's closest friends, at this moment she found him definitely *de trop*.

"My mother's devoted to roses," Blake said. "The walled garden is her scheme."

"Even from here the scent is heavenly. Close up it must outdo all the perfumes of Arabia."

Instead of following this blatant hint with an invitation to explore, preferably leaving Lambton behind, Blake actually pulled back from her. What was the matter with him? Diana knew she looked her best and she knew he admired her. Yet in a situation that should have been rife with romantic possibilities he failed to press his advantage.

"Shall we walk?" he asked. At least he offered his arm. She placed her gloved hand on it and they strolled decorously over the flagstones, Lambton keeping pace on her other side.

"If the country were always like this," Diana said, "I might even be tempted to live here."

"Don't say that, Diana," Lamb complained. "London needs you."

"I'm not serious. I can't wait to get back to town in the autumn and take my exercise on busy pavements instead of muddy fields. Not to mention that my wardrobe is in dire need of replenishment."

"Are you suggesting," Blake said, "that Mandeville Wallop cannot satisfy a lady's every whim?"

"There are certain needs that can only be met in Bond Street. I had quite enough of country life in the year after Fanshawe died."

"Talking of Wallop, are your estimable parents as singular as ever?"

"Thank you, Blake, I found them in good health." Which didn't quite answer the question.

"Mr. and Mrs. Montrose are famous in Shropshire," Blake explained to Lambton. "She is the Master of the Mandeville Hunt. Or should I say Mistress? I never quite know. Which is it, Diana?"

"I believe," Diana replied, keeping her face and tone neutral, "that she is known as the Master of the Hunt. In this she follows the example of Lady Salisbury at Hatfield."

"And does your father keep household?" Both men chuckled and Diana gritted her teeth.

"My father is of a mechanical bent," she said lightly, trying to walk the fine line between irony and disrespect. "His inventions are not always practical, or even successful, but we appreciate his ingenuity."

"What's Rufus doing these days? We used to play together as boys. He became quite a crammer at Oxford, though. Always at lectures or in the library."

"He is pursuing his classical studies abroad."

Blake sighed. "Pity. He was a regular fellow once. Then he became as bad as my cousin. Of course, Iverley never was a regular fellow. He hasn't changed since the first time he came here. We must have been ten or eleven years old and I never saw a worse seat on a horse. He couldn't stay on at anything faster than a trot. Blind too. We called him the Owl."

Whatever he'd been like at ten, Mr. Iverley could certainly ride now, but Diana didn't argue the point. The rest of the party wasn't aware he'd accompanied her that morning.

"The Owl always has his head in a book," Blake went on. "M'father thinks he's brilliant. Probably because he listens to the old man bore on about politics."

"I was at school with him," Lamb said.

"I forgot he was a Wykehamist," Blake said. "Was dear Sebastian as odd then?"

"Almost everyone at Winchester was strange. It's a strange place. He didn't stand out much then, but while the rest of us became normal once we escaped, Iverley grew stranger. He never goes to *ton* entertainments."

"He isn't interested in sports."

"And he collects books."

"Do you know what's the strangest thing about

him?" Blake asked. "He won't have anything to do with women. Famous for it. Being here with you, Diana, and the other ladies, is probably the closest he's ever been to any females. Do you suppose, Lamb, that he's *different*."

Lamb gave it some thought. "No. There were plenty of them at school but Iverley wasn't among them. Muslin company?" He spoke the last two words through a cough. While Diana appreciated his gentlemanly impulse not to talk about females of ill repute in front of her, she understood the question.

"Not that I've ever heard of," Blake said. "He claims he hates all females as a matter of principle. Probably doesn't even own a mare."

Lamb shook his head in bewilderment. "Surely he has *needs*."

"If he does he keeps them buttoned."

Diana wondered if she ought to be insulted that the men held such a discussion in front of her. As an unmarried girl she'd never been exposed to anything so fascinating and her late husband's friends, most of them middle-aged like himself, had always addressed her with perfect propriety. Sir Tobias Fanshawe had kept matters of intimacy in the bedroom. At other times he'd treated her with indulgent but strict formality. If this frankness was one of the consequences of widowhood her mother had warned about, on the whole Diana was inclined to enjoy it.

Lamb remained skeptical. "Maybe your cousin's just late to the business. My cousin Jasper was like that. Not interested until he was twenty-one. Then one day he met a barmaid with a large . . . endowment . . . and he never looked back. Had the pox by the time he was twenty-three. Iverley just hasn't yet found a woman he fancies."

"And never will, in my opinion. He's twenty-six years old. There's something wrong there, I'd wager a pony."

If there was one thing no member of Blake's set ever turned down, it was a wager. "You're on," said Lamb. "I say if a man isn't a molly he can be seduced by a woman."

"And I say there isn't a woman in the world beautiful enough to gain my cousin's attention."

"That, Blake, is an insult to womankind. Look at Diana here. Could any man resist her?"

"To get Sebastian Iverley to even kiss her she'd have to be Helen of Troy and Cleopatra rolled into one."

Diana thought of Mr. Iverley staring at her leg that morning. And the way she'd intercepted his eyes on her bosom during dinner. Blake might not believe she combined the allure of history's two most famous beauties but she'd show him.

"I'll do it," she said, without giving herself a moment to consider. "I can get him to kiss me. But not for a measly pony. I'll wager you five hundred pounds that your cousin will kiss me."

Chapter 4

Mr. Iverley was at his customary post the next morning, hunched over a volume on the library table. He'd removed his coat, thus informing the observer that his hips were very slim. The baggy breeches would never have stayed up without the leather braces that showed where the back of his waistcoat had risen up. Diana had reason to believe him more than an unmuscled weakling, but as usual his clothing did nothing to demonstrate the fact.

She swallowed nervously. She'd felt progressively worse about the wager since about five minutes after her unthinking boast. Only the recollection of Blake and Lamb's incredulity, and their strictures on honor kept her from crying off. They'd been almost insulting when they discussed the question of proof. The two men had suggested they should hide in the shrubbery and watch the "seduction." At this she drew the line. Only when reminded of her four brothers were they prepared to accept that she, a mere female, understood the sacred nature of a bet and agreed to settle the outcome on her word alone. She couldn't help but feel there wasn't a whole lot of honor in the enterprise.

"Ahem," she coughed.

Iverley spun around. "Lady Fanshawe. I thought you'd gone with the others."

"I've seen the abbey ruins a hundred times, living just ten miles away. And please, call me Diana."

He made one of his little grunting noises.

"Can you tell me where I'd find histories?"

"At the north end. Anything in particular?"

"I enjoy reading about our kings and queens. Especially the queens."

Iverley flushed. "We have that in common," he said with an enthusiasm Diana found rather endearing. "I collect royal bindings, books that belonged to royalty."

"I hadn't really thought about it before, but there are a lot of different kinds of book covers. It makes sense that monarchs would have special ones."

"Not just royalty." He pointed to a pile of volumes on the table. "See the Vanderlin arms on *Cook's Voyages*? The present duke's father bought the book when it was published and had it bound for the library here."

"Is it hard to find royal bindings? I'd expect them all to belong to the king."

"Even kings sell things, or give them away for one reason or another. The rarest binding I own belonged to Queen Catherine Howard. You can guess why that one didn't stay in the royal family."

"Poor lady."

"Yes, she didn't last long as queen. That's why the book is so rare."

"How good of Henry VIII to execute his fifth queen with such expedition. He must have had future book collectors in mind when he did it."

Iverley's lips twitched, then he smiled and Diana realized she'd never seen him do so before. His habitual expressions were boredom, irritation, abstraction, and occasionally, when engaged by a topic, alert interest. Never in their admittedly brief acquaintance had she seen his face display so much as a hint of levity. It suited him. For the first time she noticed that he wasn't a bad-looking man. His features were well proportioned with high cheekbones, a straight nose, a firm chin. Since he wasn't wearing his spectacles, she was able to observe that he had rather beautiful eyes of a silver gray, with darker rims bordering the irises. And his smiling mouth was distinctly attractive, firm shapely lips of a good color. Kissing him might not be so bad.

"Henry's matrimonial habits were certainly a boon to the collector," he said.

"Do you have examples of all six wives?"

"It happens that Katherine Parr has eluded me, but I hope to obtain her soon."

"How fascinating! Who has her?"

"A rather eccentric fellow with a small but exquisite collection of bindings. I've been trying to persuade him to sell to me for some years. I believe I'm getting close."

There was something wrong. Sebastian wondered if he were ill. He couldn't stop thinking about Lady Fanshawe. Diana.

When she joined him in the library he inwardly cursed. He should have left Mandeville that morning, as planned, after a night of heated dreams about this dangerously appealing female. It had been years since he'd woken to find a wet spot in his bed. Disgusted by this regression to adolescence, he'd almost summoned his carriage and left for Kent. It was time he had another go at persuading Deaver to sell.

That he'd mentioned the Katherine Parr binding to Diana was another symptom of insanity. The location, even the existence of the Deaver collection, was a secret known to few, and he'd almost blabbed the whole thing.

He'd only decided to remain when he learned the party had gone out for the day. Now he could hardly believe that he'd spent a full half hour talking about books to a woman. A woman who asked intelligent questions and knew at least as much about the previous owners of his royal bindings as he did. She sat with her elbow on the table, head resting on her hand, listening with apparent fascination as he spoke of morocco, gilt-tooling, blind stamps, arms, and crests. Although the Mandeville collection didn't have much with royal provenance, he was able to find examples to illustrate his disquisition.

He hoped he hadn't been talking nonsense. Her proximity made his senses swim. He ached to stroke the sweet curve of her arm, feel the flawless pale skin. He imagined it silken to the touch over warm flesh. When she put out a hand to touch a leather cover, he wanted to kiss it. The hand, that is. He wanted to draw near, to inhale her scent, to plunge his face into the enticing shadow between her breasts and breathe deeply.

He didn't want to think about what he really wanted to do with her. Suffice to say that wearing unfashionably comfortable breeches seemed like an even better idea than usual.

"But you said yesterday you'd come to Mandeville to look at atlases."

What was that? His wits had gone begging.

"What's this?" She looked at the folio volume open on the table to a map of the harbor at Genoa. Hand-drawn on vellum, the cartography was on the primitive side but the colors vibrant.

"How adorable!" she said, pointing at a mermaid who cavorted in the Ligurian Sea. "Her face is painted like a woman of doubtful virtue, but her expression is rather fetching."

He'd noted the same thing. "She looks surprised," he said. "As though her fish tail popped up through the waves and she's saying 'I didn't know I had that. What happened to my legs?'"

His face heated at the thought of legs.

She reached out her hand again and brushed against his with ungloved fingers. "This fellow must be the mermaid's lover," she said, indicating a trident-bearing sea-god puffing out his virile chest.

He was careful not to touch her again as he leafed through the volume. The next map was embellished with a sulky-looking sea monster, others with graceful sailing ships, exotic fish, or elaborate compass roses, eliciting exclamations of delight at each new illustration, in the same musical, slightly ironic tone.

"What is this book?" she asked.

"It's a portolan, an early sailing map. This one is fourteenth century and shows the coastlines, harbors, and islands of the Mediterranean. It would have been used aboard ship."

"How lovely that they added such charming decorations to a practical object."

"I expect it gets dull out at sea for weeks on end. Decorating the maps must have given a seaman with a talent for drawing something to do to pass the time."

The volume was open to the map of an island. "Elba," she remarked. "I wonder if Bonaparte regrets he didn't stay there. It must have a better climate than St. Helena."

A sentiment Sebastian could share. He hated being cold. "Without having visited either place, I'm sure you are correct."

"How I long to go to Italy. You must know it well. Is it as wonderfully warm and beautiful as it sounds?"

"I've never been."

"Surely you've visited your mother? Lady Gee says she's lived there for years."

"True."

"I suppose," Diana said, "with the political situation in Europe, travel would have been difficult until the last two or three years."

"Yes," he said without elaboration.

She looked at him with uncertainty in her eyes. Obviously she'd noted his change of mood. A good thing, really. The reminder of his mother, the Contessa Montecitta, brought the inherent treachery of the female sex forcibly back to mind.

He turned aside from his now unwelcome companion. Without blatant discourtesy he meant to convey the message that their encounter was at an end. If only she'd leave and let him get on with his work.

"Thank you for showing me the atlas," she said. "A portolan, I think you called it. I must remember the word. And for telling me about your collection. I enjoyed it."

He nodded and looked down at the table and the island of Elba, symbol of exile.

"I'll leave you to your studies now."

He grunted. She walked toward the door. He felt relieved, and bereft.

She stopped halfway across the room. "Mr. Iverley?" she said.

"Yes?"

"I intend to ride this afternoon. Will you come with me?"

He was tempted. "Will you visit your family again?"

"I meant just to take exercise."

"I'd like to see some of your father's inventions."

"We could call at Wallop Hall. I'm sure Papa would love to tell you what he's come up with since yesterday."

He succumbed. "What time do you wish to leave?"

By two o'clock it was raining. Diana didn't bother with her riding habit. Instead she changed into her prettiest muslin, a white one with pale blue figures that enhanced her eyes. Iverley didn't strike her as a man who noticed the details of a woman's clothing, so he wouldn't wonder why she'd left off the high-necked pleated chemise she usually wore underneath this gown. Without it the bodice was definitely daring for day wear. That detail any man should notice. And to drive home the point she wore her thinnest petticoat.

She descended to the hall and found him waiting. Since his garments, in various shades of mud, never changed, she couldn't tell whether he'd dressed for outdoors.

"Are you ready to go?" he asked.

"I'm not dressed for riding," she pointed out. "It's pouring with rain."

He grunted, perhaps disappointed. She wished he'd cultivate a greater degree of articulacy. When talking about what interested him he could be eloquent, but Mr. Iverley lacked fluency in the social niceties. Clearly he wasn't going to suggest an alternative, but she had a plan for the afternoon.

According to the terms of the wager *he* had to make the amorous advance. Even the boldest of men might find it hard to steal a kiss while galloping across the fields. And the Montroses would be in the way: the presence of a lady's parents was generally a deterrent to amorous advances.

"I thought we might explore the house," she said.

Another grunt.

"I'm told there are over one hundred and fifty rooms. As the duke's nephew you must know all sorts of places most guests never see."

"I wouldn't say that."

"Never mind," she said brightly. "If we get lost we can ask a servant for directions."

He grunted again. Diana, possessor of four brothers, a father, and a late husband, interpreted the

meaning as *not while I live and breathe*. She anticipated a fruitful afternoon lost in the far reaches of
the ducal mansion.

In a deserted bedroom wing they encountered a
maid armed with a duster, who politely offered to
lead them back to the principal part of the house.

"Oh no," Diana replied, as she had to the butler
and two footmen who'd already made the same
suggestion. "His Grace's nephew is showing me
around."

"You ought to stop saying that," Sebastian said.
"You know far more about Mandeville and its history than I do."

"That appears to be the case," she agreed. "Why
don't you tell me a story for a change? And not one
that involves anything found in the library."

"I can't think of one."

"Make something up."

"I couldn't do that."

"Do you always stick to the facts then?"

"I always stick to the truth," he said firmly.

"Surely there's no harm in a little fantasy intended
to amuse. Do you never read novels?"

"Books are not intended to deceive."

"Aha!" she said with a note of triumph. "You
couldn't keep out of the library after all."

"But it was you who first mentioned novels."

She laughed, and he decided, for once, to forget
that while books could always be relied upon, people
could not.

"How do you know so much about Mandeville?"
he asked.

"I lived close by all my life. As the 'big house' it was always the subject of legend."

"Yet your family's house is much older. I like it better."

"You're mad!"

He was indeed mad, but not for the reason she meant. He was well on his way to being obsessed with Diana Fanshawe. He couldn't keep his eyes off her. Unaccustomed as he was to judging feminine beauty, he was puzzled as to how to describe her allure. The best he could do, not surprisingly, was to compare her to a beautiful book in immaculate condition. Everything about her was pristine, from hair dressed in sleek mahogany waves like polished calf to pale blue slippers without a spot of dirt, like a silk bookmark. Not a stray hair nor a loose thread marred the perfection of her appearance. Her skin reminded him of the very best, softest, smoothest vellum parchment and his fingers itched to touch and stroke the curved cheeks, the pert little nose, the small yet forceful chin. Her scent drove him almost to distraction whenever he came within a yard of her.

The afternoon's exploration added a new delight and torment to his experience, the reason he was content to let her lead the way and, he feared, lead him by the nose. Each time Diana passed near a window he was afforded a spectacular view of her figure through the thin fabric of her gown.

This particular passage ended with a large Venetian window. The rain had blown over. As she walked ahead of him the sun came out. His heart hammered in his chest and he could hardly breathe. The only better sight in this world would be Diana without the semitransparent gown. And he knew what he'd like to do with her. It was too cruel that they were surrounded by bedrooms.

He beat back lust. Even were he to acknowledge his desire he couldn't act on it. Diana was a lady and not to be trifled with.

"Where shall we go now?" she said, looking over her shoulder with blue eyes rimmed by thick dark lashes. Did she have any idea what she did to him? Surely not, or she'd run in terror. "I no longer have the least idea where we are."

His response was inarticulate. She looked amused. "No suggestions? Very well, let's go up here."

Here was a narrow staircase, surely a servants' route. As they'd traveled up through the mansion the decoration became plainer. The lavish gilt, plaster-work, damask, and tapestry of the public rooms gave way to solid comfort and elegance in the family and guest quarters. Now they reached the next floor to find yet another long passage, narrower than those below, painted white with simple architraves and skirting boards.

"This is the nursery floor," he said. "It's where I stayed when I was young."

Diana looked at the pictures that lined the walls, watercolors uniformly mounted in simple gilt frames. "Most of these seem to be views of the grounds. Here is the lake, but the trees are smaller."

"No wonder. It was done sixty years ago. Maria Vanderlin, 1759," Sebastian read over her shoulder.

"And the next is by Lavinia Vanderlin, 1760. I do believe these are all by daughters of the house. What a delightful idea."

They walked along the passage, commenting on the artistic abilities of various Vanderlin ladies.

"This one is interesting," Diana said. "It's the first time I've noticed a figure in the landscape. The artist wasn't good at painting trees but the costume is quite detailed. I've seen portraits of ladies wearing habits like this."

Sebastian agreed with Diana's judgment. The drawing was stiff, save for a small figure of a woman wearing a red costume and triangular hat. Then he noticed the signature. It was absurd to be surprised, but somehow he hadn't expected it.

"Corinna Vanderlin, 1785. Isn't she your mother?"

"Yes."

"What is she like? As a girl she seems to have had an eye for fashion."

Sebastian didn't know. He hadn't seen his mother since he was six. An image, unrecalled in years, filled his mind.

A morning visit to his mother's chamber. She sits at her dressing table, occupied with potions and bottles and a huge powder puff. She draws him into her deliciously scented embrace. "My funny little monkey," she murmurs. She has forgiven him for knocking over the little statue of the shepherd god when he visited the drawing room yesterday. She cried when her ornament broke but today he's her favorite pet again. "Will you come with us to the park, Mama?" he asks in desperate hope. He holds his breath. She's going to say yes, he is sure. Then her maid enters the room, her arms full of embroidered silk and gauze. "The delivery from the dressmaker, my lady." His mother says she can't go to the park today. She has something important to do.

"Yes," he said, in answer to Diana's question. "She did have an eye for fashion."

They were standing shoulder to shoulder in front of the little picture. She angled her head to look at his face, opened her mouth to speak then changed her mind about whatever she'd been about to say. "I'd like to see the nursery," she said instead. "I love toys and I'm sure the Mandeville children had splendid ones."

Sebastian sensed a foolish shadow of reluctance as he opened the door into the day nursery and let Diana precede him into the room. It was a big, light room, warm from trapped summer heat. Though kept perfectly free of dust like every other part of the house, neglect hung in the air. He recognized some of the playthings, those too large to be stowed in the paneled cupboards that ran along one wall: a puppet theater, a model of a grand medieval keep which he now realized was copied from Warwick Castle, a huge rocking horse. This last had belonged to Blakeney who hadn't wanted to share it with his cousin. He'd sulked when the nurse had insisted he let Sebastian take a turn. Given Sebastian's desperate longing for these toys on his earlier visit, it was almost disconcerting to have no interest in playing with them now.

Diana ran her hands over the long mane of the dapple gray steed, galloping on green boat-shaped rockers. "I've never seen such a big one," she said. "I must try it. Of course I can't ride astride in this gown. I'll have to go sidesaddle." Perched sideways on the wooden horse's leather-covered back, she swayed her hips from side to side, trying to generate enough force to set the horse rocking, and succeeding only in drawing his attention to her bosom.

Let me help you with that. Sebastian was fairly sure his vocal cords never actually formed the words, though his mouth probably gaped open. He could scarcely breathe as he crossed the room, stood in front of her, as near as the rockers would allow, and placed a hand each on the horse's neck and haunch. She fell still.

Oh God. He'd had to lean over and his face was almost in her décolletage. Only a huge effort of will made him look up from breasts like living marble, pale and smooth, rising and falling gently with her breath. He dragged his eyes from the promise of the valley between, with its tantalizing invitation to explore what lay beneath fragile cloth.

Only to find her mouth, plump, red, slightly parted. The little bow shape in the center of her upper lip entranced him. He'd give anything in the world to trace it with the tip of his tongue. His upper body moved forward, his face came closer and closer. Already they shared the same air and her breath tickled his lips. Just another inch and he would inhale her heat, find out how she tasted. Surely she was inviting him to kiss her.

Then another memory intruded. Diana's dark and luscious beauty faded into the golden ringlets of Lady Amanda Vanderlin, aged seven, Blake's youngest sister.

It's his second week at Mandeville and he's hiding in the nursery, tired of being laughed at and called

Owl for his spectacles, sore from falling off an over-spirited horse, sick at heart yet dreading his return to the cold solitude of his uncle's house. Then little Amanda comes in and smiles at him. She's so pretty, as are all the girls. Mysterious, wondrous beings he has no idea how to please. "Hello, Sebastian," she says. "Come with me . . ." She offers him her hand and it's soft and small. She smells clean, not like a boy. She leads him over to the nursery closet, a small windowless room where outdoor clothing, boots, and things like cricket bats are stored. She lets go of him to turn the handle, an action that requires both her tiny delicate hands. "Go in," she says with a nod. "You first. It's a surprise."

Even sixteen years later he castigated himself for a fool. A surprise indeed. Blake awaited him in the closet . . .

Sebastian jerked his head away. Stepping backward a couple of yards he subjected Diana's expression to a keen examination. She looked both guileless and radiantly beautiful.

"Aren't you going to rock me?" she asked, brows arching over clear midday eyes. No invitation was intended and no betrayal either. She merely wished for a push.

"Of course," he said. This time he stood to the rear of the horse and set a hand to the painted wooden rump. With his help Diana got her ride. He felt foolish and perhaps she did, too, for after a minute or two she indicated she'd had enough. He held out a hand to help her dismount then rapidly dropped it.

"Shall we go down?" he asked. "The others may have returned by now."

Sebastian was desperate to escape. Diana Fanshawe might be quite sensible compared to other women. But she was appallingly attractive and that made her dangerous. The peril came, he feared, not from Diana but from his own unprecedented reaction to her. He could end up doing something he regretted.

Chapter 5

Botheration. She thought she had him on the rocking horse. He'd wanted her. She couldn't possibly be wrong about that.

In the past few months, the first season she'd spent in London without the guardianship of either parents or husband, quite a few men had tried to steal a kiss and she'd allowed a couple of them to succeed. She knew that look in a man's eye when he advanced to conquest. She'd become quite adept at gracefully avoiding most of the attempted embraces in dark gardens or deserted anterooms. And of course at stopping the privileged few before they went too far.

He wasn't the man of the party she really desired, but strangely enough she felt no reluctance about kissing him, just a mild concern that his spectacles would get in the way. While she might wish he were a little more forthcoming, she liked him. His brusque conversation was always interesting.

And he liked her. Whatever Blake claimed, Sebastian Iverley was not unaffected by female charms. So why, Diana wondered, hadn't he pressed his advantage? Perhaps he feared being trapped into marriage. Pity there wasn't some way of tactfully indicating that she wasn't seeking a long-term connection. About two minutes would be the likely length of their amorous relationship.

Excuse me, sir, but I'm only interested in a meaningless embrace without affection or vows.

Most of the men she knew would be delighted by such an offer. She thrust aside the uneasy reflection that Sebastian Iverley was nothing like any man she'd ever met.

For the rest of the afternoon and evening Sebastian avoided Diana Fanshawe. Trying not to be obviously rude, he left a room when she entered it or withdrew from a conversation she joined.

Not looking at her during dinner was a trial. It would have helped if the grand silver epergne had been placed a foot to his right and so blocked his view of her. He managed, for the most part, not to stare but still learned that she had rather peculiar eating habits. She tasted almost nothing for two courses, accepting only a morsel of poached salmon, then partook heavily of the sweet dishes that accompanied the final remove.

To his horror he found himself thinking of sharing meals with her, just the two of them. Including breakfast.

He went to bed early and the next morning actually joined the other men for a couple of hours hunting rabbits. A tedious way of passing the time, but it was the one place he could be sure not to have to fight his fascination with Lady Fanshawe's alluring person.

Yet as soon as he returned to the house, instead

of escaping to the library, he found himself following the sound of female voices to the morning room.
The terrible sisters were chattering away on one side
of the room while Diana sat in the opposite corner,
silent and beautiful. She looked up at his entrance
and smiled. Like a dog responding to a jerk of the
leash he walked over to her. At the back of his mind
he resented his compliance, but he seemed to have
lost the will to resist.

"Did you have a successful morning?" she asked.

"My efforts made no difference to the rabbit popu-
lation of Shropshire," he said.

"I should commiserate with you, I suppose, but I
am glad. Bunnies are so sweet."

Instead of treating this fatuous statement with the
contempt it deserved, Sebastian felt himself smile
back at her.

Marriage. The word circled his brain like a gnat.
Marriage. The most terrifying word in the English
language. What was it doing in his head?

For once in his life he was pleased to see his cousin
enter a room.

Blakeney came straight over to their corner.
"Diana," he said, "how beautiful you look this morn-
ing." He took her hand and, most unnecessarily in
Sebastian's opinion, raised her knuckles to his lips.
To his pleasure she appeared annoyed and retracted
her hand quickly.

"I've just been hearing about your morning from
your cousin," she said, and gave Sebastian another
dazzling smile.

Sebastian was getting used to the racing of his
heart whenever Diana looked at him, but something

about his reaction was different this time, warmer, more powerful. Blakeney, he knew, had always been pursued by women. Yet here was a woman, just about the most beautiful woman Sebastian had ever seen, showing a distinct preference for his company over that of the popular, handsome future duke.

That word again, in his ear, whispered by the devil himself. *Marriage.*

Mumbling horribly, he excused himself and fled to the library.

"This is ridiculous," Diana complained an hour later. "I follow Mr. Iverley to the library and you follow me. How can he kiss me if you are always there?"

She would have been happier to have Blake interrupt Iverley's lecture on early Venetian printers if his motive wasn't so obvious. He'd put an end to a promising tête-à-tête and succeeded in driving Sebastian from the room again.

"I have only a few hours left," she continued, "and you aren't playing fair."

"Perhaps I don't want him to kiss you," Blake said.

"I know you don't. You have five hundred pounds resting on it."

"Perhaps that's not the only reason. Perhaps that isn't the reason at all." Blake leaned against the library table with folded arms, elegance and self-confidence personified. His clothing, striking the right note, was beautifully cut, yet not as formal as he'd wear in town. He epitomized the man of fashion dressed for rustication, perfect in his imperfection, yet his neck cloth was pure white, crisp, tied in an intricate knot.

Blake's neck cloth was always pristine. Diana sometimes thought it was why she'd fallen in love with him when she was a fourteen-year-old school-girl and he a newly minted Oxford undergraduate, making his first visit back to Duke's Mandeville after the Michaelmas term. He'd almost knocked her down outside the draper's shop, probably, she realized now, because his starched shirt points were so absurdly high he couldn't see properly.

Never mind, she'd thought him the handsomest man she'd ever seen then and her opinion hadn't changed. He, of course, hadn't recognized her and he'd barely noticed when she made her eagerly awaited bow in London. Settling for second best like a sensible girl, she'd married Fanshawe and been happy enough with her affectionate older husband. But on a deep, mostly unacknowledged, level she remained enamored with Blakeney, a hopeless tendre like a favorite book, sitting on a shelf next to her bed to be taken up, reread, and enjoyed whenever she had nothing better to do.

She looked at him now, drinking him in: firm chin shaved to the smoothness of planed oak, high cheek-bones, a straight nose, forget-me-not eyes, golden hair that managed to look both arranged and rumpled at the same time, arched eyebrows several shades darker, and a mouth whose current sulky expression did nothing to diminish its beauty.

Poor Sebastian. There was no comparison. Yet that strange, oddly appealing man had succeeded in arousing Blake's jealousy. For this alone Diana owed him her gratitude. And before the night was over he would be rewarded with a kiss. Not that he would know why he was being so gifted. And if she felt a twinge of guilt at using him she dismissed it easily.

What was a little kiss, after all? He'd enjoy it.

"Why would you wish to kiss him, anyway?" Blake's question sounded querulous. For goodness sake, it was his bet.

"Men kiss for many reasons," she replied coolly. "Perhaps women do, too."

"I hope there's only one reason for you to kiss dear Cousin Sebastian."

Diana shrugged.

"Very well. After dinner tonight I shall suggest we go out. But I'll be keeping an eye on you. And my cousin."

Wives. Sebastian knew what wives did.

Not from firsthand observation. His upbringing and education had been blessedly free of feminine interference. But he had numerous male acquaintances and sometimes he couldn't help hearing about the female appendages that most of them had to endure.

Wives nagged. They demanded. They spent too much money. They wept when they didn't get their way.

A wife was nothing but trouble.

But there was one other thing a wife did. A wife shared your bed. Sebastian ached at the thought of Diana Fanshawe between his sheets.

Marriage. He couldn't leave the idea alone. It had started as a single word rattling around in his brain and grown into a full-blown concept that ousted every other thought. The vision took form. The days were a little vague. Not much would change. He'd still visit booksellers, attend auctions, meet his friends, enjoy stimulating intellectual and political conversations with his fellow men in London's masculine haunts. During this time *she* would do whatever mysterious and probably nonsensical things women did.

But the nights. The nights! He'd come home and find her waiting for him, warm, soft, perfumed. Perhaps she'd be undressed. The thought of Diana naked made him slightly faint. And she'd be his, all night long. He'd do all the things to her he was imagining now and a good many more. He had the feeling that he hadn't even begun to plumb the depths of his imagination when it came to sharing a bed with Diana Fanshawe.

Diana Iverley, he corrected. She'd be Diana Iverley.

His. Not Blake's but his.

Keeping his promise, Blake suggested the whole party tour the park by moonlight. Dinner ended late and it was almost dark, a rising moon waxing in the fading twilight, as the party took to the graveled walk that began Mandeville's carefully designed circuit of shrubbery, lake, bridge, temples, and grottos.

Diana looked for Sebastian and she believed that he looked for her. A summoning smile brought him to her side and she tucked her hand around his elbow. His arm hung awkwardly, as though unused to offering a lady support. They crossed the steep stone bridge that spanned the lake at the beginning of the walk. A hundred feet past there was a diversion from the main path.

"Shall we . . ."

" . . . take the path to the Temple of Aphrodite?"

"You know the park well," he said.

"I always took every opportunity to explore it."

"Do you suppose we ever met when I visited Mandeville?" he asked.

"If we did, I was doubtless a small, untidy schoolgirl and of no interest to boys. You are about the same age as Blake, I think."

"Exactly the same," he said curtly.

"Were you friends back then?"

"I lived with my great-uncle in the north. My uncle the duke invited me to stay at Mandeville so that I could have company of my own age."

"And that would be Blake."

"That would be Blakeney," he agreed without further elaboration.

Dusk fell fast now and the path was almost invisible. Silk slippers weren't designed for the rougher terrain off the main walk. Sebastian guided her safely along the grassy trail through a thick group of azaleas and past a climbing rose, blooming wildly as it smothered a tree trunk, its scent intensified by the darkness. She clung to his arm and took every opportunity to brush her hip against him.

The trickle of running water recalled a forgotten feature of their chosen route. "The stream," she said. "I wonder if I can find the stepping stones without getting my feet wet."

Without a word he set one arm about her shoulders, the other beneath her knees. Diana was horribly conscious that she was no feather, but she might have been made of gossamer the way he swung her up. Appearances were deceptive: clearly Sebastian was very strong. She put her arms about his neck and leaned her head against his chest, feeling and hearing the steady drum of his heartbeat. She braced herself to be dropped, half expecting a dunking in the shallow racing stream. But he picked his way sure-footed over the slippery stones that formed the path across the brook. She relaxed into his embrace, enjoying a sense of safety. In the fading light all his oddities—the old-fashioned garments, the floppy neck cloth, the spectacles, the communication-by-grunt—evaporated, leaving heat, hard muscle, and a subtle masculine scent that owed nothing to any perfumer. She had a fleeting thought that she was meeting the real Sebastian Iverley, a man of strength and dependability beneath the eccentric exterior.

Without a stumble he achieved the other side of the stream. The dome of the temple gleamed white over the dark foliage of the rhododendrons, up a shallow rise.

"Thank you," she murmured, preparing to be set on her feet. But he held on to her, taking the slope in easy strides, his only comment one of those damned indecipherable grunts.

Sebastian hardly bothered to ask himself why he carried a full-grown woman up a hill she was quite capable of negotiating on her own. He'd surrendered to the fact that where Diana was concerned everything he'd ever defined as logic, reason, and common sense had fled. Her delectable body, the subject of sleepless fantasies, clung to his own. His lips pressed against her hair, as glossy to the touch as to the eyes. Her fragrance, maddening, rich and beyond his knowledge to define, should have confused his senses like brandy. Instead his head felt clearer than it had ever been. He was in the right place at the right time doing the right thing. The predictable outcome of attempting the slimy and uneven stepping stones so burdened was a cold bath for both of them. He never feared it for a moment. Tonight Sebastian was supremely powerful. He was Atlas, Julius Caesar, Columbus, and Shakespeare. If Deaver were here he'd sell him his collection in a flash.

But holding, conquering, or discovering the world, producing great works of literature, or even buying books, were not on Sebastian's list of things to be done that night.

The path emerged into an open plateau where the little round temple stood on its square plinth. Sebastian climbed four steps and walked to the other side, which offered an open view down to the lake. A warm summer breeze carried the sounds of night. Brilliant moonlight reflected ripples of water and illuminated Diana's face. Head tilted back, shadowed eyes delved into his then dropped to his mouth. He read the enigmatic curve of her own as an invitation to do, finally, at long last, what he'd ached to do for two interminable days.

He kissed her lips, hard.

His heart plunged when her movements told him she wanted to be put down. He hadn't been disappointed at the desperately anticipated contact, but had she? She almost certainly had a greater basis for comparison than he.

She slid to her feet, keeping her hands on his shoulders. He sensed her rise on tiptoes to whisper in his ear. "Not so fierce. Softly."

The sibilants caressed him and soothed his anxiety. She offered herself again and he brought his mouth to hers, gently this time. He was rewarded by the sensation of warm satin and the sweet humidity of breath as she parted her lips beneath his. He followed her lead and shook with astonishment and delight when he felt her tongue flicker around the inner rim of his lips, kindling a sensitivity he'd never have suspected. He ventured to reciprocate and the clash of their tongues sent a bolt of lightning straight to his cock.

His arms went around her waist and tugged her against him, deepening a desire that had already reached scorching intensity. Satin-clad fingers burned the nape of his neck then cradled his skull and pulled him closer. Recalling her admonishment he tried to hold back, to emulate her own skill and give equal pleasure. Without conscious intention he brought one hand up to touch her silk-covered breast and lost any tenuous control over his own actions. Wilder and bolder, he obeyed the drive to devour and felt devoured in return. Beyond observation or analysis, he was swept into a maelstrom of wet heat and one overwhelming urge possessed him.

To make her his.

There was nothing wrong with his hearing so it must have reached his ears, but at first his mind refused to register the sound. He knew only when she stiffened in his arms and her lips fell still against his.

"Di-a-na!" The repeated call wafted up the grassy slope from the lakeside.

God damn him to hell. Blakeney. In nearly twenty years of unwelcome appearances, his cousin had made his most inconvenient yet.

Chapter 6

A comfortable chair stood in the library gallery, invisible to anyone below who wasn't looking and a perfect spot for a man who wanted to hide. There was only one person Sebastian wanted to see that morning and she wouldn't be up for an hour or so.

That ladies preferred to rise late was just one of the oddities of the female race he'd discovered in the past day or two. While he waited, he looked over the small bundle of correspondence forwarded from his London house. Only two letters were of any importance. Viscount Iverley wrote that he was dying. Lord Deaver hinted that he might, finally, be prepared to discuss a price. These two communications summoned him to Northumberland and Kent respectively so he couldn't combine the two journeys. Duty competed with inclination.

His great-uncle's news didn't alarm him. His former guardian had been dying on a regular basis for at least ten years and there was no reason he wouldn't survive to do so for another decade. Yet Sebastian owed him a visit. He hadn't faced the horrors of Saxton Iverley for over a year. As for Deaver, at any other time Sebastian would be calling for his carriage and posting to Kent to reap the reward of years of careful courting.

Both would have to wait. He had another courting task planned. This morning he would propose marriage to Lady Fanshawe. The letters fell to his lap and he relaxed into his chair, reflecting on the astonishing fact that Sebastian Iverley, lifelong scorner of all things female, was about to enter the state of matrimony. Not that his opinion had changed. But Diana was different from other women. One only had to look at her family to see that. Becoming connected to the interesting Montroses was an added enticement. What his own closest relative would say he'd rather not think about. He'd never convince Lord Iverley that Diana was an exception to his favorite precept.

He wondered how long it took to arrange a wedding. For one who'd always avoided them, he found himself eager for his own. Or eager for his wedding night, rather, and the discovery of firsthand details about Diana's sleeping habits.

He stiffened like a watchdog at the sound of the door opening below, but another look at his watch told him it was unlikely to be her. A murmur of masculine voices announced the arrival of Blakeney and Lambton. He hunched down in his seat.

"You'll have to lend me the money, Lamb." That was Blakeney, so extravagant and careless in his spending he was always short of cash. "Might as well make it a thousand. You'll have it back on quarter day."

As far as Sebastian could make out, Lambton, an ever-obliging fool, agreed to the arrangement. Not terribly interested in Blake's financial difficulties, his attention drifted until her name came up.

"What about Diana Fanshawe?" Lamb asked. "You're going about it damned discreetly." Sebastian leaned around the chair so that he could hear clearly. "Have you had her yet? Are you going to give me some details?"

"Damn it, Lamb! When it comes to one's wife the secrets of the bedchamber remain secret."

"Wife!"

"I daresay I shall marry her," Blakeney replied.

"Is that necessary?"

"If I want her, and I do, it'll have to be marriage. That or risk a scandal at Mandeville and the devil to pay with my mother."

"I wouldn't think the duchess, or the duke for that matter, would like to see that connection."

"M'father won't like it at all but my mother will like it less if I take Diana as my mistress and it becomes known."

"Which it will, of course. But why should anyone care?" Lamb sounded puzzled. "Aren't her family nobodies?"

"Not quite. They may be a shoal of queer fish but the family's been here since before the Conqueror. Or perhaps it's before the Flood. A devilish long time, anyway. The Vanderlins may be ducal now, but the Montroses were already somebody when we were living in mud huts in Holland. The country folk never forget we only arrived with William of Orange."

"Still, Blake. Marriage?"

He'll never get the chance, Sebastian thought smugly, not pretending to deny that beating his cousin to the prize added spice to the prospect of his wedding.

"She's beautiful, Lamb," Blakeney said. "Who'd have thought she'd turn out so well? Fanshawe spotted a diamond where none of the rest of us saw it. And Fanshawe's nabob fortune would be damned useful. I could thumb my nose at my father. Hey, I wouldn't have to borrow from you anymore."

"Rich and beautiful, you lucky dog."

"She wants me," Blakeney said.

Sebastian could hardly restrain his mirth. How like his cousin to be so arrogant and so wrong. It wasn't Blake Diana had been pursuing for two days. It wasn't Blakeney she'd kissed in the moonlight. Thinking of that interrupted embrace almost distracted him from the rest of the conversation.

"Seeing her with my cousin Owl was quite exciting. The idiot seemed to be getting into the spirit of things. Goes to show Diana's a hot piece."

He could have howled with humiliation that Blake had observed that moment of thrilling intimacy. His own fault, Sebastian supposed, that he'd chosen to kiss her by the light of a full moon in front of a building designed to be seen from every part of the park.

The first twinge of doubt assailed him. Had he chosen the location or had she? No. He had. He'd still been carrying her when he kissed her for the first time.

"Rich, beautiful, a hot piece, and a damn good sport," Lamb said. "Many ladies would have fainted at the idea of the wager, let alone propose it."

"Don't remind me," Blake said. "That five hundred pounds hurts. I hope Diana thinks it was worth it. Kissing Sebastian Iverley can't have been much fun."

Blake's scornful laugh pierced Sebastian's gut. "I almost wish I could tell Cousin Owl she was only making up to him to win a bet. As though Diana of all women, the picture of fashion, could ever be attracted to such a ragamuffin!"

His cousin's hateful voice faded to be replaced by Lord Iverley's dogmatic Northumbrian tones.

"Never trust a woman, my boy." If his great-uncle had said it once, he'd said it a thousand times over the years. "A woman will always betray you. It's in her nature."

Lady Georgina invited Diana to join her and Felicia on their morning walk. Covering her bets, Diana guessed, in case Diana managed to land Blakeney, or some other gentleman of a rank she couldn't ignore. Not that Lady Gee had given up thrusting her sister in Blake's direction. But she must be aware that the sweet, slightly daffy Felicia wasn't really up to snuff when it came to bearing her elder's thwarted matrimonial ambitions.

Diana looked up whenever she heard footsteps, but so far only gardeners had interrupted their desultory exploration of the walled rose garden. Lady Gee was in full flood of conversation that Diana had to admit was amusing in a cynical fashion. And she needed to keep on her toes. The lady might seem friendly, but likely it was a feint based on her growing awareness that Diana, with her looks and fortune, was strong competition in the marriage stakes.

"I noticed you only took chocolate for breakfast.

Perhaps you are on a reducing diet. I recommend you try boiled chicken and pickled beetroot. The regime did wonders for my aunt."

"Which one?" Diana asked, divided between interest and annoyance.

"Lady Stourbridge."

"Forgive me for mentioning it, but Lady Stourbridge is quite . . . er . . . voluptuous." In fact she'd had a brief affair with the Prince Regent whose tastes, everyone knew, ran to large ladies.

"She used to be much fatter," Felicia said.

"That was before Stourbridge died. After he fell off the horse, her hair turned gold from grief and she faded to a mere wisp while she waited in the country for a decent mourning period. Stourbridge was a very mean man who kept her short of pin money. There's nothing like the anticipation of a brand-new wardrobe to spur one to abstinence."

That or an officious French maid.

"Then she won Prinny's attention," Lady Gee went on, "and there didn't seem any reason for further loss. Quite the opposite. She was on the slender side for him."

"Your clothes are lovely, Diana," Felicia said. "I wish I were a widow."

"You have to find a husband before you can achieve that desirable state," Lady Gee said. "And I recommend you find one who doesn't complain about your bills."

"Husbands aren't all miserly, Felicia," Diana assured the younger girl. "Sir Tobias was always most generous, and delightful company too."

"Poor Diana. You must miss him dreadfully. And

as I remarked to Felicia," Lady Gee went on, "the little bit of extra plumpness you've gained suits you perfectly. Perhaps your lack of appetite has another cause?"

A creak of the garden gate made Diana jump again. Lady Gee smiled at her archly. "Are you expecting someone? Mr. Iverley, perhaps. I noticed the two of you were getting on very well."

Diana trusted neither of the other ladies knew exactly how well.

Thanks to Blake's premature arrival on the scene, she hadn't had a chance to deliver the planned speech in which she carelessly expressed her pleasure in Sebastian's attentions while assuring him, with a gay laugh, that she accorded their flirtation no more importance than he did. The source of her uneasiness was a nasty qualm in her stomach that told her he might have been serious. When they exchanged goodnights, in front of the whole company, he'd pressed her hand significantly. He hadn't appeared at the breakfast table, but she gathered he rose early. The other gentlemen had already eaten and were off performing manly feats of animal slaughter.

"I like Mr. Iverley," she said airily. "And of course I welcome the acquaintance of any cousin of Blake's."

"Such an odd young man. Charming, of course."

By no stretch of the imagination could any of Sebastian Iverley's interactions with the Howard sisters be described as charming. Diana, on the other hand, had discovered that he possessed a certain appeal. The truth was, she'd enjoyed their kiss. Not the kiss itself so much, especially his first attempt when he'd mashed her lips rather painfully. She believed Blake's claim that his cousin had never kissed a woman. The sequel had been better and might have turned into something quite pleasurable had they not been interrupted.

But what she'd enjoyed the most was Iverley's unexpected strength. Not only had he carried her around as easily as if she were a small child, she'd warmed to the sensation of his hard muscles, pressing herself against him quite shamelessly. Frankly, she relished his youthful virility. Her husband had been a generous and attentive lover, but not a vigorous one. And he was, when it came down to it . . . old. The next man she took to her bed would have the vital energy Tobias had lacked.

And here he was, as gorgeous as ever, the sunlight catching the gold of his hair and enhancing the blue of his eyes.

"Ladies," Blake said. "I've been searching for you."

"We've been discussing Diana's diet," Lady Gee said.

Felicia giggled.

"We were wondering where you gentlemen had hidden yourselves," Diana said.

"We've been shooting. Except my cousin. He left Mandeville this morning. He asked me to convey his regrets and farewells."

"Really?" asked Lady Gee.

"No, not really," Blake replied. "That was a liberal interpretation of one of his grunts."

"That's very naughty of you, Blake," Lady Gee said.

"Diana," Blake said. "A word with you in private. About that little matter of business."

"My, my!" Lady Gee said, her eyes round with curiosity. "What secrets do you two share?"

The last thing Diana needed was for Lady Georgina to get wind of that bet. It would be all over England within days. But she couldn't ignore Blake's offered arm. And why would she wish to? Now that Iverley and the silly wager were out of the way, she could return to her principal objective for the remainder of her days at Mandeville. "Nothing of any moment," she said lightly.

Once they were out of earshot, Blake presented her with a bank draft. "Five hundred pounds and worth every penny to see old Owlverley fall for you," he said.

Diana felt a wave of distaste for the whole business. Without looking at it, she tucked the paper into her pocket. She would, she decided, give the money to charity.

"You don't think he found out, do you?" she asked.

"Certainly not," Blake reassured her. "He hadn't an idea. A package of letters came for him today. I met him in the hall after breakfast and he told me his uncle is dying."

"Poor Mr. Iverley. How sad for him."

"Lucky Mr. Iverley! He stands to inherit a fortune."

Chapter 7

London, the Burgundy Club in Bury Street,
September 1819

Tarquin Compton, sitting with the Marquis of
Chase, hailed him the minute he walked in.
"Here he comes, the new viscount, returned from
the frozen north."

Sebastian sank into a well-padded leather chair
and looked around appreciatively at the sitting
room of the new premises. "You have no idea. I've
inherited the coldest, most uncomfortable house in
England."

"Before I start weeping, let's not forget that the
biggest coal mine in England comes with it. There's
not a collector in England who'll be able to outbid
you when there's a book you really want."

Chase, usually addressed as Cain, was a more
recent and therefore politer acquaintance than Tarquin. He nodded at Sebastian's black armband. "May
I offer my condolences?"

"Thank you. My uncle complained he was dying
for years. Turns out he was right. At least I saw the
old man before he went."

"Did you know him well?" Cain asked.

"Depends what you mean by well. I lived with him from the age of six. He was an odd fellow."

"That's one way of putting it," Tarquin said. "You could also say he was mad as a march hare."

"Over the years," Sebastian explained to Cain, "Tarquin has somehow gained the impression that the old coot was eccentric."

"Could that possibly have anything to do with the fact that he never left his house in twenty years and didn't bother to get dressed for the last ten?"

"My uncle was perfectly rational," Sebastian retorted with a straight face. "Everyone he needed to see could visit or write to him. He had no interest in mixing with neighbors or slight acquaintances. Everything he wanted to do, his mechanical experiments and clock-making equipment, were in the house. And he liked his old brown dressing gown. He said it was comfortable and didn't show the dirt."

"So you see, Cain," Tarquin said. "By the standards of his upbringing, Sebastian's clothing is an exemplar of the tailor's art."

Cain nodded. "Quite the dandy."

"Dare I enquire, my friend," Tarquin said, "if you intend to celebrate coming into your title and fortune by buying some new clothes?"

"I doubt it."

Sebastian felt better than he had since that morning at Mandeville. The work on the club premises had been completed over the summer: just a small library for reference works and subscriptions to various scholarly journals, and the sitting room for liquid refreshment and serious conversation among like-minded gentlemen. The Burgundy Club was the perfect antidote to two months of trials: the death of his uncle, of whom he had been fond in a distant sort of way; the assumption of responsibilities he hadn't thought to bear in many years; and getting over Diana Fanshawe.

The last had turned out to be impossible. For weeks he'd alternated between burning rage and rank misery: rage at her treachery and misery that he would never possess her. When he'd striven, for his own sanity, to forget her, he found he could not. Of all the unacceptable options before him, never seeing Diana again was the least palatable. Finally he had his emotions under control and his plans for the future in place.

But now, for a minute or two, he determined to enjoy a warm room and the company of friends. There could be no better place in the world than this, designed for the amusement and enlightenment of an exclusive coterie of young bibliophiles. Especially since women were not allowed to set foot in the premises, let alone belong to the club.

He noticed that Cain held a volume. "What's that?" The whole point of the Burgundy Club was to discuss books.

"The Baskerville Virgil."

"Very nice." Sebastian examined the binding before opening the volume to look at the elegantly printed pages. "Nice big copy. I love blue morocco. Where did you find it?"

"My wife spotted it." That was the one problem with Cain. He'd actually proposed his wife for membership of the Burgundy Club. Sebastian, as the new club's duly elected president, had quashed that notion in a hurry. Though, he had to admit, as women went the new Lady Chase was quite knowledgeable about books.

"You won't believe the things Cain's bought for his collection this summer, with Juliana's help," Tarquin said. "She has a magpie eye when it comes to spotting the best books in unpromising circumstances."

Juliana! Tarquin had gone over to the enemy. As far as Sebastian was concerned the former Juliana Merton was Lady Chase; he would never accept an invitation to address her informally. Beware of women who offer the use of their Christian names, Sebastian thought darkly. He only hoped Cain wouldn't have cause to regret his marriage.

"You are correct in giving Juliana all the credit," Cain said. "But we buy things together for our collection." Sebastian was nauseated by the uxorious sentiment. "She persuaded Banks to part with his Jacobean drama collection," Cain continued, oblivious to Sebastian's disgust. "I think he fell a little bit in love with her. Who can blame him?"

"Any luck persuading your mystery man to relinquish the Katherine Parr binding?" Tarquin asked.

While glad to change the subject from Lady Chase's perfections (and her irritating success in landing a collection Sebastian would not have scorned), Sebastian had nothing happy to report about the prize he'd pursued hard for five years. "He wrote to me hinting he was ready to sell. Then I had to go north and by the time I got to him, just yesterday, he'd changed his mind again."

"Annoying."

"Yes. A man should decide on a plan and stick to it. I cannot abide indecisiveness."

"Persistence, my boy, persistence," Tarquin urged. "With book collectors or with women it's the only way to win. Of course," he added, "*you* don't need advice when it comes to the so-called fair sex."

Sebastian took a deep breath. "As a matter of fact I am looking for counsel in that area. I need some hints about how to woo a lady." He waited for the expected explosion of derision and disbelief from his friends.

Tarquin obliged with a crack of laughter. "I always find offering more money works well."

"I don't think Sebastian's talking about a demirep," Cain responded softly. "He said it was a lady."

"Never say you're looking for marriage," Tarquin asked, utterly incredulous.

"I wouldn't go that far," Sebastian hedged. No indeed. He'd put that folly behind him forever, but he had no wish to describe his humiliation to his friends. "I'm not sure of my intentions but I do wish to make an impression."

"I never thought I'd see the day. You'd better talk to Cain. He's the expert."

The marquis regarded him from the depths of his chair. "I'm not sure my wife would approve of me giving you lessons in the art of seduction. She doesn't like you."

"Why should she ever know?"

"You don't know much about marriage if you have to ask. You'll find out." He gave Sebastian a piercing look. "Or perhaps not. You aren't by any chance contemplating the seduction of an innocent?"

"What would I want with an innocent?"

"I don't know, but people do marry them. Unfortunately they sometimes ruin them, though that's never been my line, nor I think Tarquin's."

"Heaven forbid," Tarquin said with an eloquent shudder. "I like a woman who knows what she's doing."

"The lady in question," Sebastian said, "knows what she's doing." On that score he had no doubt.

Tarquin beckoned to the club servant. "Go to White's and ask them to bring up a bottle of the 1795 Lafite and have it ready for dinner. We're going to celebrate," he explained to his friends. "Are you going to tell us who she is?"

"Better for the moment if I keep the lady's name out of it."

Tarquin looked at Cain. "Married," he said.

Cain nodded. "Married. Careful of jealous husbands, Sebastian."

"And Cain knows what he's talking about," Tarquin said.

"Those days are behind me, but only because I survived to tell the tale. I wonder if I ran afoul of this one?"

"There's no husband," Sebastian said, unreasonably annoyed.

"Hmm. A widow then. Splendid. There's nothing like a widow for dalliance, especially if she's rich. Who do you think it is, Cain?"

Sebastian interrupted before his friends could discuss every widow of their joint acquaintance. "I don't see what money has to do with it."

"A wealthy widow," Tarquin explained, "is less

likely to be set on marriage and I can't say I blame her. Why surrender fortune and independence to the power of another husband?"

"For love?" Cain suggested.

"Thus speaks the newly married man."

"Your cynicism is tragic, Tarquin." Cain turned back to Sebastian. "Are you in love?"

"No!" Sebastian almost yelled. His heartbeat accelerated and his breath shortened in horror at the notion he should suffer such a mawkish sentiment.

"Sebastian in love," Tarquin said. "Now that would be an interesting sight."

"May I remind you that I asked for help? Never mind. Forget I ever mentioned it."

His two friends united in protest, enjoying themselves far too much to miss the treat of contemplating Sebastian Iverley in pursuit of a female.

"How shall I start?" Sebastian said, controlling his rapidly fraying temper. "How does one attract a woman?"

"First of all," Cain said, settling down and giving the question serious consideration, "is she even aware of your existence?"

"Definitely," he replied, trying not to sound grim.

"Does she know you are interested?"

"I believe she may have some idea."

"Excellent. First of all you must, in a delicate manner, make sure you have her full attention."

Tarquin nodded his approval at Cain's recommendations. "Go where she goes, attend the same affairs. Appear frequently in her vicinity. You might even brush against her in a crush."

"But do not," Cain chimed in, "at this stage address her with more than common politeness."

"Does Sebastian even know what common politeness is?" Tarquin asked.

"Hold on," Sebastian said, extracting the small notebook and pencil he kept in an inner pocket. "I need to write this down."

The marquis gave him a look of exasperation but waited till he was ready. "Pique her interest—that's P-I-Q-U-E—but keep her guessing as to whether you are attracted. It's not a bad idea to pay some slight attention to another woman."

"Perfect!" Tarquin said. "Flirt with her best friend."

Cain shook his head. "If she's the kind of women who'll steal her friends' admirers you don't want anything to do with her, except on a purely commercial footing. But make up to her enemy or rival and you'll arouse her competitive instincts. Especially if she feels you've been ignoring her."

"Brilliant, Cain," Tarquin said. "You'll drive her mad with subtle neglect. Then it's time for a grand gesture." He looked to Cain for confirmation.

"Exactly."

Grand gesture, Sebastian wrote. "I have no idea what that would be," he said.

"Sweep her into a waltz and refuse to take no for an answer," Cain suggested.

"Buy her a gift. Diamonds."

"Commonplace. Emeralds or rubies are better."

"Or sapphires."

"Or a pet. A dog works well."

"Rescue her from an awkward social situation."

"Or a runaway horse."

"Or footpads."

"Hire the footpads if necessary!"

"She'll be ready to fall into your arms."

"And whatever it is you do," Cain elaborated, "make sure it's exactly what she wants or needs at that moment."

"And good luck knowing what that is."

"I'm sure you'll have no difficulty coming up with something."

Sebastian finished scribbling and held up a hand. "Stop!"

The others fell reluctantly silent.

"There's one difficulty. These plans involve meeting the lady in question at . . . places. You mention a ball. I don't attend such events. Even if I wanted to I'm never invited."

"Sebastian," Tarquin said patiently. "Let me explain something. You are a peer. Better yet you are a twenty-six-year-old, unmarried peer. You walk without a limp and have all your teeth. And let's not forget the huge coal mine. If you want to be invited to any event you have only to let it be known and an invitation will arrive. In fact they'll probably arrive without any effort on your part. I have every confidence that the London hostesses will be able to discover the direction of your house."

The image of a marauding pack of women beating on his door with cards of invitation beset Sebastian. Could he really be contemplating this stratagem? Was it worth it, even to have Diana Fanshawe begging for his attentions?

There was only one answer to that question.

He swallowed hard. "I'm not very good at making myself agreeable in company," he admitted humbly.

Tarquin doubled over with mirth. "The first step to reform is to acknowledge its necessity," he said, when he'd finally recovered. "Luckily you couldn't have a better tutor than me. I shall teach you to cultivate address."

Sebastian nodded.

"And don't grunt at me."

"I do not grunt."

"It's your principal method of communication," Cain said through his laughter.

"That grunt has to go," Tarquin pronounced. "Ladies prefer to be addressed in identifiable words. Better yet, complete sentences."

Sebastian said nothing. Then a warning look made him realize he had, in fact, grunted again. "Yes, Tarquin," he said meekly. "Then what?"

"Then we shall go into dinner and get roaring drunk."

"Why?" Sebastian might not know much about ladies, but he'd always had the impression they deplored insobriety in men. He had a faint recollection of his mother weeping when his sire staggered home reeking of brandy.

"Think of it as a last supper. Tomorrow I'm taking you to my tailor."

Tarquin's tailor delivered the first lot of new clothes a fortnight later.

"I'm not uncomfortable," Sebastian observed in some surprise. "I always thought tight clothes would be uncomfortable."

"Of course they aren't," Tarquin said, who'd come to Sebastian's house to render judgment. "Do you think I spend my life in a state of misery? Really Sebastian, you have the most ridiculous notions. Is that why you've dressed like a scarecrow all these years?"

Sebastian shrugged, still slightly surprised he could move in a coat that had taken considerable effort to get into. He pivoted at the waist, startled by the breadth of his shoulders and chest. "I always dressed for ease. But I don't feel bad, even though this coat is so tight."

"It is not tight. It is well cut and made to fit you by a master in the art of tailoring."

"It's rather inconvenient, not being able to dress without help. Not that I'm sorry to have you, Simkins," he added politely to his newest servant. Tarquin had exercised considerable persuasion, not to mention a large bribe, to lure Simkins away from his former employer. Apparently Simkins, like Sebastian's new tailor, was a master and needed to be addressed with respect.

Paying a valet an annual salary equivalent to the cost of a book printed by Caxton wouldn't ever have occurred to Sebastian, but Tarquin assured him it was worth it. And Sebastian meekly assented. He was bringing his full concentration to the task of transforming himself into a man of fashion, the same single-minded effort he once applied to mastering a horse. He'd been driven to become a skilled horseman by the scorn of his cousin Blakeney. His current quest was, at bottom, spurred by the same thing.

When Sebastian wanted something badly he spared

neither trouble nor expense. And he always got it.

"I look good," he said, after a careful examination of his reflection in the cheval glass. The full-length mirror was another new acquisition, arriving the same day as the valet. Apart from the coat in dark gray superfine wool, he wore a waistcoat of paler gray heavy silk, discreetly figured in silver, and thigh-hugging trousers of soft doeskin that disappeared into almost knee-high black boots. The new footwear was in his opinion particularly fine, the scent of the butter-soft leather reminding him of his collection of book bindings. He also liked the feeling of the shirt in finest linen cambric against his skin. Less agreeable was the neck cloth, starched as stiff as thick Dartford paper, which Simkins had wound around his neck and tied in a fancy knot according to Tarquin's directions. He had a notion the confection might wilt after a few hours of normal movement.

"You have to change your linen several times a day," Tarquin said, echoing his thoughts.

Good God, this dressing business was work!

Sebastian looked over at his closest friend, sitting in a casual pose with one leg crossed over the other. He'd always treated him with affectionate scorn for his devotion to his appearance. He knew Tarquin had achieved his ambition of being acknowledged as London's best dressed man, and on some level he was glad for his success. Now he felt an inkling of respect for the amount of effort that success had required. He turned back to the mirror and made a discovery.

"I don't look as good as you do," he said.

Tarquin laughed. "The fact, my dear friend, that

you realize that truth makes me hopeful that one day you may join the ranks of the well dressed. For now your appearance is adequate."

"Is it good enough?"

"There are few ladies who understand the sartorial arts as men can. They tend to be distracted by irrelevancies like good cheekbones, a charming smile, or a ready wit."

Sebastian removed his spectacles, edged closer to the glass, and took a good look at his own face. He prodded his cheeks and stretched his lips into a ghastly grin. "None of which I have," he said.

"You underestimate yourself. I believe you'll do better without the glasses. Women like to see a man's eyes so they can know if he's sincere."

"Do we want them to know?" Sebastian asked. In fact it was the last thing he wanted.

"Not necessarily. On the other hand, how can they tell? I think the whole eyes-are-windows-to-the-soul business quite overrated. But if it pleases ladies to believe it, who am I to argue?"

"I can't see more than a few feet in front of me without my spectacles."

"We'll get you a quizzing glass. Lorgnettes are for dowagers and dowdies."

Sebastian discovered there were some bounds he would not cross. "No," he said. "I'm not going to look like an affected idiot with a quizzing glass. It's bad enough having to attend parties, without doing it blind."

"As you wish," Tarquin said with a shrug. "I'll take you to an ingenious little man in Soho who can make anything. We'll see if he can rig you up more elegant frames. Those things look like something my old nurse would wear."

"I can take them off whenever a woman gets really close. That way I can see her, and she can look into my eyes and be deceived about the nature of my soul."

"That's the spirit, dear boy. It's a rare woman who can resist the dedicated pursuit of a persistent lover."

Sebastian stepped back from the mirror and surveyed his figure again. A light wrinkle in his sleeve caught his eye so he smoothed it out. He stretched his lips into the kind of bland, slightly supercilious smile often worn by his cousin Blakeney. Diana Fanshawe, like all women, valued the triviality of a man's appearance more than his true worth. If that's what she wanted, that's what he would become: a fashionable fool without a useful thought in his head. And once she wanted him as he had once desired her, he would reject her and teach her the meaning of humiliation and betrayal.

Chapter 8

"**G**ood Lord," Sebastian muttered to Tarquin as they escaped from the avid speculation in the fine green eyes of their hostess, the Duchess of Lethbridge. "I feel as though I've been stripped to my drawers."

"Many have," his friend replied. "And further. Like you the duchess is a collector, but she prefers her objets d'art young and virile."

"Has she ever collected *you*?"

"I've stayed out of the lady's cabinet of curiosities. I prefer a more exclusive environment."

Sebastian glanced over his shoulder, half afraid of being pursued by this alarming noblewoman. "I think I should start with someone a little less demanding."

"A wise decision. And don't forget, if you find yourself at a loss, think of something amusing to say about the weather."

Ten minutes later, abandoned to the mercies of a pair of dowagers who persisted in discussing every relation Sebastian possessed, including his mother, he remembered the admonition.

"I read recently," he blurted, "that a storm in

Sunbury produced hailstones so large that the bird on a lady's headdress was killed stone dead."

The more formidable of the two ladies, whose plumes he realized too late had inspired his remark, gasped. What was it with women and feathers, anyway? The other looked as though he were mad. Apparently being amusing about the weather wasn't as easy as it sounded. Mumbling hideously he excused himself and plunged into the thickening crowd. The sight of a fellow book collector came like a yard of ale to a thirsty man.

This encounter went better. The man introduced him to his wife and some other ladies. Heeding Tarquin's instruction, Sebastian remembered not to kiss the hands of unmarried women, nor to compliment the appearance of ladies he'd only just met. Not that he felt any temptation to do so. The females in the group seemed sensible, or at least quiet, and listened to the men's exchange of political gossip with every sign of appreciation.

Once he'd found his footing, the discussion wasn't deep enough to demand all his attention. Surreptitiously he searched the room. Tarquin had assured him the duchess would have invited everyone in London.

Where was she?

Even out of season the Duchess of Lethbridge drew a good crowd to a rout-party. While not as uncomfortably crushed as such an event in May, Lethbridge House, one of London's largest mansions, was nicely filled without being too noisy for eavesdropping on other people's gossip. Two people had already commented, in Diana's hearing, that half the male guests were the duchess's former lovers.

Not having ever been on the duchess's guest list before, Diana had been flattered by the invitation. Word of Blakeney's interest in her must have spread. The top tier of London hostesses, ladies too superior to invite a nabob's widow, wouldn't want to offend a woman who had a chance of becoming Marchioness of Blakeney.

She hadn't seen many people she knew, aside from a brace of well-known fortune hunters she'd shaken off on the way upstairs. Standing in the famous Adam saloon, she tried to look as though she were far too busy exchanging polite nods with her numerous acquaintances to actually conduct a conversation, and wondered which of the men in the room had bedded the notorious duchess.

She caught sight of Mr. Tarquin Compton, towering above the crowd. Had *he*? Somehow she had difficulty envisioning him without his clothes. Not that she spent much time imagining other men naked, either, but Mr. Compton seemed a particularly unlikely candidate. Without being in any way effeminate, he was just too exquisite in his attire. She'd never heard his name linked with any lady, except enviously when he commented favorably on her dress.

He'd once complimented Diana's shoes, an adorable pair of pink dancing slippers embroidered with pearls. If he'd come over and notice her headdress it would irritate Lady Georgina Harville who stood with her sister a few yards away. The three of them had done the polite nod thing and Diana wondered if she should go and speak with them. While Lady

Gee wasn't exactly her favorite person, at least she wouldn't be looking like a wallflower.

"Looking for someone, Diana?" Saved, by Marianne MacFarland, her closest friend in London.

"I was trying to imagine Mr. Compton undressed and wondering what he'll think of my hair." One of the things Diana loved about her friend was that she was incapable of being shocked. Tonight, however, Marianne refused to be drawn into a discussion of the dandy's physique.

"Oh dear," she said, as they exchanged kisses. "Please don't let him come near me. I'm a bit worried about mine."

Diana drew back and blanched at the confection on her friend's auburn head.

Marianne's eyebrows arched in exaggerated distress. "I feared it might be a mistake but Mrs. Pynchon assured me it was the latest thing. I knew I should have consulted Chantal first but she was in such a bad mood last time I asked for her advice on a hat."

"Never mind her moods. Next time, take her word over the milliner's."

"Is it that bad?"

For a moment Diana strove for tact, but some things were beyond her abilities. "It looks like a pineapple top in a dish of raspberries."

"That is exactly what Robert said."

"Forget my maid, listen to your husband. Clearly he has a better grasp of fashion than you."

"That's the saddest thing I ever heard. Is Blakeney here?"

"No, he's gone to Leicestershire for a week's cubbing."

"Lord, the sports never stop. Are you sure you want to marry him?"

"He's worth it."

Marianne leaned in confidentially. "I only ask because if you decided you couldn't bear the hours listening to him rhapsodize about the nobility of dead foxes, you might want to consider this new viscount everyone's talking about."

"Oh?" Diana murmured, only half attending. Compton was getting closer. She willed him to notice the red velvet bandeau entwined with black pearls and adorned with a diamond spray. Chantal had assured her the effect was scintillating and not at all vulgar. Chantal was never wrong.

"He only just inherited. Apparently he has a large estate and a really big coal mine."

Diana owned shares in a couple of mines and their product was far prettier. She patted her diamond necklace.

"And," Marianne continued, "he's quite nice-looking and very well dressed. Tall. Better still, Susan Bellamy says he's conversable. He had her whole group in stitches with his comments on the antics of the ministry. She said she laughed so much she hardly noticed the spectacles."

"What did you say he was called?" Diana asked sharply.

"I don't think I did. Iverley. Viscount Iverley. No one ever saw the old one who was an uncle of some sort. Lived in the north and was said to be a mad recluse."

This could not be true. Not even an enormous coal mine could make the levelheaded, if taste-deficient,

Marianne describe Sebastian Iverley as well dressed. Not to mention those powers of conversation with strangers. Of course, Sebastian had spoken quite easily with her but that was different.

Wasn't it?

It couldn't be him. Some other nephew had inherited the peerage. Another tall nephew. With spectacles. Poor eyesight must run in the family.

She looked up through a gap in the crowd and with a sense of inevitability she saw him, a tall man in beautifully tailored black evening clothes, a red embroidered waistcoat, and a new haircut. The steel-rimmed spectacles had been replaced with a striking pair carved from tortoiseshell. Yet without a doubt this vision of masculine elegance was Sebastian Iverley.

He threaded his way in her direction with a smile on his face.

Marianne sighed. "Look at the breadth of those shoulders. And his legs! I love a man with good legs. And I've never really thought of it before, but spectacles draw attention to a well-sculpted face. He has the most beautiful cheekbones. And a lovely smile. Very shapely lips."

She was right about the lips. Diana had noticed them before. More than noticed them. A glow kindled in her chest. Was it possible this transformation had been undertaken on her behalf? That was something, she had to admit, that impressed a woman.

He was quite close now. She drew herself up, preparing a welcoming smile for the man who, the last time they met, had kissed her.

He bowed. "Lady Gee," he said.

And walked straight past Diana without noticing her.

"And Lady Felicia," he continued. "I am so pleased to see you again. It's been many weeks since those enjoyable days we spent together at Mandeville."

Georgina positively simpered. "My dear Lord Iverley, as we must now remember to call you. What a delightful surprise. Those were indeed happy times."

Diana listened with growing incredulity to an exchange of reminiscences that represented, to put it kindly, a radical rewriting of history. Felicia, the idiot, giggled and made eyes at the man whom she had, as Diana distinctly recalled, dismissed as a quiz. And Sebastian—Lord Iverley!—spoke with ease and fluency as though he'd spent a lifetime perfecting the art of meaningless social discourse.

"He's quite delicious," Marianne murmured. "Were you at Mandeville at the same time? I can't believe you never told me about him."

"He was Mr. Iverley then." Diana forced a weak smile though she didn't feel like it. Heaven forbid he, or Lady Gee, should notice her chagrin at the way he'd virtually ignored her.

"Still, his looks can't have changed and they are most definitely worthy of mention."

"He looks different," Diana said. "Very different."

She wasn't at all sure she approved of the transformation. She had noticed and appreciated Mr. Iverley even as a sartorial disaster. Now, if she wasn't mistaken, *Lord* Iverley was about to become all the rage.

* * *

He studied her out of the corner of his eye as he raised Lady Georgina's hand to his lips and gave it an unnecessarily thorough kissing. She turned to the woman beside her and answered some remark that made them both smile. But Sebastian had been looking and he'd caught it: a moment of surprise followed by displeasure. Diana expected him to come to her and she hadn't been pleased when he spoke instead to Lady Gee. How fortuitous that they had been standing close by but not together, providing an opportunity to implement one element of Tarquin and Cain's strategy. Diana and Georgina might not be enemies, but Sebastian was observant enough to know they weren't friends.

For several minutes he stood and talked with the sisters. In the space of one hour at this incredibly stupid soirée, Sebastian had recovered from the weather fiasco and found that making small talk wasn't difficult, merely tedious. His audience seemed to enjoy what he had to say, but he'd bored himself almost to the point of somnolence.

Until now. Not because his current conversation showed any improvement, but because every second he was thrillingly conscious of Diana Fanshawe standing a few paces away. In three months her dangerous appeal had not diminished an iota. The first glimpse of her in the thronged saloon told him he hadn't overestimated her beauty. On the contrary, clad in dark red and diamonds, she was more ravishing than he recalled. Out of sight for so long, the details had faded from memory: the gleaming locks of dark chocolate hair against ivory skin; the soft-etched collarbones now resting beneath a web of silver and gemstones; the curve of her elbow between sleeve and glove. Could he really detect that seductive perfume at this distance, or was it etched in his memory? Either way it was above all her scent that set his body thrumming with awareness and desire.

And pain. He felt the moment of her betrayal at Mandeville anew. Deep resentment churned the jumble of his emotions. Before he met Diana he'd been content with his life.

His brain was on the sharpest alert, acutely sensitive to any indication of her thoughts and mood. Unfortunately he couldn't follow the dialogue between Diana and a lady with a strange leafy concoction on her head.

More guests arrived and none seemed to leave. Bodies crowded in on them and Sebastian awaited the right moment, when he could make it appear an accident. As though pushed, he stepped back several paces and collided with her.

"I do beg your pardon," he said, spinning around and trying to ignore the jolt contact with her gave him. "Lady Fanshawe," he cried. "I didn't see you there. What a surprise to meet you again."

Much to his satisfaction she appeared discomfited. "Mr. Iverley," she murmured. Her companion nudged her. "I beg your pardon, Lord Iverley, I believe. Should I congratulate or commiserate with you?"

"You are very kind." And couldn't think of a thing to say. Which didn't matter since engaging her in conversation was not part of the evening's strategy.

"Lady Gee," he said instead. "May I accompany you to the refreshment room? Rumor has it there is food to be found there."

Lady Georgina's titter almost rivaled her sister's. "Oh Lord Iverley! You are so very droll."

Fifteen minutes later Diana tracked down James Lambton.

"Diana," Lamb said, bowing with grace despite the burden of a glass of claret cup and a rout cake. "I haven't had the pleasure since Mandeville. Do you see who's here?" He jerked his head toward a part of the room where Sebastian Iverley, surrounded by a sizeable group, appeared to be the life and soul of the party.

"Yes," she replied.

"Hard to believe the transformation, isn't it?"

"Lamb," Diana said as calmly as she could. "Have you spoken to anyone about our wager?"

"How can you ask? Upon my honor, I said I would not and a gentleman always keeps his word."

"What about Blake?"

Lamb stared at her. "How could you even suggest such a thing?"

Diana shrugged, not wishing to stir up gossip by confessing that Sebastian had almost cut her dead. "I just wanted to make sure there was no way he might know about it."

Lamb repeated his protestations. "Look at him," he added. "Coming into the title must have turned his head. Obviously it hasn't improved his eyesight. I wonder what the viscountcy has done to his conversation."

Diana smiled and laughed as Lamb continued to elaborate on the theme but without really listening. She was too busy puzzling over the reason why a man who had kissed her so passionately no longer seemed interested in pursuing the acquaintance.

Chapter 9

The initial glow of triumph turned to ashes when Sebastian saw Diana with Lamb. They were discussing him—he could tell by the way they darted covert glances in his direction—and laughing. She was laughing at *him*, doubtless reminiscing with Blakeney's best friend about Sebastian's humiliation.

"For God's sake, cheer up," Tarquin ordered an hour later when they'd retired to his Albany rooms to conduct an inquest on the evening. "You were a success. At least a dozen ladies asked me about you."

Sebastian stared into his glass without replying. The fifty-year-old brandy reminded him of Diana's hair by candlelight.

"Wasn't she there?" Tarquin asked. "There'll be other opportunities."

His resolve hardened as his anger rekindled to a blaze. Yes, there would. He couldn't expect victory the first time out.

Tarquin echoed his thoughts. "Persistence, remember?"

"Persistence I can manage. But there's one other thing I need to consult you about. Or Cain. Once I've completed the persistent pursuit and captured the lady in question, what do I do with her?"

Tarquin stared at him. "You're not asking me for advice about a marriage proposal, are you? I've no experience there. Besides, how hard can it be to choke out what a woman is so anxious to hear?"

"No, I'm not asking about marriage."

"I've always wondered and haven't liked to ask. You've never done it, have you?"

Sebastian shook his head.

"How the hell have you stood it all these years?"

He grimaced. "A strong right hand."

"The schoolboy's best friend. Am I to understand you mean to put an end to this unnatural state of virtue? Don't worry. When it comes down to it you'll know what to do. Men have an instinct for it."

Of that Sebastian had no doubt. His "instinct" had been lately speaking to him with great urgency.

Before Tarquin and Cain had joked about widows, it hadn't occurred to him that bedding Diana was an option. He'd always assumed, naïvely perhaps, there was a clear divide between ladies, whom one married if one was foolish enough to be caught, and women with conveniently loose morals. Now he couldn't get the idea out of his mind.

"I'd like to do better than muddling through," he said, remembering his first attempt at a kiss. If he ever got Diana Fanshawe into bed—and he still couldn't believe it would ever happen—Sebastian wanted to do much better.

"It's true, the first time tends to be fast," Tarquin said. "I was so excited I lasted exactly half a minute. Of course I was only sixteen."

"How did that come about?"

"My uncle took me to a brothel."

"Uncle Hugo?"

"Good God, no. The Duke of Amesbury, my guardian. Always did his duty by me. In which your guardian apparently failed. But I suppose there wasn't much scope for dalliance on the wild shores of Northumberland."

"Wouldn't have mattered if there was. My uncle never went near a woman. Hated them."

"Why?"

"He never told me and I never asked, but I had the idea that he'd been betrayed by one in his youth."

"And you never fell for that other traditional destroyer of unwanted male innocence, the buxom maid?"

"No. I did visit a bawdy house in London once, but I found the place repulsive."

"Such places aren't to my taste, either. I prefer the more exclusive regions of the demimonde."

"Very exclusive, so I hear."

"I never thought you listened when such topics arose."

"Sometimes it's hard not to." Though he didn't mind being frank with Tarquin in his search for information, Sebastian shied from admitting how trying his celibacy had been. The choice between avoiding the female sex and using one of its members for his own physical ease had not been an easy one.

"Do women enjoy it?" he asked.

"They certainly can."

"Even ladies?"

"The sexual tastes of ladies are outside my area of expertise, but I don't see why not. They are just women after all. I can give you a few suggestions, I suppose."

Sebastian wasn't sure he was up to such frankness in conversation, even with Tarquin. "Can I learn about it from a book? All those erotic rarities you buy must hold some useful information."

"You are welcome to make use of my library. Just let me know if you need any help with French vocabulary of a specialized nature."

Chapter 10

The premises of Mr. Sancho, bookseller,
South Molton Street, London.

Minerva Montrose was bored. Bad enough that Diana had taken it into her head to visit this very dull bookshop. A greater mystery was why she'd already spent a full half hour in the place and shown no sign of concluding her business. Not that Minerva had anything against bookshops. She'd already visited Hatchard's and Diana let her buy all the latest volumes of memoirs by the people who'd peopled the stage of European politics for the past decades. Mr. Sancho stocked quaint old volumes, many in dead languages, and nothing Minerva had the least desire to read. How Diana came to have an interest in them she had no idea. Her sister's normal shopping expeditions involved bonnets, not bibliography.

The most intriguing thing in the place was the proprietor himself. Minerva had never encountered a Negro before, those of exotic ancestry being rare in Shropshire. She'd enjoyed a most interesting talk with Mr. Sancho, learning that his father had been a slave in the Indies. Before she discovered how the son came to own a bookshop in the chillier clime of Mayfair, Sancho had been summoned to attend to a customer. Now the three of them—Diana, Sancho, and a little woman with fair hair—were engaged in deep discussion of a tedious nature about printing in the age of Elizabeth.

So Minerva turned her attention to the street, or as much of it as was visible from the window. She would have liked to go outside and explore the neighboring merchants, but Diana insisted it was neither safe nor proper to go out alone in London. At that moment Min would give anything to see something unsafe or improper, preferably both.

A man walked by in a hurry on the other side of the road. Something about the tall, bespectacled figure seemed familiar. Minerva opened the door and called out, doubtless breaking all sorts of rules, if not laws.

"Mr. Iverley!" she called.

The man ignored her cry. He'd already rapped on the knocker of a door a few yards up. It opened and he disappeared inside.

Tarquin Compton collected English poetry and French novels, novels euphemistically described in catalogues as being of special interest to gentlemen. Apart from congratulating his friend on the acquisition of a bawdy treasure, Sebastian had never attended much to the latter. After a couple of days reading he'd greatly improved his French and acquired rather a special interest, not to say painful need, of his own.

He decided to attend to the matter. Then he could forget about seducing Diana, an idea he regarded as faintly dishonorable, and return to his original plan of merely breaking her heart.

He didn't know who had called out his name, though the voice was female and that was unusual. It hadn't occurred to him that No. 59 South Molton Street was just across from Sancho's establishment and there was a chance someone would recognize him. Whoever it was, Sebastian hoped she'd never learn the nature of the business conducted at No. 59, a narrow brick-faced house with a single window on each floor.

When a maid came to the door Sebastian almost knocked her over in his anxiety to get in off the street and out of sight. The young woman, little more than a child to his admittedly inexpert eyes, had a slatternly look and a developing sty over one eye. He found her unconvincing as the personal attendant to a lady of elevated French parentage, but had no trouble seeing her as doorkeeper to a prostitute.

"What?" she asked laconically.

Sebastian remembered he was supposed to practice articulacy in the presence of females. Not that this one would recognize a complete sentence if it bit her on the ankle.

"I've come to see Miss Grandville," he said, "if she's available."

The girl flashed him a gap-toothed grin. "Mamzelle ain't busy. I'll show yer up." The only part of her that moved, however, was her hand, palm upward. Sebastian gave her a small coin and followed her to the narrow staircase.

As they climbed the first flight he detected a noise behind the door on the landing, masculine groans punctuated by the occasional trill. The urgency arising from two days in Tarquin's library seemed less desperate. Perhaps, he thought hopefully, the girl was wrong and "Mamzelle" was otherwise engaged.

"She's on the next floor." He plodded on after her. "This one," she said, swinging her thumb at the door.

Since the servant's duties didn't apparently extend to the ceremonial announcement of visitors, he knocked.

"*Entrez*," bade a voice. He *entrez*-ed.

Whatever he'd expected of a courtesan's parlor, it wasn't an ordinary sitting room decorated in a style not out of place in a country manor. The only article of furniture remotely inviting lascivious thoughts or activities was a chaise longue, covered in a serviceable sage green cloth rather than decadent brocade or velvet. The upholstery looked stiff, not conducive to lounging. The room's occupant rose to her feet from a straight chair. Aside from the fact that her gown revealed a good deal of breast, she might have been a daughter of that manor. Pretty enough and distinctly unlike any whore he'd seen in London's streets. At first glance he could tell that, in one aspect at least, her description in the popular guide to females of a certain profession lied. Miss Elise Grandville hadn't seen twenty for some years. This didn't bother him since he'd selected her for another reason. A certain passage had seemed particularly apposite:

> *She is without doubt a most pleasing* Pupil of Pleasure, *and perfectly competent to the instruction of those who desire to be announced* Students *in the* Mysteries of Venus.

If "student" meant wholly inexperienced, then she was his woman. She seemed reasonably appealing. Not equal to Diana Fanshawe when it came to looks, but who was?

"My dear mademoiselle. I am honored and enchanted to make your acquaintance," he said in slow, careful French. There. That sounded polite, if not eloquent.

He didn't understand a single word of her reply. "I do beg your pardon," he said. "Though I studied your language for many years, I haven't spoken it much, and hardly ever with a native."

Following his lead, she switched to English, of a kind. An improbable kind. "Zee Englishmen zay do not speak well zee *français*." Sebastian, who occasionally attended the theater, was put in mind of a comic French character in a cheap farce.

"Excuse me, mademoiselle," he asked, "but I thought you had been in England for some years, since your father was a nobleman who escaped the guillotine."

Mademoiselle revealed good teeth in a wide smile and dropped her French accent. "Oh, that book! They just make that stuff up, you know. I wanted to be the vicar's daughter seduced by a wicked rake, but there's already one of them in this house. But I quite fancy being the daughter of a marquee who sold herself to save her family from starving. How d'you like my French?"

"I couldn't understand a word of it."

"And I didn't understand a word of yours." She sat on the couch and patted the seat next to her. "Here," she said. "Sit down. What's your name?"

"Jack," he said on impulse. "Call me Jack."

"Jack, eh? I can keep a secret, love, but if you want to be a Jack, I won't argue with you. So, *Jack*, tell me about yourself."

Sebastian hadn't bargained on having to talk so much. That's why he'd decided not to ask Tarquin for an introduction to one of the better class of courtesan. Harriette Wilson and her sisterhood expected to be wooed as well as paid, which sounded like too much trouble. Discreet inquiries at one of his clubs had steered him to *The Handbook to the Ladies of Covent Garden* (Covent Garden in this case describing a state of mind rather than geography), a volume that offered glowing descriptions of dozens of accommodating ladies.

He wondered if anything on which he'd based his careful selection of Miss Grandville was true. The episode was indeed beginning to resemble a farce, whether a cheap one remained to be seen.

Gingerly he took his place beside her, sitting straight up on the firm chaise, elbows hugged to his sides and hands placed awkwardly on his thighs. "Er, Miss Grandville . . ."

"Call me Ellie," she said in a throaty voice.

"Ellie. If you are neither the daughter of a clergyman nor an aristocrat, who are you?"

She examined his face shrewdly. "I could give you another story, but you look like man who'd as soon hear the truth."

"Yes," he said.

"It won't take long," she said, "but we might as well get comfy." And she took his hand and held it against her bosom. Though Sebastian felt silly and a little embarrassed, he kept it there, wishing he were enjoying himself more.

"My father was an ostler," Ellie said. "I was serving at the same inn when I caught a gentleman's eye. I didn't want to spend all my life in service, or marry a man like my father and work just as hard. My gent took me to London and set me up in rooms, quite proper."

"Was he a wicked rake?"

"Oh no! A good sort. When he had enough of me he treated me decent. I have some money put away. I just need to work a few more years and I'll have enough to get a little cottage somewhere and turn respectable. I've been lucky, I reckon. There's not many girls that have choices in life."

Sebastian felt a noise ascending his throat and quickly swallowed it. Lord, he missed "the grunt" as the all-purpose comment. A half-strangled "that sounds nice," was the only response he could manage to this oddly dignified confession.

"I've always been clean, so you don't have to worry about that. And I've kept myself out of the family way, except the once." A barely perceptible quaver ran through the last three words, doubtless an intimation of a longer and perhaps sadder tale. He didn't want to hear it. The woman had already become an individual to him, instead of a nameless member of a despised sex on whom he could unleash his poorly controlled desire. If he started feeling sorry for her, he'd never get the business done.

"It sounds like you know what you are doing," he said and ventured to slide his fingers beneath the edge of her gown. He found a nipple. Rather like a soft raisin. Interesting, but not particularly arousing. "Is it true you are competent in *instruction*? Was that part of your description accurate?"

She gave him rather a sweet smile. "I guessed you didn't know much. Is this your first time then?"

"Yes."

"I'll see you right. And since the first time doesn't usually last long, I'll only charge you a guinea. If you want to do it again it'll be two more. And I go up to five for anything unusual."

Thanks to Tarquin's library, Sebastian had a notion what she meant by "unusual." On the page he'd found some of the ideas exciting. In Elise Grandville's room they seemed unnerving.

"You'll probably just want the ordinary," she said. "I can tell you're a bit anxious. Don't you worry, you're in good hands." And she wasn't speaking metaphorically. He found himself firmly clasped and discovered that his physical and mental reactions could be completely divorced from each other.

While his cock sprang to interested attention, his brain was telling him to run. He tried not to think with his head. Elise indeed knew her trade and plied it with clever hands until he feared for the seams of his fashionably snug trousers.

"Shall we?" she asked finally. She hadn't attempted to unbutton him. For the bargain rate of a guinea he apparently had to take care of that task himself. "Let me get comfortable here and you come to me when you're ready."

He stood up and she arranged herself against the backrest and raised her skirts to reveal her legs, one stretched out straight along the seat of the couch, the other bent with one foot on the floor. His fingers stopped without unfastening a single button.

Suddenly he knew he couldn't do it. It was the sight of Ellie's legs. There was nothing wrong with them. No doubt they were perfectly good, shapely female legs, clad in white stockings.

Not pink, white. And they didn't look like silk.

And the legs weren't *hers*. Diana's.

He groped in the pocket of his coat and extracted a handful of gold coins. "Here," he said.

"That's too much. And you can pay me after."

"No, take it. I'm sorry. I have to leave." He dropped the guineas into her hand, fled for the door, and took the stairs two at a time. When he reached the street he stood for a minute or two, breathing heavily.

His eye caught the swinging sign of the bookshop across the way. It had been months since he'd been there and Sancho might have interesting new stock.

But his contrary brain, now it had removed him from the source of relief, was no longer arguing with his physical exigency. Sebastian was, to put it bluntly, hard, aching, and desperate. And only one woman could assuage it.

To hell with notions of honor that were doubtless antiquated. Diana Fanshawe had aroused a sleeping monster and she would have to pay the price.

Minerva had been looking out of the window while Diana conversed with the bookseller and her new acquaintance, a small blonde lady with untidy hair. Diana knew her sister was bored. She kept a wary eye on the girl. She didn't trust her not to wander back to Bond Street, hoping to find something interesting, like an errant MP escaped from Westminster.

As though on cue, Min opened the door and went onto the street, calling out to a passerby. Before Diana could retrieve her and read her a lecture on proper London behavior, Min was back.

"I just saw Mr. Iverley," she announced.

"Iverley!" the blonde lady said in a tone of disgust. "Is he coming in here?"

"No, he went into a house across the street with a red door."

"I'm sure it can't have been Mr. Iverley," Mr. Sancho said. "He wouldn't be visiting *that* house. He hasn't been in this shop for some months though he is, of course, a valued customer."

"Of course," murmured the blonde with a derisive air.

"I'm sure it was him," Min insisted. "Tall and thin with spectacles. Though he looked different. More elegant. I suppose his dress is more à la mode when he's in town."

This time the lady unmistakably snorted. "Sebastian Iverley has never, to my certain knowledge, looked either elegant or fashionable. It cannot possibly have been him."

"Is he a friend of yours?" asked Diana.

"Absolutely not. Of my husband's, unfortunately. One area in which we disagree. We simply never discuss the man. I take it you are acquainted with the Great Woman Hater."

"We met staying at Mandeville, his uncle the duke's house." She didn't mention their more recent meeting, which had both hurt and perplexed her. "As a matter of fact, he's the reason I'm here. I was interested in what he told me of his book collection, so when I came to South Molton Street to visit the linen draper and saw the bookshop, I decided to come in and investigate."

"Oh good! I must get you to join the Society of London's Lady Bibliophiles. There aren't nearly enough of us."

"I never heard of such a group."

"It's so new we haven't even had a meeting. I'm still trying to arouse interest. Allow me to introduce myself. I am Lady Chase."

Diana looked at her with deepened curiosity. The marriage of the Marquis of Chase to a widowed tradeswoman had been much discussed last season. Diana now recalled that there had been something to do with a murder and a collection of books. Being wholly unacquainted with Chase, a famously disreputable peer, she hadn't paid much attention.

"How do you do, Lady Chase. I am Lady Fanshawe and this is my sister, Miss Montrose." After the three of them had exchanged the ordinary information about themselves, Minerva declared herself bored and asked Mr. Sancho if he had any good books written by politicians. He took her off to hunt down a translation of Machiavelli's *The Prince*. Deciding to worry later about the effect of that classic on Minerva's forceful personality, Diana settled in for a chat with her new acquaintance.

"Tell me about your society."

"A group of men started a society of collectors called the Burgundy Club. Iverley refused to let me, or any other woman, belong so I decided to start my own."

"It's a lovely idea but a terrible name. The Society of London's Lady Bibliophiles sounds dreadfully dull. The men's name is much better. I suppose burgundy is what they drink at their meetings."

"Actually the club was named for a manuscript." Lady Chase sounded amused.

"But for the wine too. Because you can be sure they drink plenty of it, and I'd also wager they talk about more than just books. I think you'd attract more members if you expanded the scope. Something like the Society of Books, Bonnets, Manuscripts, and Millinery. Women all love talking about hats."

"But we want to be serious."

"Just because we love to discuss fashion, it doesn't mean we cannot be serious about books too. Think of men and their wine."

"You make an excellent argument. I could learn something useful too. I know a great deal about books and almost nothing of fashion."

Diana surveyed her critically. It was true that the marchioness, though extremely pretty, was a little unkempt. Her dress, at least two seasons old, didn't fit well and her hair was falling down, no easy feat when one is wearing a bonnet. She returned Diana's examination and concluded her appraisal of Diana's silk twill street dress topped by a midnight blue velvet spencer with mink trim.

"How," she asked with a little sigh, "do you manage to look so . . . sleek? It's the only word I can think of. Everything about you—shoes, dress, gloves, hair, hat—everything is perfect. I always look as though I just got out of bed."

"Your husband must enjoy that."

Lady Chase grinned wickedly. "He does. But speaking for myself, I'd just as soon present myself to the world as a person who deserves to be seen outside the bedchamber. You must tell me your secret."

"It's simple. I used to look quite ordinary, you know. The key is, in a single word, Chantal. My maid."

"She must be French."

"French, weighs about six stone, dresses entirely in black and is more terrifying than anyone you'll ever meet. She's also a genius and I pay her enough to maintain the army of a small country."

"How does one find such a gem?"

"As soon as Bonaparte fell, my late husband ordered his French business correspondent to find the best dresser in Paris. She's been with me for five years and I've fought off numerous efforts to lure her away. Two duchesses only last week."

"Yet she remains loyal?"

"She'd love to dress a duchess." Diana looked down modestly. "I'm doing what I can to help her achieve her ambition."

"Really? You are being courted by a duke? What's he like?"

"A duke's heir, the Marquis of Blakeney. Iverley's cousin."

"Already I don't like him, if he's related to that man."

"Iverley doesn't like him, either." Diana couldn't suppress a gasp of laughter at her new friend's single-minded scorn for Sebastian.

Lady Chase smiled. "In that case I have no doubt he's a splendid gentleman. Is he handsome?"

"Divinely so. And such address."

"Nothing like his cousin then. Does he collect books?"

"I'm pretty sure he doesn't."

Lady Chase shrugged. "Nobody's perfect. And that can change. Cain, my husband, only bought books to read before he met me."

"I used to think books were meant to be read, too, until Mr. Iverley told me all about his collection of book bindings."

"I will allow Iverley to be a discriminating bookman. But otherwise there's nothing to be said for him at all. You'd do much better to stick with your duke."

Chapter 11

Diana's willingness to follow Lady Chase's advice and stick with Blakeney was thwarted by the abundance—or perhaps elusiveness—of Leicestershire's foxes. But while the marquis was absent from London's drawing rooms, the new Lord Iverley became something of a fixture.

The second time Diana saw him enter a room—at Lady Storrington's musical recital—she was prepared to forgive his previous discourtesy. Towering over the other new arrivals, he surveyed the guests as though searching for someone. He saw her and unmistakably he paused for a fraction of a second, unnoticeable had she not been looking. Then his gaze moved on until he spotted his quarry.

Lady Georgina Harville.

Diana was so distracted she allowed Mr. Chandler, a handsome fortune hunter she despised, to find her a seat and join her for the soprano's performance of which she heard not one single note.

Later, trying to shed him, she joined a group in which, it turned out, Iverley and Lady Gee were the center of attention.

"I do believe peacock feathers are becoming more popular than ostrich," he drawled.

Unbelievable! Iverley talking about millinery. And in such an affected voice.

"My friend Compton assures me that peacock will be all the rage next season," he continued.

The surrounding ladies clucked avidly at a prognostication Diana didn't believe for a moment. Tarquin Compton's taste was impeccable and peacock feathers, in her opinion, were dreadfully vulgar.

"What do you think, Lady Gee?" he asked with a smile that Diana could only categorize as roguish. "Your headgear is always most striking."

Striking indeed! While not quite as deluded as Marianne MacFarland, Lady Gee was notorious for the excessive ornamentation of her bonnets. Mr. Chandler entered the lists on Diana's behalf.

"No one in London," he said, "has more elegant hats than Lady Fanshawe."

"Indeed," Iverley remarked with a nod of the head in her direction, then turned back and continued his conversation with the rest of his company.

Her original idea that he had changed his appearance and manners to impress her was revealed as sheer vanity. She could only now conclude that his inheritance had gone to his head.

She turned to Mr. Chandler and asked him to take her to find a glass of champagne, though she knew she'd regret it when the tiresome man started proposing marriage again. It would do Sebastian Iverley good to see her flirting with a good-looking gentleman, and show she didn't care a jot for him. Why should she? His small talk might be as modish as his attire, but he was no longer the thoughtful, intelligent, grunting man she'd known at Mandeville.

Sebastian watched them leave, his inane chatter covering scorching anger. He prayed his spectacles disguised the hunger in his eyes as he saw Diana flirt with that worthless idiot Chandler. The fact that he had to ape the conduct of such fribbles was another charge to mark up to her account.

Meanwhile he continued to pontificate about hat trimmings, shocked by how easy it was to behave like a fool. Later he'd break the news to Tarquin that he'd launched a new fashion for peacock feathers.

"Enough of my hunting stories," Lord Blakeney said. "I'm sure you must be bored to death. Let's talk about something else."

Yes, please, do let's, Minerva silently begged.

"Oh no, Blake," Diana said. "Tell us about the third run."

Nooooo!

And he was off, with a minute by minute account of each field crossed, every fence jumped. Minerva would have been bored to death had she bothered to listen. Of all Diana's friends who called at the Portman Square house, Blakeney was the most tedious. Diana, on the other hand, was gazing at their visitor with a look of utter fascination plastered over her face.

What was the matter with her? She loathed and detested hunting and never ceased to complain about their mother's passion for the sport. If she married the marquis was she prepared to spend the rest of her life hearing about ditches and oxers, coverts and earths?

Diana had been glad to invite Min to live with

her so she could dispense with the presence of their mother's elderly aunt, who had kept her company at Portman Square during the previous season. Minerva had to pay the price of listening to her sister talk about her longstanding infatuation with Blake.

Personally she couldn't see the point. He was of course marvelous to look at. That part of his appeal Minerva understood. But the Montroses had been brought up to judge appearance of little importance. Intelligence, education, and character were what mattered in a man. And in a woman too. On the evidence so far Minerva found Lord Blakeney lacking in all three. It did cross her mind that Diana's passion for him seemed more a habit than deep-seated affection. But Minerva would be the first to admit that at the age of sixteen she was observing the couple from a position of ignorance. Her own parents had completely different interests and got along perfectly well.

Nevertheless Minerva was disappointed that the son of one of England's most prominent political figures so lacked interesting conversation. The Duke of Hampton was immensely influential and had almost become Prime Minister. If his heir should follow in his footsteps, *then* Minerva would be impressed.

"And we lost the scent and while the hounds regrouped my groom brought up my second mount."

"Did they find it again?" Diana asked.

Longingly Minerva eyed *The Times*, sitting on the table next to her chair. Blakeney's arrival in Diana's drawing room had interrupted her reading about the petition for an enquiry into the conduct of the Manchester magistrates. Diana insisted it was rude to read while they had callers, but she wasn't looking and Blakeney certainly wasn't. She picked up the newspaper and was soon engrossed in the political aftermath of the recent massacre, now dubbed Peterloo.

In years of living with her mother, Diana had perfected the ability to listen to hunting anecdotes with an air of spurious interest while half her attention was elsewhere. Elsewhere in this case being contemplation of her companion's appearance. He'd seated himself next to her on the sofa and his proximity let her enjoy his lovely blue eyes gazing appreciatively at her face while her mind contemplated the joys of being a duchess. A vision of Lady Georgina Harville groveling for an invitation made the subject of the third, and even the fourth run bearable.

Finally Blake exhausted the subject of his recent sojourn in Leicestershire. "Guess whom I ran into at White's this morning? My cousin Sebastian Iverley."

"I saw him at Lethbridge House," Diana said with an indifferent air. "And once or twice since."

"I hadn't laid eyes on him since Mandeville. He's quite transformed. I wouldn't have believed it possible."

"I suppose he has neatened his appearance somewhat. I hadn't really noticed."

"You know, Diana." He moved a little closer and lightly touched her knee. "Had I realized the old Owl could cut such a good figure I wouldn't have encouraged him to . . ." He broke off, throwing a quick glance in Minerva's direction. He also, alas, replaced his hand on his own thigh.

Minerva looked up from the newspaper, which

she thought Diana hadn't noticed her reading. "You didn't tell me you'd seen Mr. Iverley."

Minerva had, for some reason, taken a fancy to him. She'd asked about him several times since they arrived in London. Diana hadn't been able to bring herself to explain that their shabby guest had become the *ton*'s latest darling, a fashionable viscount who showed no signs of wishing to renew his acquaintance with Diana.

Diana didn't understand why it bothered her and she was beginning to find her preoccupation tiresome. It wasn't as though she wanted him for herself, or ever had. She was, she thought with a flash of rueful self-knowledge, piqued that he seemed to have got over their encounter so thoroughly.

To think she'd worried he might take their kiss too seriously! No chance of that. The new Lord Iverley appeared gratified to receive overtures from a dozen women, not all of them single. The interest of the unmarried girls was understandable. But quite a few married women were also in the hunt. Nothing demonstrated Sebastian's transformation better than the fact he was now considered lover or flirt material.

Minerva looked at her reproachfully. "I really liked him. Does he know I'm staying with you? He told me he'd call."

Blake turned to Minerva, whom so far he'd mostly ignored. "He said that to you? He never speaks to females if he can help it. Especially young ones. You should have seen the way he ran away from my sisters when we were young."

Minerva looked at Blake coldly. "I suppose they teased him."

"We all did," Blake agreed. "But he's a grown man. He should have got over it by now."

"If by getting over it you mean his dislike of women," Diana said, "it seems to have happened. Lord Iverley is flirting quite shockingly with Lady Georgina Harville. All the gossips are agog."

"Lady Gee! I can't wait to ask Harville what he thinks of old Sebastian making up to his wife. What a joke!"

"I don't believe Lady Gee is serious in encouraging his attentions."

"Of course she isn't. And it wouldn't do her any good if she was. My cousin can't have changed that much."

Diana wasn't sure he was right about Sebastian, though she agreed that Lady Georgina probably wasn't looking for an affair. Conducting an open flirtation with the new Lord Iverley would do wonders for her reputation as a dashing young matron. Diana was beginning to find the whole subject irritating.

She was thus grateful when Minerva decided to practice her political hostess skills on Blake, though Diana could have told her she wasted her time.

"Tell me, Lord Blakeney," Minerva said in her best sixteen-going-on-sixty voice, "what do you think of events since Peterloo? Do you feel the government has responded with unnecessary harshness to the radical threat?"

"Good Lord, Miss Minerva. That's no question for me. I care nothing for politics. Just ask my father."

"I would be honored to hear his opinion but I am not acquainted with the duke," Minerva said hopefully. She was dying to meet and converse with Blake's powerful father.

In one sense the entire Montrose family, as neighbors, knew Blake's family. Diana had called on the duchess during the season and they exchanged polite greetings when they met. But her position didn't extend to arranging such a meeting for a sister who wasn't even out.

Despite Blake's failure to rise to her bait, Minerva hadn't given up. "A petition for an enquiry is to be presented at the Home Office tomorrow afternoon. The organizers have obtained thousands of signatures. I would like to see it delivered."

"I'm sorry, Min," Diana said. "I promised to drive out with Lord Blakeney tomorrow."

Minerva looked beseechingly at their guest but it was clear, though he was too polite to say so, that he didn't give a damn what the magistrates had done and wouldn't care if they marched in triumph down the street with a fanfare of heavenly trumpets.

"I'll pick you up at three, Diana," he said and took his leave very correctly after a half hour's visit.

"Sorry, Min," Diana repeated, once they were alone. "I could have asked him to drive both of us to Whitehall but he'd be bored. Wait until I've married him. Then I'll make sure you meet the duke. And with those connections you'll have your choice of every up-and-coming young politician in the country."

Sebastian had taken the day off. No morning calls, no afternoon breakfasts. No driving in the park with Lady Georgina Harville, an experience he fervently hoped never to repeat. If he didn't get Diana's attention soon he would either die of boredom or burst from frustration.

His life, his very thoughts, had become dominated by his need to impress a woman who both fascinated and repelled him. When he entered a drawing room he sometimes felt like an automaton going through his clockwork social paces until Diana's presence brought him to life. Too much so. At the sight of her he'd be thrown into a maelstrom of contradictory emotions that set his head spinning in a manner quite foreign to the experience of his well-ordered masculine existence.

Three hours browsing the superb books in the library at Westminster Abbey soothed him. Tonight he had a choice between a musicale and a card party, either of which Diana might attend. But maybe he'd take the evening off too. He might track down Tarquin for dinner and a strategy session. Or dine at home and read. An evening spent forgetting he'd ever set eyes on Diana Fanshawe would be a relief. There were moments, and this was one of them, when he wished he could make that state of oblivion permanent.

As he strolled up Whitehall toward Charing Cross he became aware of a commotion ahead of him, shouts arising from a crowd outside the entrance to one of the government buildings. Sebastian went on the alert, knowing how much unrest simmered beneath the surface of the country's peaceful society. He thought the government's proposed measures likely to provoke the very violence it aimed to combat.

Most of the gathered crowd were men, but he noticed one female hovering on the fringe. Drawing closer he realized she was no servant girl but, from her clothing, a lady. And a young one. Long fair hair emerged from her bonnet to cover her back. He recognized her just as a boy ran past and grabbed her reticule, breaking the string that was looped over her arm.

"Hey!" shouted Minerva Montrose. He might have predicted she'd neither take such treatment sitting down nor resort to tears. "Come back! Stop! Thief!"

"Miss Montrose," he said, stepping in rapidly to prevent her taking off after the boy.

"Oh! Mr. Iverley. Quickly, that child has my reticule. Help me."

"He's well away and you'll never catch him. Besides, he'd lead you into a maze of streets and some company you'd rather not encounter."

He'd known from the start Minerva was a sensible girl. She nodded. "There wasn't much in it, just enough money for my fare back to Portman Square. I'm going to have a long walk."

"I'd offer to take you in my own vehicle, but I'm on foot myself. Let me find a hackney and see you home."

"Thank you. Diana's butler will pay for the carriage. There's no need for you to come with me."

"It would be my pleasure."

She gave him a big smile. "Good! It would be my pleasure too."

"You are staying with your sister?"

"I told you I would. You promised to call."

Sebastian felt quite incapable of offering any explanation for his neglect, and certainly not the true one. "My apologies" was all he could manage.

"Shall we walk part of the way?" Minerva asked. "It's a lovely day."

He offered his arm and they headed up Whitehall together while she filled him in on the reason for her presence in Westminster that afternoon. They'd exchanged viciously critical opinions of government policies before it occurred to Sebastian that there was anything irregular about Minerva's expedition. He stopped abruptly outside the Horse Guards.

"Why did you come alone? It's not safe."

"I was fine."

"You were robbed. What was your sister thinking?"

"Well, actually she wasn't. She thinks I'm upstairs in my room with one of my headaches."

"My God! Minerva, she must be worried sick. I must get you home at once."

"Mr. Iverley," she began. "I beg your pardon, my lord."

"I don't give a damn what you call me. I care that Lady Fanshawe may be pacing around her house wondering where her little sister has gone to unaccompanied by so much as a maid. Why didn't you take a footman?"

Minerva had the grace to look a little ashamed. "I knew if I took one of the servants Diana would find out and stop me."

With a harrumph of exasperation Sebastian turned away and hailed a hackney, headed down the street in the wrong direction. While the driver maneuvered the turn he turned back to Minerva whose expression had progressed to defiance.

"To think I thought you a sensible sort of female," he said. "I should have known better. You are just as boneheaded and totty-brained as any of them."

"Why are you so angry?" Minerva demanded. "You didn't seem to think me totty-brained when I told you about the petition."

"How can you be so heedless of your sister's feelings?" he demanded, as he bundled her into the hackney.

Minerva settled back in the seat, folded her arms and thrust her lower lip forward. "I tell you, she'll never know. She's out driving with Blakeney this afternoon. I won't even be missed."

"Blakeney!" Sebastian almost shouted. "She's driving out with Blakeney?"

His plans for a peaceful, woman-free evening melted away. Not having seen Blakeney in Diana's company at any event, he'd assumed his fickle cousin was no longer interested. It was time to make the next move before Blakeney's position became entrenched.

Minerva's rebellious pout softened to a demure little smile. "You are right," she said. "And I was wrong. Very wrong."

Shock, combined with a lurch as the carriage made the turn into the Haymarket, nearly landed him on the floor.

"I shouldn't have risked worrying Diana," she went on, "although I still say she'll never know. But I'm sorry I did it. I thank you for rescuing me and for your escort. And I am grateful to you for making me see the error of my ways."

Sebastian eyed her suspiciously. Was she serious?

"Diana is giving a dinner party to celebrate my birthday. I would like to invite you to join us."

At four o'clock precisely Diana's butler opened the door to admit the Marquis of Blakeney.

"Is your mistress ready?" he asked. "I don't like to keep my horses waiting."

Diana, pacing nervously in the hall, rushed forward and grabbed his arm. "Thank God you are here, Blake."

"Didn't you get my note telling you to expect me at four instead of three?"

"Yes, of course. Minerva has disappeared. I'm worried to death something may have happened to her."

Blake patted her hand. "Do you need to sit down?"

"No! I want to go out and look for her."

"First tell me what happened."

"Two hours ago she said she had a headache and went to her room. She gets headaches sometimes, though she's very brave and ignores them more often than not."

"Yes, yes, go on." Blake sounded impatient.

"When I received your note postponing our drive I went to my own rooms to attend to some matters there. A quarter of an hour ago I crept into her room to see how she was and she wasn't there."

"Where in blazes would she have gone?"

"She wanted to see the petition delivered to the Home Office. My guess is she's gone to Whitehall."

Blake slipped an arm about her waist but she was too agitated to enjoy the sensation. "Cheer up, my dear. We'll pop down in my curricle right away."

"Oh yes, please let us leave at once. I fear something may have happened to her."

"I doubt it," Blake said, rather carelessly in Diana's opinion. "And I'll be sure to give her a good scolding for such a hoydenish escapade. She's ruined our afternoon."

"I should have arranged for her to see the petition delivered, then she wouldn't have had to resort to this deception." Although Diana knew Min had behaved badly, she found Blakeney's attitude galling. She had every intention of punishing her sister, but it was her job, not Blake's.

"The main thing is that we find her safe," Blake said, thereby retrieving his position. He put his other arm around her shoulders and kissed her forehead. "Let's go."

Even as he spoke there came another knock at the door and the butler opened it at once to admit Minerva, smiling broadly and clinging to the arm of a tall gentleman with spectacles.

"Look who brought me home," she said cheerfully. "Sebastian, I mean Lord Iverley, has agreed to come to my birthday party."

"Lord Iverley," Diana began, then faltered when she saw Sebastian's expression. What she read there certainly wasn't boredom or indifference. Neither was it the admiration and desire she'd seen at Mandeville. Even through the glass of his spectacles she couldn't mistake the raw fury in his eyes.

It only lasted a moment then he smiled blandly and inclined his head. "Lady Fanshawe. Blake. I've had the honor of escorting Miss Montrose home."

* * *

Sebastian strode through Mayfair, the walk to Piccadilly only increasing his seething hatred.

"I need to learn how to box."

"Nice to see you, too, Sebastian," Tarquin drawled in response to Sebastian bursting into his dressing room without so much as a word of greeting. "Obviously you need a drink." He nodded at his valet, who laid down the waistcoat Tarquin was about to put on.

The man returned a minute later with a decanter of sack and Sebastian tossed back a glass, the dry but rich wine enhancing the feelings of aggression that already expanded his chest.

"You look as though you want to kill someone," Tarquin said calmly.

It wouldn't come to that, Sebastian assumed. But he wasn't guaranteeing that he wouldn't inflict considerable bodily harm on his cousin Blake before this was over.

He growled.

"I suppose I could arrange some lessons," Tarquin continued. "Meet me at Jackson's tomorrow at noon. Now get out and let me dress in peace."

Chapter 12

"Lord Chase is a marquis," Minerva said.

"Yes," agreed Diana and wished she hadn't punished Minerva for her escapade by depriving her of newspapers for a week. Her sister had too much time to brood. Tomorrow, thank the Lord, she could go back to reading *The Times*. Meanwhile she sat in the drawing room looking bored and worrying about the seating arrangements for her birthday party.

"And so is Lord Blakeney. But he will be a duke one day."

"Quite so."

Minerva, Diana observed with interest, was kicking her heals against the legs of her chair. She'd never actually seen anyone do that.

"So is Blakeney's precedence higher?" Min asked. "Or is Lord Chase higher because he's a real marquis, not just one by courtesy? Or is precedence decided by the date of the title's creation? And if so, which title?"

"For the hundredth time, Min. I don't know and I don't care."

Minerva looked sulky. "I bet Lord Blakeney cares. He's quite full of himself."

Diana set aside her embroidery, which she hardly worked on anyway. She'd never learned to sew as a child, neither Montrose parent having regarded stitchery as a necessary skill. She'd taken it up to please Tobias who thought she looked pretty bent over the frame, fussing with colored silks.

"Stop making nasty little remarks about Blakeney, who may be about to become your brother-in-law. I know you have this ridiculous notion that I should prefer Lord Iverley but it will never happen. Not least because Lord Iverley is not at all interested in me."

"Yes he is."

"No. He isn't."

"Well, he was. Before, when he came to see us at Wallop." Minerva saw a good deal too much.

"If he was, he isn't anymore. He scarcely speaks to me when we meet."

Minerva gave her a hard look. "Did you do something to offend him? Because if so, you should apologize."

Cringing inwardly, Diana tried to shake off her guilty conscience. He couldn't have found out, could he? Apart from her, only Blake and Lamb knew about the bet and they swore they hadn't said a word. But nothing else explained the way he almost snubbed her. And she hadn't imagined his anger when he brought Min home.

Her sister wouldn't leave the subject alone. "You just prefer Blakeney because he's going to be a duke. Isn't a viscount good enough for you?"

"That's absurd. You know I've wanted Blake for years. And it's too much coming from you. I'm not the one who's obsessed with precedence." There were times when Minerva was too annoying for words.

The arrival of visitors saved Min from grave injury and put a temporary end to the sisterly wrangle. Diana's new friend Lady Chase was accompanied by her sister-in-law, Lady Esther Godfrey, who was the same age as Minerva.

"Thank goodness you've arrived, Juliana. We are about to have a small luncheon. Will you join us? Minerva's driving me quite mad. Perhaps you can settle her questions about the order of precedence."

Lady Chase, or Juliana as she had become over the course of a couple of meetings of the disorganized, sparsely attended, and still unnamed Books and Bonnets Club, looked alarmed. "I seriously doubt it."

"But you are a marchioness," Minerva said.

"A very new one. Esther might be able to help."

Lady Esther was admiring Diana's gown and disclaimed any special knowledge in the area.

"I'm trying to decide on the seating arrangements for my birthday party," Minerva explained.

"I thought it was to be a small, informal affair since you aren't out," Juliana said.

"Di said I could have it the way I wanted and I wish to practice for the future. There will only be about a dozen at the table but I want to get it right. You will be the highest ranking lady present."

"I hope that doesn't mean I have to go into dinner with Sebastian Iverley."

"No," Minerva assured her. "Probably Lord Blakeney. I'd *like* to sit next to Lord Iverley."

"It's your party. Why don't you?"

"I have no rank at all. I shall be at the very bottom of the table, next to Mr. MacFarland. That's all right. He's great fun."

"You'd never guess," Diana remarked to her visitors, "that my sister is a Radical."

"In order to exert influence," Minerva said earnestly, "you have to win the ear of those in power and you do that by playing by their rules in inessential matters."

Juliana regarded the girl with awe. "Is she always like this?"

"I know," Diana said with a nod. "She's terrifying. But I love her anyway. Most of the time."

Marsden arrived to announce the meal and the four ladies descended to the dining room where cold meats, salad, and fruit awaited them.

"We came to issue an invitation of our own," Juliana said. "We're removing to Gloucestershire at the end of the month. Cain and I thought we'd invite some friends to visit us for a week or two. Please say you and Minerva will join the party."

Diana accepted with pleasure. Markley Chase Abbey was a famous Elizabethan house that few people ever visited.

"I shall be glad to have the support of a friend," Juliana went on. "My mother-in-law just moved to the dower house and this is the first time I shall be the hostess at the Abbey. You seem to have a much better grasp of entertaining than I do. Look at this lovely array of food, just for chance callers. Not," she added, looking at Diana's plate, "that you seem to be taking advantage of it. Is that beetroot?"

Diana looked down at the slice of boiled chicken

accompanied by three unappetizing slices of carmine vegetable that bled into the white meat. "It's my new reducing diet," she said. "The old one, where I only ate foods I enjoyed, didn't work. No danger of that with this regime."

"I can't imagine why you think you need a regime," Juliana said. "You always look beautiful."

"Thank you for saying that, but Chantal doesn't agree and I am in thrall to my maid."

"I'll make sure we have plenty of beetroot in the house when you stay with us."

"I wish I could feel more grateful," Diana said. "I really don't like it very much."

"She'll probably have changed her diet by that time," Minerva remarked. "This is the third one she's tried."

"Enough of your impudence. Try a little respect for your elders!" Diana said severely, then spoiled the effect by laughing. "Min's right, unfortunately. But I really think this one is working. I feel thinner after only two days. Beetroot must have some magical reducing property. Chantal says I need to lose an inch off the bosom to make the new fashions drape correctly."

Juliana looked at her quizzically. "I doubt Lord Blakeney would agree with that opinion."

"Nor Sebastian," Minerva muttered.

"Should we invite Blakeney to Markley Chase? My husband is acquainted with him, I believe."

"He won't come unless you have lots of hunting, shooting, and fishing," Min said. "The more animals he can kill the happier he is."

"Be quiet, Min. It's entirely up to you, Juliana. I'll

just say that things are progressing well in that area. Very well indeed."

Without going so far as to claim enjoyment, Sebastian was beginning to find his excursions among the *ton* at least bearable. To begin with, he no longer felt any awkwardness in company. He could talk to anyone with ease. And though much of what passed for conversation in the vast ocean of society was insipid, he discovered islands of sense, not all of them male.

He accepted an invitation to dine at the house of a married acquaintance and found it quite endurable, despite the presence of his friend's wife and sister-in-law. To his surprise he learned that Diana wasn't unique in all her sex in possessing the ability to conduct an intelligent discussion.

The company went on to the theater and, making the promenade in the interval between the tragedy and the farce, Sebastian caught sight of Diana as he descended the grand staircase. Lady Georgina had seen him and thrown him an encouraging smile, but suddenly he couldn't stomach another exchange with the woman. Pretending not to notice, he marched past her in the crowd and forged on in Diana's direction so that he could brush her arm in passing. He'd become quite an expert at the maneuver but the thrilling shock of her touch never diminished.

"I beg your pardon, Lady Fanshawe," he murmured.

"Lord Iverley," she replied. She looked at him warily, as though expecting a snub, and started to turn away.

On impulse he decided to alter his tactics. She was certainly puzzled and probably annoyed at the way he had almost ignored her. Now that he'd secured an invitation to her house, it was time to move on from subtle neglect and start charming her in earnest.

"I am looking forward to Miss Minerva's dinner party," he said.

She turned back to face him and smiled, awakening a swarm of butterflies in his breast. "I'm glad you are able to attend. Minerva is delighted. She's never stopped talking about you since you called on us at Mandeville Wallop. I don't know what you were discussing out in the garden, but it made a big impression."

"Er . . . good." What was the matter with him? She seemed pleased to see him yet he could barely manage a coherent sentence, let alone a charming one. Damnation, he needed to demonstrate that he was a gentleman of wit and fashion, the kind of creature she admired.

She looked at him quizzically, as though she could tell the thud of his heart was drowning his thoughts. "What do you think of the play?" she said after an endless silence.

He'd had some opinions on the performance of Richard the Third and expressed them cogently to his companions in the box. Now he couldn't remember a single one.

"We've been having very fine weather for October," he said. "It must be a full week since it rained."

Chapter 13

Considering the slightly motley collection of guests, Diana thought Minerva's first dinner party was going well. Her birthday gift for her sister, the latest edition of the peerage, had settled the vexing question of precedence. Diana, as lady of the house, had been led into dinner by the Marquis of Chase who, according to Mr. Debrett, outranked Lord Blakeney.

Around the table, conversational balls were happily rolling. Marianne's husband, Robert MacFarland, entertained the youngest members of the party, Minerva and Lady Esther. Juliana Chase was talking to Blakeney about fifteenth-century printing, and Blake was listening with every appearance of enjoyment. Diana might have been more impressed had Lady Chase not been wearing a new and very low-cut gown of silver tissue, ordered on Chantal's recommendation. With her tousled golden curls she looked like a tiny and delectable fairy queen. Diana could hardly blame Blake for giving her his undivided attention.

"Your wife looks beautiful tonight," she whispered to her neighbor.

"Blakeney seems to think so," Chase said.

"I don't believe Lady Chase is at all impressed with Blake."

"I am absolutely sure my wife has no idea that he keeps eyeing her chest. She thinks he's actually interested in Gutenberg."

"All things are possible, although not, I grant you, likely."

Chase stopped gazing at Juliana and gave his hostess his full attention. "She says Blakeney's intentions lie elsewhere. That's why I invited him down to Markley Chase."

Diana lowered her eyes demurely. "That was very good of you."

"We have plenty of room. Now tell me, what do you think of Sebastian's transformation? You knew him before he acquired a viscountcy and a new wardrobe."

"It's quite a change. I always thought him a good-looking man but I had no idea how handsome. He pays for the dressing."

"What of his manners?"

"They are certainly much more polite." Diana wasn't about to admit that she found them rather repulsive.

"And he's become quite a talker. He used to be economical with words, even when discussing books. On any other subject he was miserly. Now, just listen to him chatter away."

Diana had listened. Sebastian had warmed up a trifle since accepting Minerva's invitation. He'd crossed paths with her in the crowd at the theater earlier in the week and, instead of excusing himself with a polite nod, he'd engaged her in conversation.

They'd enjoyed a scintillating ten minutes discussing the unusually dry autumn weather. Now she listened again, straining her ears to overhear what he had to say to Marianne.

"The duchess has departed for Devonshire? How very singular," he said in a fashionable drawl. Marianne looked quite amused but Diana strongly suspected her friend was enjoying his broad chest more than his discourse.

"I think he disposed of his brain along with his old clothes," she said.

Lord Chase laughed.

"Oh dear, perhaps I shouldn't have said that. I know he's a friend of yours."

"I had the impression most ladies like a man to present a good appearance and a polished address."

"Are you suggesting we prefer style over substance? That doesn't apply to your own wife."

"You think not? She married me after all."

"Quite," Diana said, giving the well-tailored marquis a mocking examination. Though he was a very good-looking man and certainly not lacking in style, she suspected Chase of possessing a sharp intelligence. Why else would he have attracted the scholarly Juliana?

She looked down the table at Sebastian who responded to some remark of Marianne's with a cynical-looking grin. She couldn't tell if his bespectacled eyes matched the rest of his expression. His clothing and linen were impeccable and he leaned back in his chair with the relaxed air of a man at home in his surroundings. She had a sudden recollection of a very different man: shabby, a little awkward, never glib, not even articulate, but always sincere.

"Much as I concede the improvement in his appearance," she said, "there are things about the old Mr. Iverley I miss."

"He used to grunt quite a lot."

"True."

"Is that what you miss?"

Diana laughed. "The grunt I can live without. But he was never dull."

"Don't tell my wife," Chase said, "but I always liked him, too, even with the grunt." He gave her a look of approval with flashing sky blue eyes that posed a danger to any woman whose heart wasn't engaged elsewhere.

Diana had a vision of dark-rimmed silver eyes that the world rarely saw, gazing at her with unalloyed admiration.

She gave herself a mental shake. The servants were bringing in the second course and it was time for everyone to switch partners. She turned to the man seated on her left, easily the handsomest man in the room and one with dark blue eyes as fine as Chase's. Blakeney. He was the man she wanted.

Sebastian wasn't sure how much longer he could stand it. He'd managed to chat with Mrs. MacFarland for half an hour by dint of applying one of his new methods of polite social intercourse: think of a predictable observation on a commonplace subject and deliver it with enormous confidence and a cynical edge.

Watching Diana converse with Cain was bad enough. He wasn't sure his friend was wholly on his side. Lady Chase, he knew, was firmly in the enemy camp. Now Diana had turned to Blakeney. Seeing them together stoked his resentment to white heat. His cousin looked down at her with a possessive air that made Sebastian itch to test his fledgling pugilistic skills. And Diana smiled back with that glowing look Sebastian knew too well. He could only hope she was as insincere in her attentions to Blake as she had been with him.

Thanks to Minerva's invitation he'd carried the battle into her territory. He'd get a little closer after dinner, attempt to judge if there was a chance of her falling into his arms. Forget "chance." Failure was not an option. To judge if she was ready to fall. And this time he wouldn't relapse into tongue-tied idiocy in her presence.

He had no need for his planned tactics. Diana made the first move when the gentlemen returned to the drawing room for coffee.

"Would you come to the library?" she asked him. "I'd like your opinion on a book I've acquired."

For a moment he was surprised she even had a library. But judging by the furnishings of the large modern house, her late husband had been a man of taste and education as well as wealth. Naturally he would own books, even if he didn't collect the kind of rarities Sebastian regarded as necessary for a library worthy of the name. He followed her into a large well-appointed room lined with fully stocked shelves.

With a tremor of excitement he wondered if

Diana's request was an excuse. Her new friend Lady Chase was more than capable of rendering a verdict on any unusual volume. Minerva had told him about the Ladies' Society of Bibliophilia and Fashion, or whatever ridiculous name they'd come up with.

A book lay open on a table in the center of the room. Sebastian removed his spectacles and skimmed the text. It was a copy of Debrett's *Peerage* open to the entry for the Dukes of Hampton, Blakeney's family. His anticipation ebbed a little.

"What do you want to show me?" he asked.

Instead of fetching a book, she came and stood next to him, so close he could sense her warmth and fragrance, close enough that she had to tilt her head to meet his eyes.

"Have I done anything to offend you?" she asked.

He almost reverted to the grunt. "Why would you think such a thing?" he answered cautiously.

"I thought we were friends. Then you left Mande-ville without a word."

"I was called to my uncle's deathbed." His grip on his spectacles tightened.

"I understand that. I'm sorry." She touched his hand. "But I have the impression you've been avoid-ing me since. Even that you were angry. Were you? Are you?"

Blue eyes gazed into his as though seeking to read his soul. He kept his expression neutral. "Why should I be angry with you?" he asked in feigned bewilder-ment. "Is there a reason?"

He concentrated on her sweet, lush, lying lips. They parted, so slowly it seemed to take an age. Hardly breathing, he awaited her answer. Would she confess her perfidy?

He hoped not. Because if she were honest with him now the game would be over and Sebastian wanted to keep playing to the end. The only danger was he'd play too fast. With endless patience he'd achieve the satisfaction of full and final victory.

She was the one to break eye contact. "No reason that I can think of," she said softly, lowering her chin.

She wasn't the only liar in the room. "There is no reason," he said. "We had a flirtation at Mandeville. I should be grateful. Astonishing, really, that you took the slightest notice of me."

Her blush fueled his exhilaration and lent veracity to his performance.

"I was such a bumbling idiot then," he said.

"No," she said faintly.

"Yes. I hate to think of how I was then, how I looked. A clodhopper!" He shuddered theatrically. "My clothes. I had to burn everything."

"You've changed."

"Of course. Why, I was almost incapable of conducting a civilized conversation." He was warming up now, and beginning to see the appeal of the career of an actor. "I never accepted invitations or consorted with people of refinement."

Her eyes widened and her mouth parted. He wished he could kiss her but it was surely too soon. Letting his spectacles fall to the tabletop he clenched his fist, digging the nails into his palms. *Patience.*

"Why did you decide to change?" she asked.

"Why do you think?"

"I don't know."

He said nothing, instinct telling him this was a moment to be mysterious. Still flushed, she examined his face, which he kept carefully impassive. She opened her mouth to speak a couple of times, then changed her mind.

He'd flustered her.

"I must return to my guests," she said finally.

He followed her back to the drawing room where the two youngest members of the party played a duet on the pianoforte and Cain sat on a sofa between his wife and Lord Blakeney. Sebastian gave his friend a nod and the marquis excused himself and accompanied him out of the French doors that led to a terrace overlooking the garden.

"Cheroot?" Cain asked.

"No thanks, I don't."

"I thought you'd acquired all the fashionable vices."

"Filthy habit."

"You almost sound like the old Iverley," Cain said, leaning against a stone balustrade, apparently unbothered by the late October chill.

Sebastian shivered. "I wish I could be. I miss him." He also missed the flannel waistcoats he used to wear.

"You're not the only one."

"What do you mean?"

"Lady Fanshawe misses him too."

"Why should I care about that?" If it was too dark to see him shrug, he hoped the sense of it was carried in his voice. He barely restrained the urge to demand an explanation but he disdained to expose his feelings.

"Oh please, Sebastian. She's the one you've been working so hard to impress. It took Tarquin and me a while to guess because we'd expected someone more brazen. But Diana Fanshawe is altogether delightful. I had quite the wrong idea of the kind of lady you'd fallen for. I congratulate you on your good taste."

Sebastian caught himself about to acknowledge Cain's compliment, a ludicrous impulse because it was based on a misreading of her character. Diana had them all fooled, much as he had been at first. His friends didn't know that underneath her perfect exterior lay a heartless tease.

"If I'm not mistaken," Cain went on, "you've just been alone with her. Any progress?"

"I'm not sure. Since you ask, I'd like you to find out what she thinks of me."

Cain laughed. "And how would I go about that?"

"Be tactful. Ask her if she likes me."

"I could torture you for another ten or fifteen minutes and amuse myself enormously. But being a man in whom the milk of human kindness flows deep, I'll tell you that I already know. She likes you."

"Are you sure? How do you know?"

"She told me."

"Then it worked?" he said, astonished. "The plan worked."

"Yes indeed. She said she had no idea how handsome you were and you pay for the dressing."

Of course, Sebastian thought cynically. She liked his new wardrobe.

"But . . ." There had to be a but. It couldn't be that

easy. "But," Cain said, "there are certain aspects of your new guise she's not so sure about."

"Oh?"

"She thinks you have become boring."

"That makes two of us," Sebastian said with real fervor.

"My advice is to keep the clothes and the good manners, but return to your former mode of conversation. God know why, but I always found it entertaining."

"Do you mean I can grunt again?"

"Definitely not. Lady Fanshawe specifically excluded the grunt from the list of your traits that she misses."

He hadn't really thought he'd be allowed to retain the grunt. What mattered was that she liked him. And to his surprise there were things about his true personality she liked. The real Sebastian. The bumbling idiot, the clodhopper. For a moment a sweet melody sang in his heart, a tiny pure flame kindled in his heart, like a distant star on a moonless light. Then a triumphant gong boomed through his chest, a victorious sunrise dispelled the starlight. Total conquest would soon be his, along with the humiliation of his cousin.

Except that logic and all evidence told him that Blake was very much in the race. Most likely he was ensconced on a sofa with Diana at this moment.

Cain interrupted his thoughts. "You're frowning. Why?"

"Blakeney. I don't understand his appeal. If she thinks *I* have turned into a bore, can't she see that he's always been one? I've never heard him say anything intelligent or original."

"There's no better-looking man in London," Cain said.

What a fool he was. Diana might have enjoyed his conversation, but appearances mattered more. Without his improved looks he'd never have a shot at defeating Blakeney.

"And he's going to be a duke. But if I read the lady correctly, rank isn't of paramount importance. I feel sure," he continued with a grin, "she'd be content to be a viscountess."

Momentarily nonplussed by the marquis's assumption that his aim was marriage, Sebastian almost missed Cain's next revelation.

"I have bad news for you. Lady Fanshawe and her sister are to be our guests at Markley Chase Abbey next month."

"Yes?"

"And Blakeney is coming too. He agreed to come for a week on his way to Badminton for the hunt."

"You have to invite me."

"My wife'll kill me. She's firmly on Blakeney's side."

"Please, Cain. And I'll be nice to Lady Chase. I'll talk to her about books."

"You were devilish rude to her when she was a bookseller. She isn't one of those sweet women who refuses to hold a grudge."

"You know I may have been wrong about her in the past." Cain had to be appeased. "She is fairly knowledgeable about books."

Cain raised an eyebrow.

"Very knowledgeable." Cain waved his hand, demanding more.

"And I was very, very wrong. Completely mistaken."

"All right, you can come to Markley Chase. But don't say anything. I'll wait for the right moment to break the news to Juliana. And when you arrive at the Abbey you will tell her what you just told me. You will grovel."

"Yes, Cain. Thank you, Cain," Sebastian said, crossing his fingers behind his back. "You won't regret this."

"Don't forget what comes next. The Grand Gesture."

Back in his own library Sebastian found his notebook and studied Tarquin and Cain's list of grand gestures.

Sweep her into a waltz. He'd been determined from the beginning to get through this whole affair without having to set foot on a dance floor. He wrote a large X next to that item.

Diamonds, emeralds, sapphires. Diana's late husband had a nabob's fortune and her jewels were superb. But he hadn't seen her in sapphires and they'd match her eyes. He put a question mark in the margin.

Dog or other pet. Sebastian disapproved of pets on principle as being bad for books. He'd once seen a perfectly nice copy of the *Nuremburg Chronicle* with a large hole in the cover pecked by the owner's wife's parrot. *No.* Double-underlined.

Save from socially awkward situation. Until a few

weeks ago Sebastian had himself epitomized social awkwardness. He'd come a long way, but not that far. *Impossible.*

Save from runaway horse. Too hard to set up, since Diana was a brilliant horsewoman.

Save from footpads. Hmm.

Hire footpads if necessary. It sounded like a completely stupid idea. On the other hand, his friends' advice had proved sound up to this point.

Chapter 14

"**H**ow much longer?" Minerva asked, peering out of the closed window at the twilit Cotswold landscape. On the second day of their journey to Gloucestershire, Minerva seemed to be losing a year of maturity every ten miles. Luckily they were in the final stretch, or Diana feared they'd reach Markley Chase with her sister a mewling and puking infant.

"Five minutes less than the last time you asked," Diana snapped. "For heaven's sake, Min. I've never known you so fidgety." Traveling was always tiresome, but there was little to complain about a journey on excellent roads in the comfortable and well-sprung coach that had been one of Sir Tobias Fanshawe's wedding presents to his bride.

"I wish we were in London. I only just escaped from spending my entire life in the countryside and now you're making me go back. You're taking me away from pavements and people and returning me to plows and pigs. I can almost smell the dung already."

Diana laughed at Minerva's horrified expression. "I don't believe Markley Chase Abbey is set in a farmyard. The house is reputed to be quite lovely and the party should be amusing."

"We both know why *you* are looking forward to it. Days and days of listening to your darling Blakeney rattle on about pigeons and partridges."

"If you work at it I'm sure you can come up with a few more things you hate beginning with *P*."

"I can think of one I don't hate! Parliament. There's going to be a special session and I shall miss everything."

"It's not as though you can attend," Diana pointed out. "You can read the reports in *The Times* just as well in Gloucestershire."

Minerva was not to be consoled. "If the Chases bother to have it delivered. Lady Chase probably only subscribes to some tedious journal of bibliographical enquiry."

"You'll have plenty of time to enjoy London next year when you come out. And as I keep telling you, having Lady Esther to share your debut will make you much more comfortable. I wish I'd had a close friend during my season."

Minerva leaned back in her seat and frowned. At least she wasn't whining anymore. "I'm not sure I want to come out next year. I don't think I want to marry yet. I don't want to settle for someone whom I'll have to live with for the rest of my life without looking around first."

"That's just what I want for you," Diana agreed. "You certainly don't have to wed anyone unless you truly wish to. You'll have the comfort of waiting as long as necessary. And you'll have lots of choice, I promise. There's nothing I won't do to ensure your season is a triumph."

Minerva must have heard the bitterness in Diana's voice. "Was yours so very bad then?"

Diana shuddered at the memory. "Going to London was all I dreamed of since I was fourteen years old. All I wanted to do was have fun and then get married, preferably to Blakeney. I looked forward to the season so much and I hated every moment. My clothes were wrong and we weren't invited to the most *tonnish* events. I hardly met anyone. I spent most of the time at balls sitting with the chaperones while Mama talked to elderly gentlemen about horses when she should have been finding me partners. She had no idea how to meet the right people."

"Is that why you married Sir Tobias?"

"He was the only person who took any notice of me. He was kind, and he adored me. By the end of one month in town I knew marrying Blakeney was as likely as traveling to the moon."

"I don't understand it, Di. You are so beautiful."

"No, Min. You and Mama and the boys are beautiful—and handsome. I take after Papa. My face is too round, my hair a dull brown, and my figure tends to plumpness. I spend a fortune on clothes, thanks to Tobias, and I've learned how to dress well thanks to Chantal, but underneath my looks are no more than passable. It's all in the presentation. But you, with your golden hair and tall, slim figure, will take the *ton* by storm. Particularly since your clothes will be unequalled by any young lady in London."

Minerva looked troubled. "I don't want to win a

husband with my looks. You know I wish to wed a man of substance who will appreciate the help I can give him in his career."

"And so you shall, my dearest. But I'm afraid men are fundamentally shallow. It's always the appearance that attracts them. Only then will they take the trouble to discover what's underneath the surface."

"That's so sad."

"Not really," Diana said with a shrug. "It's just life. And I'm not clever like you. I was always the ordinary one in the family. Thank goodness Tobias saw something in my unpromising exterior. I shall always be grateful to him. I only wish I could have given him the heir he wanted."

"I'm sure that wasn't your fault. He was so much older."

"He never blamed me. As you know, he was married twice previously without any children. He believed an illness in India during his youth may have rendered him infertile. Dear Tobias. He was always a reasonable man. There are many gentlemen who would refuse to entertain the notion that the fault was theirs."

"Was he . . . capable?" Minerva asked delicately. Rather a shocking question for a girl of her age, but Minerva had spent a lifetime listening to their mother discuss the successes and failures of equine and canine liaisons.

"Yes."

"You know I'd like to know more about . . . er . . . marriage between human beings."

"I promise you, Min. When you marry I shall tell you all about it. Mama told me I had nothing to worry about and it was just like animals. That turned out to be rather inadequate information."

"Was it terrible? The dogs don't seem to enjoy it much. Not the females, at least. They seem to be hating the whole business."

"To put it delicately, there's a reason I want to be married again."

Minerva's eyes widened and she nodded silently. "I see," she said after a moment or so. "Perhaps I can finally understand what you see in Blakeney. I don't suppose the marriage act requires much in the way of conversation."

Considering Diana had spent quite a lot of time over the past year in contemplation of the marriage act with Blake, it was strange that the face—and body—this exchange brought to mind was not that of the marquis. She envisioned a taller, less exquisite figure. Brown hair, not blond. Not blue eyes but gray, and concealed by *steel-rimmed* spectacles.

Peculiar enough to be thinking of the Viscount Iverley in this context. Odder still to be thinking about Sebastian Iverley as he'd been when she first knew him: shabby, unpolished, and inarticulate. And generating a familiar and delicious physical heat. She recalled the ease with which he'd carried her up the path to the temple, the hard strength of his arms around her. The interrupted kiss.

She shook her head to dispel the inexplicable image and was thrown into a corner as the carriage came to a sudden halt.

"We're here," Minerva cried and wrestled open the door.

"Impossible," Diana said. "It's another ten miles

at least." But Minerva, without waiting for the footman to get down from the box and lower the step, leaped to the ground.

Diana snuggled under her fur rug. "You're not even wearing a bonnet. Get back in and close the door. You're letting the cold air in."

"We're in the middle of a wood."

"I told you we hadn't arrived. Ask John why he stopped."

"I'll go and look."

Before Minerva returned, the coachman appeared at the door. "I'm sorry, my lady. There's another vehicle blocking the road."

"An accident?" Diana asked, leaning forward.

"Don't know, my lady. There's nobody here and no horses. Maybe they rode for help."

"Can you get by?" Diana felt a chill that had nothing to do with the season. The armed outriders she'd hired for the journey were some miles back, with the baggage coach. The last time they'd changed horses there had been some minor problem with the wheel of that vehicle. Rather than wait for it to be adjusted, she'd elected to travel on ahead. At the time it had seemed sensible to leave the guards with Chantal, and Diana's jewel case.

"That's strange." Minerva's voice came from a few yards distant. "There's someone among the trees. Hey there! Is this your carriage?"

"Min! Don't!" Diana cried, tossing aside her blanket and sliding over to the open door. "Help me down," she ordered and grabbed the coachman by the shoulders. Her terrified premonition was justified. As she let the servant swing her to the ground, a masked rider emerged from the woods, stopped his horse next to Minerva, and pressed a pistol into the girl's blond head.

"Stand and deliver!" he commanded in rough accents. "Bring your valuables here."

They were powerless. The coachman had left his gun on the box and even if the footman who rode with him could reach it, he couldn't fire at the highwayman without endangering Minerva.

"Don't shoot!" Diana yelled. "Let me get my purse. There's not much in it but what there is you can have. John, Matthew, don't move." At her command her servants became statues.

"Don't try anything funny," the rogue growled as Diana scrambled back into the carriage. "Any trouble and I'll shoot the girl."

The sight of that cruel gun barrel thrust into Minerva's curls robbed Diana of rational thought. Sobbing with terror, she wrestled with the strings of her reticule, which became entangled and knotted in her haste. She kept thinking about how she would break the news of Min's death to her parents. And how stupid it was that her sister might die because all she found, once she ripped open the purse with the strength of the demented, were three golden guineas, a handful of lesser coins, a jar of rouge, and her silver etui. The latter was a pretty thing, large enough to hold a small pair of scissors as well as needles and thread, but worth only a guinea or two.

Most of the currency she'd brought for travel expenses and vails was in her well-guarded jewel case, along with a fortune in precious stones. Leaving the guards with those valuables had been a foolish choice.

What was jewelry compared to her sister's life?

"I'm coming back out," she said in a clear voice, struggling for calmness as she prepared to explain to the robber why such a luxurious equipage yielded so little of worth. And, just in case an opportunity presented itself, secreted the tiny scissors between her thumb and the palm of her hand.

"That's right, lady, just bring out your baubles and young miss here won't get hurt."

"You are hurting me!" Minerva said, sounding less frightened than annoyed. She glared up at her persecutor. "Your gun is digging into my head."

"Hush, Min!" Diana warned but the complaint seemed to have an effect. The brute pulled his gun upward, away, thank God, from Minerva's head and pointed it at Diana instead.

"Look, sir," she said. "I'm very sorry but I don't have much money with me. You are welcome to any of it. And my earrings. They are only garnets but I don't wear my good jewelry when I travel." As she bent her head to remove the earrings she found further inspiration. "I have jeweled buckles on my boots. They're diamonds. Worth a fortune!" She assumed they would have long parted company by the time he discovered they were paste. She should have claimed the garnets were rubies.

She didn't notice the approach of a horse up the road behind them, until it sped to a gallop. What followed was something of a blur.

Shouts.

"Stop, you rogue!"

More shouts.

Min screaming as she hit the ground. Two horses

thrashing about. Diana's servants coming to life and joining the melee.

By the time Diana had a grasp on the situation, the highwayman had galloped off as though pursued by hellhounds and their savior had swung down from his own mount and was picking Minerva off the ground.

"Are you hurt?" he asked.

"I'm fine," she said, brushing dirt off her clothing. "That was exciting."

He turned to face Diana, a tall gentleman in a dust-covered multi-caped great coat. Her reticule dropped to the ground as he strode over and took her nerveless hand in one of his. The other held his own gun, pointing at the ground.

"It's all right," he said in a gentle voice. In the confusion, or perhaps during the final charge to the rescue, he'd lost his hat but his spectacles remained in place.

"Oh Sebastian," Diana cried and flung her arms about his neck.

"Ouch," he said. "What's that?"

"Sorry," she said and threw her scissors down before tightening her embrace. "Min might have been killed. You saved us!"

Over refreshments served in Markley Chase's magnificent scarlet saloon, Minerva and Lady Esther cornered Sebastian on a sofa and pestered him with questions about his dramatic rescue.

"I suppose," Juliana Chase whispered to Diana, "I have to be grateful now that Cain invited Lord Iverley to join our party."

"I certainly am."

"I'm so used to despising the man I find it inconvenient to change my stance."

"I hope you will," Diana said earnestly. "I believe he is a true hero."

"Come with me." Juliana led her to a glass-topped display table in the farthest corner of the room, away from Sebastian and his youthful admirers, and the other gentlemen who stood in front of the fireplace, half listening to the sofa group, occasionally exchanging desultory remarks.

"These are all Tudor miniatures," she said, then lowered her voice. "Is it possible you are *interested* in Iverley?"

Juliana's tone of incredulity made Diana smile. "I told you I was grateful to him."

"Not more than that? When you all arrived together you clung to his arm as though he were your last hope. I thought I detected a bit more than just gratitude."

Not wishing to give Juliana the wrong idea, Diana framed her response carefully. "I like Lord Iverley but I can't make him out. You've known him longer than I. Perhaps you can throw some light on his character."

"I've told you about the things he used to say to me when I was a bookseller. The man has absolutely no respect for women. He does appear to be changing, but it remains to be seen whether the transformation goes deeper than his wardrobe."

"I've known men who fail to appreciate that ladies can be anything but ornamental broodmares, but with Sebastian the prejudice seems to go beyond that. Do you know why?"

Juliana raised an eyebrow at Diana's unconscious use of the Christian name. "I've asked my husband that very question. Cain says Iverley doesn't talk much about himself but he does seem to have had an unusual upbringing."

Diana shifted sideways so she could glance at Sebastian, who was chatting to Minerva with some animation. "He's a mystery," she said, shaking her head.

"You're looking at him again."

"So what?"

"I'd expect you to look at Lord Blakeney that way. Now *he* looks jealous. Is that your aim?"

Diana realized she'd forgotten Blake was even in the room. "Maybe. Thank you again for inviting him. I realize neither you nor Lord Chase has much in common with him."

"I quite like Blakeney. I think he's more intelligent than he shows. It reminds me a little of how Cain used to be, playing the fool to disguise the truth about himself."

"Why would Blake do that?"

"I have no idea, but if you're going to marry him you'd better find out."

Diana wished she felt more enthusiastic about the prospect. To her surprise she was more curious about Sebastian's unknown past.

Sebastian was enjoying himself so much he forgot to feel even a twinge of guilt.

The tale, which lost nothing in Minerva's increasingly dramatic retellings, seemed a source of unending fascination to the ladies. The younger ones,

Minerva and Lady Esther, sat on either side of him on a sofa, pelting him with questions.

And Diana. After her initial heartfelt and delicious expression of gratitude, Diana let the others do most of the talking but she gazed at him with stars in her eyes. Really, the company of ladies, even in plural numbers, was tolerable when one was the object of their collective adoration.

As for Blakeney, he slouched against a caryatid that held up the gigantic marble mantelpiece, folded his arms, and scowled.

Sebastian felt ten feet tall.

The only shadow over his enjoyment of this moment of glory had been Lady Chase's tiresome insistence that her husband summon a magistrate to take information leading to the arrest and execution of the malefactor. Her bloodthirsty enthusiasm for the gallows, which Sebastian thought excessive in a gently bred lady, made him nervous for the continuing health of his head groom. That useful servant had disposed of his mask and Sebastian's old topcoat and was now lodged in the Markley Chase stable quarters.

And now Lady Chase had drawn Diana off to the other side of the room. From the glances the two of them sent his way, he gathered he was the topic of conversation. He hoped their hostess, whom he hadn't yet had time to butter up, wasn't turning Diana against him.

Sebastian also had to endure some cynical looks from Cain and Tarquin, the latter having been persuaded to join the party despite Gloucestershire's unfortunately rural nature. He wasn't surprised when his friends, acting in tandem like a pair of Welsh sheepdogs, cut him away from the pack of women and herded him into the library.

"We're safe from your cousin here," Cain said. "But we'd better hurry or my wife will be in to see if I'm showing you our new books without her. And," he continued with a glare, though Sebastian hadn't said a word, "don't forget you are here only on sufferance. You still have some serious groveling to do, and don't think your so-called heroics have let you off."

If Tarquin could have rolled his eyes further they'd have disappeared into his brains. "What a hero! Playing silly games with firearms. Someone could have been hurt."

"Neither of the guns was loaded, my groom's nor mine. There was no danger."

"What about your poor groom?" Tarquin asked. "His weapon may not have been loaded but I wager the Fanshawe servants' were."

"I was lucky," Sebastian admitted, "that the outriders remained with the other coach. I wasn't sure I could manage the robbery until that happened. The whole business was harder to arrange than I anticipated."

"Why arrange it at all?"

"You said I should hire footpads. I decided to take advantage of the journey and used a highwayman instead."

"He actually said 'stand and deliver.' Couldn't you have come up with something less hackneyed? The whole affair has a regrettably farcical quality."

"To hell with that," Cain said. "Poor Lady Fanshawe was terrified for her sister's life. I have a sister.

I know what that would feel like. You were cruel to pull such a trick."

Sebastian was astonished. "It was your idea!" he insisted.

"Sebastian," Tarquin said patiently. "Can't you understand a joke? I recall we made all sorts of ridiculous suggestions that day."

Sebastian felt himself color. He had taken all of his friends' suggestions in earnest. "I think it went splendidly," he said defensively. "My grand gesture was just what you said it should be. I provided exactly what she needed at that moment. Her sister was threatened, I saved her."

"Except," said Tarquin, "that her sister wouldn't have needed saving if you hadn't created the threat."

Cain shook his head in disgust. "You'd better pray she never finds out. I can promise you she will not be amused."

"She won't," Sebastian said. "She's never seen my groom and he was masked. She'd never recognize him. Besides, why should she suspect? I think your idea was brilliant."

Escaping further criticism, Sebastian left the room, only to meet Diana in the passage just outside the door. Judging by her welcoming expression, she hadn't overheard any part of the recent conversation.

"Lord Iverley. I was looking for you."

Each time he saw her, however brief their separation, he was astonished anew by her beauty, as though in her absence he'd forgotten her. Just a glimpse and his chest tightened.

"Yes?" he said, resentful that she still affected him so deeply. Her smile faded to uncertainty and he gentled his tone. "What can I do for you, Lady Fanshawe?"

"Do for me? How could I ask for anything more? I wanted to again express my most profound thanks."

Perversely he now felt uncomfortable at her misplaced gratitude. The words of his friends needled at his conscience. Besides, the false rescue had served its purpose and he'd just as soon not think about it anymore.

"Please don't mention it again," he said gruffly. "I am glad I happened along the road."

"I shall never in my life forget that moment when you galloped up and drove off the villain. I was terrified for Minerva's life and you saved her. I will never be able to thank you enough."

She stood in the shadowy corridor, the blue of her gaze intensified by emotion. His heart leaped when she moved closer and placed a hand on his shoulder. His throat tightened. "It was nothing," he rasped.

Her voice dropped. "I wanted to thank you while we were alone." She raised a hand to touch his cheek with cool fingers, then rose on her toes to brush warm lips over the same spot. "Thank you, Sebastian," she whispered then turned abruptly and left him.

He watched her walk away, the graceful sway of her hips reminding him of their afternoon spent exploring Mandeville. It was a lucky recollection since it brought back the source of his resentment. But the encounter disquieted him. For the first time a shade of unease tempered his anger.

Chapter 15

"**W**hat would anyone like to do today?" their host enquired.

"Minerva and I are going to the stables to see Octavo's puppies," Esther said.

"Octavo?" Diana asked.

"Octavo is Quarto's wife," Minerva explained. "She has—how many puppies?"

"Seven," Esther said. "They are quite adorable. Here, Quarto. Do you want to come and see your children?"

Quarto, Juliana's bulldog, was stretched out asleep in front of the fire. He opened a single uninterested eye then sank back into slumber.

"Apparently not. A typical fashionable father, I see," remarked Tarquin Compton.

"I'm afraid he shows remarkably little interest in his offspring," Juliana said.

"Or his 'wife' for that matter," said Cain. "Except during that particular time, of course."

Juliana glanced at the two girls and gave her husband a warning look. "*Pas devant les jeune filles*," she said softly.

Not softly enough. "It's all right, Lady Chase,"

Minerva said. "My mother breeds foxhounds so I understand about bitches in season. I also understand French, perfectly."

"Why don't you leave now, Minerva," Diana suggested, before the gentlemen could erupt into unseemly mirth.

"Will you come with us?"

"No thanks. You know what Chantal's like about dog hair."

Juliana and Cain offered a visit to the library to see a collection of plays they'd recently acquired. Sebastian and Tarquin were, predictably, interested. Blakeney was not.

"Would you like to go for a ride, Diana?" he asked.

A week ago she would have been thrilled by such an opportunity for a tête-à-tête. "I think I'll join the library party," she said. "I've become quite interested in books."

"In that case," Blake said, "I shall take Chase up on his offer of some shooting."

"My gamekeeper will be delighted," Cain said. "He keeps trying to tempt me with tales of pheasant by the hundred but my interest in sports is limited. Come with me."

Blake gave her a significant look as he followed their host from the room. She should be flattered by his very presence in Gloucestershire. Since he was barely acquainted with the Chases she must be the reason he accepted their invitation. While he'd pursued her in London, his courtship had been maddeningly slow, halfhearted even, with bursts of attention followed by days of neglect.

Now, unless she was very much mistaken, he would soon be making her an offer. Diana couldn't understand her lack of enthusiasm. About to achieve the thing she'd dreamed of for years, she did everything to postpone the moment.

She looked at Sebastian out of the corner of her eye and discovered him looking back at her. The presence of his spectacles, which most of the time she no longer noticed, prevented her from reading his eyes. She still didn't know what he thought of her. Or what she felt for him, for that matter, beyond gratitude for his rescue. Infuriating man to be so unpredictable!

Then she realized something strange: she cared a great deal about Sebastian's opinion of her. When she thought of Blake, she wondered only if he would propose marriage. She was so used to her single-minded pursuit of Blake as a husband, she never questioned what he thought of her. Yet surely she ought to care if he loved her.

"I've changed my mind," she said, pushing back her chair. "If you'll excuse me, Juliana, I think I'll see the library another time. I need a walk and I daresay it will rain later." What she needed was some time alone to examine her feelings.

Her hostess looked out the window at leaden skies and fallen leaves blowing about the lawn. "Are you sure? But if you need exercise I will go with you."

"There's no need for you to get chilled. I won't go beyond the gardens."

Before Juliana could argue, Sebastian stood up. "I would like to keep you company, Lady Fanshawe, if you will allow me."

Her sensible resolution flew out of the window.

What better way to gauge Sebastian's feelings for her, and hers for him, than to spend time together? Which was why, half an hour later, she found herself walking through the shrubbery with him, talking about books.

"How's the pursuit of Katherine Parr going?"

"The owner is still a little coy but I believe he's ready to surrender."

"So you should have the lady in hand soon. I do trust she won't prove disappointing."

"I shall be disappointed only if I fail to win her."

"Once you have her I am sure you will provide her with a good home."

Sebastian had to admit that talking with Diana was much more exhilarating than discussing the same subjects with his male friends. She had a sweet, mischievous wit that made him want to smile, even when the subject was perfectly serious, and inspired him to respond in kind. This, he realized in a flash of enlightenment, was flirting. Another new experience courtesy of Diana Fanshawe.

Somehow the conversation came around to earlier English monarchs, and thence to her family. "I believe I heard somewhere they go back to the Normans," he said.

"The first Montrose came over with the Conqueror. My brothers are named for the first kings: William, William Rufus, Henry I, and Stephen."

"And you all use the shortened form of your names as nicknames?"

"Well, Will doesn't object and Step's the youngest so no one would care if he did. Rufus doesn't mind being called Ru if he's in the right mood. But no one calls Henry 'Hen' twice. Will claims he decided to become a doctor so he can learn how to cause the greatest pain."

Sebastian found the Montrose family fascinating. "Your father must be very proud of his ancestry."

"Not really." She placed a hand on his arm, leaned in confidentially, and looked up at him. "To tell you the truth, I think my parents were pleased to come up with a formula so they wouldn't have to keep thinking of names."

He lowered his head, so their lips were but a few inches apart. "I can see," he said gravely, "that naming six children could be fatiguing."

"Exhausting," she agreed, her mouth curved in a smile that sent a sensation straight to his groin. They gazed at each other foolishly for moment or two. "Is Sebastian a family name? Or were you named for the saint with all the arrows stuck in his body?"

They'd been conducting a very enjoyable flirtation but, as usual, when Diana raised the subject of his family Sebastian withdrew. Without outright avoiding the subject, his answer was barely informative. "I was named for my father."

Diana refused to give up. "How old were you when he died?"

"Five."

"So young. You must have missed him."

"He was a virtual stranger to me." His voice took on a bitter tinge. "The great military hero."

"Was he killed in battle?" she asked, assuming his father must have served abroad.

"Nothing so honorable. As a matter of fact he was defenestrated in Piccadilly."

She clapped a hand over her mouth. "A defenestration? I thought that was something that happened in history books, and only ever in Prague. Someone pushed him out of a window?"

"He wasn't pushed, he fell. He wagered he could drink a whole bottle of brandy while standing on the sill of a third-floor window. He lost."

She didn't for a minute credit this careless dismissal of his father's demise. She wound her arm around his. "That's a terrible story. What a tragedy for you and your mother."

"As I said, I hardly knew him. He was, as Tarquin would put it, a fashionable father. In fact both my parents were highly fashionable. Darlings of the *ton*. Major Sebastian Iverley of His Highness the Prince of Wales's Own Regiment and his beautiful wife, Lady Corinna. No invitation list was complete without them."

"And your mother? When did she go to Italy?"

"A little later."

Without shaking off her arm he placed some distance between them and, not for the first time, shied away from the subject of his surviving parent. How had the son of what sounded like a brilliant social couple become the shabby inarticulate man he'd been until recently? And which was the true Sebastian Iverley, the interesting reclusive bookworm or the strangely disappointing fashionable viscount? She really wanted to find out.

"Enough about me," he said, his lips curving though she couldn't tell if the smile reached his eyes. "How did you and your sister avoid royal names and become Roman goddesses instead? Shouldn't you have been Matilda, for England's first reigning queen?"

Recognizing that the moment for confidences had passed, she answered in similar vein. "I am glad to have been spared that. Min always says she's relieved not to have been named for Bloody Mary, but I secretly think she would have enjoyed it. It seems my father took one look at me and pronounced me his little goddess. Probably because I'm the only one of his children who looks like him. All the others are beauties like Mama."

Sebastian stopped abruptly and swung around to face her. A gust of wind wrapped the skirt of her pelisse around her bottom, and blew a chill around her ankles. As she looked up at him she hunched her shoulders into her fox fur collar and buried her hands in the matching muff. Sebastian seemed unaffected by the breeze disturbing his long topcoat. He removed his spectacles, tucked them into his pocket and looked intently at her face.

"You *are* beautiful."

Diana felt a little warmer. It was the first time she'd ever received a compliment from him. And he uttered it in the gruff voice that recalled the way he'd been at Mandeville, the old Iverley, not the smooth-talking viscount.

"How can you tell without glasses?"

"I don't need them to see up close," he said softly, moving nearer until there were but inches between them. She looked into his eyes, deep, gray, intense and felt she was gazing into his soul.

"I love your mouth," he murmured. He removed his glove and his skin was firm and a little rough as he traced the bow of her upper lip with his forefinger. "So perfectly shaped here. And smooth and rounded like a ripe fruit here." The edge of his thumb stroked the length of her lower lip.

The wind and the chill, damp atmosphere receded and it might have been summer. His breath felt warm on her cheek. Her lips parted in anticipation. He was going to kiss her again.

"Hey! Diana!" the voice came from some distance.

Sebastian raised his head and said something unrepeatable. "No one in history has been cursed with a cousin as inconvenient as mine," he said, swinging around and stepping to the side so that three feet of air separated them.

"Richard II might disagree with you," Diana replied in a slightly wobbly voice. "Wasn't it his cousin who drove him from the throne?"

"This is not the moment to display your knowledge of English history." He sounded as irritated as she felt.

"I don't see why not. Blake will be with us any moment and I don't think we can return to our previous topic."

Sebastian grunted which, under the circumstances, Diana found forgivable, even pleasing.

"James II was deposed, too," she remarked.

"By his son-in-law."

"So he was. What about Edward II?"

Sebastian thrust his hand into his pocket to retrieve his spectacles and put them back on. "I don't remember and I don't damn well care."

Blake strode across the field toward them, gun over

arm and a spaniel at his heels. Long before he reached conversing distance she could read the displeasure on his face.

"Blake!" she called. "We're discussing annoying cousins in history. Can you remember how Edward II lost his throne?"

"Certainly not."

"I remember," Sebastian said. "Not who did it but how. I know it hurt."

Diana bit her lip, having realized she perhaps should not have raised the subject of this particular monarch. Poor Edward had been executed by means of a red-hot iron plunged up his fundament.

Blake's frown melted into a pained grimace. "Ouch. Was he *that* one?" And for a fraction of a second the cousins put aside their rivalry in favor of an exchange of masculine empathy.

But not for long. "I'm about as interested in Edward II as I am in that German printer Lady Chase keeps talking about," Blake said. "I thought you were going to spend the morning looking at books." His remark was addressed to Diana but he glowered at Sebastian as he spoke.

"Diana decided to come for a walk with me instead," Sebastian said. He folded his arms and rocked back on his heels with a self-satisfied air. It was the first time in many weeks he'd used her Christian name.

"*Lady Fanshawe*," Blake said, "generally prefers to take her exercise on horseback. But I suppose she accommodated your limitations by agreeing to go on foot."

"*Diana* may be as skilled a huntress as her namesake, but I think I'm up to the challenge of matching her pace."

"Even a goddess like *Lady Fanshawe* needs the escort and protection of a competent horseman."

Diana was aware of two facts. The first, less important though mildly surprising, was that Blake had heard of the goddess Diana. The second was that Blake and Sebastian teetered on the brink of physical combat. The latter hadn't moved but she knew his relaxed air was a pose. His eyes seemed to blaze through the glass of his spectacles. By contrast Blake's body tilted forward, equally still but coiled for attack. Diana eyed the shotgun slung casually over his arm. Country-bred, she knew a serious sportsman like Blake wouldn't point it at another human under any circumstance. Yet the atmosphere between the cousins was so thick the presence of the weapon made her nervous.

"You're both talking utter nonsense," she said in a burst of irritation. "If I want to ride I can do so perfectly well without an escort." She glared at Blake, not remotely impressed by his jealousy.

She swung around to look at Sebastian, who stood beside her and was scarcely less annoying. "And I can walk quite well by myself, too." She would have demonstrated the truth of her statement by stalking back to the house, had Sebastian not arrested her by grabbing her arm. He did not, however, address her.

"Mounted, on foot, or in a carriage, I am more than capable of protecting Diana," he said.

"Prove it!" Blake said.

"I rather thought I had. A little matter of driving off a highwayman."

Blake's teeth ground audibly. "There's a neatish course around the Markley Estate. I challenge you to a race."

Sebastian uncoiled from his stance of exaggerated relaxation. "What horses?" he asked. "The mount I brought is a road horse, lots of stamina but no jumper. What's in the stable here?"

"No need to bother Chase. I have my hunters with me, fresh and recovered from the journey by now. You may take your choice. I can beat you whatever you're riding."

"Done."

"Good," Blake growled. "Let's settle the matter once and for all."

Diana didn't know exactly what "the matter" was. She was part of it, yes, but the rivalry between Blake and Sebastian was older and deeper than one for her favors. She was fairly certain this race—just like a pair of men to come up with such an ridiculous method of solving their differences—was not going to settle anything, once *or* for all.

Chapter 16

He had to hand it to Blakeney: his cousin knew how to pick a horse. Warrior, a coal black miracle of muscles and sinew with the endurance of a prizefighter and the heart of Satan, soared over the penultimate jump. Sebastian wondered if he could persuade Blake to sell him the beast.

Probably not. Without Warrior Sebastian wouldn't have a chance in the race. Even with him, his probability of winning was slender. Though Blake only led by a couple of lengths, his mount was faster on the flat than Warrior, whose strength lay in the ability to jump anything. Only one fence remained, at the end of a long grassy avenue.

"Come on, boy," Sebastian urged. Warrior had no need of the crop. The great horse had thrown his heart into every obstacle once he discovered Sebastian could master him. And now he was ready to pursue and defeat his owner, streaking ahead of them on his stablemate.

Sebastian had to admit that his despised cousin was a superb horseman, perhaps the best he'd ever seen. Even with the superior mount he couldn't match the speed and skill with which Blake steered the bay around the course, finding the shortest path, never missing an opportunity to shave a few seconds off the journey, to cut into the lead Warrior and Sebastian built up in the early stages. He'd finally passed them and since then his advantage had gradually and inexorably increased.

Sebastian told himself he had nothing to be ashamed of. Blake had expected him to fall at the first fence. In mastering Warrior he'd shown his cousin that he was no longer a bespectacled grinder but a man capable of challenging the best.

A lump of mud thrown up by the leading horse landed on his cheek. He looked ahead to the arrogant ease of Blake's perfect seat. It was all so damned easy for his cousin, the golden-haired wonder, born to strawberry leaves and adulation. He had everything he wanted and deserved none of it.

Well, Blake wasn't going to win this race. And he most definitely wasn't going to win Diana Fanshawe.

He gave Warrior just a touch of the crop. "Let's go, old fellow."

"As far as I can tell they're neck and neck." Tarquin Compton, the tallest of the company even without the advantage of sitting on the biggest denizen of the Markley Abbey stable, had seen the competitors emerge from the trees. "By God!"

"What's happening?" Diana and Minerva spoke together. The two of them had ridden out with Compton and Chase to stand level with the final fence, a few hundred yards from the finish line.

"Sebastian's pulling ahead, but only just."

"I wonder if Blakeney regrets giving Sebastian the

choice of his hunters," Chase said. "He didn't hold back from picking the best."

Tarquin grinned. "That's our boy. He doesn't like to be beaten."

"The black is definitely ahead," Minerva said. As the riders drew nearer they could hear the creak of harness, the shush of equine breath, the rumble of galloping hooves. "Come on, Sebastian!" she yelled. "You can do it!"

From the moment she heard of the challenge, Minerva had made no secret of where her allegiance lay. Diana remained silent.

The thunder of thousands of pounds of powerful horseflesh drew nearer. Diana sucked in her breath and held it as the black stallion took off. She was enough her mother's daughter to appreciate the way Warrior made the four-foot fence look like a puny log, and the grace and strength with which his rider held his seat, controlled the landing and adjusted to urge the horse into unobstructed parkland. She scarcely registered that the bay, less than a length behind, was mastered by a horseman at least as skilled. In a flash both accelerated away from the fence in a shower of flying sod. The din of hooves diminished as fast as it had crested.

"Come on, Di!" her sister said. "Admit it. You want Sebastian to win. Look at him ride."

"Yes," she said. "I do. I do hope Lord Iverley wins."

"Let's go to the finish."

Chase and Compton were already on the move. Minerva and Diana kicked their mounts to a canter and followed them to the pair of oaks that marked the finish line, not far from the ha-ha that separated the gardens from the greater park. Juliana and Esther, hunched in fur-trimmed coats, stood the other side of the ditch.

The competitors had still to circle the edge of the open meadow. As they rounded the final bend the spectators could see that Warrior and Sebastian were just holding the lead."

"Sebastian!" Minerva yelled.

Neither man watching expressed his preference, but Diana guessed they were hoping for their friend's victory. They maintained a steady commentary.

"He's still ahead."

"The bay's getting closer."

"The black's holding him off."

"Not for much longer."

Diana's fingers clenched on her reins. *You can do it you can do it you can do it.*

She could hardly stand to watch and closed her eyes as the pounding hooves again approached. All the others were shouting, creating a cacophony around her from which she felt oddly detached. Because while she prayed desperately for Sebastian to hold off Blake's challenge, a corner of her mind was asking why she cared so much. Or even at all. It was only a horse race with nothing at stake beyond male pride. If Diana had a preference, logically it should be for Blake, the man she'd adored since she was fourteen. The man she wanted to marry.

But she wanted Sebastian to win, no question, and she had a feeling she knew why.

He'd won. Only by a nose but nevertheless a clear victory, and a sweet one. Never in his life had he ridden so fast over such a challenging course. He was enveloped in congratulations: hearty from Cain and Tarquin, boisterous from Minerva, grudging from Blakeney and Lady Chase, quiet from Diana.

Diana's radiant smile warmed him to the core. Unlike her sister's bubbling glee, her words were spoken softly and he could find no hidden meaning in the conventional words of applause. Yet he had the sense that she had cared about the result of the race. As he galloped to the finish, urging Warrior to extend his long powerful neck and reach his nose over the line, out of the corner of his eye he'd glimpsed her, elegant in dark green on a gray mare. Her eyes had been closed, her expression intent, as though the outcome mattered too much for her to watch. He wished he'd seen her face when she learned that he had won. Then perhaps he would know whose victory mattered to her so much, whether her words were heartfelt, or as perfunctory as Blake's.

He had to hand it to his cousin. He was both a gentleman and a sportsman. Sebastian had no doubt that it took every scrap of schooling in both areas for Blake to offer his felicitations with good grace.

"I would never have won without the better horse," Sebastian replied truthfully. "The victory belongs to your Warrior."

This acknowledgement seemed not to provide Blake with any comfort. "Your riding's improved," he said curtly.

Sebastian shrugged. "We don't remain ten years old forever."

Minerva nosed her horse alongside his.

"Brilliant race." She beamed.

"Thank you."

She looked at Blakeney with some remark on the tip of her tongue then apparently thought better of it.

Blakeney responded to her derisive glance. "Don't you have a sampler to sew? Something to knit or tat? I'm surprised your governess lets you out with the grown-ups."

Minerva's eyes popped with indignation but Diana intervened before bloodshed could ensue. "Come back to the stable with me, Minerva. I'm cold."

This drew Blake's attention. "A word with you, if you please Diana, before you go."

"Go along, Min," Diana said. "I'll catch up in a minute."

Diana and Blakeney rode off a short distance. Minerva gave Blakeney a dark look that Sebastian could appreciate, but put up no further argument and followed the other ladies in the direction of the house.

"One day, and a day not too far off," Tarquin remarked, "Minerva Montrose will be a great beauty."

"No question about it," Cain said.

Sebastian had to argue the point. "Not as beautiful as her sister."

Tarquin shook his head. "Lady Fanshawe is no beauty. But she is," he added before anyone could remonstrate, "one of the most desirable women I've ever seen."

Sebastian didn't know who he wanted to hit more, his cousin, chatting away with Diana, out of earshot, or his best friend.

"Don't worry," Tarquin said, saving himself

from assault. "Purely an esthetical judgment on my part. I never allow myself to lust after marriageable females."

He cast Sebastian a quizzical look and Sebastian wondered again what had drawn the notoriously rural-shy Tarquin away from Piccadilly to this unfashionable house party. Curiosity to observe the denouement of his courtship of Diana Fanshawe, he suspected. Now it occurred to him that Tarquin, no less than Cain, might disapprove of his ultimate intentions.

Whatever those intentions were. They seemed to change hourly, swinging madly from dishonorable to honorable with an occasional detour into call-for-my-horse-and-get-the-hell-out-of-here. The closer Sebastian came to achieving revenge, the more ambivalent his feelings.

Then he heard her laugh. With Blake. Pain and humiliation came roaring back.

"I'm going back to the stables," he announced. "The ladies were correct. It's damnably cold out here."

Having relinquished Warrior to the care of a groom, he headed back to the house, looking forward to a hot bath. As he left the stable yard Minerva emerged from a sheltered recess and grabbed him by a button of his coat.

"Why are you still here?" he asked, smiling at the girl. "You must be chilled to the bone. Let's keep moving."

She let him go and they resumed the walk to the house. "I wanted to talk to you. I'm glad you won."

"Thank you, again."

"Blakeney's an ass."

"You are right," he said, unbothered by her un-maidenly language.

"Diana was glad too."

He stopped. "Was she now?"

"Yes." She gave him a piercing look. "You like my sister, don't you?"

"Er . . . yes," he said evasively.

"It's all right. I know."

God, he hoped not.

"I know the highwayman was your groom."

"Nonsense. You're imagining things."

"I thought at the time the man didn't seem like a criminal. He looked like an ordinary servant."

"Much you know about it," Sebastian scoffed. "Do you think highwaymen go around with the letter *H* emblazoned on their foreheads?"

"No, I don't, but I expect them to wear masks."

"He was masked."

"Not when I first saw him in the woods, getting ready."

Damnation. Minerva was much too sharp for her own good, or his. He waited for the axe to fall on his hopes.

"Then," she concluded smugly, "I recognized him in the stable when we went to see the puppies. But I already suspected."

"Why didn't you say anything?" he rasped. "Do you mean to tell your sister?"

Minerva shook her head. "I know why you did it and I won't say a word. I'm on your side. I don't want Diana to marry Blakeney. I want her to marry you."

Chapter 17

"**L**et me in," Minerva demanded. "I don't care if you aren't dressed. It's not as though I've never seen you in your chemise."

Diana tried once more to make Minerva go away. "I'm trying to get some peace and quiet, something that seems to be surprisingly difficult considering there are very few people in this very large house."

Since Min's banging persisted, Diana descended from her bed, thrust her arms into the sleeves of her dressing robe, and stamped across the room, trailing silk and lace. "What?" she demanded, turning the key and wrenching the door inward.

Minerva almost fell into the room. "I want to talk to you."

"So I gather." She placed her hands on her hips and glared at her little sister.

"I don't want you to marry Blakeney."

"Because of what he said to you yesterday, after the race? He was just upset because he lost."

"I know that. But I think it was rather small of him, just because Sebastian beat him. It revealed something about his character."

"Nonsense. You've never liked Blakeney. And you

aren't the one who'd marry him. But you'd certainly benefit. Think what his father could do for you."

"I don't care. I'll manage without him." Diana couldn't help a smile at Min's determined scowl. Yes indeed. Her sister could manage anything.

She wandered over to a low-seated carved walnut chair and sank into the cushioned seat. "I'm still not sure Blakeney will make me an offer," she said, leaning back and crossing her ankles.

Minerva tossed her head, the fairy-tale profusion of her golden hair contrasting with her fierce expression. "Now you are talking nonsense. He's hardly left you alone since we've been here. When he asks you, please say no."

"You know how I feel about Blake."

Except that she didn't know herself. Not anymore. She feared she was trying to convince herself, more than Min. She'd spent so many nights since Tobias's death wishing for a companion, wishing for one particular bedmate, imagining the touch of that well-honed sportsman's body. But lately another face, another body had invaded her daydreams, and her sleep, too.

She'd woken at dawn flustered and perspiring, aching with frustration because she was alone in bed. Because, unlike in her dream, Sebastian Iverley wasn't there.

"I think you prefer Sebastian." Minerva couldn't have been reading her thoughts, surely. Diana blushed at the very idea.

"You know I want to be married again," Diana said, her shaking voice matching her inner turmoil.

"But Sebastian Iverley will never marry. He doesn't like women. He's famous for it."

"That's rubbish. He likes me and he definitely likes you."

"I'm not so sure. He avoided me when he first came back to London."

Minerva was in pursuit of her own train of thought. "Do you know what I've noticed about him? He speaks to me as though I were a person of intelligence, not a child or a girl. It doesn't matter to him that I'm female, even though he has a reputation for despising us. I've seen no evidence of it. He just likes me and he cares about what I say and think."

Diana nodded. She'd thought the same thing, with the difference that Sebastian had definitely noticed *she* was a woman.

"The opposite of Blakeney," her sister said, folding her arms with a self-satisfied expression. "As I'm sure you'll agree."

"My dear Min. I'm not going to choose my husband based on your opinion of his conversation. Besides," she continued, after Min had regarded her in silence for a period, "it's most unlikely he will offer for me."

"He will."

"Oh? And what brings you to that conclusion?"

"I've been watching him for the last twenty-four hours. He's been paying as much attention to you as Blakeney has. He's just a bit more understated about it."

Diana remembered how Sebastian had brushed against her in passing, touched her fingers when handing her a cup, met her eyes across the dinner table as he raised a wineglass to his lips. There had been several such instances, any one of which could have been purely accidental. He'd been driving her to distraction, wondering if he meant those subtle advances or whether they were a product of her imagination.

Perhaps Min was right and his actions were deliberate. Still, her sister was so engaged by the notion of having Sebastian as a brother-in-law she might be indulging in wishful thinking.

She shook her head hard to clear her brain. "Go away, Min. Let me rest."

"Very well. But I'm going to give you a chance to get Sebastian alone after dinner."

"I don't want to be alone with him."

Minerva merely looked at her, her smile eloquent with disbelief.

"How?" Diana muttered.

"I'll draw off Blakeney by asking him about hunting. Lucky I've had so much practice with Mama."

"My goodness, Min. You *are* serious!"

"For you, Diana, no sacrifice is too great."

"You're a madman! It's November and it's dark. I'm not going outside."

Sebastian had lured her to the great hall under false pretenses. Once there he showed absolutely no inclination to inspect the Elizabethan tapestries. Instead he asked a footman to send for Diana's cloak.

"It's a clear night," he said as he wrapped the garment around her shoulders and tied the strings. "Do you know what that means?"

"Frostbite?"

"The conjunction of two red bodies."

"What?"

"I'll tell you outside."

"How can I resist an invitation like that?"

"That was my idea."

Once the door closed behind them, shutting in the glow of lamp and candle, the light of a million stars illuminated the mist of their breaths, mingling in the dry, crisp air. Diana was more than adequately protected by fur-lined velvet. She shivered when Sebastian put an arm about her shoulder and drew her close, but not from cold.

"Look," he said. His movements directed her eyes to a certain section of the sky. "Do you see those two red stars?"

Diana had never been good at identifying the constellations. Her knowledge of the heavens began and ended with the Great Bear. "I think so," she said, following where his finger pointed. "They're only inches apart."

"So it appears. In reality it's millions of miles."

"Are they always like that?"

"No. That's why I brought you out to see them. Mars is a planet and Antares a star. Without a telescope they are the two brightest red objects in the sky. The ancients named the star the anti-Mars or the foe of Mars."

"How do you know about such things?"

"I've always been interested in astronomy. I had a telescope as a boy. Unfortunately where I lived I rarely enjoyed nights as clear as this."

"Where was that?" Diana knew almost nothing of Sebastian's upbringing.

"A long way away," he said.

They continued to stare at the sky in silence for several minutes. She was scarcely conscious of the dark mansion looming behind them. The two of them seemed alone in the universe with only the stars for chaperones. She felt tranquil and comfortable in his company, with an edge of excitement. His arm held her, casual yet a little possessive. She thought of the last occasion when she'd been alone in the dark with Sebastian Iverley. Her lips tingled. She wasn't averse to repeating the experience. But first there was something she'd like to know.

"Why did you ignore me in London?" she asked. "You hardly spoke to me for weeks. You told me before I hadn't offended you, but I still don't understand."

"I suppose I'd better admit the truth. Someone told me that was the way to gain a lady's attention."

She gave a little huff of annoyance. "That's a very calculating attitude. I'm not sure I approve." Despite her words a seed of joy germinated in her breast.

"Did it work? Do I have your attention?"

"You had it without having to play games. I don't know why you should have thought otherwise."

He tightened his embrace and used his free hand to take one of hers. "Would it help if I apologized?" he murmured into her hair.

"An apology is always acceptable," she said softly.

Her lingering fear that somehow he'd known about Blake's bet dissipated. More than ever, she hoped he'd never find out. Foolish as the business had been, had she known how powerful was the antagonism between the two cousins, she'd never have agreed to the wager.

In a blaze of enlightenment Diana realized how much more important Sebastian's opinion and feelings were than Blake's. More important than just about anything she could think of. And he felt the same way, surely. Why else would he have gone to so much trouble to impress her? And he hadn't only brought her out here to show her the stars. Or even just to kiss her. Though she hoped he would do so.

She returned the clasp of his hand then twisted in his arm and tilted her head. She wanted to see his face, to read his expression, but it was too dark. Freeing her hand, she reached up to caress his cheek. Carefully she removed his spectacles so they wouldn't be in the way when they kissed.

"Diana," he breathed, drawing her closer still and nuzzling her temple and then her forehead. When he spoke again his voice was shaky. "There's a question I want to ask you." He sounded unsure of himself, a little anxious.

Involuntarily her mouth formed a self-satisfied smile. It made sense for Sebastian Iverley to be nervous about a proposal of marriage. "Yes?" she asked, deciding not to keep him dangling too long for an answer. She'd put him out of his misery quickly and proceed to kissing. Perhaps to more than kissing. The very idea had her flushed with pleasure. She'd been a long time without a man in her bed and she was ready.

Sebastian knew he'd won when she caressed his cheek. He couldn't have explained why, but at that moment he knew. In the dark he imagined the expression on her face. The same look of besotted joy he'd doubtless worn at Mandeville during those few brief hours when he believed he'd found a woman he could trust.

The knowledge shook his resolve. For a minute as they stood in the moonlight he thought about scaling back his revenge. Perhaps it was enough merely to reject her love. Or even, a whisper of a thought came from the part of his brain that governed his heart, accept it.

At the very least he could ask her what she'd been about at Mandeville, give her a chance for an honest accounting of the events there. If she admitted her fault and apologized, perhaps he could forgive her.

Before he could even frame a question, history repeated itself. Again. A swath of light fell onto the flagstones as the door opened.

"Diana?" Blake called.

Minerva's voice spoke from within. "I told you she wouldn't go outside in this weather. Diana hates being cold. Let's try the library."

"There you are," Blake said. "I wagered your sister I'd find you out here."

Sebastian dropped his arm and they turned to face him. "A wager?" he said. "What was the stake?"

Minerva joined them. "I never bet for money. Certainly not about something so stupid."

"Your teeth are chattering, Min," Diana said. "You aren't dressed for outside. Would you take her back in, Blake? Please? Your cousin and I will be right behind you."

Blake looked as though he'd like to send Minerva to perdition but was too polite to say so. "Come on, Miss Montrose," he said, unable to ignore a direct request. "You're a devilish nuisance. Back inside with you."

Too late. Blake's appearance had killed Sebastian's impulse to forgive. He stoked his anger by reliving—for the thousandth time—that moment in the library when he learned Diana and his cousin had conspired against him, laughed at his infatuation. Blake he wanted to kill. For Diana, he'd be satisfied if her pain equaled his own.

"He'll be back. We only have a minute." Diana pulled his head down and whispered in his ear. "Do you know where my room is?"

Chapter 18

"**D**id you pack my pink stockings?"

"Why?" Chantal said, shaking out Diana's evening gown with her usual deft motions. "They don't go with the dress you said you want for tomorrow."

In actual fact Chantal had decided Diana should wear the sage twilled silk. Just once it would be nice to have a servant who didn't believe she was the one in charge.

"Where are they?"

Chantal turned and looked at her mistress with a beady eye. "I'll be annoyed if I find my drawers *dérangés*."

"They're my favorites. I only wanted to be sure you packed them."

The Frenchwoman gathered up the twilled silk and Diana's discarded undergarments to take them below stairs for pressing and laundry. From the suspicious glance she gave her mistress from the doorway, Diana feared she knew exactly what was going on. Chantal hadn't spent more than twenty years as a dresser, most of them in Paris, without learning a thing or two about intrigue. Nevertheless, Diana did her best not to disturb things as she searched through a large commode and extracted the hosiery and a pair of matching lace garters.

A few minutes later she surveyed herself in the tall glass with satisfaction. Her most luxurious robe of heavy ivory satin, embroidered in white silk and profusely trimmed with Belgian lace, hung open. Pink feet peeped out from the hem of her nightgown of finest white lawn whose gathered neck was tied so loosely it would slither off the shoulders at a breath of wind.

Not perhaps the most conventional ensemble for receiving a proposal of marriage. Her first husband had, very properly, spoken to her father first. Then she'd put on her best morning dress (a wretched ill-fitting garment made by the village dressmaker at Mandeville Wallop) and demurely accepted the offer to become the eighteen-year-old bride of a forty-five-year-old baronet. During five minutes alone in the drawing room of the Montroses' rented London house, Tobias had celebrated their engagement with a chaste kiss on the hand and very correct expressions of esteem.

In the bedchamber, as Diana discovered to her surprise and pleasure, Tobias was far less restrained. Which was why, on this occasion, she decided to cut short the time between proposal and bedding. She was now an experienced widow, not an innocent maiden, so surely she was allowed some latitude. And since she knew that Sebastian had little or no experience with women, she would have to lead the way, an idea she found both alarming and exciting.

*   *   *

He could scarcely believe she'd invited him to her room. Yes, he'd fantasized about seducing Diana but he realized he'd never entirely believed he could. He had the sense of hurtling down a road, at gathering speed, soon to lose all control. This was the last moment to turn back. He should, he knew that now, but that would mean not seeing Diana again.

It would mean not seeing Diana tonight.

Even as he wrestled with his conscience, he crept along the passage, carefully counting the doors, his heart banging to wake the dead. Without much interest, Sebastian had heard tales of *affaires* carried on during country house parties. Not, it now occurred to him, an enterprise without risk. All doors looked the same by candlelight. Entering the wrong room might disturb Minerva or Tarquin, or, worst of all, Blakeney. He turned the handle of the fifth door on the left, mentally preparing excuses should the room house a young girl or a gentleman. As soon as he cracked the door ajar he relaxed. He'd recognize that scent anywhere.

"Sebastian?" Her voice was soft and low and promised unimagined delights.

Well, not unimagined. Never experienced but most definitely imagined.

A fire flickered in the hearth providing the only light, aside from a branch of candles on a side table. Quite enough to see her, seated on a sofa near the fireplace. He was aware of long dark hair over pale-clad shoulders before his gaze fixed on a sight that went straight from his eyes to his groin. Half aroused even as he crossed the threshold, he felt those delicately crossed ankles clad in pink bring his desire to an unequalled intensity.

"You're wearing pink stockings," he rasped.

She smiled, and if he didn't know better he'd have sworn she was nervous. "I put them on especially for you. I was wearing them the first time we met."

"We met in the library."

"Not really. I shall always think of that time in the stable yard as our first meeting. Do you remember? You adjusted my stirrup."

As though he could ever forget the dizzying moment that changed his life. Had she already made the bet with Blakeney when he found her there? When she displayed her leg had it been deliberate?

Two overwhelming desires—to punish her and to possess her—merged into one. A flicker of compunction somewhere deep in his brain was brutally extinguished. He'd reached the point of no return. Right or wrong, he had to have her.

He stood in the middle of the room and looked at her, drinking in silk and lace, gleaming brown locks, carmine lips that offered all he ached for from a woman and everything he'd resisted. The atmosphere was thick with promise and his newfound facility for idle talk had vanished.

"Would you like to sit down?" A prim invitation, appropriate for a morning call to a drawing room. But it was midnight and her bedchamber.

Bypassing a conveniently placed chair, he lowered himself beside her, his thigh only inches from hers. She shifted and her loose robe fell further open. The stuff of the garment she wore beneath was white and so finely woven as to be almost transparent. He could see the pale pink of her knees, the place just above where her stockings ended, and a dark shadow at the junction of her legs. His breath caught but he dragged his eyes up to her face.

She looked back at him, her expression bright and unguarded. She seemed to be waiting for something. After a while she spoke. "I had to ask you to come here because I knew I'd never be able to get away from Blakeney."

"I was flattered."

"I thought you might not come."

He almost laughed at the idea. He'd spent an hour pacing around his room, counting the endless minutes till the household was safely retired for the night, wondering what he should wear, or not wear. In the end he'd removed only his neck cloth.

"I wasn't sure what the correct dress was for calling on a lady in her room at night," he said hoarsely.

"It isn't a habit of yours?" she asked in that teasing way she had.

"No." He raised a hand to his open neck. "I apologize if my informality is inapposite."

She smiled at him with lustrous eyes: warm, inviting, seemingly guileless. He thought he'd die if he didn't touch her. Greatly daring, he bent his head and placed his forefinger on her knee then drew it up her leg, over the bump of her garter, until he felt warm, smooth flesh though thin linen. The rate of her breathing accelerated, matching his own. Her hand entered his line of sight and covered his, pressing it against her thigh.

"Kiss me," she whispered.

At last, an unequivocal invitation. Cupping her

head in his hands he drew her near. Her hair was like satin beneath his fingers, her scent a drug to his brain. Remembering the lesson of their first kiss he held himself back, sipping lightly at her lips, relishing her sweetness, venturing only to trace the edge of her mouth with the tip of his tongue. As she opened at his unspoken request, his response was restrained and unhurried. She was the one who demanded more, pulling him closer and deepening the kiss until his spectacles got in the way.

She drew back and gave a shaky laugh over his murmur of protest. "I think you'd better remove them." For the first time he regretted turning down a quizzing glass. He unhooked the ear pieces and tossed the glasses aside.

His naked eyes focused on the skin of her neck, harmonizing in ivory perfection with the lace trim of her garment. With trembling fingers he tried to push the robe aside but found his hands as clumsy as if they wore gloves.

"I'll do it," she whispered. She stood and turned her back on him. At a shrug of her shoulders the slippery silk robe slid to a pool at her feet.

Sebastian found it difficult to exercise restraint when confronted with Diana's figure backlit by the glow of the fire. Her full-length night garment was like a gauze veil, blurring but not hiding the feminine curves of her waist and hips. She returned to sit beside him on the sofa. Her neckline was low, revealing the swell of her bosom, but to his regret the cloth was heavily gathered and covered the rest of the breasts quite efficiently.

"You are so beautiful," he said. Trite, inadequate

words. Again he raised a hand to her shoulder and found he'd regained the use of his fingers. He traced the tender indents of her collarbone with his thumb while using his other hand to pull on the ribbon between her breasts. The bow dissolved and the neckline widened, gradually at first then faster as the weight of the material descended the slope of her shoulders.

Sebastian Iverley was a well-educated man, a gentleman of culture with an appreciation for the arts. As such he'd seen any number of female nudes depicted in paint and canvas and in sculpture. Nothing had prepared him for the sight of Diana Fanshawe naked to the waist. No marble goddess, however perfect, could equal the flesh-and-blood reality of creamy flesh, the lower curve more pronounced than the upper and each exquisite fruit capped by a pink circle surrounding a pert red nipple.

Awed into silence, he ventured to touch. He cupped silken weight in his palm and felt the firm peak under his thumb. Experimentally he flicked it and it hardened further. As though in sympathy he felt his cock and ballocks ache.

A sound emerged from her throat, one with the emotional message if not the timbre of a cat's purr. Doubling his efforts, he applied his other hand to the second breast, gently kneading rich flesh and stroking the stiff crests.

"Don't you want to see my stockings?" she whispered.

He couldn't speak. He merely freed one hand from its duty and tugged at her skirt, dragging it up to thigh level. And reaching down to grasp her ankle then explore the entire length of her leg. Because, he discovered, he was much less concerned with seeing her stockings than he was in touching them, and feeling what the stockings contained. And when his hand reached their end he quite lost interest in the topic of hosiery since the skin of the inner thigh was softer, smoother, and warmer than satin.

He felt her shift, sink lower. Her legs parted. His fingers crept higher and touched a nest of dark hair, the gateway to a woman's secrets, ventured farther and found wet heat. He knew it by a number of names, both crude and poetic. The "cradle of delight" was the one that came to mind.

In his researches in Tarquin's library, he'd read accounts of a hundred seductions. His theoretical knowledge of how to satisfy a woman was immense. His brain emptied. He could remember none of it. All he knew was that he needed to possess her. Now.

Without any pretense at finesse he kissed her: her temples, ears, neck, hair, frenzied stabbing kisses all over her face, and finally her lips. They kissed deeply while he tugged at his own clothing. Dimly he realized she was trying to help. She'd freed his shirt from the waist of his trousers and he felt her caress his back.

He managed to pull back with the greatest reluctance. He didn't want to stop, even for a second, but there was something he needed to reveal.

"I've never done this before," he said, his breathing harsh.

If she laughed at him he'd die. But she didn't.

"It doesn't matter," she whispered. "I have." And reached for him again.

She started tugging at his waistcoat buttons but

undressing didn't go well when they were entangled on the sofa, trying to kiss and embrace at the same time. Finally she pushed him away.

"We'll be better off in bed," she said with a little breathy laugh.

It took him so little time to shed his clothes that Diana had barely climbed onto the mattress when he joined her. Any notion of finesse vanished. He'd waited a lifetime for this.

The feeling as he entered her exceeded even his own fevered expectations. How had he lived twenty-six years without this? He must have been mad.

He muttered something incoherent. Her name?

She said his.

He feared it was going to be over all too soon. He knew a man was supposed to last longer. But he was ready to explode almost as soon as he felt her slick heat encompass him.

By a miraculous effort he seized back a measure of the control he'd relinquished and saved his pride from incineration. He ceased his thrusts and looked down. Diana's head was tilted back, her eyes closed, her lips parted, her breathing fast. Though it was hardly news to him that she was the most beautiful woman in existence, her face caught in the act of love rendered him breathless.

Her eyes opened, pure and blue. "Lovely," she murmured. Silken limbs wound around his thighs, inner muscles clenched and pulled at him. "You feel so good. Don't stop."

He kissed her, deep, wet, and long, but he had no more inclination or capacity for restraint. Three minutes, he lasted, at the most. He supposed he should be thankful it hadn't been three seconds. As he lost all control she gave a cry that sounded like ecstasy and her body stiffened. He collapsed into bliss.

He'd done it.

At that moment he had no idea what came next.

Chapter 19

Diana sighed happily. She propped herself up on one elbow and surveyed the man lying beside her, eyes closed. One arm curved on the pillow above his head, a position that emphasized the muscles of his chest and arms. Her former scarecrow was no weakling. She knew that. At Mandeville he'd carried her up a hill. And he was a good-looking man, too. How had she ever preferred Blakeney? Sebastian's face had character and strength and intelligence, like him. She'd chosen well.

She leaned over and kissed his chest, inhaling his musky scent. It had been too long, much too long. She very much hoped her wait for a repeat would be a matter of minutes rather than hours, let alone days or years.

He wasn't asleep, she thought, just relaxing. She'd put that satisfied look on his face. And she'd do it again. In the meantime they could get on with the proposal of marriage. Make it slightly more proper.

Slightly. She'd never have let Blakeney into her bed before they were married, let alone betrothed. But she trusted Sebastian. Thank God she'd come to her senses in time and realized her tendre for Blakeney was nothing but a long-ingrained habit. She'd picked the better cousin, a man worthy of her love. She wanted to hug herself with glee.

Sitting upright she considered, and dismissed, the notion that she should wear a nightgown when he made his offer. She merely tidied her hair a little, stretched luxuriously, and rubbed her foot along Sebastian's thigh. "I know you're awake. Sit up and talk to me."

He opened his eyes and tilted his head. His happy look faded and the expression in his eyes was flat, unreadable.

"Do you always order people around?" he asked.

"No!" she said. "As a rule I'm a most amenable person, as you must be well aware."

Something was wrong. It occurred to her he might be worried about his performance. He had been a virgin and surely not only females worried about their first time. It had taken her quite a few times to enjoy being with Tobias.

She smiled at him. "That was wonderful," she said in an encouraging voice. "And next time will be even better. I can't wait."

"Is there going to be a next time?"

Oh dear, she thought, *he's afraid he has disgraced himself.*

"Of course there is," she hastened to assure him. She wished he'd take her in his arms. Given the trend of the conversation she hesitated to make the first advance and appear domineering.

He grunted. Sebastian seemed to have regressed to his former state of inarticulacy. And while that might be indicative of a flattering exhaustion, it was inconvenient when she expected him to have something particular to say to her.

"We never had a chance to finish our conversation on the terrace."

Instead of taking the hint, his only response was another grunt. Then he hauled himself upright and sat on the edge of the bed, on the opposite side, with his back to her.

"What were you going to ask me when we were interrupted tonight? You said, just before Blake came out, that you had a question for me."

There! She could hardly be blunter than that.

He didn't look at her and he seemed to think about his answer for a long time. "I remember," he said finally. "I was going to ask why you smell so good. I'm not good at naming scents."

"There's nothing else you wanted to ask me?"

"No." His voice was dull.

Diana began to feel a little panicked. She crawled across the bed and knelt at his back, putting her arms around him and resting her chin on his shoulder. "Stop teasing," she said.

"Teasing?" His muscles tensed in her embrace.

"Why did you come to my room tonight?"

"Because you invited me."

"But why did you accept?"

"I find it impossible to believe that any man has ever turned you down."

The insolence of his tone was like a slap. She jerked backward and scrambled off the bed to find her robe. Once covered she returned to stand in front of him, lifted his chin in one hand, and engaged him eye to eye. His gaze was guarded, perhaps a little wary.

"You are the first man, aside from my husband, I've ever invited to my room," she said tremulously.

He shook her off and looked away. "I'm honored to be the first. There's a certain poetic quality to the fact, don't you think, since you are *my* first? I don't suppose either of us is destined to be the other's last."

She stood there, stunned, taking in the meaning of his words. "I think you'd better go," she said, striving to speak calmly as she knotted her sash with a vicious tug. "You . . . you . . ." she stammered, vainly seeking a suitable epithet.

He left the bed and gathered his scattered clothing. Diana went over to the fireplace and stared at the glowing coals, unable to comprehend the disastrous turn the night had taken. She barely resisted the urge to snatch up a bottle of perfume and hurl it at him. Her scent! She'd give him scent. Either that or burst into tears.

She still couldn't believe she'd been so mistaken in Sebastian. He was the last man in the world she'd have supposed an amoral rake, yet that was how he was behaving.

Her eyes narrowed. Something didn't add up. How could he be a heartless womanizer when she was the first woman he'd ever had? Without pretending to be an expert on the subject, she was sure men had to work up to rakehood.

She spun around. "Sebastian."

He looked up quickly and stopped fastening buttons. His eyes seemed almost eager, and he was himself again.

"Why?" she asked. "Tell me what this is about, and please, tell me the truth."

For a moment he appeared uncertain, then she watched as the warmth faded from his eyes and she saw nothing but pain. "Five hundred pounds was, I believe, your payment for kissing me. I'm prepared to call us even."

Leaving her speechless, he collected the rest of his garments and left the room.

Chapter 20

Diana spent the day curled up in bed, huddled in misery. *That smell* lingered, reminding her of her folly. She couldn't have the linens changed. Chantal would know immediately what she'd been doing. Most likely the servants already knew; they always found out.

As darkness fell her hostess would no longer be denied and Diana told Chantal to admit her.

"Are you truly unwell?" Juliana asked in obvious concern. "Shall I send for a physician? Minerva's very worried about you. We all are."

Diana had stirred herself to put on a dressing gown—not the ivory satin but a sensible blue one—and let Chantal comb her hair. But she knew she looked terrible: pale and hollow-eyed.

"I'm a little better," she said dully. "It's nothing that needs a doctor."

"Are you hungry? I hear you've taken nothing all day but tea. Will you come down for dinner?"

"Maybe. Probably not." Definitely not. Nothing would persuade her to share the same room, let alone a meal, with Sebastian Iverley.

Juliana climbed up to sit on the bed and gave Diana's

hand a comforting squeeze. "Female problems?"

"Male problems."

"Iverley!"

"How did you know?" For one horrified moment Diana imagined Sebastian swaggering about the breakfast room, hinting at his conquest.

"He left this morning without warning or credible explanation. Something must have happened."

Diana nodded and could no longer fight back her tears.

Juliana crawled over and put an arm around her. "It's all right," she murmured.

"I can't believe he would do such a thing!" Diana sobbed.

Her friend let her weep for a while, and when the sobs subsided, found her a handkerchief. "You must forget all about him," she said. "He's just a worthless poltroon."

Diana managed a watery smile. "Did you just use the word *poltroon*?"

"Unfortunately I've never had the opportunity to do so before. But if ever there was a candidate for the insult, it's Sebastian Iverley."

"He's worse than a poltroon," Diana said. "He's a blackguard."

"A scoundrel."

"A caitiff."

"One of my favorite words."

"A scurvy varlet." Diana mopped her eyes and blew her nose hard.

"What did he do? Would it help you to tell me about it?"

She hadn't meant to, but Diana found herself telling the whole story.

"He deserves to be torn apart by wild horses," Juliana exclaimed when she heard of Sebastian's final exit the night before.

"It's true I did make that wager with Blake and I shouldn't have," Diana said. "That was wrong of me, very wrong."

Juliana dashed aside this attempt at an excuse for Sebastian's behavior. "Since when was kissing a man a crime? A kiss, for God's sake! He should be grateful."

"That's just what I thought."

"Any man would be delighted to kiss you."

"Exactly," Diana said, her spirits reviving. "And even if I hurt him, and I suppose I did, his reaction was quite excessive."

"Cain is constantly at me to give the man a second chance, but I was right about him from the start. I always knew there was something very wrong with Sebastian Iverley."

"What?"

Juliana had nothing new to impart that Diana hadn't heard before. She'd already heard how her perfidious lover had failed to appreciate Juliana's talent as a bookseller.

"Is that all?" At this point Diana was ready to hear something much worse: spying for England's enemies; torturing children or small animals; at the very least cheating at cards.

"I'll ask Cain," Juliana promised. "I'll make him tell me all their male secrets."

Diana's momentary animation faded and she returned to reality. "Are you going to tell Lord Chase what happened?"

"I won't if you don't wish it, but I think he should know. And Tarquin, too. Let the members of their precious men's book club know what a snake they have in their midst."

"Being thrown out of the Burgundy Club would really upset Lord Iverley," Diana said. "Book collecting is important to him."

"But he's the president of the club," Juliana reflected gloomily. "Even if Cain and Tarquin vote him out, the other members won't. Not without a reason and you don't want everyone in London to know what Iverley did to you."

"Certainly not."

"But we have the right idea. The way to hurt Iverley is through his collection."

"Do we really want to hurt him?"

"Diana! How can you ask?"

Diana thought about it and decided she did, almost certainly. "How could we use the books?"

"The man prides himself on always getting a book that he truly wants. He hates to be beaten by other collectors. I wonder if there's anything particular he's pursuing."

A knock at the door heralded the appearance of Minerva.

"Diana," she cried. "Sebastian's left and he wouldn't tell me why." She approached the bed and gave her sister a ferocious glare. "Did you refuse him? Please tell me you didn't turn him down."

"I didn't refuse him," Diana said quietly. "He didn't make me an offer."

"But he wanted to, I know he wanted to. What did you *do?*"

Since she could hardly reveal the truth to a seventeen-year-old girl, she didn't know how to defend herself.

"Minerva," Juliana interjected firmly. "Lord Iverley has behaved very badly." Diana shook her head to warn her not to go on. "I can't tell you the details . . ."

"I suppose it's one of those 'not in front of young girls' matters," Minerva interrupted sulkily.

"Exactly. Don't ask questions because you won't get answers and you'll make things worse for your sister than they already are. She has every reason to be extremely angry."

Minerva had her faults but stupidity wasn't one of them. "Oh goodness! Did he . . . ?" She covered her mouth.

"We shall not speak of Lord Iverley or this matter again," Diana said firmly.

Astonishingly, Minerva burst into tears, something Diana hadn't witnessed since her sister was in the nursery. "It's all my fault!" she said through her sobs.

The need to comfort her sister got Diana out of bed as nothing else had all day. She put her arms around the weeping girl. "It's not your fault, darling. I know you liked him. He deceived us both."

"I wasn't deceived. I *knew.*"

"What do you mean?"

"The highwayman was Sebastian's groom. The whole rescue was a counterfeit. I knew it but I didn't tell you. He wanted you to believe him a hero and I didn't see the harm in it."

Diana hadn't been entirely sure she wanted retribution. Some part of her understood that Sebastian's actions had been motivated by the desire to pay her back for what he saw as her own betrayal.

Now she remembered her terror that the robber would harm Minerva, her deep relief and gratitude at Sebastian's rescue. Her anger burned bright and clean, dispelling the sadness and self-reproach that had haunted her sleepless night and solitary day.

She turned to Juliana. "He told me about a book that belonged to Katherine Parr. The last volume he needs for his royal binding collection."

Juliana smiled. "Am I right in thinking, Diana, that you have a great deal of money?"

Sebastian welcomed the driving rain that penetrated his topcoat and made the journey a misery.

He'd returned to his room the night before aglow with righteous triumph at a mission fulfilled, congratulating himself that he'd overcome a last-minute impulse to mercy. Diana would experience the same pain she'd inflicted on him. They were even. He could return to London and get on with his life.

But the farther he rode away from her, the more she invaded his thoughts. He recalled all the enjoyable times he'd spent in her company. Most of all he remembered the way she'd felt in his arms.

Despite every effort to dwell on practical, useful things as befit a man of logic and common sense, he found himself wondering what Diana was doing, what she was thinking, even what she was *wearing* for heaven's sake.

And with whom she was talking. His closest friends remained at Markley Chase. And so did Blakeney.

Sebastian began to fear he'd made a terrible mistake. And the icy water descending his neck seemed a deserved, if inadequate, punishment.

Diana accepted Blakeney's invitation to walk in the garden during a dry interval after two days of steady downpour. The dank weather had matched her own mood and she hoped a little air would improve it. More important, Blake was the only member of the house party who didn't treat her with exaggerated solicitude.

Cain and Tarquin were either offering her their arms, as though she were too weak to cross a room without support, paying her outrageous compliments, or trying to raise her spirits with a relentless string of jokes. She quite enjoyed the jokes, but the rest was becoming tiresome.

Minerva and Esther brought her puppies. She had to admit she liked the tiny bulldogs with their wrinkled skin and squashed noses and clumsy paws. The feel of a baby dog snuffling into her neck brought back memories of her childhood, and her mother's calm presence when things went wrong.

When Juliana wasn't scribbling letters to various booksellers of her acquaintance, she coaxed Diana to abandon her reducing diet and accept the comfort of cups of chocolate and the bounty of the Markley Chase pastry cook. Diana accepted the former but hadn't the appetite for sweetmeats, fruit cakes or much else, one positive result of her humiliation.

Blakeney treated her exactly as he always had. Now she no longer fancied herself in love with him, she realized that his manner was a combination of admiration and disengagement. He liked her, yes, but not enough to let it interfere with his own concerns. Only a man as self-absorbed as he could have failed to notice something amiss. She found his indifference soothing.

He tucked her hand into his arm and looked down intently. He was staring at her bosom with a warm look in his eye. Not the most respectful behavior, but at least he didn't expect her to collapse into hysterics at a moment's notice.

"What a fine view," she remarked.

"What?" he said, then looked up and grinned. "Superb," he agreed. "Couldn't be better."

Lord, he was a handsome man. Too bad looking at him no longer increased her heartbeat.

"I've had difficulty getting you to myself," he said. "Everyone else in the house seems extraordinarily anxious for your company."

"Very strange," she said dryly.

"Sorry. Very understandable, of course. Even old Sebastian Owlverley was sniffing around you lately."

"I don't believe so."

"I'm not so sure. That kiss you gave him must have got him interested."

Anger and mortification, blended with a tinge of guilt, gnawed at her insides. Without thinking she increased her pace, kicking frost-crisped leaves before her.

"Hey, Diana. Slow down!"

"Can't you keep up with me?"

"Of course," Blake said. "But there's a question I want to ask you. I expect you know what."

His words were almost the same as Sebastian's that night, when he'd been about to ask her why she smelled so good. She felt like laughing hysterically and giving Blake the name of her perfumer. How ironic that he was finally making the offer of marriage she no longer desired.

She could be wrong of course. Her judgment was faulty in this regard. Perhaps his proposal would be more of a proposition.

"Yes?" she said.

"Will you marry me, Diana?" Not a poetic offer, but she appreciated the lack of ambiguity.

"Thank you for asking, Blake," she said. "Why?"

"Why?" Her question took him aback. "Because I want to, of course." Perhaps realizing his words lacked fervor, he seemed to search his brain for appropriate vocabulary. "I would be honored and you would make me the happiest of men."

No longer trusting her own judgment of anyone's words or motives, she wanted to know exactly where things stood. "Why would marrying me make you happy?"

"You know how I feel about you."

"Actually I don't." He looked so dumbfounded she decided to help him along. "Do you love me?"

"I admire you enormously and take great pleasure in your company. I know we should deal very well together."

"In other words, no, you don't love me." She quelled his protest. "It's all right. I don't love you, either."

"You don't? Does that mean you won't marry me?"

"I haven't decided yet."

"Uh, when do you think you might decide?"

"I'd like to ask some questions first. Maybe you'd like to as well. I believe when it comes to marriage everything should be out in the open."

"I like that. No opportunity for misunderstanding."

He was taking this very well. Now that she was no longer in love with him, she began to find him likeable.

"You're the most eligible man in England, Blake. Why have you chosen me?"

"You are very beautiful. And I desire you." He searched her face. "You don't mind me saying that, do you? You're a widow so you know what I'm talking about."

"I appreciate your frankness. And your interest, too. And let me return the compliment. You are a very handsome man."

Blake eyed her a little nervously, not certain whether his ardor was reciprocated. Diana didn't elaborate, purposely. "What else?"

"Well, since we are being frank . . ."

"And open."

"Your money would be useful. This isn't the main thing, I assure you, but it is a factor."

"Your father is one of England's richest men. While I perfectly understand that well-endowed brides are always preferred, the heir to a dukedom would have no difficulty marrying a fortune that isn't tainted by trade."

"I like the fact that your fortune is your own, not a dowry to be negotiated by your father and mine. I'm tired of living under my father's thumb and having to beg him for every penny."

"I confess I'm surprised. I had thought the duke a liberal man."

"The duke would like to dictate the course of my life. Let's say that our ideas differ as to how that course should run."

Diana nodded, intrigued by this new view of Blakeney. "I'd insist on having my money settled on me. And any children, of course."

"I have no argument with that. I shall inherit the dukedom eventually. I only need the use of your income in the meantime."

"One other thing. Minerva will make her debut under my aegis next year. She'll be living with me most of the time until then, and probably until she marries. You and she don't get on very well."

"My dear Diana! I'm not about to interfere with your family affairs. I trust your sister and I could rub along well enough. Are you going to say yes?" he coaxed with a smile. "I wish you would."

Diana closed her eyes for a minute and thought about the advantages of wedding Blake, a consideration for the first time uncolored by infatuation.

She'd be a marchioness, eventually a duchess, her position in the world elevated and unassailable. She'd be able to do so much for Minerva, for her brothers, and for others, too. The marriage settlement could be written to make sure she retained ample resources to continue her gifts to charity. She would have children, at last. And while the begetting of those offspring no longer filled her with unadorned anticipation, Blake was still highly attractive. She looked him up and down through slitted eyes. Bedding him would hardly be a punishment. Just because she at present lacked all enthusiasm for the idea didn't mean she'd always feel like that.

She took a deep breath and prepared to make a giant leap of faith. "Yes. I'll marry you."

With his usual physical grace, Blakeney swept an elegant bow and kissed her hand. "You won't regret it."

If Diana expected a wave of euphoria at her betrothal to the man she'd wanted for so many years, she was disappointed. She felt curiously apathetic about her dazzling future.

"May I kiss you?" he asked.

She nodded. He leaned over and placed his mouth on hers for a long though not deep kiss. There could be no doubt of Blakeney's skill and experience. And it left her cold. She refused to recall less skillful kisses and the good-for-nothing louse who bestowed them.

"One thing, Blake."

"Anything, my love."

"We shan't . . . do anything until we are wed."

"Certainly not. I have far too much respect for you."

"I know it can be hard for men. Perhaps you would wish for an early marriage."

Blakeney smiled. "Naturally I am not without recourse but you can be assured of my discretion. I shall never embarrass you."

Diana hadn't quite expected that level of frankness. "Er, thank you. I'm sure you won't."

"And I have every confidence you'll extend the same consideration to me. Once we've bred an heir or two, of course. We'll get that done quickly and after that you'll find me the most complacent of husbands." Just for a minute his eyes narrowed and he looked anything but complacent. "Don't have an affair with my cousin Sebastian, will you?"

"I can safely promise I won't do that."

She refrained from asking if there were any other men on the proscribed list when it came to her future adultery. Compared to Blake's, Tobias's proposal had been a young maiden's romantic dream.

"How soon can we be married?" Blake asked.

"What do you have in mind?"

"Let me see. I'm expected at Badminton in a day or two. I'll spend a couple of weeks hunting with the Beaufort, then come back to London and talk to my father, if he's in town. If not I'll see him at Mandeville at Christmas. He may kick up a bit of a fuss but he'll come around. With any luck all the folderol with lawyers and so forth will be taken care of by spring and we can be married before the beginning of the season."

What an ardent lover she'd pledged herself to! Two weeks with the Duke of Beaufort's Hunt was clearly more important than discussing his marriage with the Duke of Hampton. She had a feeling Blake wasn't going to let marriage unduly interfere with his life.

Good. She wouldn't let it interfere with hers, either. She'd have higher rank, a regular bed partner (when he wasn't having *recourse* to his mistress), and eventually children.

This, she supposed, was wedded life among the high aristocracy, what she'd always aspired to. And if it was even less like the cozy intimacy of the Montrose family than she'd expected, so much the better. All very polite and fashionable with none of those untidy emotions that made her want to burst into tears.

Chapter 21

Tarquin cornered him between two shelves at Mr.
Rice's bookshop.

"I've been looking for you all over town. At St.
James's Square they keep telling me you're out."

"I am. Most of the time." This was a lie. In the two
weeks since he returned to London, Sebastian had
spent most of his time brooding in his own library
and denying callers.

"God knows where. Certainly not anywhere I'd
expect to find you."

"I'm always pleased to see you." Another lie. He
didn't want to see anyone ever again, and certainly
not Tarquin who must, by this point, be acquainted
with what he had done.

At the moment, however, he had no choice. Tarquin blocked his exit and glared at him down his
prominent nose. "Why did you do it?"

"What does it matter to you?" he snarled. "Did
you suddenly become an archbishop?"

"You're a damn fool and you've behaved like a
scoundrel. Let me tell you what I think of men who
seduce respectable ladies *and* deceive their friends
into helping them."

Tarquin's reputation as a supercilious arbiter of manners was well-known, but Sebastian had never been on the receiving end of his snubs. While he could have made the case that Diana had done the seducing, he recognized the argument as specious. He took his medicine in silence like a man.

"And," Tarquin concluded, "I strongly advise you to keep out of Cain's way. You'll be lucky if he only refuses to speak to you. The alternative to the cut direct would be far worse. Cain doesn't fight nicely."

Sebastian couldn't think of anything to say to his friend that didn't lead back to the same subject, the subject he both longed to broach and avoided like the plague, the object of his constant thoughts.

He wanted to know how Diana was, whether she had remained in the country with the Chases, how she looked, what she said about him. No, not the last. He could guess that.

He didn't dare ask.

After his verbal thrashing by Tarquin, Sebastian retreated to Gentleman Jackson's looking for a physical beating. He selected one of Jackson's assistants, a particularly brutal oaf with a crooked nose and grotesque ears, as a sparring partner. A couple of hours at the boxing saloon rendered him sweaty and bruised but didn't succeed in driving Diana Fanshawe from his mind.

What he ought to do was leave London and go back to Saxton Iverley, where numerous decisions arising from his great-uncle's death awaited his attention. Putting three hundred miles between himself and the victim of his misdeed might be healthy. But he simply couldn't face the great empty mansion.

The only bright spot was another letter from Deaver, who wrote that he was at last ready to sell the Parr prayer book, along with other treasures, including something Sebastian had never seen. He hinted that this would be the last chance and Lord Iverley should act fast or forget the whole matter. But Deaver had toyed with him before. He liked to play games and it wouldn't be the first time Sebastian had hurried to Kent at his invitation, only to be fobbed off.

The truth was, even the anticipation of filling this important gap in his collection failed to excite him. Armorial bindings had lost their charm. In his library he glanced through the newspaper, unable to get interested in the special parliamentary session for passing repressive measures against a restless populace.

He could just imagine what Minerva would have to say on the subject. He'd enjoy hearing her rant. And watching the indulgent, proud, and slightly exasperated look on Diana's face as she listened to her sister.

But neither Minerva nor any other member of her family would ever speak to him again.

Tossing aside *The Times*, he opened another newspaper and the name leaped off the page at him. *The Morning Post* reported, in strict order of precedence, notable members of the audience at a performance of *Don Giovanni*. With much of the beau monde leaving town, Lady Fanshawe, the widow of a mere baronet, was quite high on the list. He recalled her mentioning a fondness for opera.

Instead of posting down to Kent, he bought a ticket

to the last opera before Christmas, an interminable performance of *La Clemenza di Tito* featuring a fat soprano in breeches. Sebastian hardly noticed. His attention was fixed on Diana, sitting in a box with the MacFarlands and Blakeney, damn his eyes. As far as he could tell from his seat in the pit, she appeared to be in spirits though pale, just as beautiful as usual, but perhaps not quite so blooming.

The intensity of his gaze must have penetrated her consciousness. Just as the curtain fell for the interval she picked him out of the crowd and their eyes locked for a few seconds. Then she looked away and started flirting at Blakeney over her fan.

The enormity of his error hit him. He was in the pit by himself while Blakeney, lord of all he surveyed, sat in a private box with Diana. The prize. Sebastian had got his revenge, but against the wrong sinner. And the one he'd punished most was himself.

He wished with all his heart that he could return to that moment when he'd asked her if there was going to be a "next time."

Of course there is.

When she said it his heart had lifted. It hadn't been too late to halt his revenge. He could have been happy, and enjoyed a lifetime of "next times." Instead his obstinacy had made him carry through the rest of his plan, mortally insult her, and ensure his eternal misery.

Unless . . . No. How could she possibly forgive him?

An apology is always acceptable, she'd once said. In that case the offense was trivial in comparison. Nevertheless, he wouldn't give up without a fight.

* * *

After being denied for two days, he was admitted to the Portman Square house and shown into the clean, bright, ground-floor sitting room. The fire blazing in the hearth and a forest of candles dispelled the gray late afternoon gloom. She rose to greet him, that maddening perfume wafting across the room. His breath caught at the sight of her and his heart beat a little tattoo.

"I'm pleased you called again," she said. "I've been away from town."

"I see," he managed. "I assumed you were refusing to receive me."

"Why would I do that?"

The unexpected question deprived him of coherent speech. He could read nothing in her face. Neither the justifiable anger he expected, nor the forgiveness he hardly dared hope for. Her expression was entirely blank.

"Won't you sit down?" She gestured to a chair and settled in its twin, the other side of a mahogany whatnot.

He had no idea how to react to her eerie calm. Instead of reciting his carefully rehearsed apology, like a coward he retreated to small talk. "I trust you are well. How was your journey from Gloucestershire?"

"As tolerable as one can expect at this time of year."

"Did you spend the night at Hungerford?"

"At The Bear."

"An excellent hostelry."

"Indeed," she said. "The sheets are always dry and they make a particularly good eel pie." He rather had the impression she was laughing at him, but not in a friendly way.

"Uh. Did Minerva return to town with you? I'd like to see her."

She smiled faintly. "My sister is here. I won't send for her. She doesn't reciprocate your desire." Finally a hint of steel. Regret pierced him at the confirmation that Minerva knew about his behavior, and had no doubt told Diana about the little secret they shared.

"I'm sorry about the highwayman," he said.

"Such a splendid joke. You must have been most amused to see me so thoroughly taken in." He welcomed the edge of anger in her voice, wished she'd berate him as he deserved, instead of treating him with this maddening indifference. But her face regained its previous unearthly tranquility.

With an elegant shrug she took an embroidery frame from the second shelf of the whatnot, exposing a leather bound book. It was second nature for him to pick it up. His head reeled.

Dark red polished calf glowed like young wine. In the center of the cover the royal coat of arms was instantly recognizable. And at each corner a Tudor rose was tooled, together with the interlocked letters *H* and *K*. There was no need to open the book to know what he'd find. He looked up in disbelief.

"I see you've noticed my latest acquisition. I thought you'd appreciate it. It's a prayer book, you know. A wedding gift from Henry VIII to his last wife, Katherine Parr."

"So I see," he said grimly.

"I found it in Kent, during a visit to my estate there."

He hadn't believed it when told she was out of London. For the first time in years he'd been outmaneuvered in his pursuit of a book.

"How?" he croaked. "No one except me knew Deaver had it."

"You underestimate my friend Juliana's deductive abilities."

Diana wasn't the only woman dealing in revenge this afternoon. Other chickens had come home to roost.

He replaced the book on the shelf. "I'm surprised Lady Chase isn't here to witness my defeat."

"She'll be sorry to miss it. But I shall be sure to give her a full report. By the way," she continued. "I asked Lord Deaver why he hadn't sold you the book. I gather you've visited him several times over the past five years and he seemed unimpressed with your powers of persuasion. I, on the other hand, found him quite amenable."

A spark of anger kindled. "I'm intimately acquainted with your powers of persuasion . . ."

"Tsk. I think you should stop before you say something you regret, Lord Iverley. You really don't want to insult me again. All I meant to imply was that you hadn't offered him enough money. Let me show you another little treasure I *persuaded* Deaver to sell."

Sebastian was fairly certain he wasn't going to like what came next. He had the impression she followed a carefully prepared script, that from the moment he walked into the room he'd been her puppet.

She opened a deep drawer in the whatnot and extracted another volume. At a glance he could tell the binding was even older than the Katherine Parr, late fifteenth-century.

"What is it?" he asked, dry-mouthed, about to learn the nature of Deaver's secret treasure.

Without letting him touch it she showed him the dark blind-stamped pigskin then opened it to the first page. He recognized the famous book at once.

"The Caxton Chaucer," he said. "The first printed edition of *The Canterbury Tales*."

"Yes, it's a very important book," she said, for all the world as though she'd ever heard of a first edition before he'd instructed her in the library at Mandeville. "But what will particularly appeal to you is its history. You see, Lord Iverley, it belonged to Elizabeth Woodville."

King Edward IV's wife. It would be the crown jewel of his collection. And if he'd never met Diana Fanshawe it could have been his. Since his uncle's death he had the means to meet Deaver's doubtless extortionate price.

"What do you want for it?" he said. "How much?"

"Really Lord Iverley! I wouldn't expect you to be so crude in your approach. As though one could put a monetary value on such a treasure."

"I'll warrant Deaver did."

"That is true. But you and I are beyond such mundane considerations. The worth of these books is not to be measured in gold."

"What do you want?" His mouth parched, he could scarcely get the words out.

She replaced the book in the drawer and pretended to give consideration to his question, but he could tell it was playacting. She knew what she wanted.

"Neither is for sale. I have decided I shall give them to my future husband as a wedding present. Most appropriate in the case of Katherine Parr's volume, don't you think?"

He was unable to credit the implications of her statement. Did she expect him to offer her marriage? A wild hope fought disbelief. He wanted to marry her, and not just to gain possession of the books.

He wanted her for her warmth, kindness and wit; for the way she surrounded herself with beauty and comfort; for the intelligence and curiosity she'd inherited from the most interesting family he'd ever encountered. And, not least, because he wanted to share her bed, all night and every night.

Or perhaps she lured him to propose to her so she could turn him down flat. If so, he could scarcely blame her.

"Your future husband?" he said cautiously.

She beamed at him, her smile at its most radiant, her eyes dreamy with desire.

His heart stood still. He desperately wished to believe in the promise of those eyes.

"You shall be the first to congratulate me," she said. "No one else knows, but you are a member of the family, after all. I am engaged to Blakeney."

His heart descended to his boots and he felt like dashing his head against the wall. Fool, fool, fool! Suddenly, once again, she was little Amanda Vanderlin, luring him to his doom and the ridicule of Blakeney. For the last time, he swore. Never again would he let her, or any woman, dupe him.

Chapter 22

"**I**t cannot be true. Try it again."

Chantal pursed her lips and ran the long strip of cloth marked with inches around Diana's waist. "The tape does not lie," she said. "One inch more. You have been eating pâtisserie again."

"I haven't," Diana wailed. "I promise."

"Have you changed your regime? The beetroot seemed to work well, at first."

"I'm tired to death of beetroot. It makes me feel sick. I have no appetite." Diana groped for her handkerchief and couldn't find it, since she'd stripped to her shift for the measuring session with her maid. She gave an inelegant sniff. Not only was she frequently queasy, she'd developed a tendency to burst into tears for absolutely no reason.

"Let me measure the bust now."

Diana feared the worst. Her breasts had felt swollen for days. She braced herself for another scold. "How much have I grown?"

"It is as I thought," Chantal said.

"What?"

"The lady's maid is always the first to know."

"Know what?" she shrieked. "That I'm swelling up like a balloon?"

"Does milord Blakeney know?"

"I doubt he'd notice an inch or two. Men don't, you know." She glared at Chantal. "Only interfering French maids constantly harangue one about such things."

Chantal ignored this show of temper. "You will have to hurry and have the wedding. No more waiting for permission from *monsieur le duc*."

"What," Diana said carefully, "are you talking about, Chantal?"

"Milady, you are increasing."

"Impossible!" Even as she ejaculated her denial, Diana knew the truth. She'd last suffered her monthly flow before the trip to Gloucestershire.

Chantal snorted. "*Madame*, I have been in service for twenty-two years and I know well the signs. You would not be the first to claim yourself a victim of immaculate conception. *Quant à ça*, it is not for me to say. But I have never been wrong. When Chantal says you are enceinte, in a few months, if all goes well, there will be a child."

The house had seen better days and those days were long past. While Diana assessed the crumbling mortar and peeling stucco of the once handsome building from the shelter of the hackney carriage, Chantal went to the door. The maid's negotiation with the servant who answered her knock was apparently satisfactory. She nodded at her mistress and Diana climbed the steps to enter a shabby hall before removing her heavy veil. Even with Chantal to keep her company her present quest edged on impropriety. In St. James's Square it was all too likely that some passerby would recognize her.

A footman in old-fashioned livery as faded as the furnishings returned to the hall. "His Lordship will see you in the library."

"Thank you. Please find somewhere comfortable for my maid to wait."

She followed the servant, dreading the coming confrontation. During her last meeting with Sebastian she held the upper hand. His bafflement, without compensating for his sins, had been deeply satisfying. Today she had no idea what to expect, how he would react to her tidings.

Taking a deep breath she prepared to carry the battle into enemy territory, alone and unarmed.

Two things transcended the aura of decades-long neglect the library shared with the exterior of the house. Serried shelves of books glowed in a subdued rainbow of colored leathers decorated with old gold. And the room's master was as orderly as his cherished collection.

He stood to greet her dressed in garments that wouldn't have disgraced Tarquin Compton. The perfect tailoring was worn with the same comfort and ease he'd once lent his old-fashioned breeches and loose coats. Since Sebastian had updated his wardrobe only for the nefarious purpose of impressing her, the sight gave her no pleasure. There were few places in the world she wouldn't prefer to be.

He didn't look pleased to see her, either. "Have you changed your mind about the books?" he demanded, not troubling with the niceties. "You are lucky you caught me. I plan to leave for the north tomorrow." He folded his arms and frowned. "I'd have called at Portman Square had you summoned me. You shouldn't have come here."

"I wanted to see your house." Taking her time, she took in faded curtains and bare patches in the carpet. "I think I prefer mine."

"As a matter of fact, so do I."

Her eyes scanned a scattering of mousetraps around the wainscoting. "Why don't you move?"

"Since I left Cambridge I've had the use of the house at no expense to myself. Before that it hadn't been lived in for some fifty years. My great-uncle never came to London."

"Now that you own it you could make a few repairs."

Even through his spectacles, his eyes were steely, unwelcoming. "I don't believe you came here to lecture me on building improvements. Why don't we get to the point?"

"I have changed my mind about the books." His smile of satisfaction annoyed her and she was pleased to think she was about to erase it. "I've decided not to give them to my future husband after all."

"Good. The idea of a yahoo like Blakeney owning Elizabeth Woodville's Chaucer is a travesty. Buy him a nice set of hunting prints instead."

"You misunderstand me. I may still give Blake the books. I haven't decided yet. But I'm taking a different husband." She paused. "You."

That silenced him. He no longer looked either forbidding or smug.

"Believe me," she said, "I'm not happy about it

but we need to be married. Unless you are prepared to have your child born a bastard. And for my sake I'd prefer it was soon. There's something so vulgar about an obviously pregnant bride."

She took a risky approach. Conciliation might be more effective. But pride demanded she not beg, even though she had more to lose. If he refused to marry her some might frown on him; she would be utterly disgraced. She preferred not to acknowledge that he held the upper hand.

When she named him as her husband Sebastian's heart missed a beat. Then incipient pleasure at the prospect was rapidly quelled by Diana's obvious disgust. She spoke as though marrying him was the worst fate she could imagine.

"Are you quite sure I am the father of this infant?" he asked bitterly. "If it actually exists, that is."

He felt ashamed of himself even as she launched herself at him with a strangled cry. He stepped back barely in time to avoid her slap, then managed to catch her before she fell. "Careful," he said more gently, her nearness having its usual effect on his senses. "You had better sit down."

Having settled her in a wing chair, he propped himself against the library table and crossed his ankles, trying to address the matter calmly. "Now, tell me about it."

She regarded him resentfully. "You are most certainly the father. There is no other possibility. Do you honestly believe that had I . . . engaged in intimacies with Blake that I would be proposing to wed you instead of him?"

He winced. "I am guessing the answer is no."

"Do you know that it has been my greatest ambition since I was a girl to marry him? Thanks to your vile scheme of revenge for something that most men wouldn't think twice about, my life is ruined! Why did you do it? Was kissing me such a dreadful experience?"

"I am sorry." The simple apology was all he could manage. And one true fact. "Kissing you was as good as anything I had ever experienced until . . . well . . . you know."

"Neither of us considered the consequences," she said on a ghost of a sigh. "And now we must pay."

Stupidly, like the protagonist of a bawdy novel, he'd never given a thought to the frequent result of lust indulged. And like those fictional debauchers he was taken by surprise.

"Tell me how you know." He retreated into practicalities. "My ignorance of the business is profound, but I'm aware it takes nine months. It has only been six weeks. Are you absolutely certain?"

"I'm afraid there's very little doubt." He listened as she described her symptoms and some details about female physiology with which he guessed she meant to embarrass him. The whole monthly bleeding business was mildly repulsive, but Sebastian always found the acquisition of knowledge worthwhile. He made a mental note to buy a book on the subject.

"Are you unwell?"

"Most of the time not. The nausea comes on without warning."

He eyed her a little warily. "Can I get you anything? A glass of wine? Tea?"

"Not now, thank you. I'd rather settle what we should do."

Carrying on his line for posterity wasn't something Sebastian had ever wished for, or even considered. And when it came to the matter of human reproduction the male of the species was involved only at the outset (in his case for a very short time). After that the business passed to the feminine realm and there was nothing for a man to do except await the dubious pleasure of seeing himself duplicated in miniature form.

There was, however, one duty that he couldn't avoid: to give this future product of his flesh and blood a name.

"When do you wish to marry?" he asked. "And where?"

So it was done. In this matter at least Sebastian proved a gentleman. For the second time, Diana found herself betrothed to a man she'd once believed she loved. What would it be like, she wondered, to receive a proposal of marriage from a man she *did* love, and who returned her sentiments? She would never know.

She longed for a gesture, for him to offer even the smallest hope that they could move forward together without disaster. He remained leaning against the table, shoulders hunched, arms folded.

She spread one gloved hand in front of her and examined it carefully for flaws. "I would like to marry at Mandeville Wallop," she said. "I had planned to travel to Shropshire for Christmas. Since there will be no time to call the banns, you will have to obtain a special license." She looked up, but his face told her nothing. "Do you know how to go about it?"

"I'll find out. Shall you tell your parents the truth?"

"They'll eventually suspect when the child is born so soon after the marriage, but I think I'd prefer to let them believe we have an affection for each other. It would upset them very much to see me forced into a marriage I didn't want. My mother and father will both welcome you to the family. They liked you."

His voice thawed a couple of degrees. "I liked them. They are interesting people."

"A few things I'd like to make clear," she said. "I have a large fortune. For my protection I would like it to be settled on me and my children. Blakeney agreed to the condition."

"I have sufficient funds. You can keep the whole lot as far as I'm concerned."

"I don't like this house." She sniffed and checked the mousetraps, thankfully still sitting idle. "Would you consider moving to mine? We can expand the library."

"Agreed. I meant it when I said I liked yours better." So far he was proving amenable.

"One other thing. Our sleeping arrangements. Until the child is born I would prefer to sleep alone."

A quiver in his throat was the only perceptible reaction for a few moments. "Is it better for the infant?" he asked finally.

"I don't know. But it's better for me. Naturally if the child should turn out not to be a boy, I shall readmit you to my bed until you beget an heir."

Sebastian didn't give a damn about begetting an heir. Did she mean that the only way he'd be allowed to make love to her was if she kept on producing girls? And forget the future. The birth was months off.

"Why?" he said. He wanted to assure her that with experience he would become a better bed partner.

"I'm sorry," Diana said. "But I can't forgive your shabby behavior. I hope I may be able to in the future."

That poured cold water on any inclination he had to beg. *His* shabby behavior! Yes, he'd been wrong. Very well. He was willing to admit it. Like a man.

"I owe you an apology for what happened at Markley Chase," he said. "I should not have behaved as I did."

"You mean seducing me for reasons of petty revenge?"

He nodded.

"Don't you think that was a little excessive? All I did was make you kiss me. Was that such a dreadful sin?"

Pride wouldn't let him protest how much that kiss had meant, or how devastating had been the discovery that she was trifling with him. "Again, I apologize."

"And I apologize for the original bet. It was a jest in poor taste and I have long regretted it. And I suppose I'm sorry about the books, too, though under the circumstances I do believe you deserved that."

All he could manage was a nod.

She sighed. "I feel like we are a pair of children, forced by our mothers to make up our differences, to utter apologies that we don't mean because there is no true forgiveness. Perhaps like children we can forget in a day or two."

She tilted her head at him, expecting a response. "Since we are to be married," he said, "it would be better if we were on cordial terms." There! That was a sensible and mature aspiration.

"I can't argue with you. Nevertheless, I'm not yet ready to engage in normal marital relations."

"I would never force myself on you," he said coldly. "Am I permitted to state a condition of my own?"

"That would only be fair."

He was about to ask her for the books, but his mind rebelled. The pleasure in owning them would be tainted by being obtained as part of this bitter fight. He didn't want them as spoils of war. Let her give them to Blakeney, rather. See how the boob enjoyed such an esoteric gift.

Blakeney.

Blakeney wanted to marry Diana. Blakeney was presumably going to be quite sorry when she broke their engagement. And furious when he learned his cousin had stolen her from under his nose.

"It doesn't matter," he said. "I have no condition."

"You summoned me. What can I do for you?" Blake gave her a careless kiss on the cheek and dropped a long narrow package into her lap.

Another fan, she guessed. In the period of their betrothal he'd surprised her with any number of elegant, though inexpensive trifles. As an affianced husband he'd turned out to be attentive, even affectionate. Much more so than his unromantic proposal had prophesied. She had all his gifts gathered in a box, ready to return to him.

"Please sit down. Shall I ring for tea?"

"No thank you."

"Wine? Brandy?"

"Diana. It's not even eleven o'clock in the morning. Are you offering me a sop in advance of a scolding? I do have news. My father is in town. I shall call on him today."

"Knowing how little you look forward to that, I can at least relieve you of the necessity."

"What's this? Are you suggesting we marry without his blessing?" He grinned. "The notion is not without appeal. We could go to Gretna Green and shock the world."

He'd probably do it, and she was tempted. Then ashamed and horrified at herself for even contemplating the deception. She couldn't foist another man's child on him. Careless as Blakeney appeared in many ways, he'd object to the dukedom of Hampton passing to a cuckoo. A cuckoo sired by his despised cousin.

She stood up, walked over to the fireplace and took a deep breath. "Blake," she said, turning to face him, "I can't marry you. I'm breaking our engagement."

He gawked at her. Even through her anxiety and embarrassment she couldn't help a twinge of amusement at seeing the all-powerful Marquis of Blakeney's shock at being jilted, not something he'd have expected in a decade or a hundred years.

"Why?" he asked finally. "What have I done?"

"Nothing. It's just that I have decided we shan't suit after all." She might as well get it over with. "I'm to wed someone else. Your cousin. Lord Iverley. Sebastian."

She watched a parade of emotions cross his face:

shock, disbelief, scorn, and finally mirth. "Owl? You are marrying the Owl instead of me?" He burst out laughing, making her feel a lot less sorry for him.

"And why should I not wish to marry Lord Iverley? He is a man of superior intellect and solid fortune." Having seen his house, she wasn't sure of the latter, but he was certainly reputed to be a wealthy man.

"Oh, please, Diana. I know you too well. You are a woman of the world. You want the fashionable life. Owl may have tidied himself up but he's still the same odd fellow underneath. I don't understand you."

Eventually he'd guess the truth, when the child was born seven months after the wedding, but for the moment she wouldn't admit it. Not only did she distrust Blake's discretion, she didn't want to own that the wedding was a forced one, for the sake of her own pride, and Sebastian's too.

"When we made that bet, I got to know Sebastian and since then I have come to value him. I wasn't aware until yesterday that he shared my sentiments. Indeed I hardly knew my own heart. I owe you a sincere apology but it isn't as though our betrothal was a formal one. No one knew about it, including Sebastian, or he would never have spoken to me."

Blake shook his head in bafflement. She could tell he didn't entirely credit the little romantic fiction she'd woven, yet there was little he could do but retire from the field.

"My dear Diana, I can only wish you every happiness in your future with my Cousin Owlverley."

"Why do you persist in calling him that idiotic name?" she demanded, irritated by his smirk.

"Just a childhood habit. I suppose you're going to

spoil my fun and insist I refer to your new betrothed with respect."

"Why don't you like each other?"

"I don't know. We never have."

"He never talks about his family but Minerva looked him up in Debrett and found he's the last of the Iverleys. Your family are his only living relations."

"My father thinks the world of him. He was always telling me to be more like him." This was the first indication Diana had that the aversion on Blake's part derived from anything more than the scorn of the sportsman for the intellectual.

"And that upset you?"

"When he visited Mandeville we were both about ten, I suppose. The duke droned on about how much more advanced Sebastian was, how he spoke Greek like Aristotle and Latin better than half a dozen popes. I never could get very interested in languages spoken by a lot of ancient fellows dressed up in sheets. The Owl—excuse me, Sebastian—couldn't do anything I liked." Blakeney scowled. "Somehow he learned to ride."

"Not as well as you."

"Not quite, but almost. I have to be fair about that. My sisters and I used to tease him about how he sat on a horse like a sack of potatoes."

"Did he dislike girls then?"

"He quite liked them at first, used to trail after them. They laughed at him. He was such a scrawny fellow with funny clothes and those big glasses over his eyes." He gave a rueful laugh. "We played a trick on him. Hadn't thought of it in years. I got Amanda, m'youngest sister, to promise him a kiss."

Diana felt a chill that had nothing to do with the early winter weather. "What happened?"

"When the nurse was out of the room she lured him into the nursery closet where I was waiting with the older girls. We took away his spectacles and locked him in."

"That was unkind."

"That's not all." Now Blakeney sounded distinctly sheepish. "We removed some of his clothing, too. We knew the duke and my mother were coming up to the nursery, which wasn't something that happened often."

"Good heavens."

"He yelled to be let out and the nurse came back and opened the door just as they arrived. I can still remember his face when he had to greet his uncle and aunt without his breeches."

"That was a horrible thing to do, Blake."

"I know. But it was a long time ago. We all got over it."

Diana wasn't sure Blake had got over it and she was certain Sebastian hadn't. At least it explained his reaction to their wager about a kiss. Blake and a girl plotting to make a fool of him, all over again.

Chapter 23

Two carriages waited at the door, Diana's luxurious chariot, familiar to Sebastian from the highwayman imbroglio, and a plainer vehicle, which a footman was stowing with luggage. Two large cloak bags and several boxes still awaited loading. The horses snorted, expelling their breath into the cold morning air. A small woman dressed in black descended from the house, carrying an expensive green leather dressing case and a hat box. He recognized the maid who had accompanied Diana to his house.

"Another one?" asked the footman with an air of disbelief Sebastian could appreciate. Was it possible for two smallish women to require this much baggage for a couple of weeks in the country? He apologized mentally to Minerva, whose contribution was likely modest. Diana, on the other hand, rarely appeared in the same garment twice. And nothing better illustrated the carnage she'd wrought in his peaceful life than the fact he'd noticed.

"Mamzelle Chantal," said the coachman, stamping his feet on the pavement. "How much longer will my lady be? It's too cold to keep the horses standing long."

Mademoiselle Chantal shrugged off the requirements of mere animals. "Milady will be ready when she is ready." She addressed Sebastian. "Will you wait inside, milord?"

He dismounted and commissioned a crossing sweeper to walk his horse for a few minutes, wondering if married life was going to entail a great deal of waiting around.

The hall contained a number of servants running back and forth and Minerva, dressed for travel, seated on a bench reading a book.

She looked up and a guarded expression crossed her pretty face. "Lord Iverley."

"Please, Minerva. We are to be brother and sister. You used to call me Sebastian."

"That was before." She looked at him with such disappointment in her eyes he felt the veriest scoundrel. "I helped you by not telling her about the highwayman. You used me."

A lump rose in his throat. "I'm afraid I did."

"And that night, I drew off Lord Blakeney so you would be alone with her. I thought I was helping my sister and instead I allowed you to hurt her."

Nothing had made Sebastian feel worse. Diana and he were adults and both had engaged in antics that were more or less reprehensible. Minerva, for all her intelligence and air of sophistication, was barely out of childhood, an innocent who hadn't deserved to be drawn into their conflict.

"You mustn't blame yourself." The words seemed inadequate.

"I wanted you to marry her," she said sadly.

"And that is just what is going to happen."

She shook her head. "Not like this. This isn't right."

They'd spoken softly, though the bustling servants were too busy to attend them. Sebastian got down on his haunches and met her eye to eye on the same level.

"I promise you one thing, Minerva. I will do my best to take care of your sister."

She gazed at him, hers eyes bright with anxiety and hope. "Do you swear?"

"I swear to God."

He had the uncomfortable feeling she examined not just his face but his soul. After a few moments she nodded. "Thank you, Sebastian." And leaned forward and kissed his cheek.

"You're here, my lord." Diana reached the bottom of the stairs, an empress swathed in velvet and sables. "Well, you two. What are we waiting for? Let's be on our way."

Sebastian and Minerva got to their feet as Diana swept out of the front door.

Minerva pulled a face. "She always takes hours to get ready so we're late," she said. "And then she blames me."

For two days Minerva was grateful for her foresight in bringing three books with her. Diana spent much of the journey sleeping, and when awake tended to be querulous. Though life at Wallop Hall had given her a detailed knowledge of the habits of pregnant horses and dogs, Minerva had no firsthand acquaintance with increasing females of the human variety. Still, she'd kept her eyes and ears open over the years and had a very good idea what ailed her sister. But she acquiesced in the fiction that she had no notion why Diana had suddenly broken her engagement to Lord Blakeney and was to marry Sebastian in a week.

The former fact pleased her. She didn't believe Diana would ever be happy with a self-centered idiot, however good-looking and ducal. About Sebastian as a husband for Diana, she had her reservations. Before he revealed his feet of clay she'd thought him perfect for her sister. Now she suspended judgment and hoped for the best. It was all she could do since the marriage was inevitable, indeed essential.

The third and last day Diana's stomach and mood improved and the weather worsened. Driving rain persuaded Sebastian to join them in the well-heated carriage where Diana proposed they pass the time playing games.

As Minerva set up the carriage's clever folding table, she began to have serious questions about her future brother-in-law's upbringing. He displayed total ignorance of the simplest childhood word and card games.

"You don't know Pope Joan?" she asked. "You must."

"Everyone knows Pope Joan," Diana and she said in perfect unison.

"Aristotle's Beard!" they yelled, also together.

"Shakespeare!" Minerva said, a fraction of a second before Diana.

"Bother," said her sister. "You beat me. That means you'll get a letter tomorrow."

Sebastian stared at them as though they were talking gibberish. "You're talking gibberish," he said.

"Aristotle's Beard is the phrase we use in our family when two people say the same thing at the same time," Diana explained. "What do you use?"

"Nothing. I've never heard of such a thing."

"But you must have!" Minerva said. "Everyone has one. Our neighbors the Loaches use Robert the Bruce because their mother is Scottish. Our mother's family uses Oyster Stew which is quite common in Essex where they live, but she adopted Aristotle's Beard from the Montroses."

"What does Shakespeare have to do with it?"

"The first person to say Aristotle's Beard wins, but if we say it together, as Di and I just did, we move on to Shakespeare. The first person to say it is sure to receive a letter the next day."

"What happens if you say Shakespeare at the same time?"

"We both get a letter."

Sebastian shook his head in wonderment. "Does it work? Do you always get a letter?"

"Always," Minerva assured him.

Diana laughed. "Sometimes."

Minerva was about to argue because, though she knew Diana was right, she still liked to pretend that Aristotle's Beard was an infallible presage of correspondence. Then she realized she had lost the attention of her companions. Sebastian was gazing at Diana as though he'd never seen anything so amazing in all his days and Diana returned his look with a smile on her lips that Minerva could only describe as naughty. Had they not been closed in a moving carriage she would have discreetly withdrawn from the room. Instead she looked out of the window.

"Let's teach Sebastian to play brag," Diana said after a little while. She pulled a pack of cards from a compartment under the seat.

The Montroses took their games seriously and didn't believe in letting considerations of sportsmanlike behavior get in the way of total conquest. They cheered when they won, cursed at every reversal, and when all else failed argued about the rules. Neither Diana nor Minerva had ever received a minute's consideration from their brothers because of their sex or youth. They'd never been allowed to win a single hand until they earned it by beating the older boys fair and square. Diana had been a little kinder to Min when she was very young, but there was no need anymore.

Sebastian might not know any card games but he learned fast. In a remarkably short time he was lying like a Montrose born in pursuit of vast sums of imaginary wealth. While not quite as noisy in his triumphs and despair as the others—Diana had a special crow of victory like a demented rooster—he more than held his own, displaying an appropriate sense of brutality when taunting his opponents as losers destined for a sad lifetime of indigence and madness. Minerva's eyes widened in respect. Sebastian might even surpass Rufus in the art of the insult. Of course Ru's invective was delivered in several languages, including Turkish, Greek, and Coptic. But Sebastian demonstrated enough imagination to challenge the acknowledged family champion.

Sebastian was almost sorry as they passed Much Wenlock and the journey drew to an end. Carriage travel, which he generally loathed, was quite bearable as arranged by Diana. She had a talent for comfort and luxury. And for the first time since their forced betrothal Diana appeared happy. In his more optimistic moments he hoped her prickly attitude was largely the moodiness and irrational emotions attributed to pregnant women, and not because she hated him. Today she'd been in a delightful humor.

And there'd been a moment when their eyes had met across the carriage. Sebastian wasn't quite sure what he'd do if she stuck to her decision to ban him from her bed, but he feared he might become a worthy candidate for a lunatic asylum.

Both the older Montroses, along with young Stephen, came out to greet them with much embracing and kissing and hand pumping all around. About the warmth of his reception he could have no complaint. During dinner, served soon after their arrival, the enthusiasm expressed at welcoming him to the family made him feel like a fraud.

"Now!" Mr. Montrose said, after the last cover was removed. "It's time for you girls to be weighed. Iverley, too, if he wishes. In fact," he added with satisfaction, "you're a member of the family so I'm not giving you the choice." Totally oblivious to the disgust on his daughters' faces, he emitted a rumbling laugh.

"Perhaps not tonight," Sebastian said quickly. He and Diana had agreed to keep their secret to themselves and present themselves as a happily engaged couple, eager to marry quickly. He didn't know about the rate of weight increase during pregnancy, but even at this stage the infant had to count for something.

Diana wouldn't wish to be interrogated on any extra pounds.

Her father was not so easily deterred. "It won't take a minute, and I'd like to show you my new improved bootjack, too."

Despite her obvious reluctance, she was about to give in. Diana liked to grumble about her parents but Sebastian knew it was all bark and no bite. She wouldn't stand up for herself if it meant disappointing her father.

"No," Sebastian said. "Diana is tired after the journey. She needs to rest." He took her hand from her lap and lifted it so their clasped fists were visible to all at the table.

"Quite right!" Mr. Montrose beamed his approval of this loverlike behavior. Sebastian felt even guiltier.

Life at Wallop Hall was a bit like living in a foreign country. Aristotle's Beard was only Sebastian's first encounter with a body of language peculiar to the Montroses. Sometimes it was an idiomatic, though comprehensible, usage of common words. But he also heard Minerva and Stephen conduct an entire conversation which meant something to them but to him sounded like "eggy-peggy."

Diana merely shrugged when he commented on the phenomenon. "All families do it. The only difference is that the Montroses are more bizarre and annoying."

"It has stopped raining," Minerva interrupted. "Time to go out and gather greenery to decorate the house. Only two days till Christmas and if we don't do it no one will. Mama's too busy preparing for the meet the day after to even think about it. If it were up to her we'd get dog food for Christmas dinner. Are you two coming?"

"No thanks," Diana said. "I'm much too comfortable by the fire."

"Lazybones."

"I plead guilty."

"Come on, Min," said Stephen. "I'll race you."

After they left the room Sebastian stood in front of Diana's sofa and frowned. "I think you should come out. It will be good for you."

She pouted. "I don't want to."

"Exercise is good for pregnant females."

"Oh? Who says so?"

"Dr. Thomas Denman."

"Who's he?"

"An authority on pregnancy and childbirth. His book came highly recommended and I've been working my way through it. He says a generally healthy woman will have a much easier time of it if she takes regular exercise."

"That's not what I've heard. I think I'll have a little sleep this morning."

"Denman has based his conclusions on his observation that the lower class of women, who work in the open air, do much better than the more affluent who are encouraged to be idle. I am afraid I must insist." He held out his hand. "Come. You'll feel better. You look pale."

She grumbled but assented and half an hour later her color had improved. She positively glowed as she directed him to cut a particularly thickly-berried branch of holly.

"Ouch," he said. The prickle had penetrated his glove. "Why do I have to do this?"

"Because you are so much taller than Step and can reach higher."

"I mean, why gather holly at all? It appears to be a dangerous enterprise."

"We can't have Christmas without holly."

"I don't see why not. I've survived twenty-six years of Christmases without so much as a prickle."

"You are so strange, Sebastian," Minerva said. "I suppose you don't know about mistletoe, either."

"I believe it is a parasitical plant used in various medicines."

They all laughed at him and he didn't mind.

"What?" he said.

"Nothing," Minerva said.

"We're not letting any of that stuff in the house," Diana said.

"Yes we are," Minerva and Stephen responded.

Which set off a whole new round of Aristotle's Bearding and presumably a deluge of correspondence.

Sebastian continued to fend off Mr. Montrose's attempts to weigh and measure Diana. For himself, he confirmed he was six foot one and one half inches and hadn't changed his weight since the summer.

"Come into my study, my boy," Mr. Montrose said after he'd recorded the information. "I wish to talk to you."

His host cleared a place for him to sit, among the books, papers, and miscellaneous and mysterious objects that cluttered the small room, then took his own place behind the desk. There wasn't usually anything formidable about Diana's father. That Christmas Eve afternoon, however, his stern expression made Sebastian feel like a scrubby schoolboy.

"So you intend to marry my daughter in three days," he began.

"Yes, sir. I am so fortunate."

"Diana is of age, of course, and her own mistress, but I would be remiss in my duty as a father were I not to enquire into the circumstances."

"I'll do my best to answer your questions," Sebastian replied cautiously. "Some information you require may be more properly obtained from Diana herself."

"Hmm. You must be aware that Diana is a very rich woman. Fanshawe left her his entire fortune. I don't like to think of her being married for her money."

"Have you heard of the Saxton coalfield?"

"I believe not."

"It is located in Northumberland on the Saxton Iverley estate and belongs to me. It is highly productive." He named a sum that made Mr. Montrose whistle.

"Good Lord. Your income is even greater than Diana's."

"I'd take her without a single penny."

"You love her then?"

Sebastian could only manage the same promise he'd made Minerva. "I will always do my very best to take care of her."

"I know it's hard for we men to speak of our feelings but it's all right, Sebastian—I may so call you, no need for formality here. It's all right because I can tell that you do love my daughter."

Sebastian felt unable to deceive this kind, affectionate man a minute longer. If they were to be related for their remaining mutual lifetime, almost father and son, he preferred it to be based on honesty.

"I hate to confess this, and perhaps I should let Diana do so but I fear she will not. Our marriage is not her choice. She is with child."

Montrose didn't insult his daughter by asking if Sebastian was the father. "I see," he said, pursing his lips and stroking his whiskers. "This isn't news to gladden a father's heart but since you are to be married, there's nothing I can do but rejoice in the prospect of my first grandchild."

"Thank you, sir."

"All's well that ends well." He chuckled. "That explains why Diana is so crotchety. I sympathize, my boy. I've been through this a few times myself. I can tell the marriage is *your* choice."

"But not hers," Sebastian blurted miserably. "She wanted to marry Blakeney. I ruined it for her."

"Blakeney? Oh no! Of course she had a girlish tendre for him but he would be quite wrong for her. He needs to grow up."

"He's two months older than me."

"Years don't always matter. Blakeney's still a boy and Diana needs a man. You, my boy, are a man."

Chapter 24

"I hate Dr. Denman!"

"Try not to get upset. Dr. Denman says it's bad for pregnant females."

Diana gritted her teeth and prepared to dig in her heels. The rest of the family, including Henry who had surprised them by arriving from Edinburgh late on Christmas Eve, had already left the breakfast room.

"How often must I tell you, Sebastian, that I cannot bear to eat any of this food."

"That," he replied with odious patience, "is because it's all animal food." He waved at the array of breakfast dishes laid out on the sideboard. "Dr. Denman says pregnant females will often eat vegetables and fruit when everything else disagrees with them."

Diana began to feel an inkling of respect for the doctor, despite his obnoxious use of the phrase "pregnant females," as though she were a member of a herd of milch cows.

"I'm not going to eat vegetables for breakfast," she said with diminished vehemence.

"How about some fruit?"

"Maybe. Grapes would be nice. I love grapes."

"I hate grapes," he said.

"That's ridiculous. No one hates grapes. Not that it matters. We won't have any unless someone robbed the Mandeville hothouses."

He rang the bell for a maid who looked dubious when asked what fruit the kitchen might have. "Maybe Cook has some stewed prunes."

Diana's stomach lurched. "No thanks. I could eat an orange." It sounded delicious. "Are there any left?"

When the fruit arrived Sebastian insisted on peeling it, a task he performed with deft efficiency. "There. Once you've eaten it you can change into your habit and we'll follow the hunt for a while, at a gentle pace of course. No jumping."

"My mother will think we are cowards."

"I can't live my life worrying about other people's opinion of me, and neither should you."

"I was thinking of you. I certainly don't care what Mama thinks."

"So I noticed." His tone was even drier than usual. "And since you don't care if you are branded a coward, there's no reason not to go out."

Half an hour later Sebastian gave her a leg up onto her horse and they left the stable yard to join the hunt gathering in front of the house. In spite of the irritating Dr. Denman, Diana admitted to herself that she was coming to appreciate the care of this man who would become her husband the next day.

He looked good on a horse. In fact, he looked good to her almost everywhere. She still felt bruised by the events that had led to their forced marriage but began to see the possibility of forgiving him, of putting it all behind her and achieving a mutual accommodation. Or something even better. Perhaps they could be happy together.

Once she stopped feeling sick she'd probably rescind her prohibition on bed sharing. She hardly yearned for a life of celibacy. She peeked sideways at the way his thighs straddled his mount and felt an answering throb in her own body.

Maybe it wouldn't be too long.

At dinner that night, Sebastian's wedding eve, Mr. Montrose drank to the health of the bridal couple.

"This is the second time I've had to give away this daughter," he said with suspiciously shining eyes. "I shall never forget the day my little goddess was born." He groped for his handkerchief and applied it to his nose with a loud snort. "I always miss her when she isn't here but I couldn't relinquish her to a better man. And I expect you to visit us often."

Diana looked as though she were about to cry, too. Sebastian took her hand and gave it a squeeze. "We will, sir," he said. "On one condition." A flurry of protests rose around the table. "You must agree never to weigh Diana again."

"Thank you!" she said, and Minerva cheered.

Her father surrendered with grace. "I announce a new rule. In future married women need not be weighed unless they wish it. It's the same rule I've always had for Mrs. Montrose." He raised his glass to his wife with a look of great affection. "You, miss." He turned to Minerva. "In the hall, after dinner."

"There's an incentive to find a husband, Min," Diana said.

"Minerva, married!" Stephen taunted. "Who'd marry her?"

"I'd like to welcome Sebastian to the family, too." Henry Montrose was a big man, both tall and broad. His incisive intelligence and mordant wit gave him a maturity beyond his twenty-four years. "I wish you years of joy and want to assure you that if you make my sister unhappy I shall dissect your body for anatomical study while you still breathe."

Sebastian wasn't sure he was joking.

Mrs. Montrose, who tended to be lost in her own world of horses and dogs, frowned at her son. "This is no time for threats. I suppose we should be grateful William and Rufus aren't here to disgrace us. Sebastian, the first time you came here I told Diana she ought to marry you. This is the only time she's taken my advice since she was ten years old."

Immensely touched, Sebastian noted that his betrothed was blushing but not, he thought, unhappily. A strange emotion welled in his chest. He couldn't identify it, but he did like it. Then he noticed that Stephen had slipped away from the table and Minerva grinned like a mad thing.

"You're about to find out what mistletoe's for," she crowed.

Twisting his head he saw the youngest Montrose standing behind him and Diana, flourishing a sprig of green with pale berries. "Kiss her, Sebastian!" Minerva ordered. Diana regarded him with huge blue eyes and parted her lips.

This was a Christmas custom he could learn to love. Cupping her flushed cheeks in his palms, he brought his mouth to hers. She tasted of brandy and spices and her own indefinable sweetness that seemed to dispel the bitter memory of earlier kisses and promise a new beginning.

He was sure the kiss, accompanied by a chorus of cheers, jeers, and whistles, lasted longer than was proper for a public mistletoe kiss.

He wished it could last all night.

Sebastian spent much of his last night as a single man perusing the work of Dr. Denman. He learned things about pregnant females he'd rather forget, such as their tendency to suffer from a variety of unappealing conditions like costiveness, hemorrhoids, and dropsy.

But the good doctor was distressingly, maddeningly, inexplicably silent on the only subject that currently interested Sebastian: Could pregnant woman safely indulge in marital relations?

There was a moment of almost unbearable excitement when he read that they were often prone to *depravity of appetite.*

God, he hoped so.

On further reading he learned this promising phrase merely referred to a whimsical desire to consume certain foods.

Dr. Denman, *accoucheur extraordinaire*, had let him down.

But surely, he reasoned, if making love to one's pregnant wife was inadvisable, the doctor would have said so.

Chapter 25

Diana's first wedding, performed with maximum pomp at St. George's Hanover Square, had been very different. So had her feelings on the occasion.

She'd been filled with excitement about becoming a married lady with a title and pin money to buy whatever she wanted. Her bridegroom, though she liked him well enough, seemed almost irrelevant. But what did an eighteen-year-old girl know about marriage, or anything else for that matter?

Today she was too exhausted for an emotion as heightened as excitement. Anxiety and nausea had played havoc with her rest in recent weeks and she'd barely closed her eyes the previous night.

The cause of her sleeplessness stood beside her at the altar, tall and unsmiling. He spoke his vows firmly but without inflexion, and when the time came slipped a gold ring on her third finger. It fit perfectly. Later she learned he'd sent a messenger to Chantal to discover the correct size. And when she had a chance to examine it, she found the ring chased in an exquisite design on the outside and the inner circumference engraved with their names. Not for the first time,

Sebastian revealed himself to be both efficient and thoughtful.

This time the person of her bridegroom filled her thoughts to the exclusion of all else. In many ways he mystified her. She was an open book, standing here in the village where she'd grown up, surrounded by her family and their household staff. She'd attended services in Wallop's ancient parish church almost every week of her life until she left home. Sebastian was alone, without anyone to stand up with him. He'd declined to invite the Duke and Duchess of Hampton, his uncle and aunt, although they were in residence at Mandeville. (Blakeney, she'd learned with relief, had not joined his family for Christmas.)

Whether he wanted one or not, he had a family now. Not only had her eccentric clan embraced him, he had a wife and would soon become a father. Diana began to hope she and Sebastian might be able to put their various transgressions behind them and make something of their marriage.

But she needed to understand what had made her new husband the man he was. Only then could she truly know him.

Once again Sebastian found himself sharing the breakfast parlor with one other person. The morning after his marriage his companion was not his wife. He'd left her sleeping in their shared bed.

Henry Montrose munched his way through a plate heaped with roast beef and eggs while perusing a book propped against the coffeepot.

"Sorry to disturb you, but may I?"

Henry grunted and tilted his book, replacing it

once Sebastian, who decided he liked his brand-new brother-in-law, had poured himself coffee. Given his mood, the company of a grunting, reading male was about all he could abide. He drank his coffee and brooded, until the subject of Henry's volume caught his eye: a treatise on diseases of the lung.

"Do you know the work of Dr. Thomas Denman?" he asked.

Henry closed his book, marking his place with a finger, and held it on his lap. "*Introduction to the Practice of Midwifery*. A respected work on the subject. Why do you ask?"

"Just married, you know. Thought I'd better be informed."

As a student of medicine Henry was likely one of the few men in the world who would find this explanation credible. "Good idea," he said.

Diana had felt very hot last night. Unfortunately she'd also been unconscious, all night. She was already asleep when he entered the bedroom and his deliberately clumsy preparations had failed to waken her. So he'd lain at her side feeling heat pouring off her body while he tried to quell his lust with a recitation of Dr. Denman's symptoms: costiveness, hemorrhoids, dropsy, plus diarrhea, vomiting, and blotchy skin. None of these often contradictory ailments did a thing to lessen his burning desire. He didn't believe he could survive another night like that without either jumping on her like a mad bull or suffering spontaneous combustion.

How could she lie there and sleep when he felt like this? She must, he decided, be unwell.

"According to Denman," he said, "women often

become feverish because of the way their blood thickens during pregnancy."

Henry nodded. "A result of the interruption of the menses."

"Denman advocates bleeding to alleviate the condition."

Henry frowned. "I'm no expert on the subject, but I'd be careful of that. You know Denman's daughter married Croft who followed his father-in-law's precepts."

"Croft?"

"Princess Charlotte's physician. He bled her frequently during her pregnancy."

Sebastian's heart jolted. He'd been following the advice of a man whose ideas had led to the death in childbirth of the Prince Regent's daughter, the heiress to the throne of England.

All his life he'd relied on two infallible sources of logic and common sense: good books and his own sound brain. And now, when it really mattered, when it might literally come down to a matter of life or death, they had failed him. He'd promised to take care of his wife, and instead he might have killed her.

When Diana awoke she first assessed the state of her stomach and found it to be good. This was one of the days she didn't need to hold her head over a basin. A glance at the clock told her she'd slept for almost twelve hours.

She stretched, contemplated rising, and dismissed the notion. Rolling over she noticed a distinct indentation in the pillow on the other side of the bed and caught a whiff of an alien yet familiar scent among the bed linens. Apparently she had not slept alone.

Poor Sebastian, she thought ruefully. What a wedding night! His bride had remained unconscious throughout.

Of course he had no right to expect otherwise, and he'd only joined her because it was expected. The large spare bedchamber had been lovingly prepared by the housekeeper: the finest sheets, a blazing fire of sweet applewood logs, and arrangements of dried flowers and a bowl of potpourri from the still room. Something told her Sebastian had not greatly enjoyed these humble luxuries.

Perhaps she'd make it up to him later, if she continued to feel as well as she did now.

"Come in!" she called. Not Chantal with tea, alas. Her maid wouldn't have knocked. The door opened to admit her husband.

While his morning and evening clothes were now always impeccable, Sebastian looked best when dressed for riding. Which was strange in a way because he wasn't by habit a countryman. His tall, wiry figure in a bottle green coat, buckskins, and top boots made her mouth water.

"How are you this morning?" he asked with the concentrated concern she found touching, though occasionally irksome.

"Excellent. I slept like a top."

"I noticed." She was right: he hadn't appreciated her unbridelike behavior.

She stretched her arms high and gave a little wriggle so the covers fell back, revealing the shape of her breasts beneath her nightgown. "No wonder I slept so well. This is a very soft mattress, don't you agree?"

Sebastian's jaw discernibly clenched.

"But perhaps you don't. You came to bed so late and got up early. Were you uncomfortable?"

She hadn't heard the sound in weeks but under stress he reverted to the grunt, the grunt tinged with a new quality of desperation. Though it was cruel to torture him so, she wanted to laugh.

She also wanted to invite him to join her. But at this time of day there would be maids going about their business upstairs. She couldn't face the idea of servants who'd known her as a child overhearing her engage in marital relations.

Besides, she wasn't quite ready to forgive Sebastian. It was his fault she was in this condition and he deserved to be punished a little more. She wriggled again.

"I have to go to Northumberland," he said, abruptly. "To Saxton Iverley."

She stilled her provocative movements. "When?"

"At once. I have business I should have attended to weeks ago but things came up."

"You might have mentioned this before," she said, dropping her arms.

He put his hands in his pockets and looked at the floor. "I didn't think of it."

"Married people," she explained patiently, "generally inform their spouses of a few basic facts, like which county they plan to stay in. I assumed we'd remain here for a week or two then return to London."

"You can still do that. It's a long journey and I'll travel faster alone."

"You don't wish me to accompany you to your home?" she asked. "I've been looking forward to seeing it."

"No, you haven't, believe me. Saxton Iverley is not a place you want to spend the winter, or any other season for that matter."

She pulled up her covers to her chin then changed her mind. Her mind spinning, she got down from the bed, pulled on a dressing gown and stood to face him, hands on her hips.

"It's going to look very odd, you going off after the wedding and leaving me behind. I know neither of us would have chosen this, but I thought we were managing to rub along well enough."

Better than well enough. He wanted her, she wasn't mistaken about that, but that meant nothing. He was a man and men always wanted to bed her. More important, his solicitude for her health and well-being had moved her, even when the precepts of Dr. Denman drove her to distraction.

Apparently she was wrong: He didn't care enough to wish for her company.

"You need to see a doctor," he said.

"They must have doctors in Northumberland."

"Not good ones." A feeble excuse.

"I am perfectly healthy, aside from the obvious disadvantages of my condition. I have no doubt that women by the thousand give birth to children in Northumberland every year."

"I'd rather you stayed safely with your own family. Your father already knows you are with child and you should tell your mother."

"You told Papa? That was high-handed."

Sebastian folded his arms defensively. "He is delighted to be expecting a grandchild."

The sense of well-being that started the day with such promise began to unravel. "I don't wish to spend the next seven months being weighed by my father every ten minutes and listening to my mother describe the childbirth experiences of foxhounds."

"He won't weigh you again . . ." She cut him off with a glare. "And you could ask Henry for his advice."

"I'm not going to take medical advice from my little brother."

"He's older than you."

"By *eleven months*. He has barely started to shave."

Sebastian looked at her in bafflement. "But they love you. And you love them!"

"Of course I love them but that doesn't mean I want to live with them. I'm a grown-up woman with two houses of my own. If my husband doesn't want to share his with me, then I shall just have to make my own way."

"You're behaving irrationally."

Diana knew that once a man accused a woman of being irrational there was no point in further argument. The combined reasoning of every great philosopher and scientist in history wouldn't convince him to change his mind.

"Go!" she said, flinging her arm toward the door.

"Go to Northumberland. Don't worry about me. I shall stay here a little longer then I'll decide what to do. I shall keep you informed in which county I am residing."

"You will be careful, won't you?"

"If you are so concerned, stay with me, or let me come with you."

He turned away. "You're better off without me."

Abandon hope, all ye who enter here.

The first time Sebastian returned to Saxton Iverley from Winchester after being introduced to the works of Dante, he realized the Italian poet had given voice to his dread. The words might as well have been carved along the frieze of the giant portico.

For weeks he'd received increasingly urgent letters from Northumberland demanding his presence there. His excuse for ignoring them had been his responsibility to his wife. He could no longer justify his absence.

For a few days at Wallop Hall he'd been happy. He'd thought himself so damn clever, learning all there was to know about his future wife's pregnancy and watching over her. Not only was he keeping his promise to Minerva and Mr. Montrose, he was being a good husband.

What did he know? There was absolutely nothing in his experience that had taught him how to make a woman happy. Diana didn't want him as a husband, and never had. Now he knew she didn't need him, either.

As he rode up the drive away from Wallop Hall he felt a chill that owed nothing to the frost in the air.

Compared to the warmth and affection that imbued
the Montroses' house, the massive stone monument
of the Iverleys seemed, more than ever, like a section
of hell, one of the frozen bits. He'd been brought there
at the age of six to fulfill a purpose and for the past
few years he'd tried to escape it. Now was the time
to embrace his fate.

Chapter 26

"**A**re you sure this is wise, my love?" Her father's whiskers quivered as his jaw worked with concern. "Sebastian said you intended to follow him north later."

That was the polite fiction they'd agreed to use with her parents, who were visibly distressed by the early departure of her bridegroom.

"That was yesterday. Today *is* later."

"I don't understand. What business was so urgent that he couldn't take the time to escort his pregnant wife?"

"As I explained, I shall take the journey in very easy stages and Chantal will look after me. I shall hire outriders in Shrewsbury so there isn't the least reason for you to worry."

"Let her alone, William," said his spouse. "She's with child, not at death's door. Just because she is increasing a woman doesn't have to be treated like an ornament. I certainly never did."

Diana's mother had greeted the news of her pregnancy with a delighted snort and a great deal of information about broodmares of the equine variety.

"A woman belongs with her husband, not her

parents," she concluded, an opinion that almost made Diana order her carriage to London instead of Northumberland.

Instead, since much against her better judgment she agreed with her mother, she and Chantal climbed into her carriage, with a minimum of luggage but every fur she possessed, and headed through the late December damp for the frozen north.

She was not going to let Sebastian avoid her for the remainder of her pregnancy, and perhaps beyond. If they were to make anything of this marriage, begun under such inauspicious circumstances, they were going to start by living in the same house.

Gray clouds swirled like a stormy ocean as the carriage passed through the gatehouse into a broad treeless avenue. Diana braved the cold to lean out of the window. If the icy wind blowing from the North Sea hadn't taken her breath away, the first glimpse of her new home would have. She'd never seen a larger house. Saxton Iverley dwarfed the ducal splendor of Mandeville.

A tall central block with a massive columned pediment dominated sprawling wings that truly defined the meaning of that common architectural term. The house resembled a giant bird of prey: dark, grim, and ready to swoop down on its victim.

The impression that she had wandered into the plot of a novel grew once she entered a front door built for a race of giants to find herself in a chamber designed to oppress the spirits of the pluckiest heroine. The three-story hall climbed in ranks of somber roman colonnades, barely visible in the afternoon gloom of a northern winter. Not a carpet, a tapestry, a painting, nor a splash of gilt relieved the iron gray stone of the arches and the vaulted ceiling. Saxton Iverley wasn't much more than one hundred years old and the architecture was classical rather than Gothic, but Diana had seen cozier castles and more welcoming ruined monasteries.

It was also freezing. As the great door clanged shut the sea gale at least was excluded. Otherwise there was little perceptible improvement in the temperature.

"I am Lady Iverley," she said to the footman who had opened the door. "Please inform His Lordship that I have arrived."

The servant, a young man who wore the same old-fashioned livery as the footman at the Iverley house in St. James's Square, said something. What it was Diana had no idea. He spoke in an accent or dialect so thick she could make out not a single word. From his face she gathered their incomprehension was mutual.

"Perhaps you could summon the house steward. Or the butler. Or the housekeeper," she suggested, slowly and clearly.

He nodded at the word butler, said something that might have been "Mr. Hedley," and left.

"*Mon dieu.*" Chantal's oath, or prayer, came out in a whisper. Diana doubted it would last, but for the moment her opinionated maid was silenced.

The two of them had ample time to further examine their surroundings. Grateful for her furs, Diana noticed that despite the pervasive gloom, the proportions of the hall were excellent and the design rather beautiful. With a few hundred candles burning, or sunshine coming through the huge arched windows, it would be magnificent. Meanwhile frost seeped from the black and white marble floor up through the soles of her boots.

Finally an extremely old servant in an ancient white wig and clothes of the style worn fifty years earlier limped into the hall.

"My lady." When he bowed Diana wanted to put an arm out to make sure he didn't topple over. "We weren't expecting you," he said, his accent thick but thankfully understandable.

"My letter must have been delayed. Please inform His Lordship that I have arrived," she said again.

"His Lordship divint in the hoose. He's doon the mine." At least, she thought that's what he said. "I am Hedley. I'm butler here."

"Have you been at Saxton Iverley a long time, Hedley?"

"Sixty years, fifty as butler."

"You must know so much about the history of the house and I look forward to hearing your stories. But for now, please take me somewhere warm, while my bedchamber is prepared."

Hedley appeared uneasy. "I don't know where a lady could stay."

Diana remembered that Sebastian's great-uncle, the previous viscount, had never married. The house had lacked a mistress for some decades. "All I require for now is a bed and a fire. My dresser, Miss Dupont, will direct the maids preparing the room and see to my luggage."

"Well. There are rooms next to His Lordship's."

"That will be quite acceptable. Now take me to whichever room has a fire."

"No fire in the drawing room." He scratched his chin and pondered some more while Diana's feet turned to blocks of ice. "Nor in the morning room. Nor in the blue saloon yet."

"Which room has His Lordship been using? Surely you must keep a fire burning there in this weather."

Hedley smiled. "The library?"

Of course. Where else? "Show me to the library, then send for some tea and ask the housekeeper to attend me there."

After half an hour the tea appeared but not the housekeeper. In keeping with what she'd so far seen, the library was constructed along monumental lines. Unlike the room where she'd bearded Sebastian at St. James's Square, it was a mess. Books by the thousand were stuck into shelves without regard to order. Many were upside down or on their sides. Volumes and papers were piled on chairs, tables, and on the floor. There were also a number of strange mechanical devices in varying states of completion, miscellaneous tools, coils, springs, and odd pieces of metal. Diana smiled as she realized the room, despite its massive scale, reminded her of her father's study at Wallop. The late Lord Iverley and Mr. Montrose had corresponded, she recalled. They must have had much in common.

At one end of the room a large ceramic stove

emitted a most welcome warmth. Diana stood near it thawing her hands. She'd never seen one quite like it and guessed it was of foreign manufacture. It was a blessedly efficient device, so effective that after a few minutes she discarded her outer garments and drew back from the source of heat. The only unencumbered chair in the room stood beside a desk that was free of heaped volumes, drifting foolscap or twisted metal. Instead it held papers tidily held down by paperweights and a pile of correspondence. Diana flipped through the letters and found her own, unopened. Whatever occupied her husband away from home, it had kept him from attending to his mail for some days.

The incomprehensible footman returned after an hour or so. She managed to discover that his name was George and he would guide her to her rooms. The heat in the library had made her sleepy and she looked forward to taking a nap in a soft bed. The journey through endless arched stone corridors dispelled her comfort. By the time George opened the door to her room she was thoroughly chilled and the sight that greeted her did nothing to raise her spirits. If this was what passed at Saxton Iverley for feminine décor, she hated to think of how the men must live.

A huge chamber, lavishly appointed with the inevitable gray stone, contained an old-fashioned fourposter bed with crewelwork curtains that, in addition to being so faded their original color was lost, appeared to have provided square meals for generations of moth. Aside from a couple of wooden chairs with rush seats, the only piece of furniture was a massive and hideous wardrobe-chest combination made from some kind of dark wood and plentifully embellished with crude carvings. Diana, who had studied such things, estimated there wasn't an object in the room less than two hundred years old and thus much older than the house itself.

The floor was uncarpeted and the large windows lacked curtains, with only wooden shutters provided to block out light and the wind whistling through the cracks. Diana crossed the endless stone floor and saw the room faced east and offered a view of the sea. Under normal circumstances she would have been delighted. She and Tobias often went to Brighton in the summer and she loved the seashore. But the North Sea in winter was a far cry from summer on the south coast: wild, dark, and vaguely threatening.

Diana began to understand Sebastian's decision not to bring her to this benighted spot. She'd taken it as an insult but perhaps he'd been doing her a favor.

"Why haven't you lit any candles?" she asked Chantal, who radiated displeasure with every movement as she unpacked Diana's underclothes.

"Tallow."

The single word was enough. With Diana's delicate stomach the gloom was preferable to the smell of cheap candles. She shuddered and walked over to the fireplace where a healthy glow beckoned. Within a few feet she stopped and clutched her belly. A particularly pungent, sulfurous odor drifted from the burning coal.

"The basin, Chantal," she gasped, lurching backward into the far corner of the room to get the stench out of her nostrils.

Alas, the room was not yet ready for a lady in an

interesting condition. She cast up her accounts in the chamber pot.

"Ring for Hedley," she ordered, huddling in a far corner of the room, as far from the noxious fumes as she could manage. "And order some firewood. And some wax candles."

"No bell."

Of course not. Nothing she'd yet seen at her husband's mansion led her to expect such a basic amenity.

"Mr. Hedley told me to tell you . . ."

"Not now." Accustomed since childhood to the Northumbrian dialect, Sebastian had no trouble understanding George, but this evening he wasn't in the mood to hear the details of a trivial domestic problem. "I need a bath as soon as possible. I'll be in the library."

Cold, hungry, tired, and above all dirty, he wondered why his great-uncle had never turned his mechanical ingenuity to the problem of an efficient hot water supply. In some houses, Mandeville for one, copper boilers had been installed on the upper floors. At Saxton Iverley the water was often cool by the time it had been carried from the kitchens in the west wing to the bedrooms, one reason why Sebastian hadn't moved from his own rooms in the west to his uncle's suite in the east. But Uncle Iverley had never been much concerned with personal cleanliness.

As he strode down the long, frigid corridor to the library, he thought about Diana's London house: new and appointed with every luxury. No waiting for a bath there, he'd wager. At once a vision of Diana naked in a tub entered his brain, the kind of invasion that occurred far too often, despite his best efforts to banish them. Every feeling of grief, frustration, and guilt about the events of the past three days unified in fury at Diana, and himself, too. Had he been attending to his responsibilities at Saxton instead of playing games of lust and revenge, tragedy might have been avoided.

Nevertheless, a flare of emotion ignited his heart when he discovered the subject of his reluctant thoughts in the library. A wild hope battled his anger and he stopped at the doorway to prevent himself from rushing forward to embrace her.

"What are you doing here?" The words came out more accusation than question.

She rose from one of the hard library chairs and set aside a book. As usual she epitomized a sleek, opulent femininity that couldn't have presented a greater contrast to her surroundings.

"I preferred not to announce to the world that my husband left me the day after our wedding," she said, her words as unruffled as her appearance.

Foolish to think she'd follow him for any other reason. He mustn't forget that his wife would rather have married the heir to a dukedom. Her standing in the polite world was important to her and he'd threatened her pride and her reputation.

He ventured farther into the room and noted the pallor of her complexion, a hint of shadow around the eyes. "You're not looking well. You shouldn't have made the journey."

"I'm merely tired."

"For God's sake, Diana." Anxiety for her health

made him snappish. "There's a freezing rain outside and the roads are a hellish mire. You could have been killed traveling in this weather."

"I survived. However, I have to say that you live in the world's most uncomfortable house."

He ignored the tinge of ironic humor in her tone and concentrated on the complaint. "I warned you. You should have stayed with your family where you would have been warm and safe. This is no place for a lady."

"You humiliated me in front of my family by leaving. I told them we'd agreed I would follow slowly."

"And you didn't think to discuss this with me?"

"Naturally I would never make an important decision about my whereabouts without asking for the opinion of my husband." The slightest arch of her eyebrow managed to convey both innocence and insolence. "But I couldn't ask for your permission because you'd already left."

"I don't believe you. You made up your mind to follow me even as I expressly forbade it."

Her only response was to raise her brows higher.

"Damn it! You should have told me."

"So that you could stop me?"

"Yes!"

Her composure seemed to grow in proportion to his own agitation. "That's why I preferred not to discuss it. You were quite incapable of rational thought."

"Irrational! Me?"

"There's no need to shout."

"I am not shouting."

"You are shouting and you are being completely unreasonable."

Sebastian clutched his head in disbelief. She gave him a sickly sweet smile. "I might have expected a warmer greeting from my husband but I can see you're not in the mood." She punctuated her remarks with an insincere curtsey. "I am pleased to see you, my lord, but for the moment the pleasure of your company has worn thin. I believe I shall retire to my room and take supper there."

Before he could think of a suitable riposte she swept out of the room and closed the door behind her with a ladylike hint of unnecessary force. Irrational! Everyone, everyone male that is, knew that men were rational and females by their nature, the opposite. Diana seemed to have no grasp of this basic fact, which only proved the thesis.

The door opened again. Hah! She was back and he could set her straight.

"Let me tell you . . . Oh. It's you, Hedley. You could have let me know Lady Iverley had arrived." Which was unfair. Clearly George had tried to inform him and he'd refused to listen. Damnation, he was beginning to behave like a woman himself.

The old man had known him far too long to heed his show of temper. "Her Ladyship has made certain requests, my lord. Am I to take my orders from her?"

"Of course," Sebastian said, then caution intervened. "Within reason. What requests?"

"A gross of wax candles. She does not like the smell of tallow."

Sebastian wasn't fond of it himself. His uncle,

who appeared to have had no sense of smell, had a penchant for petty economies and the use of cheap candles was one of them.

"Very well," he said. "What else?"

"She has requested firewood, my lord. But we have none on the estate."

"Of course we don't. We live on top of a coal-field."

"Shall I order some?"

"Certainly not."

While he could appreciate and share Diana's liking for comfort, burning firewood was a ridiculous luxury. She'd followed him to Northumberland against his orders and in this matter, at least, he determined to remain firm. She needed to learn that when you lived near Newcastle, you got your heat from coal.

This assertion of will somewhat improved his mood. He'd tried to spare her the rigors of northern life and he'd ignored him. She would have to bear the consequences. And after all they were wed and needed to find a way to coexist. He remembered his earlier vision of their marriage, before her great betrayal: that he would continue to live his life without much alteration. Unfortunately the death of his uncle meant that life would have to take place, much of the time, at Saxton rather than London, but otherwise the principle was the same.

Of course the main advantage of his original plan was sharing her bed. Having Diana in the same house, even with a couple of furlongs of corridor between them, would put a severe strain on his self-control.

* * *

The outrage in Sebastian's voice when she'd accused him of irrationality had been delightful. Nothing else about the encounter was remotely satisfactory and she wondered if she should have been more conciliatory. But much as she might wish to attain satisfactory relations with her husband, she refused to abase herself to do it. He was going to have to meet her halfway. At least halfway.

The really maddening result of her dramatic exit from the library was she'd left the only room in the house that was, thanks to the ceramic stove, both warm and free of the nauseating smell of coal.

Any hope that the firewood had been delivered was quashed when she found her room freezing. The tallow candles, while disagreeable, didn't make her sick. Only the special quality of Northumbrian coal affected her so.

"I'm going to get into bed," she told Chantal. "It's the only way to keep warm."

"This is a very strange house," her maid told her while unfastening her gown and dressing her in a flannel nightdress over several layers of shift and petticoat. "I cannot understand the language here. Is it English?"

"I barely understand it myself. Did you manage to find the housekeeper?"

"That is the most strange thing. *Il n'y a pas de femmes.*"

"No women? You mean no housekeeper?"

"No women at all. No female servants."

This was unusual, and extravagant. Menservants

were not only paid more than maids, their hiring was also subject to a tax.

Saxton Iverley seemed understaffed for such a huge house and she'd assumed it was the result of a dearth of funds, as evidenced by economies like tallow candles.

"Who does the cleaning? The laundry?"

"Men. All of them. I looked. You and I, milady, are the only women in this whole place."

Chapter 27

Sebastian didn't lay eyes on Diana again for over twenty-four hours. After another heartbreaking day at the colliery, he drove into town to dine at an inn and interview a physician recommended by the secretary of the Literary and Philosophical Society of Newcastle Upon Tyne. Dr. Harrison, who seemed an enlightened man and disavowed the use of leeches on expectant mothers, agreed to call upon Lady Iverley the next day.

Having assured himself that her health would be overseen by a competent professional, he was resigned to her presence at Saxton Iverley. Then Hedley raised the vexed topic of firewood. The old butler, obviously taken with the new Lady Iverley whom he termed a bonny lass, seemed tolerant of her desire to coddle herself.

" 'Twould be better for the bairn," he explained.

Sebastian didn't ask how the old fellow had discovered his wife's condition. "Absolutely not," he said. "I shall speak to her about it myself."

Without pausing to change his mud-splattered boots, he set out for the east wing. On the way he met Diana's French maid who gave him a dirty look along with the barest excuse for a curtsey. A muttered comment that contained the French words for *firewood*, *husband*, and *miserly* hardly improved his temper as he burst into the long-unused chamber of the lady of the house, next door to his uncle's deserted rooms.

He had, he realized, never set foot in it before. If he expected a room designed for female occupation to possess a measure of softness and elegance in its furnishings, he was quickly disillusioned. The old-fashioned bed appeared mean in the huge, almost empty chamber. Diana, huddled against the pillows under a mound of blankets with her fur-lined cloak on top, looked tiny and miserable.

"God preserve me from stubborn women!" he roared. "It must be close to freezing in this room."

He stamped over to the cold fireplace and noted that the coals in the grate had been deliberately dowsed.

"Listen, Diana, and listen well," he said, crossing the room to stand next to the bed and glare down at her. She sank further into the nest of bedclothes. "We are in Tyneside here. The principal product of the countryside is coal and coal is what we use for heating. Men have died bringing coal up from the depths of the earth so that you and I and thousands like us can be warm. I don't care what you became accustomed to with your nabob husband, or how much he spoiled you. I am going to light the coals in that fireplace and you will like it. You shall not endanger your health or that of our child by your capricious fancies."

That, he saw with satisfaction, had silenced her.

She stared back at him, her blue eyes huge and a little frightened. Then they glistened.

Hell! He hadn't intended to make her cry, merely to learn that in this house his word was law.

"Unwell," she croaked.

"You are unwell?" he said in a softer voice. "Hardly surprising given the temperature in this room. You are very foolish, you know."

"No, but I will be if you light that fire." Her voice strengthened as she pulled herself upright. "The coal made me sick. Chantal had to extinguish the fire because I couldn't stop vomiting. I don't know why," she continued miserably, "but it smells like sulfur."

Damnation! He knew about nausea from her own account, not to mention Dr. Denman's. And Saxton coal, which was indeed high in sulfur, did emit strong fumes. Once again he'd proven himself an incompetent when it came to his wife's care. Since Saxton Iverley was located on a windswept treeless bluff, there was almost no timber on the estate. He looked about the room in desperation, as though hoping for the miraculous materialization of a basket of logs.

"Don't move," he said. "I'll be back directly."

Whatever Diana expected, it wasn't the reappearance of Sebastian with a large axe slung over his shoulder.

"What do you think of that?" he asked, pointing at the wardrobe, or whatever it was. Chantal called it the *objet incroyable*.

"Hideous," she said from the bed, "though not without its uses. It holds a lot of clothes."

Opening a drawer, he removed a handful of lacy

undergarments, which he looked at with a glimmer of interest before tossing them onto the floor.

"I'll find you something else," he said as he removed his neck cloth, coat, and waistcoat and hung them over the back of a chair. He carried the empty drawer over to the fireplace. Two sweeps of his axe and it was kindling.

Two more drawers received similar treatment and in no time he had the dry wood crackling in the fireplace. But he didn't stop there. Without any appearance of haste, or even much effort, he proceeded to reduce a large piece of furniture to firewood.

As the room grew warmer, Diana emerged from her layers of blankets and sat cross-legged on the end of the bed, the better to admire the view. Sebastian might appear slender, but the casual way he swung the heavy axe gave ample proof of the muscles she knew dwelt under his shirt, especially when the sweat brought on by his labor caused the shirt to stick to his shoulders and back. Diana's eyes widened; she sucked air into her dry mouth.

Once he'd finished with the easily removable parts, he started hacking at the solid frame. He worked at a steady pace, occasionally grunting when he raised the axe above his head to tackle the upper sections. With exquisite precision he broke it down to a neat pile of boards.

Whatever Sebastian undertook, it occurred to her, he did well. Especially after a little practice.

Which was a useful attribute in a husband.

He finished the job and built up the fire to a merry blaze.

"There," he said. "That should keep you warm

tonight. Hedley will find some firewood tomorrow." He looked at her. "How do you feel?"

She felt quite extraordinarily well. She was also dressed less becomingly than she would have thought possible. Her pose on the bed should have been a suggestive, even an enticing one. Clothed as she was in a high-necked, long-sleeved flannel nightgown topped with a heavy shawl, and a pair of woolen stockings, it was hardly surprising that Sebastian regarded her with a notable lack of ardor.

"Quite excellent," she said, shedding the shawl and wondering if she could loosen the nightgown without being too obvious about it.

Much to her regret, Sebastian pulled on his waistcoat. "You should get back into bed again," he said. "You need to rest."

"I've been resting all day. Stay and talk to me."

Before she had a chance to invite him to join her in the four-poster, he sat in a chair a few feet away. His slouched position with booted legs a foot apart revealed the cords of his thigh muscles in tight buckskin breeches. The column of his neck and a hint of chest emerged from his unbuttoned shirt and waistcoat. His exertions had made stray locks of hair, usually swept neatly back, stick to his frowning brow. He looked unapproachable, even a little dangerous.

"What did you mean when you said men had died?" she asked.

His expression changed to one of grief. "An accident at the Saxton colliery last week killed three miners."

"I'm sorry." Her condolence seemed inadequate, her own concern with a little queasiness trivial in comparison. "Does that happen often?"

"More often than it should. Coalmining is a perilous undertaking."

"What happened?"

"A flood. Water broke through from an abandoned seam at a higher level and poured down though the main shaft. We were fortunate it was the end of the day and nearly everyone out. Just three miners were caught, poor devils. We brought up the bodies today."

"Did you go down the mine yourself?"

"Not far beneath the surface. But I have been working with mining engineers to detect other potential hazards before they lead to disaster."

"What can you do?"

"These abandoned shafts are a well-known danger. They can be blocked or drained. My great-uncle was always interested in innovations and he made sure miners had the latest safety lamps. But in the last year or two he was old and didn't pay enough attention. I should have spent the last few months making up for his neglect."

He had no need to state what he had been doing instead. The last remnant of Diana's resentment slipped away. She understood that Sebastian blamed himself for these unintended and tragic consequences of his revenge, a punishment worse than any she could inflict. Instead she yearned to console him.

"You can't be certain that you would have prevented this particular accident," she said, "but if you need funds to invest in improvements to the mine, please feel free to draw on my capital."

He stared at her. "Why would I need your money?"

"There's no cause for shame. The rumor among the *ton* was that you are rich, but as soon as I saw the state of your London house I suspected. The lack of furnishing and modernization here confirms it. Obviously your estate is not prosperous. Did the building of this vast place ruin your family?"

Genuine amusement restored his disposition. "You couldn't be more wrong. The Saxton coalfield is hugely productive. Don't you know? You've wed one of the richest men in England."

"Oh?" she said. "In that case, why is this house so dismal?" She poked the nearest bed curtain, raising a cloud of dust. "Look at this. Shreds! I swear this stuff was manufactured in the reign of Elizabeth. Most of the furniture, such as even exists, is older than the house itself and even more uncomfortable. And the state rooms are barely furnished at all."

"You are correct in one sense. The first viscount overextended himself when he built Saxton Iverley. I gather he was persuaded by an architect of overweening ambition to attempt to surpass Blenheim and Castle Howard."

"And succeeded. The size of the place is astonishing. I won't even need to go outdoors for exercise."

"The interior was unfinished and the furnishings left to the next generation, once the supply of cash regenerated."

"Don't you think the richest man in England could afford a carpet or two by now?"

"Assuredly. But while I can't speak for his

predecessor, I can only tell you that my great-uncle, who held the title of Viscount Iverley for sixty years, never cared for such things. In later years he only left the library for the occasional meeting of the Literary and Philosophical Society. Most days he didn't trouble to get dressed."

And this man, Diana thought, had been responsible for Sebastian's upbringing. "Why are there no female servants in the house?" she asked.

"There has never been a woman at Saxton for as long as I recall. You and your maid may be the first to set foot in the house for fifty years or more."

"Doesn't that strike you as odd?"

"Uncle Iverley didn't hold with women," Sebastian said stiffly. "He didn't trust the female sex."

"I've heard the same thing said about you. Did he teach you to think as he did?"

"I draw my own conclusions based on experience."

Diana winced. Not only had Sebastian been inexperienced with women, he'd lacked all knowledge of the sex save the prejudices of a crazy old man. Little wonder his reaction to her bet with Blakeney had been disproportionate to the offense. She slid off the bed and went over to him. "You are an intelligent man, Sebastian," she said, crouching down beside him and placing a hand on his arm. "You must know there is little truth in generalities when applied to the human condition. I fear your uncle may have been affected by some unfortunate experience of his own."

"He was a man of reason. Do you know, before I came to live with him, I had a reputation for clumsiness. I would often break things and make my mother cry."

"Your mother?"

He ignored her soft interruption. "The first time it happened here, my uncle took me to Newcastle and had a glassmaker grind me a pair of lenses. I do not believe I have walked into anything since."

Diana had the feeling he had confided something important. "Why did a young boy live with an elderly great-uncle instead of with his mother? You must have missed her dreadfully."

Abruptly he rose to his feet, shaking off her touch and almost causing her to lose balance. "Here," he said, stretching down to help her up. Once she was standing he dropped her hand and stepped back, putting a few feet's distance between them in a manner that had to be deliberate. "It's late and you should go to bed. I'll send your maid to you."

She opened her mouth to argue then changed her mind. Sebastian might be a grown man, but temperamentally he was skittish as a colt. To bring him to her side would require subtlety, patience, and a metaphorical handful of sugar.

Chapter 28

The three most respected mining engineers in the Tyne—Sebastian had refused to take the word of one alone—pronounced the colliery safe. The dead men were buried and their widows compensated, financially at least. Sebastian bathed and dressed without bothering with a neck cloth or coat, looking forward to dining with a good book and a measure of serenity.

Not that true peace of mind was possible when *she* remained under the same roof. Last time they'd been in the same room it had taken a supreme effort of self-control not to leap on his wife like a wild beast. The swinging of the axe and the wanton destruction of furniture had aroused something primitive and savage. Sebastian regarded himself as a man of reason and restraint, the product of an advanced level of civilization, not at all the sort of person who would fling a woman over his shoulder and ravish her in a cave. Yet the very thought of having Diana alone in a cave drove him to a painful level of arousal.

It might, he considered, be worth the regression to the condition of his feral ancestors if the little woman would, sated by the attentions of her virile mate, relapse exhausted onto a pile of furs and *not say a word*.

But their last conversation had made him profoundly uneasy. He hadn't forgotten Tarquin's half joking reference to a woman's desire to see into a man's soul. He had the sense that Diana wanted to do just that, to understand him, to make him talk about subjects that were far better left alone.

The memoirs of the bookseller James Lackington was an old favorite and a reliably soothing companion. He collected the book from the library and made his way to the small dining room where he and his uncle had always taken their meals. The table was bare. What on earth . . . ?

Hedley, hard on his heels, explained.

"She wants me to dine in her rooms?" Sebastian almost shouted. "Why?"

"Her Ladyship cannit wey abide the smell in the dining room."

That wasn't the question Sebastian wanted Hedley to answer. But even in this household of men, asking why a woman would wish to dine with her husband might seem unnecessary. Perhaps especially in a household of men. For the first time in his life he wondered what his servants thought about the domestic arrangements at Saxton. And how they catered to their baser urges.

"Were you ever wed, Hedley?"

"There, Master Sebastian, you know His Lordship divint allow married men in the house." The butler, who must have been eighty if he was a day, grinned to reveal a respectable set of teeth.

"Did you ever wish to?"

"Wishes bain't horses. You're a lucky man. Her Ladyship's a bonny lass."

She was indeed. Much too bonny for Sebastian's peace of mind. He should, however, find out what she wanted. And he needed to eat. And he was quite capable of resisting any discussion he found distasteful. There was always the possibility that her plans would demand more action than talk on his part.

He'd never have recognized my lady's bedchamber. It might as well have been in a different house. Nothing like it had ever been seen at Saxton Iverley.

For a start, the atmosphere was blissfully warm and redolent of burning wood. And unlike every other part of the house, nothing was gray and there was almost no stone visible. Instead Sebastian walked into a treasure house of color and opulence that would have impressed an oriental potentate. Once the initial bedazzlement faded, he began to take in the details: the walls covered ceiling to floor with fabric hangings depicting exotic scenes of life in Persia or India; the dilapidated bed curtains replaced with silk of deepest ocean blue, figured with a riot of flowers in reds, pinks, and greens; matching curtains drawn against the windows, excluding the dreary evidence of Saxton's site and season and enhancing the illusion that he had walked into a far-off country of eternal summer and magnificent luxury.

As he ventured into the room his feet encountered the muffled softness of thick carpets. Disoriented, he sought the denizen of this magnificent cave—his lips twitched at the unconscious phrasing of his thought—and found her on the floor, next to the fireplace, seated on a large pillow of pale yellow silk embroidered all over with giant red poppies.

"Come and join me," she said with a brilliant smile. "I thought we'd have a picnic."

"Does that mean we have to eat on the floor?" A table, covered with a gaudy cloth, had been set up near the fire and bore a number of covered dishes.

"We could sit on those hard chairs but I don't recommend it. Besides, it's more fun this way."

More pillows were scattered on the carpet and it didn't escape his notice that accepting Diana's invitation would bring him close to her, within easy touching distance. He settled himself into a comfortable position, half lying on his side, propped up on one elbow like a nobleman of the Roman empire. Her perfume mingled with the fragrance of the fire and the subtle scent of top quality wax candles. She wore a full-length robe buttoned from knee level all the way to the chin, and he enjoyed thinking about what the garment concealed. Her hair was pinned up but he fancied the arrangement was looser, less ornate than her usual style.

"Wine?" She filled him a glass from a decanter.

He took a sip. "Very nice."

"Hedley has a few treasures hidden away in the cellar. This claret is fifty years old."

"Either you have managed to find unsuspected riches in the Newcastle shops, or the wine isn't the only treasure you discovered." He gestured around the room with his glass. "How did you manage it?"

"I'll tell you while we eat. You must be very hungry.

George, would you bring us the food? You may lay out the dishes in front of us but leave the sweets on the table."

The footman, whose presence Sebastian hadn't noticed, did as he was asked, then Diana dismissed him.

Sebastian began to feel a low hum of excitement about the outcome of the evening, especially once he noticed Diana's healthy appetite. Not a hint of nausea. The dinner, consisting of a variety of foods that could be eaten with the fingers, was excellent.

"If picnics are always this good," he said, biting into a tiny meat pie and savoring the flaky pastry and spiced filling, "I think I like them."

"Haven't you ever had one before?"

"I don't believe so."

"Indoor picnics are my favorite kind. Outdoors can be lovely but inside one is seldom bothered by high winds, insects, or passing showers."

Something caught at his memory. "I think I did have a picnic once, when I was very young. I scarcely recall."

"Where?"

"It must have been in one of the London parks. That's where I lived before I came to Saxton."

"Did your mother take you?"

"My nurse," he said curtly, awaiting the inevitable interrogation.

She didn't press for details but talked about alfresco meals of her own childhood. He always enjoyed hearing about life among the Montroses.

"The greatest drawback to a Montrose picnic is the dogs. A good deal of vigilance is required if you are to have anything to eat at all. Tobias didn't like eating outside unless he had a fully appointed table, chairs, and half a dozen footmen. Not truly a picnic to my mind, but after losing your luncheon to a pack of foxhounds you begin to see the attraction."

"I like eating on the floor." Sebastian didn't want to be anything like Diana's first husband. Moreover his head was less than two feet away from Diana's lap and he enjoyed watching her slip morsels of food between her lips.

"Tell me how you obtained the wherewithal to create a lair worthy of a Turkish pasha."

"Not Turkish. Most of these cloths are Indian. I found them in the attics, or rather Hedley directed me to them. Great bales and crates full. There's plenty more up there, enough to furnish much of the house."

"I had no idea. I wonder how long it's been there."

"Didn't you ever go up to the attics?"

"Not that I can recall."

Diana shook her head. "This huge house and you never explored it all. It's the most fascinating place. I've scarcely begun."

"Are you well enough to climb up all those stairs? It must be cold."

She waved aside his concern. "I'm well as long as I keep out of any room with an open coal fire. In fact I feel better than I have since I realized I was with child." Placing her hand on her stomach she sighed happily. "I've eaten a huge dinner. I think I'll lie down."

She took her time about it, moving dishes out of

the way and adjusting several cushions until they were positioned to her liking. She ended up in a pose similar to his own, facing him, less than two feet of carpet between them.

He couldn't mistake her intentions, could he? Yet she was still very thoroughly dressed. He kept his eyes glued to her face, trying to read her expression.

"The one problem with a midwinter picnic," she said, "is the lack of the right fruits. I would so love some strawberries or raspberries now."

Sebastian's mouth watered at the notion of red berry juice staining Diana's lips. He got to his feet. "Let me see what we have in the way of sweets."

"I haven't visited the kitchen yet but I understand the cook is a man. He's very good."

"Northumbrian born and bred. He doesn't cook anything foreign." He returned to his place with a small bowl. "I cannot offer you fresh berries, but perhaps a cherry preserved in honey and brandy would do."

He selected one, swollen with the sweet liquor and of a red so dark it was almost black. Taking it delicately between finger and thumb he brought it to her mouth. He rubbed the plump fruit to and fro across her lips then pushed it in as they parted.

"Cook always removes the stones," he whispered.

Her mouth closed over the sweetmeat and, for a moment before he pulled them out, his finger and thumb. He sensed her bite into the cherry, savor the taste, swallow. Then she licked her lips.

Right then Sebastian made up his mind. He wasn't going to wait for Diana to lead the way or even to signal her willingness. He was sick of waiting. This time he would be the seducer and he would use every scrap of knowledge lent him by limited experience, reading, and his own imagination to make sure Diana enjoyed it. Last time he'd wanted to please her so she would regret it when the act wasn't repeated. This time he must make sure she wished for frequent, constant, and lifelong repetition.

"Would you like another?"

From the way she closed her eyes and offered him her parted lips he gathered the answer was yes. He fed her a couple more cherries. She made little appreciative "mmm" sounds as she ate them so he decided to offer her a different taste. As soon as his mouth touched hers, she placed her arms around his neck and took him with her as she relaxed on her back among the silken poppies.

They kissed for a long time. He bent over her, holding her face between his hands, saluting her forehead, her nose, the pulses at her temples, the clean soft line of her jaw. But mostly her mouth. Honey, brandy, fruit, and her unique essence mingled to madden and enchant him and impelled him to drive her to the same insanity. He'd learned enough about kissing now to know that the more you did it, the better you did it and the more you wanted it.

That rule, he guessed, didn't just apply to kissing. The fact that Diana's robe covered every inch of her flesh save hands and face began to frustrate him. Without releasing her mouth he groped for the buttons and found them to be both small and numerous.

"Damn it, woman," he muttered as he pulled back

and got up on his knees the better to work. "What is this garment? Whose devilish idea was it to use a thousand buttons? Do you mind if I rip them?"

"I'd rather you didn't because I like the robe. But I suppose it belongs to you and you can treat it as you wish."

"Belongs to me?" he growled, not really caring. He managed to free a couple of the accursed little knotted silk spheres from their loops.

"It's Indian. I found it in the attic. There's another one that will fit you. Would you like to put it on?"

"No thank you. My goal is for you to wear less clothing, not me more."

She gave that delighted laugh that always made him feel inexplicably happy. "Let me help. You start at the bottom and I'll work from the top. Race you to the middle."

The location of "the middle" wasn't specified, neither was the reward for winning this race. It was understood that both would win and claim the same prize. Just as long as the blasted robe came off. In the end urgency lent him dexterity and Sebastian had passed the belly when they met and fought over the last button, somewhere in the region of her waist.

"May I?" he asked politely.

At her assent he pushed aside the two front halves of the garment and sucked in his breath. She wore not a stitch of underclothes. He'd never had the chance to examine Diana fully naked, nor any other woman, but it had been well worth the wait.

He looked. And he touched.

His fingers explored the etched line of the collarbone and the rounded right angles of her shoulders.

He filled his hands with her breasts and let the taut nipples tickle his palms. In a dream he kissed the spot between the twin mounds then worked up the side to take a pink nipple between his lips and explore its texture with his tongue. Some instinct told him to nip it, just lightly with his teeth and he read her reaction as happy surprise. A little surge of pride subdued his purely physical desire to cut short the preliminaries. Discovering how to give Diana pleasure was worth waiting for his own satisfaction.

While his mouth attended to her breasts his hands delineated the curve of waist and hips, a line unlike anything else and so unmistakably feminine. He felt her belly, still firm with only the softest swell but soon to grow with his child, and with one finger circled her navel. Diverted from his other task, he lowered his head and rubbed a cheek against the smooth skin, kissed the neat indentation.

He looked up the length of her body, between her breasts to find her returning his gaze with smiling eyes. Her pelvis gave a little wriggle, drawing his attention to the most interesting area of the female anatomy.

He had every intention of lasting long enough for her to achieve full pleasure from his thrusts, but a little insurance never went amiss.

Threading his fingers thorough her curls he found her already wet which meant, he knew, that she was prepared for the entry of his sex. He looked, he felt, and unable to resist, he pressed his nose to her mound, inhaling the unfamiliar, intoxicating scent of woman.

Then he remembered something else he'd read

about. He wanted to taste as well as smell. Without stopping to think or ask permission, he replaced his nose with his mouth, his questing fingers with his tongue. She shrieked.

"Oh Lord!" she cried at his slight hesitation. "Don't stop whatever you do."

Thankfully he didn't. Diana hadn't expected, when she decided to let Sebastian take the lead in their lovemaking, that he would introduce her to something new. Her first husband had never pleasured her with his mouth; her second did it wickedly well. Hot hard strokes hit just the right spot with such uncanny skill that she was at once in danger of dissolving into ecstasy. Wanting to make the bliss last, she breathed deeply, relishing every caress, and groaning her delight until she could resist no more and he sent her flying.

"Where did you learn that?" she gasped, collapsed among the cushions in a boneless state.

"I'm a well-read man." She felt the movement of his lips against her ribs and his hair tickling the underside of her breasts.

She ran her fingers through the disarranged locks. "I'm beginning to see the advantages of a broad education."

"Whatever I undertake, I strive for excellence."

She became aware that a particular part of him was striving against her thigh. She tugged at his shoulders. "Show me what else you've learned."

Without delay his body enveloped her, big and warm and firm. And when she spread her legs to welcome him, his member was too. The smoldering embers of her desire reignited to scorching flame when she felt herself stretched and filled. Her hips tilted to meet him and she wished it could last all night. Her inner muscles clenched in time with Sebastian's thrusts.

Holding his weight on his elbows, he looked down at her face with fierce concentration. She read a determination to please her that warmed her racing heart. Murmuring incoherent words of encouragement and praise, she pulled his head down for a long wet kiss that went on and on as their bodies worked together, damp and slick. With almost casual ease she climaxed again and could feel by Sebastian's intensified breathing and the tension in his muscles that he was ready to join her. Instead he held back, through some effort she didn't understand, and resumed his steady rhythm. Not until she melted for the third time, with a force that made her cry out her joy, did he quicken his pace, throw back his head and spend himself explosively inside her.

It took at least five minutes before Diana was capable of moving. She propped herself up on one elbow. Sebastian lay on his back, still breathing hard and looking quite adorably pleased with himself.

"That was delicious." She traced the straight slope of his handsome nose, then the outline of his mouth, and followed the passage of her forefinger with her lips.

"So I gather," he said smugly, "judging by the noise you made."

"Was I loud?"

"I doubt there's man or beast still sleeping anywhere in the vicinity." He fended off her indignant protest. "Not that I have any complaint."

"There's a certain advantage to being the sole inhabitant of an entire wing of a mansion. In London I might wake up the neighbors."

"If you can't learn to express yourself more quietly we'll have to move to a ship in the middle of the Thames."

Although the conversation was a joking one, he spoke as though they would continue to live together, and not in the frozen wasteland of Northumberland. Diana's heart expanded and she snuggled up against his side, tucking her head in his shoulder. They lay together in peaceful satiation for some time until she involuntarily shivered.

"The fire needs building up," he said.

While he added wood to restore the blaze, she pulled on her robe again, without buttoning it, and retrieved the quilted chintz banyan she'd found in the same box.

"Try this on," she said.

The loose knee-length garment suited him, the dark red background providing a masculine contrast to the extravagant floral pattern.

"I like it," he said. "I wonder how it came to be in the attic. Or any of the other things, either." He walked over to the bed and examined one of the bed curtains.

Diane joined him. "That cloth was made for export to England. Do you see how the flowers are tulips, roses, and daisies? Not the lotuses and oriental flowers you see in some of the patterns."

Sebastian showed more interest in the recent history of the fabrics. "How long have these stuffs been here at Saxton? Is there any way of knowing?"

"Hedley says fifty years."

"In my great-uncle's time. I never knew him to be concerned with such things. I can't imagine why he would have ordered so much. But having bought it, why was it never used?"

"Hedley says the late Lord Iverley was engaged to be married and intended to put the house in order."

"Engaged? I don't believe it. He loathed women."

"Did he ever tell you why?"

Sebastian hunched his shoulders and put his hands in the pockets of his robe. His expression shuttered. "He said you couldn't trust them."

Diana wanted to probe, but instinct told her to draw back. Yet she couldn't quite leave the subject alone. "He was unfortunate in his choice," she said lightly. "According to Hedley she jilted him for a man of higher rank. She preferred the heir to a dukedom."

Even as she said it she knew her mistake. Although Sebastian would only have to question the butler to get the same information, she'd give anything to take it back. He made no response but she could sense that Blakeney wasn't far from his thoughts.

As usual, he used concern for her health as an excuse to change the subject. "You should go to bed. I'm going to read in the library for a while before I sleep."

"Fetch your book and bring it here." She put her arms around his neck. "You could read me to sleep," she whispered. "If you chose something interesting enough perhaps you'll keep me awake."

He politely but firmly withdrew from her embrace. "You need your sleep."

Two hours later she lay awake in the dark. Physically she felt splendid, couldn't imagine ever feeling unwell again for the rest of her life. Her teeming brain nagged her, asking if she'd ever make her husband see her as more than a representative of a despised sex whose bed he liked to share. She'd come to Saxton with the goal of finding a way to cohabit in a civil manner as their fortunes merged and their children were born. But her heart wasn't content with such modest aspirations.

That Sebastian could be a good lover she no longer doubted. Now he needed to learn to be a good husband. She wasn't sure he possessed the same natural talent, or an equal drive for self-improvement.

Drifting on the edge of sleep, she felt a little better when he slid into bed and flung a heavy arm about her waist from behind. A soft kiss on her neck was gentle and undemanding but his naked body didn't disguise his wishes. With a happy sigh she turned over and welcomed him.

Chapter 29

The small dining room at breakfast time was now the only reliably woman-free place in the house. Diana took her morning meal in bed and waiting at table remained a footman's job. Otherwise Saxton was infested with female servants, dusting, scrubbing, polishing, and doing whatever else was needed to bring the place to the degree of cleanliness deemed necessary by his wife.

At first Sebastian protested when she hired two maids, but she silenced him with the information that they were the daughters of one of the dead miners. Then another half dozen appeared.

"We don't have enough staff in this huge house and it's hard to find menservants. They earn more in the mines." She was good at undercutting his arguments. "I think it our duty to offer employment to women so *they* don't have to work underground."

Diana had been shocked to learn that the collieries employed women as well as men for the dangerous and backbreaking labor. She'd lost her temper when she discovered children as young as four years old were put to work alongside the coal miners, crawling through tunnels too low and narrow for adults.

Sebastian agreed with her concerns; he'd already instituted measures to improve working conditions at the Saxton mine. The recently passed factory act ruled that no children under nine were to be employed in cotton mills and older children were limited to twelve-hour days. Though the law didn't apply to mines, he felt it was the least he could do to voluntarily follow the same restrictions. He also liked Diana's proposal to start a school for the younger children, and allow the older ones a few hours off each day for education.

But while the employment of maidservants might be good policy in the wider sense, he found their presence in the house unsettling. Since early childhood he'd never lived among women.

Diana's French maid he didn't mind. She always excused herself whenever he appeared and her approving glances told him why. The French had a reputation for enthusiasm when it came to the amatory arts, a well-deserved one if the contents of Tarquin's library were anything to go by. The Frenchwoman—Chantal he believed was her name—knew exactly what he and her mistress got up to as soon as they were alone.

Which was ultimately the reason he tolerated the feminine invasion. He was beginning to fear he couldn't live without its leader. He wanted Diana just about every moment of every day and night. The nights presented no difficulty. Her amorous eagerness equaled his own. Retiring early to the Rajah's Court, as he now dubbed her bedchamber, he gave free reign to his passion. She welcomed every manifestation of his developing erotic fantasies with fervor.

But those same erotic fantasies didn't vanish with

the coming of day. As the comfort and color of the Rajah's Court extended, room by room, into the rest of the house, so did his desires. He'd retreated to the masculine sanity of the library yesterday and found curtains at the windows and a huge multi-hued carpet covering much of the floor. While he appreciated the added warmth, what he mostly wanted to do was summon his wife, strip her naked, and roll around on the rug with her.

That was not what libraries were for. And it wasn't what days were for, either, he had to keep reminding himself. He found every excuse to leave the house and as a result the industrial and agricultural affairs of the Iverley estates received more attention from their owner than at any time in history. It was the only way to keep his thoughts rational. Even now, for God's sake, as he replenished his energies with roast beef, he couldn't stop thinking about what he'd been doing two hours earlier. Her scent haunted him as though imprinted on his skin. He tested the hypothesis by taking a deep sniff at his wrist.

"Good morning, my lord."

He almost choked on a mouthful and dropped his arm to his side. Diana stood at the doorway. The tousled nymph of the dawn—warm, naked, dreamy-eyed—had given way to the Olympian goddess, dressed for Bond Street and polished to a high gloss.

"I'll have some of that ham, please, George," she said briskly, "and a couple of muffins."

She showed no inclination for breakfast chatter but set about slathering her muffins with butter and honey.

"You were hungry this morning," Sebastian finally remarked, after watching her put away a large plate of food with quiet efficiency.

"Famished."

"And not sick?" He looked over at the fireplace where sulfurous Saxton coal emitted heat and fumes.

"I haven't felt ill for several days, even in rooms where there's a coal fire. Dr. Harrison says it's normal for the nausea to end after about three months."

"You don't usually eat so much, do you?"

"Not in recent weeks. My appetite seems to have returned with a vengeance. Of course," she continued with a smoldering glance that belied her dispassionate tone, "I've been getting a great deal of exercise lately."

"Is that so?"

"Exercise is good for the health."

"So I've always heard."

"Even at night I maintain my exertions."

He kept his expression grave. "That's very commendable."

"So it's not surprising I should need added sustenance to keep up my strength."

"I have no argument with your logic." He leaned across the table with concern. "Now you've enjoyed a restorative breakfast, might I suggest a little rest." He glanced over at George whose stolid demeanor gave no indication that he understood Sebastian's present intentions.

Apparently neither did Diana, or so she pretended. "I only just got out of bed. I have all sorts of plans for today."

"In your delicate condition you can't be too careful. As your husband it's my duty to make sure you spend enough time in bed."

"I could do with a short nap," she said after a moment of exaggerated consideration, "but I think I should take a little exercise first."

Her smile went straight to his groin. Sebastian stood and offered her his arm. "Allow me to accompany you."

"That was delicious," she said half an hour later, collapsing with her head on his chest, her knees hugging his hips. They were still joined.

"Invigorating," he said, reaching to draw the covers over them. "Now rest."

The first time she'd climbed on top and indicated she wanted to make love that way, he'd been a little shocked. It seemed against the natural order of things. Once he discovered the benefits of the variant he became quickly reconciled to the supine position. And to a number of others, all highly enjoyable. But this might be his favorite, because he loved feeling her weight and her warmth envelope him as they rested afterward.

She raised her head and rubbed her nose against his. "Did you know you have beautiful eyes?" she asked.

"Me? You're the one with the eyes. Southern noon sky blue. Mine are Northumberland morning gray."

"That's quite lyrical."

He allowed himself a grunt. "Pray, don't accuse me of committing poetry."

"Your eyes aren't gray but silver, like a full moon.

I'm glad you wear spectacles because the other ladies can't tell how handsome you are."

"You're teasing me."

"Not at all. You're quite enticing enough with them. Lady Georgina Harville is mad for you."

He gave a snort of laughter. "If she is, which I doubt, it's unreciprocated. I only ever said a word to her to make you jealous."

"I don't think you should bring that up," she said huffily and rolled onto her back, leaving him chilled, despite a thick down-filled quilt.

He wanted to ask her if she regretted the eventual outcome of his deception. The fact he'd forced her into marriage was ever-present at the back of his mind. He was content, but was Diana? He wanted to ask her how she felt but couldn't think how to frame his question in a way that didn't sound weak and pleading.

He laid his palm over the slight but perceptible protrusion of her belly, proof of the accident that had brought them to this point. To this moment in a bed in huge, gray, frigid Saxton Iverley. An outcome he could never have predicted in a hundred years.

"Do you think I'm getting too fleshy?" She swallowed. "I'm afraid of what will happen now I've regained my appetite. Chantal has warned me that expectant ladies can end up very stout if they don't take care."

"I find your concern with your figure ridiculous. If there were to be a little more of you I could only rejoice."

"Thank you, my lord. That's very gallant. You are becoming quite a smooth-tongued flattering scoundrel." Her smaller hand covered his. "Do you feel it?" she asked. "I haven't felt it move yet but I should soon."

The thought of the child always disquieted him. Without being obvious about it, he turned onto his side so that he could remove his hand from the swelling lump. Thus far he'd managed to avoid much conversation about it. His wife's health in pregnancy had his full attention; the perils of childbirth and the unexplored territory of fatherhood were too alarming to contemplate.

"Do you think it will be a boy or a girl?"

This was a subject he'd definitely rather not discuss.

"Chantal thinks it's a girl because my left nipple is redder."

"Really?" he asked, perking up. He was ever happy for an excuse to examine his wife's breasts. "I can't see any difference but I'm sure I could make it so." He lowered his mouth to the jaunty pink point, then stopped. "Maybe I should encourage the right side if that will make it a boy."

"Do you hope for a boy then? I suppose all men wish for an heir."

"The viscountcy, the estate, and so forth," he said, though he didn't mean a word of it. His preference would be for a male child only because the notion was marginally less terrifying. A small boy was familiar; he'd been one himself. But a girl?

When he thought of girl children he heard giggles, specifically the giggles of Amanda Vanderlin and her sisters.

* * *

Sebastian had taken to lovemaking like a duck to water.

Diana could only hope that when the time came he would apply the same enthusiasm to the outcome of the activity. In contemplating her impending motherhood she thought of her own happy childhood and her parents, always loving and indulgent despite their respective eccentricities. Sebastian as far as she could tell had enjoyed nothing of the kind, either before or after the disappearance of his mother. Any attempt to discuss the future addition to the Iverley family aroused his best avoidance tactics and more often than not led to his departure from the room.

In fact the same applied to most conversation that bordered on the personal. Intimacy, he made it plain, was a physical not a mental state.

With some difficulty, she held to her resolution not to press him and was rewarded over the course of several weeks. He smiled frequently, laughed on occasion, and even made jokes, usually in bed in the relaxed aftermath of mutual satisfaction. When, she wondered, would it occur to her clever husband that he was happy, even in the gloomy house where he'd passed his unsatisfactory youth?

The physical gloom at least she could dispel. To her fascination, it emerged that the trove in the attics contained much that was needed to furnish the house according to the original plans discovered in the estate muniments room. The materials imported from the east which she'd first stumbled upon were a mere fraction of the riches, and intended mostly for the bedrooms. Crate after crate was unpacked to reveal wall-coverings of silk, leather, and tapestry; giant carpets from the Wilton and Aubusson factories which fit the massive rooms so well they must have been woven specially; bales and bales of costly cloth for curtains and upholstery; chairs and sofas, and tables of every kind and size.

It was going to take her weeks to sort it all out and months to find craftsmen to install what she found and to execute the elaborate gilt and plasterwork the original architect had designed.

She worked without the participation of her husband, who spent his days outside the house or buried in the estate office with his steward, not always even home in time to dine with her. Bedtime, however, he never missed, and most of their conversations were conducted in the old-fashioned bed which now boasted a new, softer mattress.

"I've decided the crimson silk must have been meant for the large dining room," she told him one night. "It complements the chair coverings in there. I wonder why that was the one fully furnished room."

"I suppose the table was too big to get upstairs to the attic," Sebastian said idly. He was fussing with the blankets to make sure she was warm enough, then dropped a light kiss, first on her nose then her lips. She relished such casual gestures of affection, separated from passion. She couldn't tell if he was aware of making them.

"It's a wonderful room," she said, nuzzling his arm. "When it's finished we must give a dinner to celebrate."

His response was predictably skeptical. "Whom would we invite?"

"The local gentry, of course. I haven't met anyone yet, but I imagine once the weather improves some of them will call."

"They never have before. My uncle didn't hold much with company."

"But you must be acquainted with the principal families in the neighborhood. You must have known the young men, at least, as you grew up."

"No."

She shouldn't have been surprised. When he wasn't away at school, Sebastian's life at Saxton seemed to have been almost totally isolated from the kind of country sociability she knew in Shropshire. Not that he'd ever told her directly; almost everything she knew about his youth had been deduced from the meager morsels of information he dropped from time to time.

"We sometimes went to meetings of the Literary and Philosophical Society," he said, a rare instance of volunteering information. "I remember going to see the wombat and the platypus."

"What are they?"

"Strange creatures from the Antipodes. John Hunter sent specimens to Newcastle when he was Governor of New South Wales."

"What else?" She was hungry for further confidences.

"I bought books."

"When did you start collecting?"

"I started by reading, history mostly, and travelers' tales. Uncle Iverley's father had bought some rarities. My uncle was happy to provide me with the funds to expand the collection and by the time I was thirteen there was scarcely a bookseller in England with whom I didn't correspond."

"The library here is disordered."

"I removed the valuable books to London. My uncle didn't care about them and his experiments might have damaged them."

"I have noticed some strange black residues on the walls in the library."

"Explosions."

"Just you wait till I finish in there. You won't believe how magnificent it will be. You can buy lots of new books."

And she resolved to present him with the royal bindings for his birthday in May. Sebastian had never once mentioned them, since the day she'd threatened to give them to Blakeney. Needless to say she'd done no such thing.

"It must have taken weeks of work planning the decoration of the house and assembling the orders to the merchants. Do you suppose your uncle did it himself?"

A valiant attempt, but as usual Sebastian refused to be drawn into any speculation on the subject. He didn't march out of the room, having learned diversionary tactics more satisfactory to both of them. Instead he dived under the covers.

Her annoyance gave way to contented resignation at the tickle of his hair against her inner thigh, his hot breath on her sex. Large capable hands grasped her hips and dragged her down to her pleasure and his.

He must be made, she decided, to take at least a modicum of interest in the improvements to his barracks of a house. Not so much because she cared about his opinion of the arrangements. She'd rather make decisions unsullied by dubious masculine taste for walls festooned with animal heads and weaponry.

It was one thing to spend most of the winter months in bed. Once the weather improved she expected to lead a more normal life and would need habitable rooms to do so. This assumed they would be staying at Saxton, or spending much time there in the future. She had no idea how long his affairs would keep him in Northumberland or when he planned for them to travel south. She'd assumed they'd return to London for the season, and perhaps for her confinement in the summer, but when she raised the subject he made infuriating noncommittal noises.

"You sent for me?" He didn't sound delighted but he was there, in the south-facing room overlooking a snow-powdered formal garden.

"I think this room would make an agreeable drawing room for family use. Not too big and with a lovely view."

"It's almost dark outside."

"The view was lovely half an hour ago and will be even more so in summer. I'll draw the curtains."

"Let me do that." He came up behind her at the window and surrounded her with his arms as he helped close the heavy blue velvet drapes.

She pivoted and found him regarding her with kindling heat. "Thank you," she said, ducking smoothly under his elbow. "When you've finished, I'd like your opinion on the position of the furniture. Do you like the armchairs on either side of the fireplace?"

"They're fine," he said.

"I like the way they look, but when we have guests more people would be able to enjoy the fire if we put the pair of settees there. And perhaps that chaise longue opposite." She pointed at the large and exceptionally wide chaise on the other side of the room. "It's very comfortable."

He stuck his hands in his pockets and gave it a cursory glance.

"Fine," he repeated.

"I don't like the old-fashioned mode of lining all the seating along the wall. The chaise was over there between the windows but because the upholstery matched the curtains it didn't stand out well. Since I moved it you can see what a handsome piece it is."

"What!" He finally showed signs of animation. "When you say *you* moved it I trust you mean one of the servants."

"Oh no! I'm quite alone here. I pushed it over myself."

"That's a heavy piece of furniture," he growled. "You could have injured yourself."

"Nonsense!" She waved her arms in the air and spun around. "Look! I'm well, I'm fit, I'm in excellent condition."

"You shouldn't have done that. You disobeyed my express command not to overexert yourself."

That seemed rather excessive, not to say heavy-handed. Diana was about to give him a sharp set-down when she noticed the hint of anxiety in his eyes had transformed to a predatory gleam.

"What are you going to do about it?"

He crossed his arms and looked down at her

sternly. "I'm afraid," he said, "I shall have to punish you."

She clasped her hands to her bosom. "Oh no! Please! Remember my condition!"

"You just told me you were in excellent condition."

"Be gentle!"

"Be quiet!" he ordered with a straight face. "And remove your drawers."

Diana was dressed for February by the sea in the northernmost part of England, but when it came to underclothes she abided by certain immutable principles. She hiked up her woolen skirts, untied the tapes and shook the garment to the floor. Neatly stepping out from the pool of lace-trimmed French lawn, she scooped it up and handed it to him with a pert curtsey.

"Thank you," he said gravely, raising it to his lips for a salute before tossing it aside. "Now, it's time to revisit the scene of the crime."

With a hand on her shoulder he marched the prisoner to the chaise and indicated the velvet seat with its gilt piping. "Kneel there with your back to me."

The soft nap caressed her silk-clad knees while she arranged her skirts neatly about her. Her racing heart and a blossoming heat between her legs fought her inclination to laugh, and won.

"Hold on to the back of the sofa." She obeyed immediately and without question. "Lean forward and rest your head between your hands."

The anticipation was almost unbearable. An age seemed to pass before he touched her and, with agonizing leisure, caressed her bottom through her clothing. She pushed back into his hands.

"Be still," he said sternly. "Move only when I say so. Do you understand?"

"Yes."

"Yes who?"

"Yes, Sebastian."

"Yes, *master.*"

"Yes, master," she said, shaking with silent mirth.

"And don't laugh or you'll get extra punishment."

She laughed out loud.

Then drew in her breath as one by one he lifted her skirts. First the gown of slate blue woven wool, followed by two fine linen petticoats, one at a time. Each layer he neatly folded over and rested on her arched back.

Cool air on her flesh enhanced her sense of exposure and vulnerability. She ached with desire and despite his admonition, strained backward in yearning invitation. In comparison Sebastian's hands were warm as he ran them over the globes of her behind, then down to her inner thighs. He pushed her legs farther apart, leaving her open and quivering with lust. *Touch me,* she begged silently and knew what would happen.

Seconds later she was proven right. A single long finger, three strokes back, forward, and back again along the length of her wet gaping sex and she came, just a little bit, a small preliminary shudder of relief that left her ready for more.

"Now," he said, "it's time for the Sacred Rod of Chastisement."

She responded with an incoherent noise: one part

excitement, one part apprehension, and one part giggle. She wasn't really afraid. She trusted Sebastian not to hurt her.

"Hush!"

She heard the rustle of his garments. Then she felt the "rod," long and hard, beating against her backside, sliding up and down the ridge of her arse.

She giggled again. And gasped.

"Quiet, wench!" But he was as amused as she, also as aroused. Grasping her hips he entered her, plunging into her damp passage. He'd taken her from behind in bed, but the pretense of domination gave the posture a new edge of excitement. Even the fact that they were both almost fully clothed and in a supposedly public place (thanks be for a shortage of servants) added to her stimulation. It wasn't long before she exploded, ripples of sensation shooting from her groin through her torso and the length of every limb. And when he reached his climax she joined him again.

Somehow they ended up entwined in a heap, half on the chaise and half on the floor. The expression of smug satiation he always wore at such moments made her smile all over.

"Well, master," she said softly, nipping at an earlobe that happened to be nearby, "what's my next punishment?"

"I've decided to grant a full pardon."

"That's not fair."

"You've exhausted me."

"I feel sure you have hidden reserves of strength." She groped between them and found that he was indeed depleted. "The sacred rod of chastisement?"

she asked with a chuckle. "Where did you get the idea for such nonsense?"

"I read it in one of Tarquin's books. In the story the rod was exercised by a French priest on a penitent lady of impeccable virtue. She didn't understand what happened to her."

"I must not be a lady of impeccable virtue."

"Thankfully, no."

"I understood exactly what was happening."

"And are you successfully chastised?"

"Oh yes."

In one sense the afternoon had been a failure. She'd failed to engage Sebastian's interest in the decoration of their future drawing room and the position they'd negotiated was not that of the furniture. But while her husband might not be willing to talk much, his actions were most eloquent and that counted for a great deal, surely. Never in her life had she felt more physically content.

Except for one thing.

"I'm hungry," she said.

"Me too."

"What's for dinner?" They spoke in unison and Diana mechanically uttered the usual words.

"Aristotle's Beard!" Another thing Sebastian had learned. He was only half a syllable behind her.

"I won!" she boasted and he graciously conceded victory.

The next day Diana received a letter.

Chapter 30

Thanks to the efficiencies of the Post Office, Diana maintained a regular correspondence with family, friends, and a widening circle of purveyors of the kind of expensive goods appropriate to the embellishment of a large house. That morning her desk bore but a single oblong of folded paper.

She expected a diatribe from Minerva, who wrote almost daily, begging Diana to return to London so her sister could be released from the rural tedium of Mandeville Wallop. But it was addressed in an unknown hand, an untidy masculine sprawl. In her experience only an Etonian education gave a man such abysmal penmanship and the arrogance to use it without shame. She broke the seal and glanced at the second page to check the signature: Blakeney.

My dear Diana.

Since we are now closely related I feel there can be nothing unseemly in our correspondence. How do you go on with Cousin Sobersides? I confess I am still surprised at your choice. You

*are not a lady I would expect to succumb to the
dreary attractions of propriety . . .*

Diana lowered the letter to ponder the acts of propriety visited on her by Lord Sobersides on the chaise
longue in the drawing room. Given the dispassionate,
not to say unromantic nature of the marquis's proposal, she doubted life would have been *less* dreary
as Lady Blakeney.

Repressing a tendency to drift into a daydream,
she resumed her reading.

> *But you are likely better off with a man of
> financial substance as events have shown. Let
> me not shilly-shally. I find myself, through my
> own folly, in need of a large sum of money. I
> cannot now explain what for, or why it would
> be most inconvenient to apply to my father for
> funds. I can only throw myself on your mercy.
> If you feel even the least compunction about so
> cruelly tossing me over for another, I abjectly
> beg you to assist me with a loan.*

She had to smile about how extraordinarily *unab-
ject* Blakeney managed to make his purported grovel.
As for the sum of money he asked for, she'd have
whistled if she knew how.

Nevertheless, it was well within her means and
she had no quarrel with Blake. A residue of her old
fondness lingered and she admired the sheer nerve
of his petition. Besides, when it came down to it, she
had treated him shabbily.

She wrote a draft on her bank and, since Blakeney

said the matter was urgent, asked a servant to take it into Newcastle to catch that day's mail coach.

All was right with the world.

Sebastian leaned back in his uncle's ancient leather chair, never minding the stuffing that spewed from cracks in the cushions and would coat his buckskins with fuzz. A couple more weeks of work and he could leave the Saxton estate and colliery in the hands of his deputies for a few months, and return to civilization. In the meantime, the library was quiet and warm. A small crate of books had been delivered from London the previous day and awaited his perusal. And his wife, who was somewhere in the house, would willingly participate in whatever amorous game his fervid imagination could devise.

Cautiously he poked at various tender spots in his soul, or rather, because he wasn't fond of that word, what the Greeks and Sir Thomas Browne (in *Hydriotaphia*, first edition 1658 which just happened to reside in this very library) termed the psyche.

He was married. To a woman. Who lived in the same house as him.

Once upon a time even one of these facts would have caused him acute distress. Today, nothing but pleasure.

She was expecting a child, possibly another female who would have to share his house.

A little alarming but why look for trouble? Diana could just as easily have a boy.

She might leave him. Uncle Iverley's betrothed had left him, for a future duke no less.

But Diana had left the future duke for him. And

she'd wed him. She appeared to like him. Still, this line of thinking made him uneasy. He needed to bind her to him so she'd never leave. But while binding Diana in the literal sense had major appeal and gave him an idea for later, he had a notion that something was required on a more spiritual level. Sebastian, not being a stupid man, knew that his avoidance of certain subjects vexed her. But it was bad enough having to examine his own psyche; he didn't want anyone else doing it.

So he had to find a way to let Diana know how much he appreciated her, and not just physically.

The days studying the business of coalmining had required such extensive memoranda he was halfway through a new notebook. The old one was on his desk among his correspondence. He leafed back to what he mentally dubbed The Seduction List.

Sapphires.

A job for Cain, he decided. In the past Lord Chase had bought jewelry for some very expensive ladybirds. And giving him the commission might help Sebastian win his forgiveness. Once he announced the wedding, Tarquin had relinquished his disapproval. But relations with Cain, thanks to the influence of that diminutive blonde she-devil he'd married, remained frosty.

He dashed off a letter and took it out to the hall where George was on duty.

"Send to the stable for a mount. I need to reach Newcastle in time to get a letter in today's mail."

"I'm waiting for one of the grooms to take one for Her Ladyship."

"I'll take it. I have affairs in town anyway."

The footman pulled a letter from his pocket and handed it to Sebastian.

Diana was dozing when he joined her in bed. She awoke to his weight on top of her and the taste of brandy in a ferocious and rather sloppy kiss. After what was, for her, an unsatisfying sexual encounter, he immediately fell asleep on his back, emitting the occasional porcine snore.

When not showing their better sides, she reflected philosophically, men could be quite dreadful.

She might have expected him to sleep off his excesses late into the morning, but he left before she awoke. When she joined him for breakfast he was a little pale, but in better condition than she'd seen her older brothers after a night's carousing.

"Good morning," she said cheerfully, pouring herself some tea. "You forgot to tell me you were dining out."

He grunted.

"What was it? The Association of Mine Owners or the Literary Society?"

This time it was more like a growl. Although determined not to be a nagging wife, she deserved better than that.

"I hadn't the impression either was a particularly intemperate group," she said, with difficulty keeping her tone light, "so I assume the occasion was a festive one."

He snarled. "I'll thank you to attend to your own affairs and not mine. Just because we were obliged to wed, it doesn't mean you own me, body and soul."

Biting back a retort she turned to the attendant

footman. "George. Please go to the kitchen and ask for some fresh tea. This is a little stewed."

As soon as they were alone she gave up all pretense of complacency and glared at her husband. "What unbelievable arrogance to assume that I'm interested in owning your soul! As for your body, after last night I'm not sure that's such a great catch, either."

"I have no doubt of that, my lady. You are just making do with me until you can get back to town and resume your affair with my cousin."

"Don't be ridiculous." At least she now knew what had set off this unwarranted attack. "You have no right to read my letters."

"Have no fear. I got your billet-doux to the mail coach in time, and I didn't read it. I, at least, am not without honor."

"Twaddle! What you call honor I call stupidity. If you had read it, you'd know there was nothing improper between me and Blakeney. Or you could have just asked me instead of falling into the sullens and going out to get drunk."

"I'm not in the sullens."

She raised skeptical eyebrows.

"And I wasn't drunk."

"If you say so."

They glared at each other. He was the first to look away.

"I'm sorry about last night," he muttered. "Was it very bad?"

"I know you can do better. Much better."

"I will," he said. "Later. Or as soon as you like."

She was not, however, in the mood to be dragged off to bed or the nearest piece of furniture. Too many questions needed answers, and this might be a moment to get some.

"Why do you continue to hate Blakeney so much?" she asked.

"I don't. He's nothing to me."

"He's your cousin. And while you may have little in common, there's no reason to go on feeling bitter about childhood quarrels."

"I know everyone else finds him so handsome and charming. I just don't happen to agree. And I am not bitter."

"Can't you see that you've won? I am your wife, not his. It's time to forget he removed your breeches when you were ten years old. Get over it!"

She clapped her hands over her mouth, but too late. He rose from the table, wiped his hands on a napkin and flung it to the floor. "What you do with Cousin Blakeney or any other man is immaterial to me, though I'd prefer it if you didn't expect me to offer my name and fortune to your bastards."

Starting to walk out, he paused for one last barb. "Let's make sure this one is the last, shall we?"

He stalked out of the house again and this time Diana didn't wait for his return. Three hours later she still burned with rage as her carriage joined the Great North Road and headed south. What he'd said was unforgivable.

Hadn't she been the sweetest, saintliest, most understanding wife that was ever provoked by an untrusting, overly reserved, coldhearted, mean-tongued, inquisitorial *man* of a husband? She wanted to scream aloud her frustration at being tied for life to such a brute, that her poor innocent child would have no other father.

By the time they stopped to change horses, her indignation had lessened and she was feeling weepy.

"Perhaps we should go back."

"No, milady," Chantal said firmly. Diana had neither sought nor received her maid's opinion, but she knew the Frenchwoman was thrilled to leave Saxton Iverley. In fact it was highly unlikely Chantal would ever agree to go there again. She'd find herself a duchess to dress and Diana would be reduced to a frump with messy hair, married to a reclusive bookworm who hated her, and live for the rest of her life in a frozen mausoleum where nobody called.

"I think milady's neck aches, no?"

Like a docile child Diana let the maid remove her bonnet then turned her back so that Chantal could massage her from behind. "Thank you, that feels good."

"I know *les femmes enceintes*. And I know their 'usbands, too. Milord Iverley will come after you."

"Do you think so?"

"I know so."

"He's very angry with me. Not that he has any right to be."

"He'll miss you in bed. I know men."

Diana gave an angry sniff. "If that's the only reason, he can stay behind as far as I'm concerned. There should be more to marriage than bed."

"He will be very worried about you. One day at most and he will follow you. Perhaps he'll catch us on the road." Chantal grinned. "I 'ope not. Once we're in London he won't make us come back here until after the babe is born."

Her maid's confidence cheered her a little. Leaving him, letting him discover he missed her, might be the best way to bring Sebastian to his senses. She refused to think about what she'd do if the stratagem didn't work.

"You're right, Chantal. We'll take a detour to Wallop to collect Miss Minerva and then on to Portman Square." Tears pricked the back of her eyes. "I'm afraid I won't be shopping for the season this year. I shall be big as an elephant by Easter."

Chapter 31

When Sebastian returned to the house that afternoon, he brushed off Hedley's greeting and strode off to the library. Like the day of another homecoming, his sanctuary had been invaded by a female, a maidservant feeding coal into the stove.

Irritated, he looked out of the window at a bleak prospect that matched his own inner landscape. He registered a blister on his forefinger, the result of hard riding around the countryside wearing the wrong gloves. He hadn't even noticed the hole in the thin kidskin until he removed them and realized his hands had been clad for a walk through St. James's, not galloping on the shores of the North Sea. No physical discomfort could match the pain in his heart when he thought of Blakeney and Diana together, sharing the tale of his youthful humiliation and laughing at him.

All this time he'd trusted her and she'd *known*.

A muted clatter of metal announced that the girl had finished with the stove and stowed the poker and shovel in their place. He waited with some impatience for her departure. Instead she approached him, looking scared, determined, and very young.

"My lord," she said in the lilting Tyneside accent, bobbing a graceless curtsey. It was the first time one of the female servants had ventured to address him. "I kna I divint ought to speak but I want to thank you."

"What for?"

"For taking me into the house after my da was kilt. Without it I'd have to go doon the pits."

"That's all right," he said awkwardly. "It was Her Ladyship's idea. What's your name?"

"Mary, my lord. Mary Ash."

"I'm sorry about your father, Mary. It was the least we could do."

"Most girls haven't the choice." She thanked him again and scurried out of the room.

He stared after her, something tugging at his memory. The whore in South Molton Street, whose name he couldn't now recall, had used similar words, had been glad to have the choice between life in service and reasonably genteel prostitution.

Coal worker or servant; servant or whore. Neither girl had any very alluring prospect, yet both were grateful for the option. A woman, he supposed, didn't often have much choice about her path in life. A ghost of a thought came to him, so light and fleeting as scarcely to be conscious. Had Lady Corinna Iverley any choice? Had she wanted to leave him behind?

He slammed the door on that corner of his mind. Thinking of his mother was something he never did. Ever.

He had to decide what to do about another troublesome female, the woman who'd had no choice but to wed him instead of the man she really wanted. Much as he'd prefer to skulk in his library, he'd better go and find his wife, though he had no idea what he would say to her.

Against all reason he felt a thrill of anticipation as he traversed the miles of echoing passage to the east wing. The fact depressed him. How could he still want her? Yet he did. The knowledge of her betrayal did nothing to diminish her fatal allure.

He wondered whether he should knock—he didn't usually—and decided not. The cowardly notion crossed his mind of pretending nothing was wrong, that he'd never seen the letter and the morning's exchange had never happened. He wondered if she'd let him get away with it. Probably not.

He opened the door and walked into the glorious luxury of Lady Iverley's chamber to find . . . nothing. No wife draped suggestively over a pile of cushions, no French maid sorting lace-trimmed undergarments. With a sinking stomach he noticed that many of the accoutrements of Diana's occupation were also missing: the silver-backed hairbrushes on the dressing table, the perfume bottles, shawls and robes carelessly flung over the backs of chairs, slippers next to the bed. The Rajah's Court was forlorn, for its Ranee had fled.

Slumped on the edge of the bed, his head between his hands, Sebastian gave way to despair. He didn't want to live in this monument to perpetual winter with only the ghost of his uncle and a pack of male servants for company. His soul howled with grief that for a brief magical time light, color, laughter, and femininity had dispelled the gloom and made

Saxton Iverley a place of joy. He'd lost it. He'd driven her away.

His eyes stung, an odd, unpracticed yet still familiar sensation. He hadn't forgotten the last time he wept. It was the day he finally accepted he was to spend his life in gray Northumberland instead of Italy, the fabled land of sunshine and heat.

Except it wasn't the same. He was no longer a boy and his uncle couldn't stop him from following her. He got up and ran all the way to the hall, yelling for Hedley and his valet.

That night, water broke through from a long forgotten horizontal mine shaft and once again flooded the Saxton colliery.

Chapter 32

Reaching London in late evening two weeks later, Sebastian decided to spend the night at his own house rather than join his wife at Portman Square. Ideally late evening would have been the perfect time for a visit, to the bedroom. But he wasn't so fool-hardy as to attempt an approach without an expensive peace offering.

One task could be tackled without delay. He ran Blakeney to earth at White's; not in the gaming room but alone for once, in a corner with a decanter for company. His cousin hunched low in a chair with legs apart, one booted foot propped against the edge of a table.

He looked up, and peered through bloodshot eyes. "Well, if it isn't Cousin Owlverley, the married man. Have some brandy and tell me all about life beneath the wifely boot. Or should I say slippers. Very smart little slippers Diana wears. All the better to show off those smart little ankles."

Sebastian stuck his clenched fists in his pockets. "Why was my wife writing to you?" he asked.

"You'll have to ask her," Blake replied with an evil smile. "You can do that more easily if you are in the same town. Diana—I beg your pardon, Lady Iverley—has been back at least a week and this is the first time I've set eyes on you. I'm told proximity assists in harmonious marital relations." He thought about that for a minute while taking a swig of brandy. "Or maybe not. What do I know of marriage? I was thinking of trying it lately but my chosen bride threw me over for another. Are you sure you wouldn't like to sit down and have a drink instead of standing there glaring at me?"

"You haven't answered my question."

"I'm not going to. It's none of your damn business."

"She's my wife and very much my business."

"I would never betray a lady's confidence. As I said before, ask her yourself." Blakeney raised his glass but Sebastian saw he wasn't as drunk as he pretended. "Do you want a drink?" he repeated.

"No."

"That's not very friendly of you."

"That's because we aren't friends. We never have been."

"No. We're just cousins. Do you want to talk about why we aren't friends?"

"God no!" Sebastian said. "I want to beat you to a pulp."

Blake put his feet on the floor and sat up straight. "Are you calling me out? Swords or pistols?"

"Certainly not. I have no desire to either kill you or cause a scandal. I am inviting you to a friendly bout at Jackson's. Tomorrow morning, ten o'clock. Prepare to be turned into pulp."

"You think you can do that to me?"

"I beat you in the horse race."

"You had the better horse. This time it'll be just the two of us."

"Suits me fine." Sebastian met his cousin's eye. "This isn't about Diana, you know."

"No," Blakeney replied. "It isn't."

Diana wasn't sleeping well. Over a week since she'd reached London and no sight nor sound of Sebastian, not so much as a scrawled note in the post. He was being stubborn, she assured herself. Eventually he'd miss her and come after her. She didn't want to even consider the possibility that he would rejoice in the departure of his unwanted wife and tiresome future offspring and sink back into his misogynistic ways.

Her sister's companionship she found to be a mixed blessing. While in Shropshire, Minerva had been driven by boredom to write to a noted Radical whose columns in *The Reformist* she admired. A lively correspondence ensued. As far as Diana could tell, Mr. Bentley was a respectable gentleman of middle years without any notion that the letters signed "M. Montrose" were written by a female, let alone a seventeen-year-old. Still, it was one thing to pen earnest diatribes on recent legislation from the rural safety of Shropshire. Mr. Bentley lived in London. Minerva had told Diana all about her new hero but said not one word about wishing to meet him in person. This restraint filled Diana with deep suspicion.

Rising at nine after a restless night, she was alarmed to hear from the upstairs maid that Min had left a note on her door, asking not be disturbed because of a migraine. She burst in and found an arrangement of bolsters under the bedclothes. She could only hope Minerva had left early that morning rather than the night before.

That wish was crushed by the delivery of a hurriedly scrawled note from Minerva. She'd been arrested the previous night for attending a seditious meeting and was currently immured at the Bow Street Magistrates' Court. Rumor had it the prisoners were to be transferred to Newgate later in the day. Minerva would very much appreciate it if Diana could come and pay her bail.

Bad enough that Minerva had spent the night in jail. She must not spend even a minute in the notorious Newgate Prison, famous for filth, disease, and corruption. What the escapade might do to her sister's reputation Diana didn't even want to consider.

Without having the least idea how to rescue a young woman from the clutches of the law, she knew that a gentleman, preferably an influential one, would have better luck. Better yet a nobleman. But her own husband was unavailable, just when she needed him most.

She considered her close acquaintances and which ones she knew to be in town, and settled on Blakeney. He owed her a favor and he could help. No one boasted more powerful connections. She dashed off a note saying that Minerva was in trouble and she needed him to call *urgently*, underlined twice. Her summons would probably get him out of bed. Do him good, she thought waspishly. He'd caused enough trouble and now he could damn well put himself out for her.

She was not amused when her footman returned with the message that Lord Blakeney had a morning engagement he couldn't postpone and would do himself the honor of calling on her later.

She'd see about that.

"Send for the carriage," she ordered.

Twenty minutes later she marched up the steps of Blakeney's Mount Street house and bullied his butler into indiscretion. Compensating the servant, now a broken man on the verge of tears, with a guinea, she directed her coachman to the lower end of Bond Street.

The effrontery of the man, to shrug her off for a sporting event!

"This is as close as I can get to number thirteen," the coachman apologized.

"Never mind. I'll walk."

The distance was only a hundred feet but Diana managed to meet someone she knew, Lady Georgina Harville of all people, emerging from the haberdasher's next door to Jackson's. Neither could ignore the other without issuing a cut direct.

"Diana," she said with a look that would turn a dairyful of cream to junket. "I didn't know you were back in London. Allow me to felicitate you on your marriage."

"Thank you, Lady Gee. I'd love to stop and talk but I have an urgent errand."

"Wait! You can't go in there."

"I'd like to see anyone stop me."

The hall porter of Jackson's Boxing Saloon, a hulk of a man with a crooked nose, did his best. But though he was no doubt equal to the task of ejecting any unwelcome man who tried to storm the premises, he'd never been faced with a determined female. His mouth worked up and down like a fish's as he sought the words to express his confusion.

"I'm here to see Lord Blakeney," Diana announced, her nose as high as she could raise it.

"You can't come in here," was all the prizefighter could manage.

"Nonsense."

She breezed past him and found herself in a large, high-ceilinged room with sawdust on the floor. The walls were decorated with paintings and prints depicting feats of pugilism. In one corner stood an all too familiar sight, a weighing machine almost identical to the one in the hall at Wallop. The place reeked of that disgusting smell emitted by the exercising male, familiar to her from her brothers' quarters: sweat and dirt.

Two or three dozen men were gathered in the place, some of them stripped to the waist. Rather a puny fellow crossed his arms over his chest in alarm at her approach. Diana rolled her eyes to the ceiling and refrained from telling him she'd seen it all before, and better. Two other gentlemen, similarly unclad, ducked out of her way with panicked croaks. *Like a pair of old spinsters*, she thought scornfully.

The majority of those present were concentrated in a group in the center of the place, among them Blakeney, who looked very good without his shirt. He was running in place while feinting punches with his hands, which were encased in funny padded mittens. The men surrounding him fell silent as she marched forward.

"Diana!" he said. "You shouldn't be here. You must leave at once."

"Boxing!" she hissed, poking him in the chest with her forefinger. "My sister is in trouble . . ." Poke, poke. "And you can't come and help me . . ." Poke, poke. "Because you have an *engagement*. A boxing match?"

"Uh . . . Diana."

"Don't. Say. Another. Word! Put your on shirt immediately and come with me."

A flurry of chatter arose among the company. She looked up and the crowd milled around to reveal another man stripped for boxing, one whose bare chest she knew intimately.

Sebastian was getting some quiet last-minute advice from Tarquin, who had sparred with Blakeney on numerous occasions.

"Overconfidence is his weakness. Keep your guard up and wait for him to drop his. Also, he tends to squander his strength in the early rounds. Keep in the fight and you'll outlast him. Look at him now, jumping up and down, the big show-off."

Sebastian offered his wrists for Tarquin to fasten his gloves and found he'd lost his friend's attention. "I'll be damned," Tarquin muttered.

Sebastian peered through the crowd of men, who were chattering like a flock of pigeons thrown an unexpected bushel of grain. Since he wasn't wearing his spectacles his vision more than three feet out was blurry, but he could tell that a woman stood next to Blake. She appeared to be jabbing at his chest and sounded highly agitated.

It couldn't be. But of course it was. Poor eyesight couldn't keep him from recognizing the way she stood, her glorious figure, the perfection of her grooming, the unmistakable scent that cut through the pleasant masculine odors of sweat and sawdust.

If he had a sword or a pistol Blakeney would be a dead man this very moment.

Then she saw him.

"Sebastian!" she cried and ran toward him.

As she came into focus he saw her face and at that moment Sebastian Iverley stopped being stupid about women. For even the world's biggest idiot, and that's exactly what he had been, couldn't misinterpret the look on his wife's face: joy, trust, and love.

"I am so glad you are here. Why didn't you tell me you were in London?" She flung her arms around his neck, gulping back tears. "Minerva's been arrested. You must help me save her."

"Of course," he said, putting one arm around her waist and shaking off his gloves. He angled around and held out a hand to Tarquin, who correctly identified his demand for a handkerchief.

"Here, my love. Dry your tears while I dress." But he didn't let her go immediately. Instead he gently mopped at the moisture gathered beneath her wide adoring eyes. "So what has your minx of a sister been up to this time? Never mind. You can tell me in the carriage."

"Wait a minute!" Blake, always at hand to interrupt a tender moment, shoved at his shoulder. "We are supposed to be having a bout. Are you defaulting on the challenge?"

"Afraid so. I have something more important to do."

His cousin looked at him with narrowed eyes, then at Diana who stood clutching his arm. His eyes dropped to the barely perceptible bulge at her middle, then back to her face, then back again to Sebastian, who could see Blakeney put two and two together and come up with the approximate date of conception.

"My congratulations, cousin," he said curtly. "Perhaps I'll see you here another day."

"Don't count on it."

Some muttering arose from the spectators who'd been laying bets on his and Blake's "friendly" bout. Sebastian ignored it.

Five minutes later he climbed into the carriage after his wife. She told him about Minerva's arrest while he buttoned his waistcoat and tied his neck cloth in a simple knot.

"It doesn't sound too serious," he said. "The new Seditious Meetings Prevention Act forbids political meetings of more than fifty people without prior permission of a magistrate. It's a monstrous measure, but if they've really arrested fifty people the authorities will have worse problems than the threat offered by one young girl."

"Will she have to stand trial?"

"I doubt it'll come to that."

"Thank God." Then, after a minute's silence, "When did you get to London?"

"Last night. I would have come sooner but there was another flood at the mine. Don't worry. No one was hurt, but I couldn't leave until I'd seen to the repairs."

"I've missed you."

"I missed you, too."

"Why didn't you come to Portman Square last night?"

"I wanted to bring you a gift and the jewelers had already closed."

"I don't need a gift. I'm just glad you are here." She leaned her head against his shoulder and he could feel her smile into his sleeve. "Though don't let me stop you from buying me something expensive to atone for your shocking rudeness at our last meeting."

"I'm sorry about that. I was so jealous of Blakeney I jumped to conclusions."

"Don't do that. In future, if you want to know something, ask. I'd have told you why Blake wrote to me."

"You don't need to."

"Did he explain?"

"No. I trust you." His head felt thick with emotion. He took her hand in his own ungloved one, and undid the tiny buttons at the wrist. He pulled off the glove and her skin was soft and smooth and a little cool beneath his lips. "I trust you and I love you," he said, the words emerging as easily and naturally as Northumberland rain. He kissed the palm before enlacing their fingers and tucking them in the narrow crevice between their bodies on the seat.

"I love you, too," she said, squeezing his hand.

Joy pierced his heart and cleared his brain. "I know," he said, grinning broadly.

"You do?"

"Yes, I worked it out all by myself."

"That was very clever of you, not that I didn't give you a few hints."

"It was about time I stopped being a fool."

"We've both been fools, right from the start. Although perhaps we should be grateful for that silly bet. Without it we'd never have got to know each other."

"And what happened afterward, I thought I wanted to get back at you, but really I couldn't bear never to see you again. I know that now."

"We should thank Blake."

"That's going too far."

She gave a hiccupping laugh. He tilted her chin up with his forefinger. "Are you crying?"

"Not really. I'm just happy. Do you think I could sit on your lap?"

Once she was settled they kissed a little but this wasn't the time or the place to get overexcited. Besides, he had something he needed to say. With reluctance he broke the embrace. "I want to tell you a story. There should be time on the way to Bow Street."

"What?" Her gaze was fixed on his face.

He looked straight ahead and took a deep breath. "When I was six my mother remarried. An Italian nobleman, Count Ugo Montecitta. Handsome devil, I suppose. I remember thinking he was like a character in a story."

She snuggled into his chest. "Did you like him?"

"I hardly knew him. But I was glad. My mother was an emotional woman. She cried a lot. After my father died she cried almost all the time for a while, but when she announced her remarriage she seemed happy again. And I was excited about going to live in Italy."

He'd spent so many years forgetting this part of the tale, his brain felt rusty. "During her visits to the schoolroom she'd tell me about it. She said in Italy it was always warm and the sun came out every day, not damp and gray like London in winter. Grapes and peaches and oranges grew outside. She taught me some Italian words, like the word for grapes. *Uva*. It's the same as the Latin. She said I could go outside and pick them straight from the vines, and eat them there, in the fields. She promised."

Diana kissed his cheek. "Go on," she said.

"The day of the wedding came. I was allowed to attend the wedding breakfast for a short while, then my nurse took me upstairs to get ready for the journey. We were to leave for Italy that day, by ship. I'd chosen my favorite books and toys because there wasn't going to be room for all of them. But now my nurse said I could take everything after all. I was so happy, poor fool. I remember it now, chattering to Nurse about Italy and boasting that I could speak Italian and telling her the words I'd learned. She didn't say anything about what was happening to me, just cleaned me up and sent me downstairs. Before I went she gave me a hug and a kiss goodbye because she wasn't coming with me. My mother and new stepfather awaited me, and Lord Iverley, my father's uncle. That day was the first time I met him. He was tall, like my father, but rail thin and seemed very old.

"My mother crouched down beside me and took me in her arms. 'I can't take you to Italy,' she said.

'The journey is too dangerous for little boys at the moment. You can visit me when you are older. You are going to live with your great-uncle.'"

He fought the pressure in the back of his nose. "That was the last time I saw her. Instead of going to Italy I went to Northumberland. You've seen Saxton Iverley. It was a disappointment." He allowed himself a small sardonic smile. "No sunshine, no grape vines. 'You are my heir. This will be yours one day,' my uncle said as the carriage came up the drive. 'One day you will be Viscount Iverley.' I hated it. It was always cold, inside and out. Instead of peaches I got chilblains."

"Did your mother write to you?"

He was so lost in his story Diana's softly voiced question almost made him jump. "I received her letters but never the one I wanted, telling me I could join her in Italy. After a while I stopped reading them. It was too painful. She still writes occasionally but I never reply."

She took his face in her hands and kissed him softly, his forehead, cheeks, and mouth. "Why are you telling me this now?"

"Because I thought of something the other day. I wondered if she'd had a choice about leaving me. Uncle Iverley was my guardian. She never said a word, but perhaps he insisted I remain in England."

She nodded. "I think we'd better go to Italy and find out."

Which was exactly the right thing to say. No wonder he loved this woman.

"I think so, too. But first we should bail your sister out of jail."

*   *   *

A few words from Sebastian obtained Minerva's release without charge.

"I think the magistrate was relieved to get rid of her," he told his anxious wife who had awaited them in the carriage. "Arresting a young girl with good family connections on such a slim basis could raise inconvenient questions." He frowned at Minerva. "Personally I wouldn't want to be responsible for keeping you in jail. I warrant the guards at Bow Street got tired of listening to you."

"What were you thinking?" Diana yelled, not ready to make a joke of the affair. "You could have been killed, going out at night like that."

"Humbug. I took a hackney and the meeting was full of the most respectable people. The magistrates *claim* there were fifty people there but I doubt it. It's my belief they acted illegally and Mr. Bentley and everyone else will be exonerated." Minerva's martyred face wouldn't have disgraced Joan of Arc. "I ought to have remained with them to share their fate."

"Being nibbled to death by rats in Newgate? I don't think so," Diana snapped. "But let me assure you that you will be locked up: in your room at night until I can find someone to escort you back to Wallop."

"Oh no! Not Wallop again!"

"You can't come out this year. It's out of the question. One whiff of this exploit and half of London will cut you dead. We'll have to wait for the gossip to die down."

"Do you think so, Sebastian?"

"That they'll find out? Certainly. Nothing stays secret in London for long. Very likely there was a reporter at the meeting and my guess is you stood out in that crowd."

They reached Portman Square to find the drawing room already occupied by Marianne MacFarland, Tarquin Compton, and the Chases.

Marianne rushed forward to embrace Diana. "I came as soon as I heard. My maid brought the news with my breakfast."

"I heard about it at Hoby's while I was measured for a pair of boots," Lord Chase said.

"The clerk at Hatchard's told me," Juliana chimed in. "And Tarquin just confirmed it."

Diana spun around to glare at her sister, who finally had the decency to look chastened. "I told you so! You're disgraced. There's obviously not a soul in London who doesn't know what you've done."

Marianne seemed baffled. "What has Minerva done? Why should *she* be disgraced?" She clapped a hand to her mouth. "Surely you didn't take her with you!"

"Me? What have *I* done?"

Marianne threw up her hands and appealed to the Chases. "We are talking about the same thing, aren't we? About Diana?"

"Yes!" they said together. "Diana," Juliana said with a nod.

"Lady Iverley," Tarquin agreed. "I was there."

Marianne looked at Diana with a combination of deep concern and avid curiosity. "Georgina Harville is telling everyone that she saw you in Bond Street this morning going into Jackson's Saloon."

"Oh! That."

"And I expect you to tell me all about it. Is it true

gentlemen box *naked*?" Every gentleman in the room flinched and lowered his hands.

"Never mind, tell me later. Now, my dear," Marianne continued sternly. "You can kiss goodbye to Almack's vouchers this season."

Minerva gave a crow of triumph and flung herself at Diana, hugging her till she was breathless. "*You* disgraced yourself! It wasn't me after all."

"I'm sorry, Min, it never occurred to me. I've ruined everything for you. Maybe I can find someone else to sponsor your season."

"I don't care. I'd just as soon wait. I think I'd like to travel and improve my languages. My German is shockingly inadequate and I believe the German princedoms will have increasing diplomatic importance in the next decade."

"As long as you don't mind, I expect it could be arranged."

"But what about you, Diana? Being accepted in fashionable circles has always been so important to you."

Sebastian, who had been a silent observer of the unfolding drama, or farce, was studying her face with an anxious expression. She could read his mind: he was thinking that had she married Blakeney she could storm every male stronghold in London and no one would dare snub the future duchess. The surge of gratitude that she hadn't wed Blake almost overwhelmed her. By a wondrous stroke of providence she'd won the much better man and muddled into a marriage that promised her everything she'd ever wanted.

And after all, the friends in this room wouldn't

give a damn if Lady Jersey and Mrs. Drummond Burrell refused to let her into their precious Wednesday night assemblies. Her family loved her and always would. She suddenly understood why her mother had regarded a successful London season with supreme indifference.

She took her sister's hand. "We're Montroses, Minerva. We don't care about such trivial stuff. The opinion of a lot of self-important strangers is of no importance to us."

Sebastian came and stood at her other side. "You're not a Montrose anymore," he said, putting his arm about her waist. "You're an Iverley."

"And do we Iverleys care about such things?" she asked, smiling up at him.

"We usen't to."

"And now?"

"Let me get this straight. I shan't be allowed to attend balls?"

"Very likely not."

"Venetian breakfasts?"

"Doubtful."

"Musicales?"

"Perhaps occasionally, if the hostess is exceptionally tolerant."

Sebastian nodded. "I think I'd be willing to share your ignominy and relapse into a state of social obscurity."

"That's very kind of you. I will endeavor to make it worth your while."

"See that you do. This is a big sacrifice."

Marianne broke in. "Does this mean I can have Chantal?"

"Certainly not. I may be an outcast but I can still be a well-dressed one."

Sebastian looked around at their visitors. "Well? Is anyone here going to refuse to consort with such a disreputable pair?" Diana thought he was half hoping they'd all leave. She knew he was anxious to get her alone and she looked forward to it herself. It had been far too long.

"Mrs. MacFarland?"

"I'd never desert Diana. And call me Marianne."

"Tarquin?"

"I don't follow fashion, I set it."

"Cain? Lady Chase?"

"We're in no position to cast stones at others."

"Have you forgiven *me* yet?"

"What do you say, Juliana?" Cain asked. Juliana looked stubborn.

"You know that female book collectors' club you were talking about founding?" Sebastian asked. "I think it's a bad idea."

Juliana lifted her nose in the air. "You are as ever, Lord Iverley, entitled to your own opinion, however ludicrous."

"There aren't enough ladies collecting books to make a good-sized club."

Juliana snorted.

"So I think you'd better join the Burgundy Club instead. I shall propose an amendment to the byelaws."

"I'll second that," said Tarquin.

Cain clapped. "An excellent notion. You've finally seen the light."

Diana intervened. "Wait a minute. Juliana, do you

really want to belong to a club with a lot of men?"

Juliana frowned. "I thought I did."

"Will they allow interesting conversation at the Burgundy Club? Will they let you talk about millinery?"

"It's perfectly all right by me," said Tarquin.

Her husband, Diana was happy to see, was indignant. Where would be the fun if she couldn't get him wound up?

"Don't make me regret my changed position on women," he said. "It's bad enough at home. I expect the Burgundy Club to be a fashion-free refuge."

"Sebastian," Cain said. "Before you go any further I suggest you recall a certain discussion on the club premises that you might not wish to have revealed."

"Very well, Lady Chase. If you want to talk about hats you may, but Tarquin will be your only audience. Because if my wife has the gall to apply for membership I shall blackball her myself."

There was only one possible response to such an outrage. Diana collapsed in a dead faint. She misjudged her fall, almost missed the sofa, and nearly spoiled the effect by laughing. She heard a good deal of clucking and fussing.

"I think you'd better all leave," she heard Sebastian say. "She's in a delicate condition, you know, and mustn't get overexcited. Minerva, why don't you go with the Chases and call on Lady Esther? I shall take Diana to her room."

Halfway upstairs he stopped and set her on her feet. "They've all left. You can open your eyes."

She gave him an exaggerated pout. "Do you expect me to walk the rest of the way?"

"Wouldn't you prefer me to conserve my strength?"

"You make a good point. You'll need it." Throwing her arms about his neck, she pressed her body to his in a suggestive manner. "By the end of this afternoon," she whispered, "you'll be begging me to join your Burgundy Club. You have no idea of the full force of my persuasive powers."

Her beloved husband laughed as though he hadn't a care in the world. "I can't wait to find out."

Epilogue

What with one thing and another they didn't get to Italy until the following year. Diana sat on the loggia of the villa outside Palermo, sharing an indolent morning with the Contessa Montecitta. Half dozing, she absorbed the dry September heat, the song of cicadas, the scent of salt and thyme on the mild Mediterranean breeze. Although she had come to love the bleaker beauty of the North Sea, Italy was everything she'd ever dreamed of.

"Ma-ma-ma." Her eyes flew open as she responded instinctively to her child who, at the age of only fourteen months, spoke in recognizable words. However much her husband might scoff at the notion, he was just as proud of their son as she was.

She arose and leaned over the stone railing. "Aldus!" she called back. He stood below in his muslin skirts, holding out his arms, a bunch of inky grapes clutched in each hand.

Sebastian picked up his small son. Fruit was crushed against their chests as they ascended the steps to the loggia. "We've been in the vineyard," he said unnecessarily. It was their favorite place.

Aldus gravely offered part of his harvest to Diana.

"Thank you, sweeting," she said. "Just one or I'll spoil my dinner."

Sebastian resisted the boy's struggles to reach his mother's arms. "Not until Maria has cleaned you up. Mama and your grandmother will not appreciate those grapey fingers on their dresses." He blew Diana a kiss. "I'll be back soon."

"I can't believe I have a grandchild at my age," the contessa said as Diana returned to her chair. "He reminds me of Sebastian but without the clumsiness."

"As far as we can tell, he isn't shortsighted."

"Funny that we never thought of his eyes when he kept running into things."

Not funny at all, in Diana's opinion. "Aldus is so adorable I can't stop looking at him. I don't know how you could bear it when you had to leave Sebastian behind in England." She tried very hard not to sound vinegary, but she needn't have worried. The contessa was impervious to criticism.

"It was sad," she replied placidly, "and I cried for days, but Iverley was his guardian and wouldn't let him leave the country. I had to go to Sicily with my darling Ugo."

"How tragic that the political situation stopped you from coming home to visit him, though I would have supposed after Trafalgar the journey by sea was safe enough."

"I hate traveling. Lord Iverley said Sebastian was doing well without me. Obviously he didn't miss me. He never wrote."

Diana bit her tongue and closed her eyes, resolving once again to follow Sebastian's example and accept the fact that Lady Corinna never had been, and never would be, the world's most affectionate mother. It was enough that neither was she the least.

The contessa was in the mood to reminisce. "I was ridiculously young to be a bride when I married Iverley." About ten years old, by her idiosyncratic arithmetic. "He was a handsome devil, very wild. Sebastian seems quite staid in comparison."

If by staid she meant trustworthy, reliable, and unlikely to fall out of a window while drunk, Diana thanked Providence. Not that her husband was without his wild streak, but she wasn't about to discuss that with his mother. She kept her eyes shut and refused to comment until Sebastian returned wearing a clean shirt.

"Time for your walk," he said.

"I don't understand why you need to be so vigorous just because you are increasing again," the contessa said. "Truthfully I find it surprising. No Iverley has had more than one child in generations. And no girls in a hundred years."

"I hope that's another tradition we will break."

Diana stood up and smiled. "Sebastian is determined we shall have a daughter this time. I confess I'm a little worried if we have to keep on naming our children after his favorite printers. I had to fight to get Aldus Manutius instead of Wynkyn de Worde or Caxton. It would be very hard for a young lady to bear a name like Baskerville."

"For girls," her husband said, tucking her arm in his and gazing down at her, the love in his eyes visible even through his lenses, "we follow Montrose tradition. Every woman a goddess."

Author's Note

Acouple of years ago, when I was helping my father move out of my childhood home, he asked me to go through a box of old family papers. Along with my grandfather's World War I diaries, I discovered a curious volume listing family members and friends and their weights. Investigation revealed that for seventy years, beginning in 1850, there had been a weighing scale in the hall of the family house in Norfolk, England. After reeling with gratitude that the practice of weighing visitors had ceased long before my time, I decided I needed to put this piece of lunacy in a book.

So if anyone reads about Diana's father and his weighing machine and thinks "that couldn't happen," all I can say is "it could and it did."

I'm nervous of listing acknowledgements, because I receive help from so many people and I'd hate to forget anyone. Thanks first of all to the ladies of the Beau Monde loop who always come up with a quick answer, or a suggestion for further research. Thanks to Janet Mullany, Nancy Mayer, Caroline Linden, and Allison Lane for specific help with this book. Thanks to Bradford Mudge of the University of Colorado for helping me find eighteenth-century pornography and to Paul Quarrie of Maggs Bros. for ideas and advice on rare books. Any errors are all my own.

I am ever grateful to my agent, Meredith Bernstein, my editor, Esi Sogah, and to Kathy, Sophia, Susan, and Jill for their constant encouragement and advice.

Finally, apologies to Count Leo Tolstoy. I borrowed Pierre's bet in *War and Peace* for the death of Sebastian's father.

Miranda

Next month, don't miss these exciting new love stories only from Avon Books

Passions of a Wicked Earl by Lorraine Heath
Morgan Lyons could not forgive his young wife's betrayal and devoted himself to a life of carnal pleasure after banishing her to the country. Claire Lyons has returned to London with one goal in mind...but can she reclaim the heart of the man she once betrayed in just one Season?

First Love Cookie Club by Lori Wilde
When Sarah Collier's unsuccessful attempt to stop the wedding of Travis Walker caused her to leave Twilight, Texas, she vowed to never fall foolishly in love again. Now a best-selling author, a fan letter brings her back to Twilight, and keeping that vow may be harder than Sarah originally believed.

His Darkest Embrace by Juliana Stone
Jagger is a creature of the night and Skye soars in the sun. Together they give each other reason to live. They are entrusted with the mission of salvation of the earth, but when Jagger seeks escape in the solitude of the jungle, Skye begins to question not only his secrets, but also her own.

Midnight by Beverly Jenkins
Beautiful Faith Kingston is a dedicated rebel spy in 18th-century Boston—until she meets Nicholas Grey, an audacious and worldly adventurer. Joined by their passions, their love is as dangerous as it is glorious...which could prove to be a disaster for them both.

Unforgettable, enthralling love stories,
sparkling with passion and adventure
from Romance's bestselling authors

At Avon Books, we know your passion for romance—once you finish one of our novels, you find yourself wanting more.

May we tempt you with . . .

- **Excerpts** from our upcoming releases.

- Entertaining **extras**, including authors' personal photo albums and book lists.

- Behind-the-scenes **scoop** on your favorite characters and series.

- **Sweepstakes** for the chance to win free books, romantic getaways, and other fun prizes.

- Writing **tips** from our authors and editors.

- **Blog** with our authors and find out why they love to write romance.

- **Exclusive content** that's not contained within the pages of our novels.

Join us at
www.avonbooks.com

AVON

An Imprint of HarperCollins*Publishers*
www.avonromance.com

Available wherever books are sold or please call 1-800-331-3761 to order.

FTH 0708